FAILURE TO PROTECT

Books by Pamela Samuels Young

Vernetta Henderson Series
Every Reasonable Doubt (1st in series)
In Firm Pursuit (2nd in series)
Murder on the Down Low (3rd in series)
Attorney-Client Privilege (4th in series)
Lawful Deception (5th in series)

Dre Thomas and Angela Evans Series
Buying Time (1st in series)
Anybody's Daughter (2nd in series)
Abuse of Discretion (3rd in series)
Failure to Protect (4th in Series)

Young Adult Adaptations
#Anybody's Daughter (1st in series)
#Abuse of Discretion (2nd in series)

Lawyers in Lust Series
Dangerously Sexy Romantic Suspense
by Sassy Sinclair
Unlawful Desires: An Erotic Suspense Novella
Unlawful Seduction: An Erotic Suspense Novella

Short Stories
The Setup
Easy Money
Unlawful Greed

Non-Fiction
Kinky Coily: A Natural Hair Resource Guide

PAMELA SAMUELS YOUNG

FAILURE TO PROTECT

GoldmanHOUSE
PUBLISHING

Failure to Protect

Goldman House Publishing

ISBN 978-0-9997331-8-9

Library of Congress Control Number: 2019912920

Copyright © 2019 by Pamela Samuels Young

For information about special discounts for bulk purchases, please contact Goldman House Publishing at goldmanhousepublishing@gmail.com or email the author at authorpamelasamuelsyoung@ gmail.com.

Goldman House Publishing, Los Angeles, CA

Printed in U.S.A.

For a fan-turned-friend,
Pamela Goree Dancy.
The world needs more caring
teachers like you.

For the two beautiful nine-year-old
girls who inspired this book,
McKenzie Adams and Madison Whitsett.
May your lives shine a light of hope
for all children who suffer in silence
because their voices are unheard.

"School administrators can't say it's up to the teachers. Teachers can't say it's not their job. And kids can't say, *I was too afraid to tell.* Every single one of us has to play our role if we're serious about putting an end to the madness. We are all responsible. We must be."

–Megan Kelley Hall
Young Adult Author
Dear Bully, Co-Editor

PROLOGUE

JUST BECAUSE I'M only nine years old, grown-ups think I don't have problems.

They tell me stupid stuff like, *Bailey, you have to learn to stand up for yourself.* Or *Try to make friends with the bully.* And the lamest one of all, *Just ignore them and they'll leave you alone.*

I tried that last one about a thousand times. It definitely doesn't work.

Even if I report Kiya Jackson to my teacher, she's not going to stop bullying me. She'll probably be even meaner.

That's what happened when I got a girl in trouble at my old school in Inglewood. She waited until there weren't any adults around and pushed me into a restroom stall and stuffed my book bag in the toilet. I never told *anybody* about that.

I want to tell my mom what's going on at my new school, but she's been super sad ever since my dad died. She always wears a fake smile, like a human happy-face emoji. I try to make her feel better by acting excited when she cooks me pancakes for dinner or buys me toys I don't even want. But it doesn't work. I hear her crying herself to sleep almost every night. I used to cry about missing my dad too. Now I mostly cry because my mom is so sad.

When she got promoted last month to be the first black marketing manager at her company, we had a fun dinner at TGI Friday's— just me and my mom. Now, she works harder than before. Even after she gets home at night, she still has more work to do on her laptop. The other night, she fell asleep right in the middle of helping me with my science project.

Ever since we moved into our new house in Baldwin Hills so I could go to a *supposedly* better school, my mom thinks everything's all good with me. But it's not. She hasn't noticed that my smile is faker than hers.

At my other school, when the principal told her that *maybe I'd be more successful in another environment*, my mom almost lost it. I was ready to lose it too. *Anybody* would be more successful if they weren't being bullied all the time.

I wish I could tell my mom how bad it is, but I can't. She wants me to be more like her and sometimes she says stuff that hurts my feelings.

I don't understand why you can't make friends.

You have to try harder to meet other little girls.

As cute as you are, all those kids should want to be your friend.

Well, nobody wants to be friends with me.

One time, I almost told her what was going on at Parker Elementary. But that would make her worry about me. So I keep it to myself. Every morning, right before I walk into school, I get the worst stomachache you could ever have. Even worse than the time I got food poisoning.

If my mom found out about Kiya spitting in my face and posting all that nasty stuff about me on Instagram, it would be one hot mess. She's usually very professional, but if she knew the truth, she would turn straight ghetto and go off on everybody at the school. Then she'd end up in jail, and I'd have to go into foster care. That's what happened to my friend Trey in first grade when his mother slapped the cashier at Walmart.

Okay, I wouldn't have to go into foster care for real. I would probably have to go live with my granny in Oakland or my Uncle Marcus in Atlanta.

If I had my choice, though, I'd rather stay with my Uncle Dre. He's really my godfather, but I pretend like he's my uncle. One time, when he picked me up from school, I tried to tell him about Kiya always roasting me. I was surprised that he didn't even know what roasting was. After I explained that it means dissin' you real hard, he hugged me and told me I had to toughen up.

You'll be okay, he said.

But he's wrong. I'm definitely *not* going to be okay.

CHAPTER

1

"PLEASE, UNCLE DRE, let me stay home with you today. Can you homeschool me? Please!"

Dre stroked his goatee and laughed. "Unfortunately, I'm not smart enough to homeschool you or anybody else."

"I'm serious," Bailey pleaded, her face twisted in terror. "Please don't make me go!"

As his Jeep inched along behind the long line of cars dropping off kids in front of Parker Elementary School, Dre peered over his shoulder at the cute little girl sitting in his back seat. Bailey's stress level was way too high. She'd had a few run-ins with a bully at her old school, but he assumed the transfer to Parker had fixed everything.

"What's going on? Why don't you want to go to school?"

Bailey hugged her book bag to her chest as if it were a life raft. "I just don't."

"C'mon, talk to me. Is somebody bothering you here too?"

After a long beat, Bailey slowly bobbed her head.

Dre had purposely used the word *bothering*, not *bullying*. He was tired of hearing all the hoopla about bullies. Kids getting picked on was nothing new. It happened in his day and would keep happening until the end of time.

Truth be told, today's kids were too damn soft. People turned backflips to protect them from the realities of life. Like everybody getting a freakin' trophy just for participating. That was the stupidest crap he'd ever heard. Sometimes life is hard. Kids need to know that sooner rather than later.

"Please don't tell my mom," Bailey begged, her brown eyes glassy with tears. "She'll fuss at me for not standing up for myself."

Dre reached back and gave Bailey's foot a playful squeeze. "No, she won't. But you do have to start standing up for yourself. If somebody's being mean to you, you have my permission to be mean right back."

He wasn't condoning violence, but if another kid started some mess, the only way to show 'em you weren't no punk was to clap back twice as hard. Most bullies were wimps. Once you got in their face, they backed off. That's what he'd taught his son to do and, to his knowledge, Little Dre had never had a problem. He would teach Bailey to do the same.

"You don't get it," Bailey huffed, her shoulders drooping. "That won't help."

They were almost at the drop-off point, when Dre steered his Jeep out of the line of cars and made a hasty U-turn in the middle of the street.

Bailey's upper body sprang forward. "We're going home?"

"Nope." Dre pulled to a stop along the curb. "I'm walking you inside. I want you to show me who's messing with you."

Bailey slumped back against the seat, her lips protruding into a pout. "That'll just make it worse."

Turning off the engine, Dre hopped out and jogged around to open the back door. "Let's go."

He took Bailey's hand as they stepped into the crosswalk. The closer they got to the school doors, the slower Bailey walked. By the time they reached the entrance, Dre felt like he was tugging a sixty-pound bag of potatoes.

"Please, Uncle Dre," Bailey whispered, glancing all around. "Please don't make me go!" Her tiny hand clutched two of his fingers.

Dre led Bailey off to the side, squatted until they were at eye level, and caressed her shoulders.

"I don't know what's going on, but there's no reason for you to be this stressed out about going to school. If somebody's messing with you, I need to know about it. What's the kid's name?"

Bailey hung her head as a tear slid down her right cheek. For a second, Dre thought she was about to come clean.

"It doesn't matter," she mumbled, hoisting her book bag higher on her shoulder.

"Yes, it—"

Bailey jerked away from him and dashed inside the school.

He was about to go after her when a woman stepped in front of him, blocking his path.

"May I help you, sir?"

The woman's chin jutted forward like an accusing finger pointing him out in a lineup. "And you are?"

"I'm Bailey's"—he paused—"uh, I'm Bailey's godfather." He'd started to introduce himself as her uncle to make himself sound more legit but changed his mind.

"Your name?" Her tone conveyed all the warmth of an icicle.

"Andre Thomas."

Dre pegged the woman to be in her early forties. Her thick, black hair fell a couple of inches below her ears in a blunt cut that matched her funky disposition. Her sleeveless, form-fitting, red dress hugged every inch of her curvy frame. Actually, she was kinda hot. Kerry Washington's classy style with Cookie Lyon's bad attitude.

"Bailey's mother didn't tell us someone else would be bringing her to school today."

She looked him up and down like he was some pedophile on the prowl for a new victim.

Dre couldn't seem to pull his eyes away. Despite an innate seductiveness, the woman still managed to carry herself with the spit-shine polish of a CEO. If professionalism had a smell, she would reek.

"Erika had an early meeting in Irvine and asked me to drop her off."

Dre ran a hand over his shaved head. Rarely did anybody—especially a female—make him feel this degree of uneasiness. "I'm sorry. I didn't get *your* name."

"I'm the principal. Darcella Freeman."

He should've guessed. *A sister with a little power.*

"I'll be dropping Bailey off and picking her up from time to time," Dre said, anxious for the chick to move out of his way so he could go after Bailey. "Erika got a big promotion. Her job's a lot more demanding now."

"Is that right?"

"Yep, that's right." *What's up with this chick?*

"Please ask Bailey's mother to email the office authorizing you to pick her up from school."

Dre nodded. "Will do."

He still wanted to go inside, but the woman stayed put like a queen guarding the gates of her castle.

Without saying goodbye, Dre pivoted and headed back across the street. As he opened the door to his Jeep, he made a mental note to have a talk with Erika. She'd been thrilled about getting Bailey into Parker Elementary because of its stellar reputation. But the place might not be any better for Bailey than her old school.

Dre also couldn't shake the feeling that something wasn't quite right. And not just with Bailey.

CHAPTER

2

BAILEY WIPED THE tears from her eyes and speed-walked down the hallway since running wasn't allowed. She wanted to look back to see if her Uncle Dre was coming after her. But if she turned around and he wasn't there, that would make her even sadder.

Farther ahead, Bailey saw her classmates lined up along the wall outside Mrs. Phillips's classroom. She spotted Kiya Jackson and wanted to throw up. She was so tired of Kiya messing with her every single day. If Bailey could turn invisible, she would hit Kiya in the head with her book bag.

At least the girl's back was turned. If Bailey walked super-fast, maybe she could make it to the end of the line before Kiya could say something nasty to her.

Picking up speed, Bailey kept her focus straight ahead. As she was about to pass the girl, Kiya stuck out her foot. Bailey's book bag flew off her shoulder and she stumbled to the ground, landing on her hands and knees.

Kiya led the chorus of laughter that followed from the rest of her classmates. "Miss Goody Two-shoes thinks she's cute, but she looks like an ugly black monkey looking for a banana."

The other kids pointed down at her, laughing so hard they were holding their stomachs. But when Mrs. Phillips ran up, it all stopped.

"My goodness! Bailey, are you okay?"

Her teacher put down the box she was carrying and helped her up. Bailey really liked Mrs. Phillips because she smiled all the time and wore a ponytail and brightly colored dresses that made her look like a teenager.

Bailey's knees burned with pain. "Yeah, I'm okay."

"What happened?"

Kiya gave Bailey the stink eye, daring her to snitch.

"I dunno. I just fell. I guess." As she picked up her book bag, she noticed that her knees were skinned and dotted with blood.

"I'm taking you to the nurse's office."

"That's okay, Mrs. Phillips. I'm okay."

The nurse would have to call her mom. Bailey didn't want to get her in trouble for having to leave the office in the middle of the day.

"Let me go get some paper towels."

The instant the teacher disappeared inside the classroom, Kiya whispered, "You better keep your ugly mouth shut, teacher's pet."

"Yeah," Morgan echoed. "You think you're all that, but you ain't."

Morgan never acted mean to her unless Kiya was around.

"You say one word," Kiya hissed, "and I'ma beat your ass after school."

As Bailey limped to the end of the line, the other kids hooped and hollered over the possibility of a fight.

Kiya was just plain evil. She wished she could be mean right back to her like her Uncle Dre wanted her to, but she was too afraid.

Gabriela Lopez turned around and whispered to her. "Are you okay?"

Bailey nodded. Gabriela was always nice to her but couldn't risk being her friend. Anybody who acted as if they liked her would be bullied too. Gabriela only talked to her when nobody else could hear.

"Don't be upset about what Kiya posted on Instagram last night," Gabriella said. "She's just jealous of you because you're pretty and smart and she isn't."

Not again. Kiya hadn't posted *#Baileygokillyourself* on Instagram for at least two weeks. Bailey assumed Kiya had stopped because she liked bullying her in person better than doing it online.

Bailey didn't understand why Kiya picked on her so much. She wasn't a goody two-shoes. And she certainly wasn't the teacher's pet. Mrs. Phillips liked all of her students.

Her teacher returned and waved everyone inside. When Bailey reached the doorway, Mrs. Phillips stooped to rub Wet Wipes across her knees, drying up the faint spots of blood.

"Are you sure you're okay?"

No, stupid! I'm not! But instead she said, "Yeah."

This had to be the third or fourth time Mrs. Phillips showed up three seconds *after* Kiya had done something mean to her. Couldn't she tell something was wrong? Grownups were so clueless. Bailey didn't know how much longer she could take Kiya's bullying and the other kids making fun of her. Instead of going to school, she wished she could stay in bed and sleep all day like her mom did on weekends.

Mrs. Phillips shut the classroom door behind her. "Did someone make you fall?"

Bailey's eyes fell to the floor. "No."

"You can talk to me, Bailey."

No, I can't.

She had told Mrs. Phillips about Kiya bumping into her in the hallway and pushing her into the wall, hurting her shoulder. That time, she almost told her teacher about the Instagram posts and all the other mean stuff Kiya was doing. Before she could get the words out, though, Mrs. Phillips said maybe Kiya accidentally bumped into her because the hallway was so crowded. It wasn't an accident. Kiya did it on purpose.

"Bailey, is Kiya Jackson bullying you?"

Her head shot up with a smile so big it made her face hurt. Bailey's smiley face was even better than her mom's.

"No, Mrs. Phillips," she lied. "I just tripped over my own feet."

CHAPTER

3

DRE TURNED ONTO Edgehill Street and pulled into the driveway of the fourth house from the corner. He cut the engine and leaned back against the headrest.

Sometimes he enjoyed just staring at the place. If his life could be described in colors, his world had gone from dingy gray to sunlight yellow since hooking up with Angela. The home they were leasing in Leimert Park possessed the perfect vibe for him: quiet and hip without feeling bourgeois. Once called the black Greenwich Village, Leimert Park remained an epicenter of the contemporary African-American arts scene in Los Angeles.

Dre had weathered a few rough spots in his life, but meeting Angela had served as a course correction. The fact that a guy with his past had a woman who was an attorney with her own law practice was proof of how far he had come since his drug-dealing days. A life so far behind him he'd need a microscope to catch even a glimpse of it.

He climbed out of the Jeep just as a moving truck eased into the driveway across the street.

Seconds later, a silver Prius pulled up to the curb and a white couple, probably in their mid-thirties like he and Angela, climbed out.

Another one?

Dre couldn't believe the number of whites moving in. He was used to seeing them in neighboring View Park and Ladera Heights because the homes there were in the seven figures. But the white flight of the fifties and sixties had left Leimert Park predominantly black, with a large smattering of Japanese Americans. Now the kids and grandkids of the whites who'd fled when blacks moved in, seemed to be returning in droves.

Once inside, he peered through the front picture window, watching the couple converse with the movers. Dre pulled out his cell phone.

"I'm calling with another wypipo alert," Dre said when Angela picked up.

Angela laughed. Dre was a big-time devotee of writer and poet Michael Harriot, a self-proclaimed wypipologist—someone who studies white people. Dre constantly quoted from Harriot's insightful and often hilarious social commentary on TheRoot.com.

"Which house?" Angela asked.

"The one directly across the street. Pretty soon, this neighborhood's going to be all white."

"I doubt that. Go over and introduce yourself."

"I'll pass on that."

"If they were black, you would've already done it. All the white folks moving in means our property values are going up."

"You do remember that we have a lease with an option to buy, don't you? I want them to stay right where they are until we own this place."

They had agreed to live together for a year, before deciding if marriage was the right move. Dre didn't need a year. He was all in.

Turning away from the window, he sat down on the living room couch. There was something he needed to tell Angela.

"I had to take Bailey to school this morning."

Silence.

"Yeah, uh, Erika had an early meeting and asked me to drop her off."

More silence.

Dre knew he should stop talking, but couldn't seem to shut his mouth. "She's still having a hard time over Earl's death. I'm just trying to help in any way I can."

"Yeah, okay," Angela responded.

He sighed. Angela most definitely was *not* okay with what he'd just told her.

Dre felt an obligation to Erika and Bailey that he could not and would not shirk. Bailey's father, Earl, had become his friend and mentor after Dre's release from Corcoran State Prison for drug dealing. Dre now had a successful house-flipping business because Earl had taken him under his wing and taught him a legit way to make a living.

Earl's death from bone cancer hit everyone hard. He was only forty-one. Dre would never forget his deathbed plea nine months ago to *take care of my girls*. Angela would have to understand.

He had tried bringing Erika and Angela together in the hope that they would bond. That hadn't happened. Initially, Dre was surprised when he'd picked up on Angela's jealousy because he'd never sensed that she was insecure about their relationship. But in the end, Dre understood that women were women, no matter how fine, how smart or how much cash they had in the bank. Angela would never admit she was threatened by Erika, but she was. For that reason, Dre always treaded lightly.

At least Angela had bonded with Bailey. Whenever the two of them were together, any observer would've thought Bailey was her child.

"I gotta go." Angela's jovial mood had vanished. "I have a client coming in."

"Okay, well—"

The phone went dead.

Dre shook his head. "Goodbye to you too."

He sent Erika a quick text asking her to email the school so he didn't have any issues with the principal in the future.

Grabbing a bottle of water from the fridge, Dre headed out. He was almost done refacing the kitchen cabinets at a duplex he was rehabbing in Hawthorne. Instead of climbing back in his Jeep, Dre placed the bottle in the cupholder and closed the door.

Angela was right. He should show a little hospitality and welcome his new neighbors to the hood.

CHAPTER

4

As soon as her class ended, Zola headed straight for the principal's office.

Although Zola couldn't get Bailey to admit that Kiya Jackson was bullying her, she was certain the child was being victimized.

Zola had tried to talk to the principal about her suspicions twice before. She'd never caught Kiya in action and had nothing more to go on than instinct. But this morning, Zola was certain she saw the girl intentionally stick out her foot, tripping Bailey. Because she hadn't been an eye-witness to any bullying, the principal brushed her off, scolding her for taking up her time.

This was only Zola's second year of teaching and she attacked it with a passion. In her mind, all any kid needed to succeed was someone to care about them. She was determined to be that kind of teacher.

As she hurried down the hallway, she gazed at all the posters lining the bulletin boards.

Bullying Stops Here!

Lend a hand to stop a bully.

Stand up, speak out. Stop bullying.

Strong people stand up for themselves. But the strongest people stand up for others.

Zola didn't understand what was going on with today's kids. Children were bullied in her day too, but schools didn't need to plaster anti-bullying signs all over the place. She stepped up to the desk of the principal's administrative assistant.

"Hey, Blanca, I wanted to speak with Ms. Freeman for a second."

Blanca peered up from her computer screen. She was a plump Latina who dressed in colorful, flowing blouses and high-heel sandals. Blanca protected the principal like a vicious guard dog.

"You know how she hates drop-ins. Why don't I make an appointment for you?"

Zola hesitated. As a new teacher, it wasn't good to make waves. Her friends who were experienced teachers warned her not to do anything to piss off her principal, at least not until she got tenure. Any time short of three years, the principal could dismiss her at the end of the school year without having to provide a reason. After the three-year mark, firing a teacher would take an act of Congress.

Zola clasped her hands in front of her. "This is important. Can you ask her if she can see me now? I won't need more than five minutes."

Blanca raised her pencil-thin eyebrows, pushed herself to her feet, and shuffled into the principal's office, closing the door behind her. After a couple of minutes, Zola began to get nervous.

When Blanca returned, the wary look on her face only heightened Zola's anxiety. "You can go in."

Darcella Freeman grimaced when Zola stepped into her office. "What is it now?"

The principal's gruff personality was just one of the reasons she didn't have many fans among the teachers. It wasn't like Zola bugged her every day.

"I'm sorry to bother you, but this shouldn't take long. When we talked about this before, you told me to keep an eye on things. Well, I'm pretty sure there's a bullying situation going on with Bailey Lewis."

The expression on Freeman's tight face went from dismissive to downright perturbed.

"Please close the door."

Zola did, expecting that an invitation to sit down would follow. It did not.

Before she could provide the facts to back up her statement, the principal morphed into prosecutor. "Did you witness another student doing something to that child?"

"Yes. I saw Kiya Jackson stick out her foot, tripping Bailey. She skinned her knees and—"

"It was most likely an accident. Did you hear Kiya say anything to her?"

"No."

"Did Bailey expressly state that Kiya was bullying her?"

"No, but—"

"What you described doesn't sound like *a bullying situation* to me. I'm so sick and tired of all this bullying mess I don't know what to do."

"If you let me—"

"How old are you, Mrs. Phillips?"

The woman knew how old she was. Zola straightened her posture. "I'm twenty-five. And what does my age have to do with this?"

"Everything. You barely have a year of teaching under your belt. It takes years of experience to become a good teacher. One day you're going to learn that you don't need to jump every time a child says *ouch*."

Zola's face colored. "It's not like that. I think—"

"I have way too much on my plate right now. The state assessment is next month and I need to complete a budget report by the end of the week. Are you forgetting that we're the only elementary school in this district to make the California Distinguished Schools list for five years in a row? We haven't had a single bullying incident and I don't intend to mar that record."

So you care more about this school's record than harm to a student?

Zola swallowed. "Aren't we required to do something if we think a student is being bullied?"

"Absolutely. But I haven't heard any evidence of that. Do you understand how much work a bullying investigation requires? We'll have to interview the students, call in their parents, get a district psychologist involved, and fill out a mountain of paperwork so we can cover our butts."

The principal's callousness shocked Zola into silence. She'd expected to be met with resistance, but this was nuts.

"If a child comes to you and says a specific student is bullying them, we'll deal with it. Based on everything you just told me, that hasn't happened."

Zola was slow to respond. "Bailey looks so sad all the time. She's always by herself at lunchtime and I never see anyone playing with her during recess."

"That child's only been enrolled here for three months. She'll make some friends sooner or later."

"Shouldn't we at least have one of the psychologists talk to her?"

"No! That child's father hasn't even been dead a year yet, but her mama had her boyfriend dropping her off at school this morning. He lied and said he was her godfather, but I know what's up. Some of these kids have a ton of issues that start at home, not at school. We're teachers. Not social workers. So go back to your classroom and teach."

The phone rang and Darcella picked it up. "Is there anything else?"

Zola stood there with her mouth agape. "I ... well ... uh, no. If you don't think this is important enough to—"

"I don't. Thanks for coming by."

CHAPTER

5

DRE PUT ON his best welcome-wagon face and jogged across the street. Admittedly, his actions were driven more by curiosity than a spirit of neighborliness.

He maneuvered around the huge moving truck and made his way to the porch. The front door was slightly ajar.

"Hello," he called out as he tapped gently on the door. His voice echoed into the empty space. "Anyone home?"

The woman he'd seen getting out of the Prius appeared in the doorway, her expression wary.

"Yes," she said, a smidgen short of curt. "How can I help you?"

"I live in the beige house across the street." Dre pointed over his shoulder. "I'm Andre. Just wanted to welcome you to the neighborhood."

"Thanks. I'm Hannah." An awkward silence filled the air until a slender man with a receding hairline walked up behind her.

"Our new neighbor came over to welcome us," the woman said.

The man stepped around her and extended his hand, something the woman hadn't done. "Thanks, man. I'm Jonathan. Jonathan Dolan."

The guy had a strong grip.

"Dre Thomas."

The woman raised an eyebrow. "I thought you said your name was Andre."

"Most people call me Dre for short." Maybe she was a lawyer like Angela. Distrust percolated in their bloodstream.

"So are you new to California?" Dre asked.

"Nope," Jonathan said. "Born and bred in Cali. We were paying crazy-high rent for a tiny townhouse in Santa Monica. This place was a steal."

The woman gave him a look that said he was giving up way too much information, but Jonathan continued anyway. "One of our friends hipped us to this neighborhood. They bought a house off Arlington Avenue about a year ago."

Dre nodded. *So the invasion was a group project.*

"Once I checked it out, I knew we had to come. Got way more bang for our buck. It took me some time to convince Hannah to make the move. But when she saw this house, it was a done deal."

Hannah gave her husband another non-verbal scolding. Jonathan either didn't notice or didn't care.

"Me and my girlfriend Angela moved here four months ago. It's a great neighborhood."

"So you're new to the area too," Jonathan said.

No, he wasn't new to the neighborhood. He grew up in South L.A. Dre let it go.

"I'm a stockbroker for Chase. What about you?"

White boys always had to compete. "Real estate. My girl, Angela, is a lawyer." *Now top that.*

"Nice, nice. Well, once we get settled, we'll have to invite you guys over for drinks."

"For sure. I guess I'll get out of your way."

Dre started back across the street. He hoped Jonathan did invite them over. He had a lot of questions about their decision to move into a black neighborhood. Dre didn't have *any* white friends. He'd love to get into their heads.

His hand was on the door handle of his Jeep when his next-door neighbor waved him over.

"I don't believe it," Chester grumbled, holding a coffee mug that read King of the Hill. "Another one. Never thought I'd see the day."

A retired Army officer, Chester was the neighborhood watch captain, an unpaid job he performed as if it came with a six-figure salary. He'd purchased his home in the late fifties and witnessed first-hand the droves of white folks fleeing Leimert Park to avoid living next door to people who looked like him.

Chester was a frequent poster on Next Door, a Facebook of sorts for the neighborhood. Although he didn't use his real name, Dre knew the racist rants belonged to Chester because he bragged about them after the fact. The changing complexion of the neighborhood concerned Dre too, but he wasn't ready to post Blacks Only signs up and down the street.

"I remember the white family that moved out of that house in 1961." Chester took a sip of coffee. "That man called himself a reverend but was as racist as Bull Conner."

Every conversation he'd ever had with Chester eventually turned to race. Dre needed to make a quick exit or he'd be trapped listening to him reminisce about the March on Washington for the umpteenth time.

"I just wish there was something we could do about it," Chester muttered between noisy slurps.

"I'm not happy with the neighborhood changing either, but it's a free country."

"For them it is."

He and Angela had moved to Leimert Park because of the cultural vibe. The white invasion would surely change that. He didn't want Leimert Park to become another trendy hotspot with coffee shops and Whole Foods on every corner.

"They comin' in here running up the prices so high black folks can't afford to live here. Jogging and walking their dogs all times of the day and night like they own the damn place." Chester shook his wooly gray head. "Never thought I'd see them coming back in a million years."

"It's a new day," Dre said, anxious to head to his Jeep. "The younger ones went to school with black kids. They don't fear black people the way their parents did."

"I don't care. It ain't right. They can live anywhere they want. Why they gotta come here?"

Dre chuckled to himself. This was enough Chester for one day. "Chill, bro. Times are changing and there's nothing we can do about it."

CHAPTER

6

BAILEY WAITED IN the cafeteria line, collected her food, and headed for an empty table. At least today they were serving her favorites, fish sticks and tater tots.

She happily drowned her tater tots in ketchup and stuck one in her mouth. When she looked up, her eyes met Kiya's and she almost choked. Bailey glanced over her shoulder. There were two teachers on cafeteria duty. There was no way Kiya would bother her here.

Seeing Kiya had ruined her appetite. She stole another look across the room. Kiya was walking toward her. Morgan and another girl were trailing close behind.

Bailey's stomach tightened. She was about to throw up her lunch *and* breakfast.

Kiya sat down across from her. "Hey, Miss Goody Two-shoes."

The other girls giggled as they took seats on either side of Kiya.

Bailey peered over her shoulder again, hoping to make eye contact with one of the teachers. Maybe they would see the fear in her eyes. Too bad Mrs. Phillips didn't have cafeteria duty today.

"I'm talking to you, teacher's pet," Kiya spat. "Don't ignore me, you ugly monkey. You need to make sure you look at Instagram when you get home."

The other girls howled with laughter.

How come the teachers didn't notice that all three of them were sitting on the other side of the table? If they were her friends, one of them would've been sitting next to her.

No matter what, Bailey was determined that this time, Kiya was not going to make her cry. And if she spit in her face again, maybe Bailey would spit right back like her Uncle Dre told her to.

Kiya pointed a finger across the table. "That's a cute sweater you got on. You should give it to me. Bring it back tomorrow in a bag."

A shiver of fear rocketed through Bailey's body. Her dad bought her the sweater right before he got sick and she loved it. It was soft and furry like a kitten. Sometimes at night, she put it on her favorite teddy bear and hugged it close, pretending it was her dad. There was no way she was giving it to Kiya.

"I'm talking to you, teacher's pet."

Bailey stared down at her plate. She wanted to get up and move to another table, but she was too afraid.

"Ow," Bailey gasped.

Kiya had kicked her already-sore right knee. She reached down to massage the spot. Before she knew it, a tear rolled down her cheek.

"Are you going to give me that sweater, crybaby?"

Bailey's tears quickly turned into hiccupping sobs as a slow rage began building in her chest. Why couldn't Kiya just leave her alone?

"Cry baby, cry baby," Morgan chanted.

"Okay, then," Kiya said, taking a packet of ketchup and ripping it open with her teeth. "If you're not going to give it to me, then I'll make sure you can't wear it either."

Kiya pointed the ketchup packet at Bailey and squirted it across the table, turning the center of Bailey's sweater from pink to red.

Staring down at her stained sweater in disbelief, Bailey's sobs abruptly stopped.

All three of the girls shrieked with laughter, failing to notice the fury in her eyes.

Bailey shot to her feet, picked up her tray and slammed it back down on the table, scattering food everywhere.

"I hate you!" she yelled, leaning into Kiya's face. "And if you don't leave me alone, I'll kill you!"

CHAPTER

7

Dre leaned against the kitchen counter of the Hawthorne duplex, examining his handiwork. He'd done an excellent job with the cabinets if he said so himself. The ringing of his cell phone interrupted his self-admiration. He pulled it from his back pocket.

Erika's panicked voice poured into his ear. There was some kind of issue at school with Bailey. Erika was already on her way. Could Dre meet her there?

According to what little information the school had given Erika, Bailey had been involved in a confrontation with another girl. Had she finally stood up to the bully? If so, good for her. It would not be good for him, however, once Erika and Angela found out his advice was the reason for Bailey's behavior.

Dre pulled into the school's parking lot within twenty minutes of Erika's call. He was climbing out of his Jeep when he thought about Angela. She wouldn't be thrilled that he was playing back-up daddy again. He needed to head off any issues. He called her as he walked.

"Hey, uh, something happened with Bailey. Erika's on her way to the school. I told her I'd head over there too."

"What happened? Is she okay?"

"She had some kind of run-in with another kid."

"Call me back as soon as you can."

Dre was grateful for her concern, but he knew that wasn't the end of it.

As he hurried down the hallway, his stride slowed as he took in all the anti-bullying posters. *Damn.* If they had to tell kids *Don't be a bully* this much, they obviously had a problem.

"Bailey's mother sent you an email giving you permission to talk to me," Dre said, the second he stepped inside the principal's office. "Is Bailey okay? Where is she?"

"Have a seat." Darcella Freeman extended her hand toward a chair in front of her desk. "I'm afraid we have a very serious problem."

"Is Bailey okay?" he asked again.

"Physically, yes. But I fear she may have some emotional problems."

Whatever had gone down, Dre was not about to let them pin it on Bailey. "What happened?"

"Bailey confronted a group of girls in the cafeteria."

Dre rolled his eyes. *Tiny, timid, little Bailey confronted not one girl, but a group of girls? Yeah, right.*

"One of the teachers on duty saw Bailey stand up and slam her tray down on the table."

"That doesn't sound like a confrontation to me. And, if Bailey did that, she had a reason. What did the girls do to her?"

"Another fourth-grader accidentally squirted some ketchup on Bailey's sweater. Her reaction was quite disproportionate. I'm very concerned about her mental state."

"Bailey's mental state is fine. Did that teacher also see that girl *accidentally* squirt her with ketchup?"

"No, she didn't."

"Of course not. Where's Bailey?"

"She's with Dr. Andrews, a psychologist from the district office."

Dre leaned forward in his chair, his jaw tightening. "Why would you think she needed to see a shrink for slamming a cardboard tray on a table? If she even did that."

"When a student threatens violence against another student, we have to take it seriously."

"*Threatens violence?* You're kidding me, right?"

"It wasn't just Bailey's actions. It's what she said that troubled us the most."

Dre was getting tired of this witch dispensing facts like cards in a slow game of poker.

"And what did she *supposedly* say?" He wasn't buying any of this crap until he spoke to Bailey.

"She threatened to kill her classmate."

Dre could tell the principal expected a reaction from him. He refused to give her one.

"*If* Bailey said that, I bet the girl was doing a lot more than *accidentally* squirting her with ketchup. She's a nine-year-old kid. You're making a big deal out of nothing."

"I beg to differ." Freeman's face glowed with smugness. "In this day and age of school shootings, we can't afford to ignore *any* threat of violence. Frankly, you should be thanking me for not calling the police."

Dre could no longer hide his irritation. "Give me a fuckin' break."

"Sir, there's no need for that kind of language. I have a responsibility to—"

There was a single knock on the door as Erika charged into the room. She glanced around the office. "Where's Bailey?"

Before the principal could answer, Dre interjected. "She's talking to a head doctor. They think she's nuts because she got upset when a girl squirted her with ketchup."

"I didn't give anybody permission to talk to my child."

Freeman clasped her hands and set them on the desk. "Why don't I start at the beginning. Please have a seat."

Erika grudgingly sat down, clutching her purse in her lap.

As the principal rehashed her little tale, Dre could hardly sit still. This was total B.S.

"May I ask you a question?" Freeman said, once she'd brought Erika up to speed. "Did Bailey receive counseling after her father's death?"

Dre jumped in. "You're not pinning this on Bailey. You've got don't-be-a-bully signs plastered all up and down that hallway out there. That tells me this school has a bullying problem."

"I can assure you that Parker Elementary doesn't tolerate bullying."

Dre angled his head. "So you say."

"Getting back to my question," the principal continued, her attitude not nearly as smug as it had been before Erika's arrival. "I understand that Bailey was very close to her father. Did she get counseling?"

"Yes," Erika said defensively. "Through our church."

"The loss of a parent is a very tragic event for a child. Perhaps you should consider a more formal counseling arrangement. I can get a recommendation from one of our child psychologists."

"Bailey doesn't need counseling," Erika snapped. "I want to see my daughter."

"I'll have my assistant ask Dr. Andrews to bring her in." Freeman reached for the phone. "But in the meantime, Bailey has to be disciplined for her behavior. She'll have to apologize to her classmates and she'll be assigned a campus beautification project. Something like cleaning a classroom or picking up trash during recess."

"Aw hell naw!" Dre barked. "She didn't even touch nobody. Is the girl who squirted her with ketchup gonna have to pick up trash too?"

"I can't discuss disciplinary actions involving another student. That's confidential."

"My daughter isn't picking up trash or cleaning anybody's classroom," Erika said. "I know my child. She wouldn't have gotten upset unless she was provoked. I think she's being bullied but is too afraid to tell anybody."

"Mrs. Lewis, I can assure you that Parker Elementary is a bully-free—"

"No, it isn't!" Erika exploded. She pounced out of her seat and leaned over the desk, pointing her finger inches from the principal's nose.

"I'm taking Bailey home and I'm going to find out exactly what's going on. And if she is being bullied, I'm suing you, this school, and anybody else who failed to protect her."

CHAPTER

8

"C'MON, BAILEY, I need you to talk to me. Why did you get upset in the cafeteria today?"

I don't feel like talking. Just leave me alone.

Bailey refused to look up at the white lady with the freckles and red hair. Her tears had all dried up, but her eyes still burned with anger. She rubbed them with the heels of both hands.

After Bailey yelled at Kiya, a teacher had marched her to the principal's office, where she sat on a hard chair for a long, long time. Then Principal Freeman came out to tell her how disappointed she was with her behavior.

And now she was stuck in an office with Dr. Andrews. She came to their school twice a week to talk to kids who were having mental problems. Everybody called her the cray-cray doctor.

Bailey didn't have a mental problem. She had a Kiya problem. The cray-cray doctor needed to find out why Kiya acted like the devil.

"Will you talk to me?"

Bailey looked up. "Okay."

"Why did you slam your tray down on the table?"

Bailey sighed. She might never get to go back to class if she didn't explain what happened.

"Because Kiya put ketchup all over my sweater. My dad bought it for me."

"Okay," the woman nodded, scribbling on the notepad on the desk in front of her. "That sweater's very special to you, huh?"

"Yeah. Now it's all messed up."

"Well, maybe he can buy you another one."

"He can't." Bailey's voice crumbled into a trembling whisper. "He's dead."

"Oh." Big red blotches spotted the woman's cheeks. "I'm so sorry to hear that."

"He had bone cancer. He got really, really skinny like a skeleton."

"That must've been tough. I bet you miss him a lot."

Bailey nodded and wiped a tear from her cheek. "Yep. But I got my Uncle Dre. He was my dad's best friend."

"That's great. What else happened that made you slam down that tray?"

Bailey hunched her shoulders. "Nothing."

She'd seen the teacher from the lunchroom talking to Kiya, Morgan, and the other girl. They were all going to lie on her anyway. It would be three against one and everybody would believe them.

"Did you tell Kiya you wanted to kill her?"

"I didn't mean it for real." Bailey touched a gooey splotch of ketchup on her chest. "I just got upset about my sweater."

It wasn't fair that Kiya got away with telling her to kill herself on Instagram all the time. But when she said it just once, she had to go to the principal's office. She wished she could have a classroom with just her and Mrs. Phillips and nobody else. She was so tired of everything. Tired of being bullied. Tired of being scared. Tired of missing her dad. Just tired of having such a sad, sad life.

"C'mon, Bailey. I want to help you."

"You can't," she whimpered. "Nobody can help me."

CHAPTER

9

THE NEWS OF Bailey's outburst in the cafeteria left Zola stunned and bewildered. For her, it was a further sign that the child was in distress. She didn't need twenty years of teaching experience to recognize a little girl's cry for help.

At least the principal had called in a mental health professional. Now they would get to the bottom of things.

Zola was packing up to leave when the classroom phone rang. She needed to report to the principal's office right away.

When she arrived, Zola was pleased to find Dr. Reese Andrews there too. That told her the meeting was about Bailey. Dr. Andrews had facilitated several workshops on bullying and childhood depression for the staff.

"Have a seat," Freeman said. "We have a problem with Bailey Lewis."

A problem with Bailey Lewis? Zola thought. *Bailey isn't the problem. You are.*

"Dr. Andrews met with Bailey Lewis this afternoon. She was about to debrief me. I thought you should be here too."

"The child is exhibiting signs of depression," the psychologist said. "She lost her father. That sweater was a gift from him. When Kiya Jackson got ketchup on it, it was a trigger. That's what provoked her outburst."

"Good, good," the principal said, nodding. "I figured there were some family issues."

Good? Zola's face contorted in disbelief. *What's good about that?*

"I spoke separately to the other girls." Dr. Andrews looked down at her notes. "They all said what Kiya did was an accident."

"Of course those girls would say that," Zola interrupted. "They were afraid of getting in trouble."

She couldn't admit it to anyone, but Kiya Jackson was her least favorite student. The girl had a surly disposition and always seemed to be at the center of any discord in her classroom. The one time she had tried to talk to Kiya's mother about her child's behavior, the woman told her to mind her own business, using more curse words in a single sentence than Zola thought possible.

Zola turned to face Dr. Andrews. "Did you ask Bailey if Kiya Jackson was bullying her?"

"I prodded her about that a lot. She denied that *anyone* was bullying her. Despite that, I do think bullying could also have been a factor in her outburst."

The principal slapped her palms on the desk and glared at Zola. "If the child didn't say she was being bullied, why in the world are you trying to put words into her mouth?"

Zola looked away.

"That girl's mother just bought a house in Baldwin Hills and is so focused on her job, she has her boyfriend bringing her to school," the principal ranted. "Too many of these parents care more about their careers than raising their children. And when something goes wrong, it's our fault. Well, I'm not having it."

A bewildered glance ricocheted between Zola and the psychologist.

"Do you know her mother personally?" Zola dared to ask.

"No. I'm just saying."

"Zola could be right," Dr. Andrews said, trying to assert herself. "Bailey might be too afraid to tell on the girls. That's pretty common. With her threat to kill Kiya and her comment to me that no one could help her, I think we should convene our threat assessment team, as well as develop some bullying-prevention steps to protect Bailey at school. I can call—"

"I don't believe this!" The principal's lips twisted into a pretzel. "That child threatens to kill another student and all we're worried about is protecting *her?* What's going to happen when Kiya goes home and tells her mama she's been accused of bullying? Then I'll have to deal with that ghetto-ass woman."

Zola gulped. She was horrified that Freeman had said that in front of Dr. Andrews. All teachers sounded off privately about difficult parents. But as African-American educators, there were some things you just didn't say in mixed company.

Dr. Andrews shifted in her seat. "Fine, I won't convene the team for now, but I do think I should develop a bullying-prevention action plan for Bailey"

The principal frowned. "I'm not sure that's the best course of action. Bailey's mother threatened to sue me. If there's litigation over this, having that plan in writing means we were on notice of this supposed *bullying.*" Freeman raised her hands and mimed air quotes.

Zola briefly closed her eyes. *How did this woman rise to the rank of principal?* She started rummaging around in her purse.

"What are you looking for?" Freeman asked impatiently.

"I'm trying to find some tissue."

Freeman pulled a box of Kleenex from her drawer and slid it to the edge of the desk.

"Wouldn't having an action plan in place help us if there is a lawsuit?" Zola asked. "It would show we were being proactive."

"Not necessarily," the principal said. "The first thing her lawyer's going to do is use it against us. It'll be proof that we thought Bailey was being bullied. But I have a trick or two up my sleeve if her mother does have the nerve to sue us."

Dr. Andrews leaned forward. "Let's be clear. Are you directing me not to prepare an action plan?"

Freeman locked her arms across her chest. "Of course not. You're the mental health professional. We have to follow your guidance on this. For now, why don't you prepare an oral report just for me?"

"Fine," Dr. Andrews said, reticence all over her face. "I'll work on it tonight. We can discuss it in the morning."

Freeman turned to the computer to check her calendar. "My schedule is packed. Let's shoot for early next week."

Zola wanted to scoot her chair back in case the demons possessing the principal tried to jump inside her body. The woman was a disgrace to the profession.

Dr. Andrews grabbed her satchel from the floor and stood up. So did Zola.

"Could you hang around for a minute, Zola?" Freeman asked, her tone suddenly syrupy sweet.

As Dr. Andrews walked out, Zola warily sat back down.

"I want to make sure we're both on the same page." The principal paused as if she was studying her for a reaction. "When you came to me this morning, you told me Bailey never said she was being bullied, correct?"

"Yes, but I did see Kiya Jackson trip her."

"As I said before, that was most likely an accident."

No, it wasn't.

"So are we on the same page?" the principal pushed.

"Um, sure, I guess." Zola swallowed. "But we spoke on at least two other occasions about my fear that Bailey was being bullied."

Freeman's head reared back like a rattlesnake poised to strike. "That's not what I recall. You simply expressed concern about Bailey being a loner and not having any friends. If you want to continue teaching here or anyplace else, your recollection had better start lining up with mine."

Zola's mouth fell open.

"Are we on the same page or not?"

Unable to speak, Zola nodded.

"We're done then."

Zola reached the door, then looked back. "When you said you had a trick or two up your sleeve, what did you mean?"

"Nothing you need to know," Freeman said with a devilish smirk. "But stay tuned."

10

BAILEY WAS SO happy to see her mom and Uncle Dre waiting outside Principal Freeman's office that she almost forgot about being in trouble. She hugged them hard enough to break their bodies in half.

Her Uncle Dre took her book bag from her hand. "You okay, squirt?"

Bailey smiled. Her dad used to call her squirt. "Yeah."

"We're not putting up with that bullying mess again," Erika said. "If I have to sue this school to stop it, I will."

Bailey's smile tumbled to the floor. "Mom, you can't do that!" She wished she could run out of the school and never come back. "Are we going home now?"

"Yes," her mother said. "And we're going to have a long talk when we get there."

It felt great walking down the hallway with her mom holding one hand and her Uncle Dre holding the other. Maybe she *would* finally tell them everything so she could transfer to another school. There was no way she could keep going to Parker Elementary if her mother sued the school.

When they reached her mother's car, Bailey looked up at her Uncle Dre. "Can I go home with you?" She wanted to avoid talking to her mother as long as possible.

"Sure, if your mom says it's okay."

Erika checked her watch. "Actually, I do need to run back to my office."

"Go do your thing," Dre said. "I got this."

Erika gave Bailey a hug, then stood on her tiptoes to kiss Dre on the cheek. "I don't know what I'd do without you."

Bailey climbed into the back of the Jeep and buckled her seat belt. She hoped her Uncle Dre didn't ask her about the cafeteria stuff. If she kept him talking about something else, maybe he wouldn't.

"Can we make peanut butter and jelly sandwiches when we get home?"

"Sure. But only if you come clean about what's going on at school."

Bailey swallowed.

"Tell me what happened."

"If I tell you, will you stop my mom from suing the school?"

"I'll see what I can do."

Bailey pointed at her chest. "Kiya Jackson squirted ketchup all over my sweater. I didn't even do anything to her. I was eating lunch all by myself, not bothering anybody."

"Why were you eating by yourself? Don't you have any friends to eat lunch with?"

Bailey shook her head. "Nope."

"That's crazy. As smart and cute as you are? Something must be wrong with those kids."

Uncle Dre was always trying to make her feel good. He had no idea what it was like to be a kid.

"So why did Kiya squirt ketchup on you?"

"Because she's the devil."

Dre laughed, which made Bailey laugh too.

"She is, Uncle Dre. I promise she is. She's mean to me for no reason at all. Right after you dropped me off this morning, she stuck out her foot and tripped me up and made me skin my knees. Then she said she was going to beat me up after school."

Bailey started to tell him about Kiya's Instagram posts. But if she did that, she would get in trouble because she wasn't supposed to have an Instagram account. Her mom said no kid should be on social media.

"Did you tell your teacher?"

"Mrs. Phillips was standing right there. She saw it. One time, I told her about Kiya pushing me into the wall and making me hurt my shoulder. But she didn't do anything about that either."

"Does anyone besides Kiya bother you?"

"Not really. Morgan Matthews always goes along with everything Kiya does. But when Kiya isn't around, she doesn't even notice me."

"We need to report Kiya to the principal."

"No, Uncle Dre, no. Please! If Kiya gets in trouble, she'll be twice as mean to me!"

"If we report her, she won't bother you anymore."

"Yes, she will. Kiya only messes with me when no teachers are around. Please don't report her."

"I'm going to put an end to this madness if I have to go talk to that girl's parents myself."

Bailey's eyes bulged. "Please, Uncle Dre!" she said, sobbing now. "Please don't do that."

His hand curved around the seat and he squeezed her foot. "Calm down. This is crazy. Ain't nobody at that school you should be *this* afraid of."

"I'm telling you, Uncle Dre, you can't do nothing. Promise me you won't tell the principal or my mom what I told you."

"I'll think about it. But you have to keep a secret for me too." Bailey could see him smiling in the rearview mirror. "Don't tell anybody I said this, but your principal is a total asshole."

"Okay," Bailey said, cracking up. "I'll keep your secret. But you have to keep mine too."

CHAPTER

11

HOURS LATER, DARCELLA Freeman was still fuming about Bailey's mother threatening to sue her.

"The nerve of that woman," she muttered to herself.

During her tenure in education, the principal had been involved in a handful of lawsuits. The first time, she'd only been teaching four years when the parents of an autistic child sued the district for failing to accommodate their son. The boy was the worst behaved child she'd ever run across and needed to be in a special class, which his parents resisted.

After two years of litigation, the district lost the case. They had to hire a dedicated aide for the boy and pay the family close to fifty thousand dollars, plus attorneys' fees.

The second time—only a year into her first job as an assistant principal—she took on the arduous process of firing an incompetent teacher. It still bugged her that the teacher got paid during the entire three-year process.

After that, Darcella began to understand the rules and was better prepared the next time around. As the school district's lawyer told her, *If it's not in writing, it didn't happen.* She had learned the hard way the importance of documenting everything. Or, in some cases—like Bailey Lewis's—not documenting *anything.*

The principal was still concerned about Zola Phillips. She'd never been involved in litigation and didn't understand how stressful it could be, how much time it took away from your regular responsibilities and, most importantly, how it could potentially wreck your career.

Darcella had strategically mapped out her professional path. She planned to spend a couple more years at Parker, then move into administration at the district level. When the time was right, she'd land an appointment to superintendent in a smaller school district. Then she'd retire early and start her own consulting firm so she could make some real money.

Darcella wasn't about to let a bullying lawsuit throw a wrench in her game plan. It was time to go on the offensive now. Not after the case was filed.

Blanca stepped up to her desk.

"Here's the phone number you asked for." She handed her a Post-it Note, an inquisitive grin on her lips.

"What are you smiling about?" Darcella asked.

"I'm curious about why you wanted that number."

"You apparently know me too well."

"Yes, I do. So what's up?"

"I'm calling to check on a student."

"Which student?"

"You don't need to know everything I know. Now get out of here and go home. Thanks for staying late."

She winked. "Anytime, boss."

Blanca was an excellent assistant, but didn't comprehend the meaning of the word *confidential*. That worked both to Darcella's advantage and disadvantage. The principal often used her to disseminate information that she couldn't publicize herself.

When Darcella caught a teacher screwing the janitor in her classroom, she wanted to embarrass the woman for her indiscretion. So she told Blanca about it and demanded that she keep it confidential.

Before Darcella made it home that day, a vice principal from another school was blowing up her phone asking for details. Blanca couldn't hold water if you gave it to her in a lockbox.

Glancing at the phone number, the principal dialed. Just as she was about to hang up, not wanting to leave a voicemail message, a woman's voice came on the line.

"Department of Children and Family Services. How may I help you?"

"This is Darcella Freeman," she said into the phone. "I'm the principal of Parker Elementary School. I'm calling to report a possible situation that I believe could be endangering the welfare of one of my students."

"The name of the student, please?"

"Bailey Lewis."

CHAPTER

12

DRE AND BAILEY lounged on the couch in Angela's office watching *Raven's Home,* munching on peanut butter and jelly sandwiches.

He noticed that Bailey was unusually quiet. Normally, the juvenile antics of the Disney sitcom had her laughing out loud.

"You're not going to tell anybody what I told you about Kiya, are you?" she asked, her eyes full of concern.

Dre placed a finger under her chin. "Do you trust me?"

Bailey shrugged. "I guess so."

"You guess so?" Dre poked out his lips in mock offense. "I thought I was The Man?"

"You can't always trust what grown-ups say."

He frowned. "Why would you say that?"

"My dad said he wasn't going to leave me, but he did."

Dre pulled her close and kissed the top of her head. "Sometimes things happen that we can't control. But you can definitely count on me. That's why I'm going to take care of this bullying madness."

Bailey started to cry. "No, Uncle Dre! If Kiya finds out—"

The doorbell rang.

"That must be your mother." He tried to get up, but Bailey grabbed his arm.

"Please don't tell my mom what I told you." Bailey started wiping her eyes. "I don't want her to worry about me."

When Dre opened the door, Bailey jumped into her mother's arms.

There was a vacant look in Erika's eyes as she embraced her daughter. "Go get your stuff."

"You look exhausted," Dre said as Bailey skipped off down the hall. "How are you doing?"

"Not good." Erika took a seat next to Dre on the living room couch. "There's this egomaniac on my team who gets off on criticizing everything I do. Yet, when our boss praises the final product, he takes all the credit."

Dre threw an arm around her and pulled her close, the same way he had comforted Bailey minutes ago. "You've made it to the big leagues, girl. You can handle it."

A second later, the front door opened and Angela stepped inside. Dre flinched as Erika pulled away from him.

Damn. He knew how this looked, but Erika was like a little sister to him, nothing more.

"Hi, Angela." Erika stood up.

"Hey." Angela flashed a phony smile back at her.

Dre watched Angela's eyes as they examined Erika from head to toe. She was wearing a dark pantsuit with a pink, satin blouse. He didn't know much about women's shoes, except that the red-bottoms Erika was wearing cost a grip.

"How's Bailey doing?" Angela asked.

"Okay, I hope," Erika said. "I'm so mad at that principal I could scream. If I have to sue that school to keep my child from being bullied, I will."

"My friend Jenny specializes in juvenile law. I'm not sure whether she's handled any bullying cases, but she might be a good person to talk to."

"I'd love to speak to her," Erika said. "Thanks."

Bailey returned to the room, her book bag hanging off one shoulder.

Angela bent down and gave Bailey a hug. "What happened to your sweater?"

Bailey looked down at her chest. "Kiya put ketchup all over it. I can't get it out."

"I'm sure the dry cleaners can fix it," Erika said. "I'll drop it off in the morning."

Erika's phone dinged. A crestfallen look glazed her face as she read the screen. She hesitated, then turned to Dre.

"I'm keeping Bailey out of school until I can figure out exactly what's going on. I just got a text asking me to attend a meeting at seven. Can I drop her off in the morning? I can pick her up before noon."

"Why don't you let her spend the night?" Dre said.

"Please, Mom, please! I have clothes here from last time."

"Thanks, Dre." Seemingly as an afterthought, Erika added, "You too, Angela."

She picked up her purse from the couch.

"Wait, Mom!" Bailey ran down the hallway, returning seconds later, wearing a red T-shirt. Her pink sweater was neatly folded in her hands. "Can you take it to the cleaners in the morning?"

Erika took the sweater and stuffed it into her purse. "She would wear this thing every day if I let her."

Bailey scampered back down the hallway.

"I'll walk you out," Dre said, announcing that solely for Angela's benefit.

When they reached Erika's BMW, Dre opened the door for her and watched as the car disappeared down the street.

Turning back toward the house, he spotted Angela's head dashing back behind the curtains of the living room window.

Dre hung his head. What did she expect to see? Him tongue-kissing Erika right in front of their house?

He blew out a long, slow breath. "Women."

Once he stepped back inside, Dre headed straight for the bedroom, prepared to face the music. Dre didn't like conflict, but when it arose, he preferred to deal with it head-on. If he and Angela were going to have another fight about his friendship with Erika, he wanted to get it over with.

Dre took a seat on the corner of the bed as Angela undressed. "Where's Bailey?" he asked.

"Watching TV in the office. She wants to sleep in there tonight. I told her that was fine."

"So how was your day?"

Angela took off her earrings and set them on the dresser. "Fine."

"Other than this thing with Bailey, mine was pretty good. I think we'll be able to put the Hawthorne duplex up for sale by the end of next month."

"Great."

One-word answers were never a good sign. Angela had her back to him now. She bent over to step into her yoga pants.

"Stop staring at my ass."

Dre snickered. "You got eyes in the back of your head?"

"Nope. I just know you."

When she finally turned around, there was a hint of a smile on her lips.

"Nothing's going on with me and Erika," Dre said.

"I know."

Then why were you peeking at us through the window?

"I promised Earl I'd look out for them," Dre continued, resenting the need to say this yet again. "That's my job as Bailey's godfather. His people are nothing but drama and Erika doesn't have any family in L.A."

"Doesn't she have any friends? Seems like you've become her ever-ready babysitter."

"She's got friends. But not anybody who can take off work whenever something comes up with Bailey. I thought you were cool with me helping her out."

"I am."

"She hasn't been right since Earl died. I think that promotion might be more than she can chew. But she walks around perpetrating like everything's all good. You know how you black women are."

"No, tell me. How are we?"

"Y'all want people to think you're stronger than Superman. You take care of everybody except yourself. I can still see the pain in her eyes. I gotta be there for her. For Earl's sake."

She turned around to face the mirror on the dresser, gathering her hair up in a ball. "I know. I'm good."

"When I suggested that Bailey spend the night, you acted like you had a problem with it."

"You know I love that little girl. So don't even go there."

That was true. He just wished she loved Erika too.

"But it would've been nice if she'd asked me about Bailey spending the night."

"I'm sure she didn't think it was a big deal."

"It wasn't. But if you want me to jump up and down and be all happy and giddy when I walk into *our house* and find *my man* hugged up with another woman, it ain't gonna happen."

Now we're getting somewhere. But Dre knew how to diffuse the situation.

"Oh, so you saying I should hug her *outside* of our house and you'd be fine with that?"

Angela didn't crack a smile. "This isn't funny, Dre."

He walked up behind her, threw his arms around her upper body, and kissed her slender neck. "You know I love you, right?"

"So you say."

He turned her around to face him and pressed his lips to hers. Angela eagerly reciprocated.

"Can we order Pizza Hut?" Bailey called from the hallway.

Once she arrived at the bedroom doorway, she covered her eyes at the sight of them kissing. "Yuck!"

Angela laughed as she pulled away. "I'll go order the pizza."

13

W HEN THE DOORBELL rang, Angela assumed it was the Pizza Hut guy. Instead, her sister Jada stood on her doorstep.

"Hey, sis," Angela said, giving her a hug. "I'm surprised to see you on a weeknight."

Jada frowned. "You must be losing it. I talked to you last week about borrowing your red, satin jacket for the hair show in Vegas? Remember?"

Her sister was a hair stylist and makeup artist with a fast-growing reputation. She had her own salon and also did makeup for a local TV morning show.

"I completely forgot."

Jada followed her down the hallway, slowing at the office door to say hello to Dre and Bailey.

"What's up with *that?*" She lowered her voice and pointed over her shoulder.

"What?"

"Every time I come over here, that little girl is here. I know her daddy died, but is Dre trying to take his place?"

"He's her godfather," Angela said defensively. "It's hard being a single mother. And she's still grieving Earl's death. Dre's just trying to help."

Jada swung her head from side to side. "My gullible, naive big sister. I've been doing my best to keep my opinion to myself since you and Dre seem so happy, but now I gotta speak my piece. Are you sure Erika and Dre don't have a past?"

"What? Of course not. Dre and Earl were best friends."

"Something don't smell kosher. A woman like Erika is used to having a man around. That's why she married old-ass Earl."

Angela retrieved her jacket from the closet. "Earl was only ten years older than her. That's not old."

"Well, she snagged one sugar daddy and now she might be hunting for another one."

Angela laughed. "Dre doesn't make enough money to be anybody's sugar daddy."

"If you ask me, Erika is relying way too much on Dre and I don't think you should be cool with that. With all the people she knows in L.A., Dre can't be the only one who can babysit her daughter."

"Stop it, Jada."

"Keep ignoring the obvious if you want to. But don't come crying to me when she walks off with your man."

"I don't need you putting craziness in my head. I trust Dre."

Jada paused as if she was trying to decide whether it was wise to proceed. She opened her mouth, but Angela flashed her palm, shutting her down.

"Whatever it is, I don't want to hear it."

"You sure?"

No, I'm not. Despite the facade she was presenting to her sister, the image of Dre and Erika embracing on the couch didn't sit right with her. She *did* trust Dre. But she couldn't say the same about Erika.

Angela placed her hands on her hips. "What, Jada? What beauty shop gossip are you dying to tell me?"

"Well, since you asked, every time Erika comes into the salon, she's constantly talking about how Dre did this and Dre did that

and how she and Bailey couldn't make it without him. I think it's
hella disrespectful since she knows I'm your sister. If I didn't know
better, I'd think she was talking about *her* man, not *yours*. I think
she wants me to tell you how she's always going on and on about Dre
so it'll create some friction between you two."

"Dre can't stop Erika from bragging about him."

"No, he can't. But *you* certainly can. If I were you, I'd put a lid
on that little threesome A-S-A-P. Hell, if she can spend three hundred dollars on that fake-ass natural hair weave, she should be able
to afford a nanny."

"I love Bailey. And I'm glad she has Dre."

"Yeah, but are you also glad Erika has Dre?"

No, I'm not. "I'm not threatened by Dre's relationship with
Erika. She's like a sister to him."

"I'm not trying to start nothing between y'all. You know I think
Dre is all that and then some. But men will be men."

"What's that supposed to mean?"

"It means that if Erika comes at him hard enough, Dre might
give in. Hell, Bailey is over here more than his own son. You might
wanna get a DNA test to make sure Bailey isn't Dre's kid."

"Really, Jada?"

"Yeah, really. Dre don't have to know. Save some of his semen.
And you could easily swab Bailey's cheek without her even knowing.
Tell her it's a game."

"It's time for you to go." Angela forced the jacket into her sister's
hands, took her by the shoulders, and spun her around. "Bye, sis."

"Let me say one more thing. Erika's image ain't as wholesome as
it appears."

"I don't care about her image."

Jada kept talking. "She's all polished and suited up with her new
BMW and her big-time job. But I bet you didn't know she used to
be a stripper."

That little tidbit stung Angela like a hard slap.

"I can see from that stunned look on your face that Dre never gave you the 4-1-1 on *that*," Jada said with a smug smile. "If I were you, I'd ask myself why."

CHAPTER

14

BAILEY WOKE UP in a haze, roused from sleep by muffled shouting.

"I'm not dealing with this right now. I'm just not."

Bailey sat up on the couch in Miss Angela's office, clutching a blanket to her chest. She didn't remember anyone putting a cover over her or turning off the TV.

It sounded like Uncle Dre and Miss Angela were arguing.

"I asked you a simple question. Why didn't you tell me Erika was a stripper?"

My mom was a stripper? Isn't that the same as a prostitute? Maybe they were talking about somebody else.

"Where'd you hear that? Your sister?"

"Doesn't matter where I heard it."

Bailey tiptoed to the office door and cracked it open. Their voices poured into the room.

"Please don't come at me with a bunch of gossip."

"Is it true?"

"Babe, please stop."

"Do you guys have a past?"

"C'mon, Angela. Don't do this."

"Do you?"

"Erika stripped for all of six months when she was barely twenty-one. I never told you because it was a long time ago. Her past is behind her. Just like mine is."

"Objection, non-responsive. I asked you a question. Maybe I need to be more clear. Did you ever fuck her?"

OMG! Bailey covered her mouth with both hands.

"Hell no! Earl was one of my closest friends."

Bailey struggled to make sense of what she was hearing. But she wasn't sure whether she was awake or dreaming.

"If you want me to trust you, you need to be honest with me, Dre. About everything."

"Can you lower your voice, please? You're gonna wake up Bailey."

"I checked on her a minute ago. She's sound asleep. Now can we finish this conversation?"

"No, we can't."

Heavy footsteps stomped down the hallway, past the office door. Seconds later, more angry footsteps retraced the same path. When Bailey heard the front door slam shut, she threw off the blanket and crept down the hallway.

Miss Angela was sitting on the living room couch, rubbing her forehead and looking sad.

"What's the matter, Miss Angela? Is something wrong?"

She bounced off the couch. "What are you doing up this late?"

"Are you okay, Miss Angela?"

"Yes."

No, you're not. Grown-ups always pretend like everything is fine. Like kids don't have a brain. When her dad died, everybody tried to keep her from knowing anything. But it was *her* dad. She had a right to know.

Bailey rubbed both eyes with her fists. "Where's my Uncle Dre?"

"He went out for a minute. He'll be right back. Let's get you back to bed."

Miss Angela took Bailey by the hand. "Are you sure you don't want to sleep in the guest bedroom?" she asked.

Bailey shook her head. "I like the office better. The couch is really comfortable."

Angela tucked her in and kissed her on the forehead.

"Can you leave the light on?"

"Sure."

Bailey planned to stay awake until her Uncle Dre got home. She laid still, thinking about everything she'd heard. Miss Angela and her Uncle Dre never argued. It sounded like Miss Angela was jealous of her mom. But her mom loved her dad, not her Uncle Dre.

She didn't care what Miss Angela said. No way was her mom a prostitute.

No way.

CHAPTER

15

DRE THUNDERED OUT of the front door, headed for his Jeep. He jerked on the door handle just as he remembered that his keys were on the kitchen counter. He refused to go back inside and subject himself to more nonsense. As mad as he was, it was a good thing that he wasn't behind the wheel.

He hit the sidewalk. A nice, long stroll would help him blow off some steam.

Angela had never jammed him up like that before and he didn't like it. He'd been a model boyfriend, happy to have a woman like Angela in his life. But jealous chicks had always been a turnoff.

Dre looked up and saw a 30-something white woman jogging toward him.

WTF?

Gentrification at its finest. But what he didn't understand was their seeming disregard for their physical safety. Why was this woman jogging alone at night? And he wasn't saying that just because this was a black neighborhood. Criminals were hard at work everywhere. He'd seen a news story about a break-in at some celebrity's house in the Hollywood Hills. A woman shouldn't be jogging alone at night *anywhere*.

The jogger was only a few feet away now. As she got closer, Dre noticed that she began to veer away from him until she was finally on the opposite side of the street. As she zipped past him, she stared straight ahead, her pace much faster now.

Maybe she did care about her safety after all.

As he turned around to see if she would cross back over to his side of the street, he spotted a white couple half a block behind him, pushing a baby stroller.

It was one thing to see whites invading their neighborhood. It was another to see them acting like they were walking the streets of Beverly Hills at high noon. Dre was almost jealous. He wished he shared their sense of fearlessness. Even now, he was on high alert, cautious of his surroundings. Almost *expecting* something to go wrong. It must be nice to never have that fear. Even on a pitch-black street in the middle of an urban area.

He headed left on 39th Street, the crisp air helping to diffuse his anger. Dre should've told Angela about Erika's past. Having her find out from her sister made it seem like he was hiding something. But it wasn't anybody's business. Dre understood what it was like to have people judge you for the mistakes of your past.

Dre made another left on Crenshaw, intending to circle back around to Edgehill. But seconds after rounding the corner, he came face-to-face with a spotlight so bright it stung his eyeballs.

"Stop! Hands up! Now!"

Damn.

Two officers jumped out of a squad car with their guns drawn and aimed squarely at him. One was a beefy white guy, the other a Hispanic female whose small stature surprised him.

Dre raised both hands in the air, his temples throbbing with rage. White folks could roam the streets, but a black man taking a stroll in his own neighborhood might get shot to death if he breathed too hard.

"Walk slowly toward us," the white cop ordered. "And keep those hands where we can see 'em."

Dre knew the drill and did as he was told, seething with every step. One wrong move and his life could be over.

When he was almost at the car, the female officer holstered her weapon and began patting him down while the other cop kept his gun on him.

"Do you have a weapon?"

"No."

After the pat down, she hurled him around and slammed his chest up against the patrol car, slapping handcuffs on him.

"You live in this neighborhood?" she asked

"Yeah."

"Where?"

"On Edgehill."

Her auburn hair was pulled back in a ponytail. Dre wondered why she wanted to be a cop. She was pretty enough to get a more feminine job.

"What's the address?" She tried to sound extra tough. Dre figured this was a show she performed daily. Women cops no doubt had to be extra tough to earn the respect of their male colleagues.

"Thirty-nine, fourteen," Dre said.

She pulled his wallet from his back pocket, took out his driver's license, and perused it. "That's not the address on your driver's license."

"I only recently moved here."

"How long ago?"

"Four months."

"That's not recent. You've had plenty of time to update your license. You wouldn't be pulling my leg, would you?"

Dre gritted his teeth and tried to maintain his composure.

The white cop, his gun aimed at Dre's head now, wasn't buying it either. "The cheapest house in this neighborhood is about eight hundred grand. How'd a guy like you make that kind of money?"

Screw you. Dre refused to respond.

"I'll run his name," the female officer said, as she headed toward the patrol car. "I got a feeling on this one."

"What are you doing out so late at night?" the white cop asked.

"Just taking a walk."

"Sure you were."

Dre's head was twisted to the left, his body pressed up against the car. His neck began to ache from the awkward positioning of his body, no doubt aggravated by anxiety. He wanted to rotate his head to the other side but didn't dare move.

"Why'd you stop me?"

"There've been a few break-ins in this neighborhood. We got a call about somebody suspicious."

"Yeah, okay."

The female officer jogged back over to them. "Bingo! Did a stint at Corcoran." She was so excited Dre almost expected her to start jumping up and down. "Drug dealer."

Ex-drug dealer, Dre wanted to say.

That life was behind him. Way behind. He was a model citizen now and he deserved to be treated like one.

The white cop snickered. "So that's how you can afford to live in this neighborhood. What's your product of choice? Crack, meth, opioids?"

Dre remained silent.

"Have a seat on the curb," the female officer instructed.

Dre wasn't sure he could manage that with his arms handcuffed behind his back. He took a backward step and tried to squat. Just as he feared losing his balance and banging his head on the concrete, the female cop grabbed his upper arm, guiding him to the curb.

"You claim you were out taking a walk," she continued. "So where are your house keys?"

"At home."

The officers moved a few feet away to huddle out of earshot. They had no legitimate reason to hold him. But the color of his skin and the mistakes of his past gave them two bogus ones.

"Give me that house number again," the female cop said. "We're going to give you a ride home."

Dre repeated his address.

The other cop snatched his arm, pulling him to his feet. He guided him into the back seat of the patrol car, a place Dre never thought he'd see again.

"I hope for your sake you're telling the truth," he said, slamming the door. "Otherwise, you're getting a ride downtown."

CHAPTER

16

BAILEY TRIED TO fall asleep, but couldn't stop thinking about the argument between Uncle Dre and Miss Angela.

If Miss Angela wasn't going to like her mother anymore, then she was going to stop liking Miss Angela. She couldn't wait to talk to her Uncle Dre. He treated her like a grown-up and never lied to her.

She could feel herself drifting off to sleep. As soon as she did, she shook her head back and forth ten times. She had to stay awake until Uncle Dre got home. She wished she had some water to splash on her face.

Bailey heard Miss Angela coming down the hallway and pretended to be asleep. Miss Angela stuck her head into the room, turned off the light and closed the door.

Bailey walked over to the window. She was confused. Uncle Dre's Jeep was still in the driveway. So where was he? Maybe he'd already come back home and she hadn't heard him. She was about to go check when she spotted Miss Angela's Mac on the desk.

It reminded her that she'd forgotten to check Kiya's latest posts on Instagram. She'd been attacking Bailey on Instagram almost from the day she started at Parker Elementary.

When she sat down at the desk and hit a key, the screen lit up.

Bailey wasn't allowed to have a phone yet. Only three girls in the whole fourth grade had cell phones. Her mom said she had to wait until she was 12. That was like a million years away.

She did have an iPad, but her mom put an app on it so she couldn't go on social media. But when her mom went to sleep, Bailey snuck to use her work laptop. Afterward, she always deleted Instagram from the browser. She learned how to do that on Google.

Bailey's Instagram account used a fake name and a pink flower for her picture. She only had it to look at other people's posts. A lot of kids in her class had Instagram accounts even though their parents said they couldn't.

She went to Instagram and searched for *KitKatKiya*. The girl's page had a bunch of selfies of Kiya and Morgan smiling and posing like they were Kim and Khloe. All Bailey saw was evil. They must not be raised in the church. Otherwise, how could they act so mean all the time?

Kiya probably used Morgan's cell phone to post stuff since she didn't have an iPad or a cell phone.

As Bailey scrolled through the posts, she began to shudder. Kiya had posted a picture of her!

How did she even get it?

Bailey could tell from the background that it had been taken in the school playground. Kiya had distorted her face to make her look like a monkey. Underneath the picture were the words *#BaileyShouldJustDie!* It had 32 likes.

What did she ever do to make Kiya hate her so much? Tears began to stream from Bailey's eyes as she read the comments other people had posted below the picture.

She looks like that for real.
Ugliest girl in the fourth grade.
Teacher's pet needs to go to the vet.
Just kill yourself.

Why would her classmates say such mean things? She took a screenshot of the picture and a separate shot of the comments.

Maybe her mother *should* sue the school. This would be some good evidence too. But then other kids besides Kiya would get in trouble for posting mean stuff. Then *everybody* at school would hate her.

Bailey lowered her head to the desk and sobbed.

CHAPTER

17

A LOUD POUNDING ON the front door startled Angela out of a deep sleep. She jumped up from the living room couch, struggling to get her bearings.

Angela remembered that Dre had forgotten to take his keys and sprinted to the front door. She trusted Dre and regretted giving him such a hard time about Erika. Her lips were poised to gush words of apology.

Once the door was open, however, she was so stunned by the image facing her, the words got stuck in her throat.

Dre stood between two uniformed cops, his hands behind his back, his jaw clenched tight enough to crush his teeth. Behind him on the street, the flashing lights of the police car heightened the gravity of the scene.

"Does this man live here?" the male cop asked, the bravado of his protruding chest mimicking the bluster in his voice.

"Yes he does."

When Dre's eyes met hers, Angela saw blistering rage. A vein the size of a drinking straw pulsed like a heartbeat on the side of his neck.

"Why is he in handcuffs?"

"For no reason at all," Dre snarled.

"There've been some break-ins in the neighborhood," the female officer said. "This address wasn't on his license."

"Do you handcuff everyone whose address doesn't match their license?" Angela demanded.

"We're trying to protect this neighborhood," the male cop said, ignoring her question.

"I'll take your response as a no. I'm an attorney. A former federal prosecutor, in fact. First, take off those handcuffs. Second, I'll need your names and badge numbers for the complaint we intend to file."

Both officers stiffened.

"Hold on while I get something to write with."

Angela stepped away from the door. By the time she returned from the kitchen with a notepad and pen, Dre was sitting on the living room couch, stewing. She took down the information and closed the door.

Angela joined him on the couch, eager to diffuse his anger. "I'm sorry. I trust you. I'm happy you can be there for Erika and Bailey."

Dre angled his head. "Happy?"

Angela smiled. "Well, not happy. But I understand."

She pulled him into her arms, his body still rigid with rage. "I'm sorry that happened to you."

"I bet the white folks I saw out taking a stroll didn't get shoved into a police car and have to prove where they lived."

Angela decided it was best to let him rant.

"I should go right back out there and dare 'em to arrest me again."

"No, you shouldn't. They could've shot you."

He pulled away from her and stood up. "I know it was some white person who called the police on me."

"You don't know that."

"Yes, I do. White people flood our neighborhood and we're the ones treated like outsiders. I'm not having it. I'm going to start taking walks *every* night."

"That's stupid." Angela glared up at him. "If you meet up with the wrong cop, you could end up dead."

"I'll be damned if I'm going to be afraid of walking down the street in my own neighborhood. If I get shot, so be it."

CHAPTER

18

THE BLINKING RED-AND-BLUE lights of the police car spilled into the room, setting off a silent alarm in Bailey's head.

What's going on?

Bailey had fallen asleep at Miss Angela's desk and her neck hurt from resting her head on the hard surface.

Cracking the door open, she could hear voices but couldn't understand what they were saying. Bailey tiptoed down the hallway and peered around the corner. Uncle Dre was standing between two police officers, his hands behind his back.

O-M-G!

Bailey was just about to run into the living room to help him, when one of the officers reached down and took off the handcuffs.

Why did they arrest my Uncle Dre?

After a minute or so, Miss Angela and her Uncle Dre started shouting at each other again. Bailey still didn't understand what was going on. This time they weren't arguing about her mom.

Then she heard her Uncle Dre say he was going to walk the streets every night and he didn't care if the police shot him.

Bailey ran back to the office, plopped down on the couch and sobbed into the blanket. She couldn't take it if the police killed her Uncle Dre. Why was he being so hard-headed when he knew the police shoot black men for no reason? If her Uncle Dre got killed, everything would be ten times worse for her and her mom.

If her dad was still here, he would tell her Uncle Dre not to act like that. Her granny said her dad was waiting for her in heaven. Bailey wished she could go live up there with him right now.

Everything was so messed up and nobody could fix it. Kiya was never going to stop bullying her.

Bailey got up from the couch and sat down in front of Miss Angela's computer again. Her eyes were so full of tears she almost couldn't see the screen.

CHAPTER

19

Zola couldn't wait for school to begin. If the principal wasn't going to do anything to protect Bailey, then she would. If she had to keep her eyes on the child every second of the day, she would.

The meeting in the principal's office still unnerved her. She thought about calling Dr. Andrews to get her take on things, but feared what would happen if Freeman found out.

Zola liked arriving at work before seven so she would have the teacher's lounge all to herself. Though it was empty now, she'd only have a few more minutes before someone disrupted her solitude. She poured herself a cup of coffee as two other teachers entered.

"Hey, Zola, give us the 4-1-1," said Tara Slaughter, a third-grade teacher. "What in the world did you do to piss off Sami?"

Sami—short for Satan's mistress—was what most teachers called Freeman behind her back.

Zola's squinted. She had no idea what the woman was talking about.

"I don't have any 4-1-1."

"You clearly did something to get on Sami's bad side."

"And where'd you hear that?"

"I can't disclose my sources. But a little birdie told me Sami isn't happy with you these days."

Zola's stomach contracted. She didn't want to be on the principal's hit list.

The other teacher, Lydia Mendez, gave her a sympathetic smile. "Tara's just messing with you. Blanca's been going around spreading rumors again."

"The principal's assistant knows everything that goes on in this place," Tara said. "So what were you and the psych doc doing in the principal's office yesterday?"

Zola exhaled a long breath of frustration. "One of my students is being bullied."

There. She'd said it.

Lydia pursed her lips. "Be careful. Sami does not like the B word."

Tara took a sip of coffee. "We're giving this bullying stuff way too much oxygen. The more we talk about it, the more kids focus on it. Kids are just being kids."

Zola almost spit up her coffee. "So you don't think bullying exists?"

"I'm not saying that. But it's not nearly as bad as everybody's trying to make it out to be. Every time a kid has a problem, somebody wants to blame it on bullying. I say you need to look at what's going on at home."

Another teacher, Malcolm Lawson, walked in on the tail end of Tara's statement.

"These days, we have to be teachers *and* therapists," he said, joining the conversation without an invitation.

"I didn't go to college for that," Tara countered.

"That's certainly not the right attitude to have. I strive to treat the whole student."

Malcolm was a goofy, sandy-haired, white guy who considered himself God's gift to teaching. He couldn't sit in a room without being the center of attention. His fifth-graders adored him.

"Have any of you had students who were bullied?" Zola asked.

All three teachers nodded.

"What did you do about it?"

"I handled it," Malcolm replied with a shrug. "I didn't run to the principal."

Did Malcolm also know about the situation with Bailey? How did this reach the entire school overnight?

"Overreacting to every minor situation will only make things worse," he continued.

Zola had heard schools were professional rumor mills, but this was the first time—at least to her knowledge—that she was the focus of one.

"How could doing something about it make it worse?" Zola asked, her defenses up.

"All the rules and regulations telling us how to handle a bullying situation were made up by people who aren't in the trenches like us," he said. "We'd never be able to teach if we had to investigate every complaint."

Malcolm grabbed two cinnamon rolls from the center of the table. The teachers took turns bringing pastries. Malcolm never contributed, but always loaded up.

"The principal has a lot on her plate," Tara said. "I can understand her not wanting to be bothered with a bullying investigation."

A minute ago, Tara had referred to Freeman by her nickname. Now that Malcolm was in the room, she'd changed her tune. He was one of the principal's staunchest allies. No one ever said anything negative about Freeman when he was around.

Zola tossed her empty coffee cup into the trashcan and got to her feet.

Both Tara and Malcolm had almost a decade of teaching under their belts. After she'd been in the classroom that long, Zola hoped she didn't end up as jaded as Tara or as full of herself as Malcolm.

CHAPTER

20

DRE GAZED UP at the ceiling as he lounged in bed. He could hear Angela in the shower. She'd slept in his arms for most of the night. He relished the comfort of her warm body, but nothing could erase the humiliation of his run-in with the cops.

Despite everything, he was glad that Angela had cut him some slack about Erika. He'd expected to return home to more attitude. But unlike most of the women he'd dated, Angela didn't have a problem admitting when she was wrong. And she never stayed mad for more than a hot minute.

He glanced at the clock on the nightstand. It was almost seven-thirty. It would be another hour before Angela left for her office. Dre hopped out of bed. He'd surprise her by cooking breakfast. Thanks to his homegirl Rachael Ray, his ham, cheese and mushroom omelets would have a five-star chef asking for seconds.

After retrieving a frying pan from the cabinet, Dre remembered that he was taking care of Bailey today. She wasn't big on eggs, so he decided to make pancakes and bacon for her.

He peered into the refrigerator, looking for the ingredients he would need: eggs, milk, ham, bacon, butter, mozzarella and cheddar cheese. He opened the cabinet next to the fridge and took out the olive oil, garlic powder, lemon pepper seasoning, and pancake mix.

Angela joked that he organized his ingredients with the same precision he used to install tile. Next, he pulled out two plastic bowls, a whisk, a large spoon, and a spatula. Bailey was an early riser and would be plodding into the kitchen any minute. He'd make the pancakes first.

Just as he stepped up to the sink, Angela let out a loud, gut-wrenching wail that washed over him like a tsunami.

"Dre! Oh, my God, Dreeeeee!"

Dre dashed toward her voice, running down the short hallway with such speed that he overshot the bedroom door. He was inside the bathroom, snatching back the shower curtain when he realized Angela wasn't there.

"Oh, my God! Help me, Dre! Please help me!"

Angela's screams were coming from her office, not the bathroom.

When he reached the doorway, Dre froze as if the scene was a mirage. Angela was standing outside the closet, cradling an ashen, limp Bailey in her arms. A red-and-white jump rope—Angela's jump rope—was tangled around her neck. It was connected to his pull-up bar which hung on the closet's door frame.

Snapping out of his fog, Dre rushed over to them, kicking his workout bench out of the way. While Angela held Bailey, Dre struggled frantically to untie the jump rope which was a jumble of knots around her neck.

"Oh, my God!" Angela sobbed.

"Hold onto her," Dre yelled. "Everything's going to be okay."

When the knots wouldn't give, he grew more frustrated. "Fuck! Fuck! Fuck!"

Darting over to the desk, he opened the left drawer and grabbed a pair of scissors. Cutting through the coarse rope was like trying to saw steel with an emery board. It took another minute before he was able to free her.

Dre took Bailey's lifeless body from Angela and laid her on the floor. "Call 9-1-1!"

But Angela backed away into a corner, curled up in the fetal position and wailed.

Dre lifted Bailey's chin and covered her small mouth with his, desperate to breathe life back into her body.

C'mon, Bailey, breathe!

This was only the second time he'd ever performed mouth-to-mouth resuscitation. Dre had rescued a child from the bottom of his cousin's pool. He'd been successful in bringing that little boy back to life and he would bring Bailey back too.

But it wasn't working.

Dre switched to chest compressions, using just one hand, for fear Bailey's tiny chest couldn't withstand more pressure. Dre tried to recall what he'd done to save that little boy. He couldn't remember how many chest compressions he was supposed to do before taking a break.

Angela stood over them, the kitchen phone in her hand, blubbering into it.

Dre continued giving Bailey mouth-to-mouth as his despair mushroomed.

Bailey's small, pale face glistened with tears. Dre's tears.

C'mon, Bailey, breathe! Please breathe for me!

CHAPTER

21

DARCELLA FREEMAN ARRIVED at district headquarters thirty minutes before the start of her monthly administrators' meeting. Getting there early guaranteed her a parking spot that would give her red Jaguar maximum exposure.

She checked her makeup in the rearview mirror as her cell phone rang.

"Have you heard?" Blanca asked as she hit the speakerphone button.

"Heard what?" Darcella uncapped a lipstick tube, rolled a layer of candy-apple red across her bottom and top lips, then blotted them together.

"About Bailey Lewis."

"What now?"

"She tried to kill herself."

"What?" Darcella turned off the speakerphone and held the phone to her ear. She listened in shock as Blanca recounted what she'd been told by one of her church members.

Bailey had been rushed to Children's Hospital and was now on a breathing machine. Her family attended First Baptist and had called their minister to the hospital. Blanca was close friends with the church's first lady.

After hanging up, Darcella leaned back against the headrest, too shell shocked to get out of the car.

"Dammit!" she hissed, pounding the steering wheel with the heel of her hand.

Darcella prayed the little girl didn't die. Parker Elementary did not deserve to be linked to a nine-year-old suicide victim. She'd read about kids killing themselves, but never imagined it could happen to one of her students.

Now her school would be the focus of a bullying investigation by the district. The news media might even turn up, blowing everything out of proportion and printing a bunch of lies.

Grabbing her phone, she called Blanca back.

"Don't mention what happened to Bailey to anyone else and definitely don't tell anyone you informed me about it. We need to wait until we get notification from official channels."

"What official channels?"

I have no idea. "Her family. And if you blab about this, I swear you'll never work another day at this school."

Her trusted assistant didn't respond. Darcella threatened members of her staff on a regular basis but never Blanca.

"Did you hear me?"

"Yes."

"I'm dead serious. So don't try me. Have you told anybody else?"

"No. You were the first person I called."

"Good. Keep it that way."

That was certainly a useless exercise, Darcella thought as she ended the call. The news would probably be all over the school before her meeting started.

She began scrolling through her contacts. There was another more important call she needed to make.

"You said you'd have that action plan for Bailey Lewis today," she said when Dr. Andrews picked up. "Let's chat about it around ten."

Dr. Andrews made a sound Darcella couldn't decipher. "Uh, I'm...You said you wouldn't have time to discuss it until next week. So I didn't work on it last night."

"You must've misunderstood my instructions. I said you could get me the *written* report next week, but I wanted an oral report this morning."

Silence shouted through the phone line.

Darcella knew the psychologist didn't have the balls to stand up to her.

"Did something happen? Is there a reason you suddenly want it now?"

"I don't *suddenly* want anything. This isn't something we should put off. So does ten work for you?"

More silence. "I guess so."

"Great, I'll call you then."

Darcella hung up. That was easy. Now she just had to make sure she got Zola Phillips in line.

CHAPTER

22

ANGELA NOW UNDERSTOOD the meaning of out-of-body experience. It felt like she was gliding through an unending tunnel, her feet off the ground, her vision blinded by fog.

The paramedics finally arrived and ushered her and Dre out of the room. When one of them blurted out that they found a pulse, Angela and Dre simultaneously gasped in relief.

For the longest time, they stood hugging on the sidewalk, no longer able to cry, their tear ducts drained by grief.

Angela couldn't remember when or how they'd ended up in their new neighbors' living room.

"Would you like some coffee?" the husband asked.

"No, thank you." Angela didn't even know their names.

The wife set two steaming cups on the coffee table anyway. She and Dre reached for them at the same time.

The couple's living room was still crowded with boxes. The four of them sat there, wordless. Dre had tried to climb into the ambulance with Bailey, but a detective insisted that he wait around for a brief interview.

Dre walked over to the window and stared across the street at their home. Two cop cars were still parked out front.

"We need to be at the hospital," he said, flopping back down on the couch next to Angela. "If they want to talk to us, they better hurry up. I know Erika is going nuts."

It was Dre who'd made the call to Erika. Angela couldn't remember much of what he said, but she would never forget Erika's wails gushing out of the phone.

There was a knock on the door. The husband opened it.

Two detectives stepped into the room. The wife hung back in the kitchen as if the ordeal frightened her.

"We know this is a difficult time for you," one of the detectives began, "but we have a few questions."

Both men were African-American, their bodies stiff and formal, their faces filled with compassion.

The taller man took the lead. He was balding and likely in his forties. Angela wondered if he had a child Bailey's age.

"Is Bailey your daughter?"

"No," Dre replied. "I'm her godfather. Her mother kept her out of school today and I was"—he choked back a sob—"I was taking care of her today."

"Why was she kept out of school?"

"Because she was being bullied."

The detective glanced at his partner but didn't speak.

"Can you tell us who discovered the child?"

Angela raised a limp hand, which fell back to her lap with a thud.

"Do you remember what time it was?"

"Seven-forty-three."

A subtle tilt of the detective's head told her he found it strange that she was able to be so exact.

"I had checked the bedroom clock right before going into the office to see if Bailey was awake yet," Angela explained.

"Can you tell us what you saw?"

Angela tried to form words but only an agonizing moan escaped from her lips. She swung her head from side to side and started to cry again. "No, no, I can't."

Dre pressed Angela's head against his chest.

"I was in the kitchen when I heard Angela scream," Dre replied, though the question had not been directed to him. "When I got to the office, Bailey was"—he paused—"she was hanging from my pull-up bar, all tangled up in Angela's jump rope."

"How was the child able to reach the bar?"

"My workout bench was in front of the closet. I'm assuming she must have stood on that."

"Was it normally there?"

"No. It was against the wall near the door."

"Who moved it?"

"I assume Bailey did. I always keep it against the wall."

"Where was the jump rope kept?"

"In the closet."

"I thought you said the room was an office. Why was a workout bench in there?"

Dre sniffed. "Because sometimes I use the room to lift weights."

"Who took the child down?"

Angela flinched every time the man said *the child*. "Her name is Bailey," she interrupted.

The detective nodded apologetically and scribbled on his note-pad. "I'm sorry."

"I got her down," Dre continued. As he told the rest of the story, he sounded like a drowsy robot.

"What time did"—the detective glanced down at his notes—"Bailey go to bed last night?"

"Around nine," Dre answered.

"Why was she sleeping in the office?" the other detective asked. "There's no bed in there."

"She likes the couch," Angela said. "She asked me if she could sleep in there."

Angela's tears started to flow again. If she had made Bailey sleep in the guest bedroom, maybe this wouldn't have happened. Bailey had to make it. Erika couldn't lose her husband *and* her child.

The first detective took over the questioning again. "Do you know any reason she may've wanted to harm herself?"

"I already told you she was being bullied at school," Dre said, his voice curt. "That's the reason."

As Dre recounted the cafeteria incident, Angela's legal senses began to kick in. The detectives' questions were becoming subtly accusatory.

Did you hear her moving the bench?

Did you check on her during the night?

How many times has she slept in that room before?

Angela could sense Dre's mounting frustration. She wished she could shut down her pain and turn on her lawyer brain. But she had no mental energy to spare.

Skepticism filled the detective's eyes. He didn't believe a nine-year-old could hang herself.

Angela couldn't blame him. If she hadn't seen it for herself, she wouldn't have believed it either.

CHAPTER

23

ZOLA WAS IN the middle of explaining a reading assignment when her classroom door opened and Tara rushed in.

"The principal needs to see you right away," she whispered. "I'll take over your class until you get back."

"What's wrong?" She immediately thought about her husband. "Did something happen?"

"I don't know."

Zola had never been pulled out of class like this before. She charged toward the door but ran back to grab her purse from her desk drawer. If there was a family emergency, she could head straight to her car.

She sprinted down the hallway and charged into the principal's office without knocking.

"What happened? Is my husband okay?"

The principal ignored her questions. "Have a seat."

Zola refused to sit until she knew what was going on. "I need to know —"

"Your husband's fine. Have a seat," she repeated in a firmer, more dismissive tone.

Zola fell into the chair, her chest heaving up and down, partly from the race to Freeman's office, partly from fear of the unknown.

"I just got a call from an LAPD detective. Bailey Lewis tried to hang herself last night."

For several seconds, Zola didn't react because the principal's words had not yet registered.

"Is she okay? Is she still..." Zola couldn't say the word.

"Yes, she's still alive. She's on a breathing machine at Children's Hospital. Let's pray she makes it."

"Oh, my God," Zola blurted out. "The bullying! That's why she tried to kill herself!"

The principal pounded the desk with her fist. "That's exactly why I brought you in here. The police may want to talk to us. If they do, we both need to tell them the truth. And the truth is, we don't know why that child tried to hurt herself. I don't want you putting words into her mouth."

"But she—"

"*But she* nothing. Nobody knows what was in that child's mind. Just like we don't know what was going on at home. So don't try to pin this on the school. If you do, you'll only be putting yourself in the line of fire. *You* are her teacher. They'll blame *you* for not knowing what was going on."

"But I reported to you that—"

"You did not report *anything* to me. And I don't want you bringing that up when we speak to the lawyer."

Zola sat more alert. "Lawyer?"

"A lawyer from the district office is meeting with us at three. For now, it's important that you don't talk to anyone about this matter, not even your husband. And you shouldn't have any contact with Bailey's mother. She might start asking questions we don't want to answer."

Zola was speechless. How deep Bailey's despair must've been to prompt her to try to end her life? And trying to hang herself no less. Zola began to weep.

"This is a time for strength, not weakness," Freeman chided her. "I'm sure she'll be fine. This was probably just a cry for help. Thank God the paramedics got there in time. Now we need to concentrate on making sure we don't get blamed for any of this. I'm having a call with Dr. Andrews at ten regarding that action plan I asked for yesterday."

Zola glared across the desk, fire in her eyes. "You said you didn't have time for that until next week."

"No, that's incorrect. You must really be stressed out about this news, Mrs. Phillips."

Zola was beginning to understand. The principal didn't call her there to deliver devastating news about a student. This was all about threats and intimidation.

"We dodged a bullet," Freeman continued, her face full of relief. "Bailey's case won't get as much media attention since she survived. Anyway, I wanted to be sure we're still on the same page."

The same page?

Anger welled up from the tips of Zola's toes. "Do you mean you want me to cover up the fact that I came to you yesterday, and two times before that, to tell you that Bailey was being bullied and you brushed me off?"

Rage crept across Freeman's face. "You made no such reports to me."

Zola sat up straighter in the narrow chair. She had no idea where her new backbone had come from.

"I most certainly did."

"You listen here, little girl. I'm not having this nonsense ruin my career. You will not tell anybody that you reported a damn thing to me. Do you understand? Not anybody."

"And if I do?"

"I have contacts up and down this state and all across the country," Freeman said, her words so cold they chilled the air, "if you cross me on this, I guarantee you'll never work in education again."

CHAPTER

24

DRE AND ANGELA'S drive to Children's Hospital was nerve-wracking and somber. For the entire trip, Angela clutched the door and begged Dre to slow down. The second time he ran a red light, she threatened to jump out of the window.

They found Erika in a small waiting room with two of her co-workers. As Dre approached, she flew into his arms.

Initially, Dre felt uneasy as he consoled a distraught Erika. But when his eyes found Angela's, they held compassion, not jealousy. Erika pulled away from him and embraced Angela too.

"This is all my fault," Erika sobbed. "I've been hurting so much since Earl died, I didn't pay enough attention to my child. I had no idea she was hurting so much that she wanted to die. I should've—"

"It's not your fault," Dre said, his voice breaking. "It's *my* fault. When I took her to school yesterday, she started going into hysterics as soon as we pulled up in front of that place. I should've known something was wrong."

"It's not helping anybody to sit here passing around blame," Angela said quietly. "Bailey's going to be—"

When Angela stopped mid-sentence, Dre and Erika turned around to follow her gaze. A dark-haired woman in a white coat walked toward them.

Dre tried to read her expression, but it told him nothing. She'd no doubt had years to perfect her poker face. The doctor wanted her words, not her demeanor to deliver the news—good or bad.

Erika ran up to her before the doctor could reach them.

The woman didn't hesitate. "I'm so sorry. Your daughter didn't make it. We weren't able to—"

Dre didn't hear anything else the doctor said. Erika's excruciating wail sucked all light and air from the room.

She sank to the floor as Angela and Dre each took an arm and carried her to a nearby couch. As Erika clung to him, Dre grew angrier and angrier.

How does a nine-year-old get to the point that she's so fed up with life that she hangs herself? Dre had been blown away by news stories about celebrities who seemed to have everything, yet took their own lives. But a nine-year-old kid? He didn't know how to hang himself. How did Bailey know?

For now, Dre would find the strength to help Erika through this. Then he was going to make damn sure Erika sued that school, the principal, and anybody else who didn't to do their job.

CHAPTER

25

Zola ENTERED THE teacher's lounge near the end of the lunch hour to find the room swaddled in sadness.

"I just can't believe it," Tara said, the first one to break the painful silence. "We keep hearing about kids doing this. But I never expected it to happen to one of ours. I can't imagine not seeing that little girl walk the halls here again."

"What are you talking about?" Zola asked, alarmed.

Tara's eyes darted away.

Another teacher walked over and hurled an arm around her. "Bailey didn't make it."

Zola collapsed into the closest chair, her body landing like dead weight. She cupped a hand to her mouth, trying to restrain her anguish. Her whole body began to tremble.

Tara squeezed Zola's shoulder. "Are you going to be okay?"

"That child killed herself because she was being bullied," Zola cried. "We could've stopped it!"

The other teachers in the room traded apprehensive glances.

"I don't think you should be making allegations like that," Malcolm said.

Zola stared up at him, disgust in her eyes. Malcolm would likely run straight to Freeman and repeat what she'd just said. Zola didn't care. It was the truth.

She stood up, a bit unsteady on her feet, and wiped her eyes. "I have to go."

By the time she got to her empty classroom, she'd received both a text message and an email from the principal.

To: All Teachers and Staff

I regret to inform you that we lost a beautiful young student today, Bailey Lewis. This loss will be devastating for both our students and staff.

Psychologists from the district office have arrived on campus and will be on hand to assist anyone having difficulty coping with this tragedy. A psychologist will be assigned to Bailey's class.

We encourage teachers who had Bailey as a student to allow her classmates to express themselves, perhaps by writing poetry or drawing pictures.

To the extent you have heard rumors or speculation about the circumstances of Bailey's death, please ignore them. You should not discuss how Bailey died or any details about what may have happened to her. Conveying such information would not be beneficial to our students.

If you have additional questions or concerns, please address them directly with me. An email has already gone out to parents.

Sincerely,
Darcella Freeman

After reading the text, Zola was seconds away from bursting into tears. Before she could, a woman stepped inside her classroom.

"I'm Elsie Espinoza," the woman said. "I understand you were especially close to Bailey. I'm here to help you and your students in any way I can."

Where were you when Bailey was being bullied? Zola wanted to shout. *And where was I?*

Instead, she nodded, too shaken to say more.

The woman squeezed her shoulder. "Are you alright?"

Zola nodded and moved toward the door. "I should let my students in now."

"I have an announcement to make," Zola began, once everyone was seated. She was suddenly having a hard time breathing.

"Good morning, kids," Elsie said, jumping to her aid. "I'm Ms. Espinoza, from the district office. I'm very sad to have to inform you that we lost one of your classmates today, Bailey Lewis."

Confusion blanketed the kids' faces.

Lost? Zola wanted to scream. This woman didn't know how to speak to fourth graders. Bailey wasn't some inanimate object that had been misplaced. The child was dead.

A girl on the back row shot her hand in the air. "You mean Bailey died?"

"Yes," the counselor said. "Yes, she did."

A chorus of gasps swept the room.

"What happened to her, Mrs. Phillips?" another student asked.

"Right now, we're going to focus on all the wonderful things about Bailey," Elise said, ignoring the question. She walked over to a cabinet and opened it. "I'm going to hand out some paper and I want everyone to draw a pretty picture for Bailey."

Zola headed for the door. "I'll be right back."

She race-walked to the closest teacher's restroom, shut herself inside a stall and silently wept.

CHAPTER

26

FOR THE NEXT few days, Angela and Dre buried their grief and poured their energy into helping Erika plan Bailey's funeral service.

While Dre handled the particulars with the funeral home, Angela made calls to family and friends, wrote the first draft of the obituary, and picked out a dress for Bailey to wear. Erika ultimately decided on a frilly, white skirt and the pink sweater Bailey cherished so much. The ketchup stain gone.

Two days before the funeral, Dre called Angela at the office.

"Can you invite Jenny over for dinner tonight? We need to talk to her about suing Bailey's school."

"Shouldn't we at least wait until after the funeral? Have you even talked to Erika about this?"

"I want to have our ducks in a row for when we do talk to Erika."

Angela wasn't sure what good suing would do. Thanks to TV and movies, non-lawyers foolishly believe that you simply file your case, tell your story, and skip out of the courtroom with a multi-million-dollar jury verdict. In reality, litigation was emotional, costly, and physically draining.

Dre, however, would not be receptive to the truth. So after getting off the phone, Angela dialed her friend Jenny Ungerman.

"I haven't handled any bullying cases before," Jenny told her, "but one of my mentors has done a ton of them. You want me to contact him for you?"

"How about giving him a call to get a feel for what Erika would need to prove. Then you can share that with Dre."

"Sure."

"And I need you to give him the pros *and* the cons," Angela stressed.

"Sounds like you don't want Erika to sue."

"You know the deal. The school district is going to pull out their big guns. I don't want her spending two or three years in litigation only to have the case dismissed. Help Dre understand that this won't be the cakewalk he thinks it'll be."

It was after seven by the time Jenny arrived. She was wearing shredded jeans and a white T-shirt, her shoulder-length brown hair shining with reflective blonde highlights.

Uber Eats had just dropped off pasta from California Pizza Kitchen. Angela and Jenny were sitting at the dining room table, when Dre walked in. Angela was not pleased to see his cousin Apache tagging along behind him.

The literal black sheep of the family, unlike Dre, Apache's criminal past remained as present as ever. Angela always felt antsy when he was around. The pair, however, came as a package deal. Dre was closer to Apache than his own brother.

"Hey, almost-cousin," Apache said, giving Angela a hug.

He was small in stature but packed a large presence. His bone-straight hair was pulled back into a ponytail, his flawless bronze skin a testament to his Indian and African-American bloodline.

As Dre headed for the bedroom, Apache treated Jenny to a much longer hug. The top of his head barely reached her chest.

"Nice seeing you again." He leaned back and gave her body a suggestive up and down. "Don't forget what I told you. If you wanna get with me, I'm still available."

Jenny giggled.

"I don't usually do white girls, but I'd make an exception for you. You ever been with a brother before?"

"Apache! Please stop hitting on my friend."

He grunted, reached for a plate, and started piling it with food.

Dre stalked back into the room. "Let's get to it. We need to sue the principal, Bailey's teacher, the girl who bullied her, and the girl's parents."

Jenny bit her bottom lip as she eyed Angela.

"What do we have to prove to win at trial?"

"Most bullycide cases settle," Jenny said. "In the few that go to trial, the schools win the majority of the time."

Apache stuffed a forkful of chicken pasta into his mouth. "What the hell is bullycide?"

"It's a suicide where bullying is believed to be the trigger."

Dre's face scrunched up. "They have a name for it?"

"Sadly, yes. The media made up the term. Mental health professionals hate it."

Dre scratched his head. "But why do the schools win?"

"Because parents have to prove that the school knew the child was being bullied and did nothing to stop it. That's a tough legal standard to meet."

"We can prove that. The day before Bailey committed—"

Dre had developed an aversion to uttering the words *Bailey* and *suicide* in the same sentence.

"Bailey told me she reported the bullying to her teacher," he went on.

"What Bailey told you won't be admissible in court," Angela said. "Your conversations with her are hearsay."

There were a few exceptions to the hearsay rule that could apply. Their conversations might be admissible to show Bailey's state of mind or for impeachment purposes, but Angela was more intent on discouraging Dre from suing than strengthening his resolve.

"No sweat. Jenny can take the teacher's deposition."

Angela couldn't help but smile. Dre had picked up a thing or two about the law since they'd been together.

"And what if she lies?" Jenny asked.

Dre scratched his jaw. He hadn't considered that possibility.

"We can interview some of the students," he fired back. "I'm sure they witnessed it."

Jenny hunched her shoulders. "Just because the students knew, doesn't mean her teacher or the principal knew."

Apache picked up a piece of sourdough bread and slathered it with butter. "I don't understand why y'all even wasting time with a lawsuit. I can take care of it for you. Want me to shoot one of 'em?"

"Apache," Angela huffed. "Could you please stop embarrassing me in front of my friend?"

He took a sip of water. "I don't have to kill nobody. For instance, I can shoot the principal in the kneecaps so she'll have a permanent limp. Let her know karma's a bitch."

"Stop it, Apache. That isn't funny."

He spread his hands and shrugged. "I was just offering."

Jenny's eyes widened as she seemed to realize that Apache might be serious.

"Let's do a little role-playing," she said, getting to her feet. She towered over Dre like a prosecutor glaring down at an accused criminal. "Pretend you're on the witness stand."

"Okay. I'm game." Dre squared his shoulders. "Throw it at me, counselor."

"Mr. Thomas, you contend that you were aware that Bailey was being bullied when you took her to school for the last time, is that correct?"

"Yeah. She was terrified. I practically had to drag her inside."

"And what about when you picked her up from school that day? How was she then?"

"She was worse. That's why she went off in the cafeteria."

"Had she been afraid to go to school on other occasions?"

"Yes."

"So, you were concerned about her well-being?"

"Yes. Very concerned." Dre sat up taller, certain that he was scoring big points.

"So after you picked Bailey up from school that day, how did you address your concerns about her emotional state?"

Dre paused, rubbing a hand across his shaved head. The wary look in his eyes told Angela he realized he might be walking into a trap.

"I spent time with her. I tried to make her happy. We bought pizza and watched a TV show she liked."

"Did you have any idea that Bailey was going to kill herself?"

Dre's nostrils flared. "Of course not. No one could know that."

Jenny moved in for the kill.

"*Exactly*, Mr. Thomas. You spent far more time with her than anyone at school. Yet, *you* didn't do anything to prevent her death. So why would you think the school could've done something?"

"Aw man!" Apache pressed his fist to his lips. "She got your ass good. Led you right up to the cliff and pushed you off."

Dre's jaw tightened and, for a second, it seemed as if he was testifying for real.

"Everything started with the bullying," he insisted, his voice bloated with bitterness. "They could've stopped Kiya Jackson from messing with her."

"But *you* knew Bailey was being bullied, yet *you* didn't do anything to stop it."

"We were going to meet with the principal the next day and—"

"Oh, c'mon, Mr. Thomas." Jenny folded her arms and increased the incredulity in her voice. "If you *really* thought Bailey was in danger, why didn't you keep her at home?"

"Bruh," Apache said, cracking up, "it's time to fold. If the glove don't fit, you must acquit." He turned to Jenny. "Girl, you're a bad ass. I'ma start calling you white lightning. What's your phone number? I might need to call you the next time I shoot somebody."

Jenny cringed and turned her attention back to Dre. He still hadn't answered her question. She waited, her eyes boring into his.

"It don't matter what I did and didn't do," he said, the tenor of his voice seesawing between anguish and rage. "That school let Kiya Jackson bully Bailey day in and day out. So they bear some of the responsibility for what happened. And I plan to do everything in my power to make sure they pay."

CHAPTER

27

ZOLA CLIMBED THE steps of First Baptist Church with the unstable gait of a senior citizen. Concerned about her emotional state, her husband Brock took the day off so he could attend Bailey's funeral along with her.

The pair met at a church retreat and recently celebrated their second wedding anniversary. An accountant at a small CPA firm, Brock was the most ambitious man Zola had ever met. They were now in the process of getting pre-qualified for their first home.

An easel with a poster-size photograph of Bailey's smiling face greeted them in the vestibule of the church.

As Zola stared into Bailey's bright eyes, her heart ached in a way she had never experienced before. If only she had made different choices. Instead of going to Freeman with her concerns, what if she had called Bailey's mother? Or one of the district psychologists? The principal was right. She didn't know a darn thing about teaching. If she'd had more experience, she wouldn't have kowtowed to a woman the teachers had nicknamed Satan's mistress.

"C'mon, babe, let's go inside." Brock took her hand, trying to lead her away from the photograph. Zola didn't budge.

"Give me another minute," she mumbled, unable to take her eyes off of Bailey.

When they entered the sanctuary, Zola was surprised by the sparse crowd. She'd never attended a child's funeral before. Why weren't any of Bailey's classmates here? On second thought, maybe the nine-year-old brain wasn't developed enough to experience the sad ritual of saying goodbye to a loved one. At least not one who'd gone to the extreme of taking her own life. The parents of Bailey's classmates probably didn't want them to attend her service for fear it would put the idea of suicide into their heads. Better to pretend her death never happened.

If Bailey had been an adult, the circumstances of her death would've still been shrouded in the kind of secrecy reserved for AIDS victims. When that disease took Zola's cousin last year, her aunt told everyone it was bone cancer. If his death had been by suicide, cancer still would've been the cover story.

They took a seat on the right, behind two rows of pews that had been roped off for family members.

A silvery pink casket sat below the pulpit, surrounded by sprays of tulips. Zola had never seen such a tiny coffin.

When she spotted Darcella Freeman dressed in black sitting near the front of the church, Zola wanted to vomit. Darcella had no right to even be here. Bailey might be alive if she had only...

Zola shook off the thought. She could not blame Freeman without blaming herself too. They were equally to blame.

An organ began to play as a small procession of ministers and family members paraded down the aisle. Zola knew instantly that the weeping woman being propped up on both sides was Bailey's mother. She wore a bright-pink knit dress. Bailey loved pink and her mother's dress was a touching tribute.

A woman sang a rendition of *The Lord's Prayer* that was so moving, Zola could not control her own tears. Brock pulled her closer as she wept against his chest.

Zola half-listened to the scripture readings and two more songs before the minister asked the audience to share memories of Bailey.

At first, it appeared that no one would speak. Then a boy, not much older than Bailey, walked up to the microphone, shadowed by a woman who was likely his mother.

"My name is Andre Thomas, Jr. Bailey was like my little sister because my dad was her godfather. I showed her how to play video games. She could also run fast. Almost as fast as me. She was really nice and fun and I wish she was still here." The boy threw his arms around his mother's waist and sobbed.

When the minister invited more speakers to come up, Zola wanted to rise but feared she would stand up there and blubber. Still, didn't she owe it to the family? She could tell them how Bailey always volunteered to read aloud and how she loved decorating the classroom walls.

As Zola tried to coax herself out of her seat, Darcella Freeman headed for the spotlight.

"As the principal of Parker Elementary, I'm here on behalf of the school and all of our students, teachers, and staff who loved Bailey so very, very much." Darcella lifted her head and pointed her chin in an almost-regal manner. "Bailey was a smart, beautiful child who excelled at reading and math. I know she was truly destined for greatness."

You phony bitch, Zola wanted to shout. *You have no right to be standing up there!*

"Losing a child so young and so precious is an unimaginable tragedy. Our heartfelt prayers go out to—"

Bailey's mother shot out of her seat. "You need to get—"

A man sitting next to her snatched her back down and cradled her head. Her sobbing was so loud it sounded like it was coming through the speaker system.

Darcella smiled nervously and rushed through the rest of her remarks. "We encourage you to reach out to the Parker Elementary School family. We are here for you now and in the future."

"Let go," Brock whispered. "You're going to break my fingers."

Zola didn't realize she had such a tight grip on her husband's hand.

Brock freed his fingers from her grip and began flexing them.

"That woman is a lying, pretentious, narcissist!" she murmured. "If Bailey's family does file a lawsuit, I'm going to tell them everything I know."

28

Dre was in meltdown mode by the time Darcella Freeman stepped away from the microphone.

"She don't have a right to even be here. Erika should've kicked her ass out."

Angela squeezed his forearm. "C'mon, Dre. We're in a church."

"I don't care!"

She placed a hand on his right knee, stilling his bouncing leg.

Dre had never felt so outraged in his life. When his niece Brianna had been kidnapped by sex traffickers, he'd experienced more desperation than rage as he scoured the streets of L.A. searching for her. Now, desperation had been replaced by helplessness. There wasn't a damn thing he could do to bring Bailey home.

Dre wanted to share all the fun and funny things he knew about Bailey. Like how she laughed at *Raven's Home* or how she would beg him to order a pizza for breakfast.

But once he got up there, Dre feared he would break down. Or worse, if he caught a glimpse of Darcella Freeman, he might just start in on her. The nerve of her to even walk her ass into this church. No, it was best that he stay put.

By the time the services ended and they'd completed the short ceremony at Inglewood Park Cemetery, Dre had a throbbing headache. The day had been one long, painful blur and he wanted it to be over.

"I wish we hadn't agreed to host the repast," he complained to Angela as they made their way from the gravesite. "All I wanna do right now is go home and climb in bed."

"You'll be able to do that in a couple of hours," Angela said. "I'll drive. Give me the keys."

Dre scoffed. "I'm fine. I can—"

"Give me the keys."

When Angela's voice took on a hard edge—like now—it was fruitless to protest. He pulled his keys from his pocket and handed them to her.

They drove home in silence.

"What the fuck?" Dre shouted.

Three cars crowded their driveway.

"Why didn't they park on the goddamn street?"

Angela squeezed his hand. "Probably because they had to carry the food inside. It's no big deal."

She found a parking spot near the end of the block. Cutting off the engine, she turned to face him. "Dre, I need you to be okay. At least until everyone's gone."

"I'm good."

In truth, he was not good. And he wasn't going to be good for a long, long time.

"I'm fine." His lips angled into a smile. "But if that principal has the nerve to show up, there might be some fireworks."

Angela shook her head as she opened the car door. They walked the short distance hand in hand.

Before they left for the services that morning, several women from First Baptist commandeered their kitchen. Large aluminum tins of food crowded every inch of counter space. Through the French doors, they could see people sitting at tables in the backyard.

No one was eating yet, as it was a sign of respect to serve family members first.

Dre walked up to Erika's mother as she left the bathroom. "Where's Erika?"

"Back there in the bedroom with her brother." She gave Dre and Angela a hug. "I really appreciate you. My baby wouldn't have nobody in this city if it hadn't been for you two. You're family."

"They should go ahead and start serving," Angela suggested. "I'm sure everyone's hungry."

"Yeah," Dre said. "The sooner we feed 'em, the sooner they can leave."

"Dre!" Angela said.

Erika's mother smiled, then laughed. "I was just thinking the same thing."

Dre cocked his head and smirked, then followed Angela down the hallway. They found Erika in the guest bedroom, wrapped in her brother's arms.

"Thank you guys for everything." Erika gazed up at them with agony-filled eyes.

Angela bent down to embrace her. "We're glad we could be here for you."

"You want something to eat?" Dre asked.

Erika shook her head. "No, I'm fine."

"All you had this morning was half a cup of coffee," her brother said. "You need to eat something."

Erika exhaled. "Yeah, okay. I guess I should put something on my stomach."

"I'll go ask your mother to fix it," Dre said.

As he trudged down the hallway, he heard two of the church women speaking to one of the deacons. Their words rocked him.

"It's a shame the way they raising kids these days," the older of the pair said. "You never heard of no kids hanging themselves when we was growing up."

The deacon stood in front of the kitchen island, chomping on a chicken leg. "Spare the rod, spoil the child. Everything turned to crap when they took prayer out of schools."

Both women nodded.

The deacon continued on, smacking as he spoke. "And all of these mothers letting their kids watch anything they want on TV and givin' 'em computers and cell phones with no supervision."

"It's because they don't raise 'em in the church like we was raised," the older woman said. "That's why they're cutting up their arms and trying to kill themselves. And the same thing for all this talk about autism. Ain't nothing wrong with these kids that a good butt whipping wouldn't fix."

"I heard the mama wasn't never around," the deacon said, lowering his voice. "Got some big promotion and never took no time with her daughter. Ain't no reason for just a woman and child to be living in a house as big as the one they got in Baldwin Hills. Parents today don't know how to—"

"You need to leave," Dre bellowed, moving swiftly toward them.

The deacon stopped mid-bite. "Excuse me, sir?"

"I said get out."

Angela rushed into the kitchen, followed by Erika's mother and brother. "What's going on?"

Tears trailed down Dre's cheeks. The first tears he'd cried since trying to breathe life back into Bailey.

Dre stared at the deacon with venom in his eyes. "You're standing here passing judgment like what you think matters. We just lost a child. This ain't what we need. And this ain't what you so-called Christians are supposed to be all about."

By now, several people from the backyard had filtered inside, attracted by the commotion.

"Sir," the deacon said. "I know you're grieving and you're upset. Please forgive us if we misspoke."

"You didn't misspeak. You were being mean and nasty. Now please leave."

The deacon picked up his plate, seemingly out of fear that he might have to leave it behind. "Sir, maybe you should—"

Dre lunged forward, slapping the plate out of the man's hand, spraying food everywhere.

"*I* don't need to do a damn thing!" Tears soaked Dre's face. "But what *you* need to do is get the fuck out of my house!"

CHAPTER

29

A COUPLE OF DAYS after Bailey's funeral, Angela decided to work from home. Dre's escalating despair made her nervous about leaving him alone.

"I'm fine," he insisted, when she rolled over in bed and told him she wasn't going into the office. "I don't need a babysitter."

"Maybe I'm the one who's not fine," she admitted.

It was as if Dre recognized for the first time that he wasn't suffering alone.

"Babe, I'm sorry. I've only been thinking about myself."

Angela's lips began to quiver. "I can't seem to erase the image of walking into that room and seeing Bailey's tiny body hanging there."

Dre pulled her into his arms as she wept.

"I spoke to Erika last night," Angela said after a while, resting her head on his chest. "She wants to sue. She also asked me to handle the case."

"That's what I want too. But how do *you* feel about it?"

"I think we should hire Jenny's mentor. It's better to have someone who's experienced with bullying cases."

"But what if he won't take it?"

Angela hadn't considered that possibility. "If he decides not to take it, that would mean he doesn't think it's a winner."

"So what? He could be wrong."

Angela sighed. She prayed he would take Erika's case because Dre was not going to let this go.

"Are you reluctant to do it because you don't think you could handle it emotionally?" he asked.

"It certainly wouldn't be easy."

"Well, I'd feel better if you were handling it. And I know Erika would too."

Angela nodded. She decided not to mention to Dre that her discovery of Bailey's body might mean she'd have to be a witness in the case. That could potentially prevent her from also litigating it.

"In the meantime," Dre said, hopping out of bed. "We need to lift the mood around here. Let's go see a movie."

"What?"

"I'm tired of moping around. Let's find something funny. My homegirl Tiffany Haddish has a new movie out."

Actually, that wasn't a bad idea. She retrieved her phone from the nightstand to check the movie listings. She had forgotten to plug it in the night before and it was dead. Without thinking, she headed for the computer in her office, but froze when she got to the door.

Dre walked up behind her. "You good?"

"I was going to use my desktop to check the movie times, but..." Her voice trailed off.

"We can't keep using this room as a shrine to Bailey." He reached in front of her and pushed it open. "I used to love working out in here and I'm going to start doing it again."

Dre took Angela's hand and gently pulled her across the threshold. "Go ahead, check your computer." Dre plopped down on his workout bench. "I'll wait right here while you do it."

Angela examined the room as she sat down at her desk. When had Dre straightened it up? She forced thoughts of the last time she was in this room out of her head.

Tapping a key to wake up the computer, she was poised to type *Cinemark at Howard Hughes* into the search bar. But when the screen came to life, Angela cringed and backed away from the desk. "Oh, my God!"

"What's wrong?"

Dre was at her side in a flash. When his eyes settled on the screen, she could feel his body shudder.

"What the fuck!"

The headline of the article stretching across the screen seemed to make the room tilt. *The 5 Best Ways to Kill Yourself.*

Angela pressed both palms to her cheeks. "Bailey must've looked that up."

"She learned how to kill herself on the goddamn internet? Are you kidding me?"

Angela began to tap more keys.

"What are you doing?"

"I want to see the rest of Bailey's search history."

"How do you do that?"

Angela ignored his question and continued typing. She abruptly stopped and glanced up at Dre. "Bailey had an Instagram account?"

"Hell if I know."

Angela tried to access it, but the account had timed out. "I don't think Erika would've allowed her to be on Instagram."

"Maybe she didn't know," Dre said. "My niece had a Facebook account my sister knew nothing about."

Angela went back to scanning the search history, but other than the article and the Instagram page, the rest of it belonged to her.

"What are you doing now?"

"Getting screenshots. This is valuable evidence. A kid who searches the internet to figure out how to kill herself is obviously traumatized."

When Angela navigated to the desktop to retrieve the screenshots, she spotted two additional files that she didn't recognize.

She clicked on the first one. A distorted image of Bailey's face appeared.

"What the hell!" Dre said. "How did they mess up her face like that?"

"Instagram has this thing called face filters," Angela explained. "You can do all kinds of silly things to pictures."

"How did that picture get on your desktop?"

"I don't know. I didn't put it there. Maybe Bailey did." Angela hit some more keys. "Yep. It was saved the night before we found her."

"That must be Kiya Jackson's page," Dre said, pointing at the name KitKatKiya above the picture of Bailey.

Angela noticed the hashtag underneath the photograph. "Oh, my God!"

"*#BaileyShouldJustDie!*" Dre yelled. "Who would say that to somebody? This is nothing but cyberbullying."

Angela opened another file and both she and Dre gasped in unison at a closeup shot of four comments posted underneath Bailey's picture.

"This is crazy!" Dre pressed a fist to his lips. "What kind of kids are these?"

Angela didn't respond for a long time. "Bailey's helping us," she said quietly.

"What are you talking about?"

"Bailey left us solid evidence that she was being bullied. If Kiya Jackson was bold enough to post something this cruel on Instagram, there's no telling what she was doing to Bailey at school."

CHAPTER

30

"I CAN DO THIS. I can absolutely do this."

Erika repeated the mantra aloud as she drove into the employee parking lot at Top Management Marketing. Three weeks was long enough. Neither Earl nor Bailey would want her balled up in the fetal position for the rest of her life. If she didn't fight back, grief would eventually suffocate her.

Cutting off the engine, Erika turned to grab a bag she'd placed on the floor behind her seat. When her eyes focused on the empty space where Bailey normally sat, heartbreak punched her in the chest.

She saw her beautiful daughter licking an ice cream cone, singing off-key, or begging to sit in the front seat. Tears began to flow, streaking her flawless makeup.

"I can do this," she wept. "I *have* to do this."

Erika knew there would be more days like this. Days when the pain would swallow her whole. But she was determined not to be like her Aunt Florida. A week after her husband's funeral, her aunt gave up on life. Her fun-loving, hilarious auntie never laughed again. Ever.

If she could make it through the day, she could retreat to her bed and cry herself to sleep at night.

The first step was walking back into work and doing what she had to do. It was time.

"Oh, baby!" Renetha, the security guard, ran up to her as soon as she stepped into the lobby, pulling her into a suffocating hug. "I'm sorry for your loss."

If there were any words Erika wished she could ban from the English language, it would be *I'm sorry for your loss.* She had no idea what she wanted to hear instead, but those five little words didn't do it for her. Silence would've been better.

"Lean on Jesus, baby," Renetha said. "It don't seem fair for you to have another loss like this, but He's got you. Just trust in Him."

Erika unfurled herself. "Thanks."

She wasn't sure anymore about the depth of her Christian faith. Not with the double whammy she'd been hit with. As she waited for the elevator, she placed her phone to her ear, pretending she was talking to someone. She hoped to make it to her office without another *Sorry for your loss.*

Hopping off the elevator, she rushed down the corridor. Her only mistake was not taking out her key ahead of time. As she fumbled around in her purse, she could hear someone approaching from behind.

When she peered over her shoulder, her tension eased away.

"Hey, girl." Natalie, the only co-worker she truly wanted to see, was a tall, thick-boned white girl who was far too wise for her 23 years.

They stepped inside and closed the door. Natalie pulled her into an embrace so genuine and comforting, Erika didn't want to let go. Both of their eyes glistened with tears.

"Girlfriend, I have so much gossip to tell you!"

Natalie seemed to have a gift for knowing the right thing to say in any situation.

"Just tell me they fired Jack," Erika said, taking off her jacket and placing it on a hook behind the door.

"That'll take an act of Congress."

As Erika turned around, her eyes landed on a framed picture of Bailey on the credenza behind her desk. She froze. Her beautiful child was gone.

"Breathe," Natalie said softly. "Just breathe."

Erika tried, but the air would not leave her chest. "I don't know if I can."

"Yes, you can."

Natalie lost her fiancé to suicide a year ago. She understood what Angela was going through.

Erika picked up the photograph. "I loved my baby so much." Her voice grew weepy.

"Are you sure you don't need to take a little more time off?"

"Why? So I can sit home and cry all day *and* all night? I'd rather be here. Even if it means dealing with Jackass. I mean Jack."

They both laughed.

Erika placed the picture near her computer and sat down behind her desk.

"This is going to be a hard day," Natalie said. "Everybody's going to be coming in here telling you they're *Sorry for your loss.* All you can do is breathe. And when you need to have a good cry, go to your car and let it rip."

Natalie's fiancé had been battling depression. Her grief was even harder because she didn't get along with his family. She wasn't allowed to play any role in planning his funeral service and was given two weeks to move out of the condo they'd shared for five years.

"Does everyone know?"

Erika could tell from Natalie's expression that her friend knew precisely what she was asking. Not whether her co-workers knew that Bailey had died, but whether they knew *how* she died.

"Yeah. And you have nothing to be embarrassed about." Natalie paused for a few seconds, then continued. "I'm about to ask you something and I want you to seriously consider it."

"Okay," Erika said tentatively.

"I know you dismissed this idea after Earl passed, but how about going to my grief class with me?"

Erika waved off her suggestion. "My husband and my daughter are gone. I have to move on. I don't want to sit around with a bunch of strangers whining about something I can't change."

"It's nothing like that. Just think about it."

"Yeah, okay. How did the McIntyre presentation go?"

"Awful. Jack had three typos in his PowerPoint and couldn't answer a single question without checking his notes. He raised your net worth around here by at least three-hundred percent. After the meeting, he dropped by my cubicle to ask when you'd be coming back."

Erika smiled.

"Knock, knock," Jack called out as he barged in. "Glad to see you're back, kiddo. We have a boatload of work to do."

"I'm glad to be back," Erika said.

The room turned awkwardly silent.

"Uh...I...uh," Jack scratched the back of his head. "I wanted to say I'm sorry for—"

Natalie cut him off. "Hey, let's go get some coffee before we get started."

Erika launched out of her seat. "Great idea."

CHAPTER

31

DRE CAREFULLY SCRUTINIZED Zola Phillips as she opened her car door. Bailey's teacher was a lot younger than he'd expected. He was glad that he'd come so early. Only ten other cars dotted the school parking lot.

He hid behind a column so she couldn't see him. Dre knew he might frighten her, but there was no way around it. Zola would have to pass by him to enter the building.

She retrieved a bag from the back seat and locked the car. When she neared the side entrance of the school, he stepped into the middle of the walkway in full view.

Zola froze, her eyes swelling with panic.

Dre raised his palms in surrender. "Mrs. Phillips, I'm Andre Thomas. Bailey Lewis's godfather. I was hoping to talk to you for a second."

The woman didn't relax one bit. At least she hadn't screamed or run away. Encouraged, Dre took a few steps closer, still leaving a comfortable distance between them.

"I wanted to talk to you about Bailey. She told me you were her favorite teacher and that you were always nice to her."

That did nothing to thaw the chill on her face. Though she had yet to speak, Dre still interpreted her muted response as a positive.

He moved closer.

"If you want me to leave, I will. Just say the word. I'm not here to frighten you or to cause you any harm."

"I have to get to my classroom." Zola clutched the strap of her purse and resumed walking toward the school. "What do you want?"

Dre was beside her now, walking in lockstep. "Everybody's struggling to understand why Bailey did what she did. Did she ever mention any problems she was having at school?"

Zola's head whipped around to face him, her gaze harder than granite. "I can't talk about that."

Dre had expected her to deny that Bailey had even talked to her. The teacher's admission that there actually was a *that,* only emboldened him.

"She told me she was bullied by Kiya Jackson." Dre walked in lockstep alongside her. "And that you saw it happen."

Zola tugged at the strap of her purse. "I have to go."

Okay, Dre thought. *So you definitely know something.*

Zola picked up her pace.

"What's going on? Are you okay, Miss Zola? Is this guy bothering you?"

A man wearing a beige workman's uniform with *Damien* stenciled on his shirt pocket approached them as they reached the entrance. Dre assumed he was part of the custodial staff.

"Everything's fine," Dre said.

The man acted as if he hadn't said a word.

"Are you okay?" He inserted himself between Dre and the teacher. "You need me to call security?"

For the first time, the teacher's eyes met Dre's and he saw pain as profound as his own.

Talk to me. Dre wanted to grab her by the arm and make her talk.

"I'm fine," Zola said, snatching open the door. "This is Bailey Lewis's godfather. He was just about to leave."

CHAPTER

32

"DON'T FORGET WHAT I told you," Jenny said, looking from Angela to Erika as they entered the swanky office building. "Sidney tends to be very straight to the point. So don't take it personally."

"That's the third time you've said that," Angela pointed out as they headed for an elevator. "Is the guy really that bad?"

"He can come off a little crass if you don't know him."

"How can an attorney with that kind of personality be so successful?" Erika asked.

"In the courtroom, he's freakin' amazing. It's like he flips a switch and turns off his crotchety lawyer persona and goes into soothing minister mode."

When Sidney Meltzer walked out to greet them, Angela was taken aback. Based on Jenny's warnings, she'd expected a balding man in his fifties or sixties. Meltzer was rock-star handsome with the lean body of a runner. He didn't look a day over thirty, though he was likely a decade older.

He eagerly shook hands with Erika and Angela, but pulled Jenny into an affectionate hug.

"I take a lot of the credit for the brilliant attorney this woman is today," he beamed with genuine pride. "I practically raised her in the law."

Jenny tried but failed not to blush.

Meltzer's office was spacious in size but minimalist in decor. A single abstract art piece took up the north wall. The only items on his desk were a computer monitor and a framed crayon drawing that could have been the work of a five-year-old kid.

"I took a look at the information you sent," Meltzer began once they were seated. "I do believe Bailey was bullied. I've handled enough of these cases to read between the lines. When a kid was as terrified as she was about going to school, there's a reason."

Angela smiled, relieved that she was off the hook. "So you think Erika has a case?"

"Hold on a minute." He held up his palm to them. "I also suspect there was some negligence on the part of the school." He addressed his next words directly to Erika. "But as far as having a case, this one won't be easy to win."

"But you just said the school was negligent," Erika challenged him.

"Knowing it and proving it are two different things. There's no evidence that the school was on notice of the bullying."

Erika's brows furrowed. "What about those vicious Instagram posts telling Bailey to kill herself?"

"The school can't control what kids do at home," he said. "That's on their parents."

"Well, then," Erika pressed, "we can sue the school *and* Kiya Jackson's parents."

He grimaced. "I generally don't like to do that unless there's clear evidence of very egregious, long-term bullying. The jury will put themselves in the place of the parents and shy away from bringing down the hammer. I've only gone after a bully's parents twice. One case I lost, and in the other won, the jury decided in favor of my client. Ultimately, winning didn't matter because the kid's parents didn't have any money to pay the jury award."

"This is not about money," Erika said.

"The legal profession is a business, Mrs. Lewis. No good attorney's going to take a case if the possibility of a financial payoff is a gamble. As a solo practitioner, I only take on cases with strong evidence in my client's favor."

"Where's the ladies' room?" Erika huffed.

Angela bounced to her feet. "I'll go with you."

"No," Erika said. "I'd rather go by myself."

Meltzer walked to the doorway to point her down the hall and returned to sit behind his desk.

"I'm sorry if I upset her, but I prefer to give it to people straight."

"You certainly did that," Angela said facetiously.

Despite his blunt demeanor, Angela got the sense that Meltzer was genuinely concerned that he'd hurt Erika's feelings. Dre had planned to come with them, but there was a problem at the duplex he was rehabbing. Angela didn't even want to imagine how Dre would've reacted to what they'd just heard. Thank God for small favors.

"Her case would be a lot more viable if she had a live child rather than a dead one," Meltzer continued. "I know that sounds insensitive, but there's no other way to say it."

Angela begged to differ. She could think of several ways Meltzer could have rephrased his crass statement.

She stole a quick glance at Jenny, who looked as appalled as she was.

"And why's that?" Angela asked tightly.

"Let's say Bailey came home with a bruise on her arm because another child pushed her down. Or even called her a name—to her face or on Snapchat or Instagram. And let's say this happened eight times over a three-month period. I can make the jury understand why that shouldn't happen. That a kid shouldn't be tormented at school or online. But when a child goes to the extreme of taking her own life, the jury is much more apt to shrug and say, *Well, no one could've known she was going to do that. Her own parents didn't know."*

From a legal perspective, Angela understood his point, but his delivery rubbed her the wrong way. Erika was probably in the restroom in tears. If she didn't return soon, Angela would go check on her.

"Jenny told me you've won a ton of bullycide cases," Angela said. "So you've obviously represented parents whose kid's took their own lives. What made you take those cases?"

"The schools were *extremely* negligent. I had one case where the parents were down at the school complaining nearly every other day. They even sent multiple letters pleading for help. Instead of disciplining the bully, the principal told the parents their child was too sensitive. The principal also failed to follow the school's own bullying protocol. That little boy hanged himself too."

"So if there's no extreme negligence, the school gets off?" Erika was standing in the doorway.

Angela wondered how much of their conversation she'd heard.

"No. I'm just saying that cases without extreme negligence are much harder to win. Now, if your daughter was in a protected class, that would help."

Erika squinted. *"A protected class*? What's that?"

"If she was gay, for example, and she was bullied because of her sexual orientation. That would get us somewhere. We don't have a race claim because the girl who bullied her was also African-American."

Erika remained standing, her hands gripping the back of her chair. "What about plain old right and wrong?"

"That's the stuff of TV dramas, Mrs. Lewis. Not real life."

Angela didn't like Meltzer's crudeness, but she didn't disagree with his rationale. Many solo practitioners accepted any case that came through the door, taking ten-thousand-dollar retainers from clients who had no chance of prevailing. Sidney was sitting in this ritzy office building because he knew how to pick winners.

"So I guess you're not taking my case," Erika said, though that was already clear.

For the first time, Meltzer's face reflected genuine compassion. "I'm sorry, but I can't."

CHAPTER

33

ZOLA WAS STILL rattled by her conversation that morning with Bailey's godfather. What had Bailey told him?

"You better shut up! You stupid ass!"

Zola swung around to see Kiya Jackson pointing her finger in Gabriela Lopez's face. Kiya had already found herself a new victim.

She marched up to them. "Kiya, please come with me."

Zola took the girl off to the side. "That's not the way you talk to someone. Do you understand?"

"Yes, Mrs. Phillips. I'm sorry."

"If I ever hear you speak disrespectfully like that again, you're going to the principal's office. Do you understand?"

"Okay, Mrs. Phillips. You look pretty in that dress."

Zola loathed the little girl's insincerity. "Thank you, Kiya." She pointed to a bench. "Now sit over there until recess is over."

The girl sulked away and flopped down on the bench.

After talking with Gabriella to make sure she was okay, Zola needed to sit down too. Now she would have to start watching Gabriella. She wanted to tell Freeman that Kiya was now bullying another child but knew it wouldn't do any good.

Since Bailey's death, the very sight of Kiya Jackson prompted a rush of emotions. She resented the child and hated herself for feeling that way. She could not blame this troubled little girl for the misfortune of being raised by a woman who had no business being a mother.

As Zola was about to instruct her students to line up so she could escort them back to class, Freeman appeared out of nowhere.

"I'd like to speak with you," she said. "It'll only take a minute. Ms. Taylor will escort your students to your classroom."

Zola followed Freeman to an empty section of the playground. When the principal folded her arms across her chest, Zola braced herself.

"I expected you to drop by my office during your free period."

Deep lines creased Zola's forehead. "Did we have a meeting scheduled?"

"Nope." Freeman's ominous smile made Zola uneasy.

"Then why were you expecting me to come to your office?"

"To notify me about the confrontation you had in the parking lot this morning with Andre Thomas."

Zola gulped. Damien, the custodian, had blabbed.

"It wasn't a confrontation."

"Oh, so you had a conversation with him? What was it about?"

"We didn't have a conversation either."

Zola wasn't sure how much Damien had heard. "He asked me if I saw Bailey being bullied by Kiya Jackson."

Freeman's nose turned up in a snit, but her voice remained sweeter than sweet.

"And what did you tell him?"

"I didn't tell him anything."

"Damien said you two spoke for quite a while before he intervened. He said he thought the man was about to attack you."

"That's not true."

"So what did you tell him? And I mean precisely. Word for word."

"I told him I couldn't talk to him."‘

"Why didn't you tell him that Bailey had never been bullied?"

Because that's a lie.

"Avoiding his question," the principal went on, "might lead him to believe you have something to hide."

"I didn't think I should be talking to him at all. I brushed him off and went straight to my classroom."

"I'm disappointed that you didn't come to me."

"I had to get to class."

"You could've sent me an email."

"The man is grieving the loss of his goddaughter. He's trying to understand why she took her life."

"Well, nobody at this school can answer that question. Unless you think you can."

"No," Zola said, avoiding her gaze. "I can't."

"You need to be very careful, Mrs. Phillips. We wouldn't want something you told that man to come back and bite us if there's a lawsuit."

"I better get to my class."

Zola headed inside. The principal strolled alongside her.

When Zola entered her classroom, Freeman stepped in behind her and began glancing around the room.

"Have you taken down everything that might remind the students of Bailey?"

"Yes," she lied.

A spelling contest which included Bailey's name along with four other high-scoring students was still on the back wall. Zola needed it there for her own healing.

Bailey's artwork, three English tests with perfect scores, and a Disney poster Bailey brought in to share with the class were neatly stacked in her bottom drawer. Zola had wanted to give them to Bailey's mother, but she figured Freeman would object.

"The next time that man or anyone else approaches you about Bailey Lewis, you need to report it to me. Immediately. Do you understand?"

Zola nodded.

"Enjoy the rest of your day."

34

ANGELA, JENNY, AND Erika walked out of Sidney Meltzer's office like priests leading a funeral procession. Once they reached Angela's SUV, other than the clicking of their seat belts into place, no words passed between them until Angela pulled up in front of Erika's house.

"Thanks for trying." Erika climbed out of the back seat and spoke to them through Angela's open window. "Maybe this is a sign from God that I need to move on. But Dre was so adamant that I should sue."

"And he was right," Angela said. "And we *are* going to sue."

Jenny, who was sitting in the passenger seat, gave her a strange look.

"But who's going to handle the case?" Erika asked.

"I am."

"But what about everything that attorney said?"

"He said it wouldn't be easy. He didn't say we couldn't win."

Angela could sense Jenny's disagreement though she hadn't said a word.

"This wouldn't be the first time someone told me my case sucked and I proceeded anyway. And most of the time, the naysayers were wrong."

Erika leaned through the window and hugged her. "Thank you!"

Jenny waited until Erika was almost at her front door before speaking. "So you're really going to do this?"

"Yep."

"But you've never tried a bullycide case before."

"It's basically about negligence and harassment. I've handled plenty of those cases."

"You could be called as a witness. You'll need to have Erika sign a waiver of potential conflicts of interest."

"That shouldn't be a problem. Since the cause of Bailey's death isn't in dispute, the likelihood of my having to testify is slim."

"This could be a tough one to handle by yourself."

"Who said I'm handling it by myself? You'll be at my side."

Jenny's expression turned wary. "Somehow I knew you were going to get to that."

"We can do this," Angela insisted. "Maybe we can get Meltzer to consult with us."

"Maybe he would, but one thing I've learned is that you don't know what you don't know, which is why I'm reluctant to do it."

The best attorneys Angela knew practiced in one area of the law and rarely stepped outside of that circle. They would have a high learning curve, but were smart enough to maneuver it.

"I don't think Bailey's case is as weak as Meltzer claims it is," Angela continued. "We could end up uncovering a lot of helpful evidence during discovery. Who knows what Bailey's teacher is going to say when we take her deposition?"

"*We?* I haven't agreed to join you yet."

"C'mon, Jenny, you have to do this for the sake of my relationship."

"*Your relationship?*"

"Absolutely. If I tell Dre that Erika's not going to be able to sue that school, there's a good chance he'll put me out."

CHAPTER

35

Erika viewed herself as a remarkably strong woman. She'd survived growing up in a pretty rough part of L.A. and had shaken off some bad life choices. Her high-paying corporate job would have seemed out of reach even five years ago.

But she knew she wasn't alright. The pain stemming from Bailey's absence in her life was a stronger, more profound ache than she had experienced after Earl's passing. She still managed to climb out of bed, put one foot in front of the other, and stand up in a meeting and make a lucid point. But every task she performed felt like a phantom experience. Like she was watching someone who looked like her and sounded like her, yet wasn't her.

Erika realized she was close to her breaking point. She also knew she had to do something about it. Grief was seeping into her psyche like trickles of acid, slowly eating away at her from the inside out.

Steering her BMW into the church parking lot, she turned off the engine. Erika wasn't the support-group type, but Natalie had finally convinced her to attend a meeting. If she chose not to participate, no one would force her to.

As she got out of the car, she spotted Natalie standing on the church steps, smiling and waving.

"I was worried that you'd changed your mind," Natalie said, hugging her. "I'm glad you came. You won't regret it. I promise."

Natalie looped her arm through Erika's and the two women stepped inside the church. They turned down a long hallway and found a small room which held about a dozen people, all but two of them women. Everyone smiled and welcomed her. They all embraced Natalie.

A slender white woman with graying blonde hair extended her hand to Erika. "I'm Jodi, the group leader. We're glad you're here. Feel free to join in or just sit back and listen. Grab some coffee or soda. We're about to get started."

Erika felt like she was on display as she took a seat in one of the folding chairs gathered into a circle.

"We have a guest," Jodi began. "Her name's Erika."

"Welcome, Erika," the group said in unison.

Jodi glanced around the circle. "Any victories to report?"

An older black woman timidly raised her hand. "I went back to church this past weekend," she said with a smile. "Not my own church. But a friend's."

Jodi clapped. "*That* was indeed a victory."

The woman went on to explain that she'd spent the last year being mad at God. Between snatches of her conversation, Erika came to understand that the woman's daughter had been a victim of domestic violence, shot to death by her estranged husband.

The more people spoke, the more Erika began to feel at ease. People shared funny stories about their loved ones. Sad ones about picking up the phone to call a parent, then remembering they were gone.

About twenty minutes in, during a long gap of silence, Erika blurted out, "My husband died of bone cancer almost a year ago. Then about a month ago, my daughter hanged herself. She was bullied at school. She was only nine."

Erika's eyes watered and she stared at a spot on the floor.

There. She'd said it out loud. Her husband was gone and her only child too. No one could possibly top her grief.

Natalie stuffed a tissue into her left hand. Still staring at the floor, Erika continued.

"I was an awful mother. I had no idea Bailey was in that much pain because I was too consumed with my own grief. Disease or another person took your loved ones. But my child took her own life. I should have known."

"You couldn't have known," said a male voice. "And your child had a disease too. I'd bet she suffered from depression."

Erika looked up to meet the welcoming gaze of a soft-spoken black man, probably in his sixties.

"My wife took her own life too. I knew she was depressed, but she'd been taking her medication, so I thought everything was fine. We celebrated our thirtieth wedding anniversary two days before. For a long time, I blamed myself for not knowing she was in such a dark place. Don't do that to yourself."

Erika's shoulders heaved as tears started to fall. Natalie scooted her chair closer and embraced her.

"We don't understand depression." The man wiped his nose with a handkerchief. "Hell, a lot of black folks don't even believe depression is an illness. They think it's something people can just snap out of. But they're wrong. No healthy person takes their own life. Stop blaming yourself and stop blaming your daughter too. She wasn't well."

Erika nodded.

"There's no magic pill you can take to reduce the pain. But it will get better. I can promise you that."

"When?" Erika blubbered, a smidgen short of angry. "I need it to get better *now*. It's still hard to even get out of the bed in the morning."

Jodi stepped in. "Unfortunately, there's no timeline for pain. You'll have some great days and you'll have some awful days. But confronting your grief will open the door to your healing. Being here today is a start."

Erika let the tears flow hard and heavy. She appreciated the silence from the group.

"Crying can be cleansing," Jodi said gently. "Don't ever deprive yourself of that."

Erika finally composed herself. "I didn't mean to hog the floor."

"There's no such thing as hogging the floor in this room," Jodi said with a chuckle. "You're with people who understand."

"Amen on that," someone said to her left.

"Ain't no shame in your pain," called out someone else.

Erika dried her eyes. "Thank you."

"Tell us about Bailey," said the woman who'd lost her daughter. "What do you miss most about her?"

Erika smiled, then started to laugh. "Bailey loved the TV show *Raven's Home*. I'd tape it and on weekends we'd make it part of our girls' day. We'd make popcorn and grape Kool-Aid. And we would watch it over and over and over again. One time she looked up at me and said, *Mom, you're the best.*"

"My grandbaby loves that show too," someone said.

"Those are the memories you should hold on to," Jodi said. "On your most difficult days, they'll get you through."

CHAPTER

36

ANGELA ALWAYS EXPERIENCED an intellectual high at the beginning of a new case. For her, it was like plotting out moves in a chess match before the game even started.

She and Jenny huddled in Angela's Inglewood office for their first case strategy meeting.

"I spent the night scouring Kiya Jackson's Instagram, Facebook, Tumblr, and Snapchat accounts. Instagram was the most active." Jenny slid a folder across the desk. "Take a deep breath before you open it."

The folder held color screenshots of dozens of posts about Bailey, calling her names and urging her to kill herself.

"They go back almost three months," Jenny said. "Kiya is destined for a psychiatric ward."

"I feel so sad that Bailey had to endure this alone." Angela found it hard to breathe as she perused the screenshots. "Where do kids get this from? I can remember telling somebody to *drop dead* when I was a kid, but I didn't mean it literally."

"Well, *kill yourself* happens to be a rather dope phrase among today's kids. Here's the definition from the Urban dictionary."

"It's in the friggin' dictionary?" Angela said, taking a page from her. "No way."

She quickly read the definition.

*A term meaning "I respectfully disagree with your opinion".
Believed to have originated on Tumblr, but most often seen on
YouTube.*

"Oh my God! Are we just old, or what? This is outrageous."

"Whoever said words matter," Jenny said, "was telling the truth.
Kids are telling other kids to kill themselves and they're actually
doing it."

"This is too much. I need a breather."

They walked downstairs to Subway and bought sandwiches and
chips.

"What did Erika decide about going after Kiya Jackson's parents?" Jenny asked, when they returned.

Angela rocked back in her chair. "Kiya's mother works as a security guard at the Westfield mall in Culver City. There's no father in
the picture. It's not worth it to go after her. Erika's okay with that."

Angela handed a document across her desk. "Take a look at these
jury instructions for negligence."

She always began a case by studying the jury instructions for
each cause of action. That ensured she understood the burden of
proof she had to meet.

"Too bad Seth's Law doesn't apply," Jenny said.

That section of the California Education Code requires any
school employee who witnesses an act of bullying to intervene when
safe to do so. But it only applies to students bullied on the basis of
gender, sexual orientation, gender identity, race, nationality, disabil-
ity, or religion.

"This is so depressing," Angela said, unable to stifle a surge of self-
doubt. "I keep seesawing between excitement and fear. Can we really
convince a jury that the school is responsible for Bailey's death?"

"Wait a minute. You were the one all gung-ho about doing this
case. We don't know what evidence we're going to uncover during
discovery. Let's not throw in the towel before we even get started."

"I know, I know. I guess I'm just nervous about whether this is the right thing for Erika."

"It is," Jenny declared.

"How can you say that with such certainty?"

"I read an article last night that said a lawsuit is the best anti-depressant on the market for the parents of a bullycide victim. It helps them feel like they're fighting back."

Angela mulled that over.

"And win or lose," Jenny continued, "dragging the school through this process means the next time a kid complains of bullying, they'll take it seriously. Take a look at this."

Jenny handed her a Centers for Disease Control report entitled *The Relationship Between Bullying and Suicide: What We Know and What It Means for Schools.*

"The CDC studies bullying? Are you kidding me?"

"Yep. As it relates to suicide. Take a look at the paragraph I highlighted on the second page."

Angela perused the document, then looked up, alarm filling her eyes. "This report cuts both ways." She read it out loud.

We don't know if bullying directly causes suicide-related behavior. We know that most youth who are involved in bullying do NOT engage in suicide-related behavior. It is correct to say that involvement in bullying, along with other risk factors, increases the chance that a young person will engage in suicide-related behaviors.

"I know," Jenny says. "The school district's lawyers will be focusing on the *other risk factors,* saying that's the reason why Bailey killed herself."

"Like the loss of her father."

"Exactly. So we have to be prepared for that." Jenny opened another folder. "I started working on some discovery requests. I've asked for Bailey's school file, all bullying policies and training-related material given to teachers and staff, as well as all reports of bullying made by any student in the last ten years. We also need to see Kiya Jackson's school file. I bet she bullied other students too."

Angela scanned the documents. "You're certainly on top of things."

"And then there's our most powerful weapon." Jenny waved a single sheet of paper in the air.

"What's that?"

"A press release," Jenny said with a blazing smile. "This is the perfect case to litigate on the six o'clock news."

CHAPTER

37

A HYSTERICAL CALL FROM Erika interrupted their meeting. Dre had gone to Parker Elementary and supposedly harassed Bailey's teacher.

Angela hung up and dialed Dre's cell. He didn't pick up. She texted him and waited. No response.

"Approaching that teacher doesn't sound like Dre," Jenny said. "Is he okay?"

"He absolutely is *not* okay, but you can't tell him that. He won't even consider getting counseling. I'm just grateful the principal called Erika and not the police."

Angela cut the meeting short and rushed home, hoping Dre would be there. His car was not parked in his usual spot in the driveway.

She called and texted him again. Again, the calls went straight to voicemail. Her texts went unanswered. Angela changed into sweats and decided to cook dinner, something she rarely did on a week-night. Dre loved her fried pork chops, cabbage, and cilantro rice.

As the hours ticked by, Angela's worry increased in matching increments.

Where is he?

Dre's refusal to answer her calls pissed her off as much as it worried her. Around eight, she sat down to eat alone. She prepared a plate for Dre, covered it with foil, and placed it in the refrigerator.

A million scenarios raced through her mind. Maybe he'd been in a car accident. Or blew up at someone and gotten arrested.

It was well past eleven when Dre's Jeep pulled into the driveway. The relief that swelled in her felt like someone had wrapped her in a warm blanket.

When Dre opened the front door and saw Angela curled up on the living room couch, he simply nodded and headed for the bedroom.

After a beat, she followed after him. He was sitting on the edge of the bed.

"Are you okay?"

"Nope."

Now we're getting somewhere.

"Anything I can do to help?"

"Nope."

"The principal called Erika about your visit to the school."

"Yeah, I figured she would."

"She claims you accosted Bailey's teacher."

"Bullshit." He started untying the laces of his work boots. "I didn't *accost* nobody."

"So what *did* you do?"

"I asked her if she saw Bailey being bullied."

"And what did she say?"

"She refused to answer one way or the other. Which tells me she did."

"Did you really think she was going to be honest with you?"

Dre shrugged. "Bailey liked her a lot. I figured she cared about Bailey too and would be straight with me."

"We'll find out what she knows when we take her deposition."

"Yeah, okay." He kicked off his shoes and stripped off his socks.

"C'mon, Dre. You know how litigation works. Going down there and frightening that woman like that was crazy. What were you thinking?"

"I guess I wasn't thinking at all."

"You're scaring me, Dre. Tell me what I can do to help you."

He looked up at her with glassy eyes.

"Babe, I wish I *could* tell you how to help, but I have no idea."

CHAPTER

38

ZOLA'S HEAD SWIVELED with the ease of a human globe as she exited her car in the school parking lot. Since the run-in with Bailey's godfather a week ago, she was much more observant about her surroundings. Nobody was going to ambush her like that again.

A couple dozen cars were scattered around the lot. Zola relaxed a bit. After the stink Freeman made, she was sure Andre Thomas wouldn't come within five feet of her again.

Since Bailey's death, teaching had lost some of its joy, and she had no idea how to get it back. What she couldn't understand was how everyone around her, the principal, other teachers, even Bailey's classmates, could move on as if she had never been part of their world. A child was dead.

Once inside her classroom, Zola locked the door, then sat down behind her desk. She closed her eyes and prayed, then set the timer on her phone for five minutes. Sitting erect in her chair, she took in a big gulp of air, then exhaled long and slow. The short morning meditations she'd started a week ago hadn't yielded the promised benefits yet, but she was determined not to give up.

When the soft chimes signaled that the five minutes had ended, Zola opened her eyes and picked up the day's lesson plan from her desk. It was then that she remembered a poster she'd forgotten to retrieve from her car. She grabbed her keys and headed out.

As she shut the trunk, Zola noticed a young woman standing near the side entrance to the school, smiling and waving at her.

Zola didn't recognize the woman, at least not from this distance. She half-heartedly waved back. The woman seemed to be waiting for her.

A bolt of fear shot through Zola. Was this somebody else from Bailey's family trying to get information from her?

Zola tried to quell her anxiety. Maybe all the stress she'd been under was impacting her memory. Considering the enthusiastic way the woman waved at her, she must know her.

"Good morning, Zola," the woman called out as she got closer.

Zola remained cautiously suspicious. "Do we know each other?"

"I have something for you." The woman shoved a manila envelope into her hand and started walking away.

"Wait," Zola called after her. "What's this?"

The woman ignored her and hurried out of the gate.

Zola stood there for a few more seconds, then rushed back to her classroom. She tore open the envelope and pulled out a thick document. Scanning the first page, she could tell that it was a legal document because of the numbers running vertically down the left side of the page. But why had the woman given it to her?

She glanced at a box on the right. *Negligence, Failure to Supervise, Negligent Infliction of Emotional Distress*

Then she saw her name on the left-hand side.

Bailey's mother wasn't just suing Parker Elementary, the school district, the superintendent, and the principal.

She was also suing *her.*

CHAPTER

39

DRE SPENT THE morning tinkering around in his garage, organizing his tools. Mindless busy work helped him block out thoughts of how he'd failed Bailey.

When he glanced up and saw Chester coming his way, coffee cup in hand, he winced.

"Hey there, Mister Dre. Good morning to ya." Chester stepped uninvited into the garage. Dre greeted him with a curt upward nod. He didn't want any company.

"Bet you missed me, huh? I've been with my daughter and my grandbabies down in Nashville. I heard there was a whole bunch of commotion over here while I was gone. What happened?"

"I'm not up for talking right now." Dre turned his back to Chester, hoping he would get the message and leave.

"Well, you need to know everybody on this street is gossiping about it. Said you ran across the street to the white folks instead of coming to one of them."

Dre froze. *Ran across the street to the white folks?*

He could barely remember leaving the house that morning. He was in such a fog someone could have led him to the middle of the Harbor Freeway and he would've willingly followed.

Dre kept quiet, anxious for his neighbor to leave.

"I just thought you should know about all the rumors. They also said that little girl I see you with all the time hanged herself. Now *that*, I know was a lie. Ain't no way a child that young could know nothing about hanging herself. I don't know why folks even start talk like that. Must be because they have nothing going on in their own lives. When I was growing up, a child—"

"Chester, I don't want to talk about this." He had yet to turn around to face him.

"I was just making conversation. I didn't mean to upset you. I was—"

Chester caught a look at Dre's perturbed expression.

"I said I don't want to talk about this." Dre turned back around, picked up a wrench, and tossed it into a toolbox.

The old man stayed put. "Well, you don't have to tell me nothing twice. I was only—"

Dre spun around. "Did you hear what I said?"

The anger percolating through Dre's body must have oozed out of his pores. Chester took a step back.

"Well, fine." He hurriedly shuffled back to his house.

Without warning, a sharp, hot pain propelled Dre into a bent position. It felt like a ball of fire was swirling around in his chest. Was he having a heart attack?

Dre braced himself against the garage wall with one hand and clutched his chest with the other. The pain was still intense, but he could tell it was easing up. He pressed his back against the wall, glad that it was there to keep him from falling.

"You don't look too good. Do you need me to call 9-1-1?"

Dre struggled to catch his breath. It was Hannah from across the street.

"No, I'm fine," he sputtered.

"I was headed to the grocery store when I noticed you out here all bent over. Are you sure you're okay?"

"Yeah. I'm fine."

For several painful seconds, neither of them said a word as Dre slowly regained a normal breathing pattern.

"I know what you're going through," Hannah said in a calm voice. "I can't tell you exactly when it's going to get better. But it will."

Now Dre was more than pissed. First Chester's nosy meddling, now this.

"Lady," Dre spat, his voice cracking, "you don't even know me. You have no fuckin' idea what I'm going through."

Hannah didn't flinch or show any sign of offense.

"Actually, I do." Her eyes softened, amplifying the empathy in her voice. "My only child died by suicide. He was ten."

CHAPTER

40

THE LAST THING Zola wanted to do was talk to Darcella Freeman. But after getting reamed for not telling her about Andre Thomas's visit, she couldn't put this off.

When she got to the administration office, Blanca wasn't at her desk. Zola headed toward Freeman's open door.

"Do you have a minute?" Zola asked.

"Sure. Come on in."

Zola stepped inside and shut the door behind her.

Freeman eyed the large envelope in her hand. "Oh, I see you got a little surprise present today too. Got mine at seven o'clock this morning. I was in my driveway, climbing into my Jag. When'd you get yours?"

"A few minutes ago. In the parking lot."

"I bet it was a bit of a shocker to see your name on the front page of that lawsuit, huh?"

"Yes, it was."

"Have a seat."

"I've never been involved in a lawsuit before," Zola began. "So I'm not sure how this works. Will one of the school district's lawyers represent me?"

"Probably," Freeman said. "The district has to provide legal representation for an employee who's sued for something occurring in the course and scope of their employment."

Zola vaguely remembered hearing that term during her business law class in college.

"What do you mean *probably?*"

"In most cases, the same lawyer will represent all defendants. But if they have conflicting defenses, that won't be the case."

"What do you mean by conflicting defenses?"

"Well," Freeman leaned forward and smiled, "if you admitted that you saw Bailey being bullied and didn't do anything about it, that would create a conflict. So you might have to hire your own attorney."

Freeman was so viciously relentless in her efforts to force Zola to toe the line that it made her sick to her stomach.

She might as well have said, *Unless you back up my lies, you're on your own.*

"I don't anticipate needing a separate attorney," Zola said. "I'm sure we're all going to tell the truth."

The smile on the principal's lips melted away. "For sure."

"Why wasn't Dr. Andrews included in the lawsuit?" Zola asked.

"Why would she be?"

"She had suggested convening the threat assessment team and preparing an action plan to—"

"I have no idea what you're talking about. And if you ask Dr. Andrews, she'll say the same thing. It's better to just leave her out of this."

The evil fermenting in the principal's dark eyes dared Zola to defy her. Freeman wasn't Satan's mistress. She was his mama.

Zola had no doubt that the principal had bullied Dr. Andrews into developing a case of amnesia regarding her initial plans for addressing the situation with Bailey. Since the psychologist didn't want to be embroiled in a lawsuit, she was apparently happy to follow orders.

Zola inhaled. "When will we know who's representing us?"

"I've already called Legal. Somebody will contact you."

Zola's face was etched with worry.

"Are you okay?" Freeman asked. "You seem upset."

"I'm just a little rattled about being sued. Aren't you?"

"Not at all. That lawsuit is frivolous. I'm sure whoever the school district hires to represent us will get the case resolved in no time."

CHAPTER

41

DRE INVITED HANNAH inside for coffee. They sat across from each other on stools around the kitchen island.

"Sorry about going off on you like that," Dre said. "It's been kinda rough lately."

"No apology necessary. If you'd been around me for the first six months after Dylan died, I would've bitten your head off for looking at me the wrong way."

"How long ago did you lose your son?"

"Three years. But it still feels like yesterday."

Dre poured coffee into two mugs and handed one to Hannah.

He had a ton of questions but was nervous about the one he most wanted to ask.

Hannah seemed to read his mind. "Dylan also hanged himself."

"Damn! Was he bullied?"

"Relentlessly. At school and on social media. We didn't find out about the worst of the cyberbullying until after his death."

"Did you sue the school?"

Hannah shook her head. "There was no way I could've handled the stress of a lawsuit on top of losing my child."

"Well, Bailey's mother is going to sue and I'm glad she is."

"Do you have evidence that Bailey was bullied?"

"Yep. Hold on a minute." Dre disappeared down the hallway, returned seconds later, and slapped a folder in front of her. "This is what we found on Instagram. Can you believe this madness?"

Hannah examined the pages. "Actually, I *can* believe it. The kids at my son's school told him to his face to go kill himself."

Dre scratched his chin. "When did kids become so cruel?"

"It's because they're exposed to violence and depravity every day of the week. TV, movies, music, video games. Look at how nasty politics has become. Why wouldn't our kids copy that behavior?"

"Nobody's on TV telling people to kill themselves."

"There's a cumulative effect. Think about all the reality TV shows. The primary goal is to embarrass, ridicule, and degrade. The more malicious the better. People troll Twitter and Facebook attacking complete strangers. Kids see live shootings on the six o'clock news. My parents made us leave the room when certain stuff came on television. Parents today don't do that. Our kids are exposed to too much."

"That's not it." Dre vigorously shook his head. "Today's kids are too damn sheltered. They never get a chance to develop any coping skills because they've never heard the word *no*. So when they finally have to deal with disappointment, they have no idea how to handle it."

"I agree with you to a point because I was one of those helicopter parents. But other factors are at play too."

"Being too soft on our kids is the biggest factor," Dre insisted. "When I was growing up, nobody needed a support animal to get on a damn airplane or a quiet room at college."

Hannah couldn't help but laugh. "You, sir, have some very strong views. Wait until you're a parent."

"I'm already a parent. And you can bet my ten-year-old son knows that life can be rough. He also knows that if he comes home with a trophy, it better be because he did something to earn it besides just being on the damn team."

"The real issue," Hannah said, "is untreated childhood depression. Initially, I thought bullying was the cause of Dylan's death. I now understand that the bullying exacerbated his pre-existing depression."

"How can *any* kid these days be depressed? Their parents give 'em everything they want."

Hannah's tone grew serious. "You can't dismiss this. I bet you didn't know that the number of black kids under twelve who die by suicide is twice that of white kids. You can't blame that solely on bullying or poor parenting."

Dre couldn't speak for a second. "That's crazy. Are you serious?

"Yep. Google it."

He paused. "I need to ask you something, but I don't want it to come off the wrong way."

She took a sip of coffee. "Go ahead."

"Why do you say *died by suicide* instead of *committed* suicide."

"I've been through a ton of therapy," she explained. "Saying my son *committed suicide* places the blame on him. Dylan suffered from depression. That's an illness. We don't say people *committed* cancer."

"Okay, okay. I get it. But I still don't understand what a ten-year-old kid has to be depressed about."

"You're not hearing me. Depression is the result of a chemical imbalance. It's an illness just like cancer or diabetes."

Dre's cynical expression only deepened.

"If Bailey had broken her arm," Hannah continued, "you would've rushed her to the ER. But I'm going to bet that she didn't get any counseling after her father's death, right?"

Dre hunched his shoulders. "Other than talking to her minister, I don't think so."

"Both Bailey and her mother needed counseling from a therapist with expertise in grief and depression, not from a minister. We have to start treating our mental health as seriously as we do our physical health."

Dre still wasn't buying it. "But when she was around me, she was always happy."

"So was Dylan. Most of the time. But there are highs and lows with depression."

A hush fell over the room until Dre's unwavering voice broke it.

"Depressed or not, if the school had kept that bully from harassing her, Bailey never would've committed—" Dre hesitated and took a breath. "Bailey never would've died by suicide."

CHAPTER

42

THE MINUTE SHE walked out of the principal's office, Zola headed to her car and wept like a two-year-old. Then she called her husband for the kind of comfort only he could provide.

"Sweetie, what's wrong?" Brock said, alarm in his voice. "Stop crying and talk to me."

"Bailey's mother filed a lawsuit."

"You told me you thought she might do that. Why are you so upset?"

"Because she's not just suing the school, she's suing me too!"

"What? Are you sure?"

"Of course I'm sure! I have the lawsuit right here in my hands. I can't believe this!"

"Neither can I. You were the only one who tried to help that little girl."

"And now Freeman's pressuring me to lie. But I'm not going to do it. I'm going to tell the truth."

Zola waited for Brock to tell her that was exactly what she should do. Instead, radio silence blew up the telephone line.

"Brock, are you still there?"'

"Yeah, I'm here."

"So say something."

"Let's talk when we get home."

"Why can't we talk now?"

"Because you may not like what I have to say. You've been personally named in a lawsuit. That changes things."

"How?"

"You're a defendant. If the district loses the case, you'll—correction—*we'll* have to pay damages."

The implication of what Brock was saying shook her from the inside out.

"Are you saying that since *we*"—her words were doused in sarcasm—"could be on the hook for damages, I should go along with the principal and lie?"

"I'm just saying we might need to look at things a little differently now. It's just that..."

Heat inched up Zola's neck as Brock's voice trailed off. Her handsome, supportive, by-the-book husband was never at a loss for words.

Zola waited, her disappointment spiking along with her blood pressure.

"That lawsuit might prevent us from getting pre-qualified," he said.

"What? Why?"

"Because we'll have to disclose it as a potential liability when we fill out the loan application."

"Okay. And?"

"I'll have to contact the broker to find out what this all means for sure."

Zola swallowed. "I'm not going to lie, Brock."

"That little girl is dead and nothing's going to bring her back. The only thing you saw was the child being tripped up. It could've been an accident like your principal said."

"And it also could've been bullying," she fired back. "And I believe it was."

"Stop trying to be a martyr, Zola," Brock practically shouted. "That girl's death is not your fault."

Who is this man?

The couple rarely argued and never spoke harshly to each other when they did. Zola had always viewed Brock as an ethical, Christian man. But if he was willing to put their personal interests ahead of what was right, he was no better than Freeman.

"We'll talk about this some more when you get home," he said. "I gotta go."

Before Zola could respond, he'd hung up.

Did her husband really want her to get on the witness stand and lie? Or perhaps fudge the truth? And what if she refused?

There was no way she could make it through this without Brock in her corner.

Absolutely no way.

CHAPTER

43

"ARE YOU SITTING down?"

Angela was in her bedroom undressing when she received Jenny's call.

"Nope."

"Well, you might want to have a seat."

She kicked off her heels and started unbuttoning her blouse. "Is this a good sit down or a bad sit down?" She hit the speakerphone button and tossed her cell phone on the bed.

"A bad one."

Angela ignored Jenny's directive to sit down. She pulled a cotton sundress from the bottom dresser drawer and wiggled into it. "Let's hear it. I can take it."

"I just got off the phone with the school district's lawyer. The same attorney is representing all parties."

"Isn't that normally the case unless there's a conflict among the defendants?"

"That's not the bad part."

"Jenny, please stop stringing me along. Just spit it out."

"Ethan Landers is handling the case."

"And who is Ethan Landers?"

"An attorney who's made a name for himself by flying all over the country defending school districts in bullying lawsuits. According to his website, he's never lost a bullying case."

Angela paused. Not because this news concerned her, but because of Jenny's reaction to it. Jenny sounded fearful. Fear was not something Angela had ever associated with her friend. A week ago, Jenny was the one pumping her up.

"So he's good. So are we. Have you been up against him before?"

"Yeah. Only once."

"I'm assuming you lost."

"Nope. We settled the second day of trial. A settlement that my client was pretty happy with."

"Then why all the concern?"

"Because he tried my last nerve."

Angela laughed.

"He has this clean-cut, prestigious image," Jenny said, her scorn for the man unmistakable. "He dresses the part, looks the part, and acts the part in everyone's presence except his opposing counsel's. You can trust him about as far as you can throw him."

"So you're saying he's unethical?"

"Yeah, but never enough to get caught. He'll walk right up to the line, but won't step over it. He does things not because it will advance his case, but because he gets a hard-on by messing with his opponent's head."

"Doesn't scare me. I'm ready for a fight."

"You don't understand," Jenny said exasperated. "This man is going to be our worst nightmare."

"Relax. We've both gone up against plenty of jerks before."

"Not like this one. Another attorney warned me to be prepared to work harder than I'd ever worked before. And he was right. Landers likes to file motions just to keep you doing busy work so you'll be off your game."

"You're getting me fired up," Angela said. "Bring it on Ethan Landers."

"Alright," Jenny said with a weary sigh. "Don't say I didn't warn you."

CHAPTER

44

ZOLA HAD WORRIED herself ragged since the filing of the lawsuit. Now that she was sitting in a lawyer's office with Freeman inches away, her anxiety had to be approaching stroke level.

"I'm Ethan Landers," the well-dressed man began.

Landers shined with a confidence that strengthened his eye-catching, physical traits. His dark brown hair was moussed up in age-appropriate spikes. Warm, greenish-blue eyes balanced a smile that seemed deceptively comforting. The obstetrician probably looked at him in the delivery room and proclaimed, *TV lawyer for sure.*

"I wanted to have a short introductory meeting with the two of you, followed by separate, more in-depth interviews. You should plan on being here until about one o'clock today."

Freeman shot Zola an I-told-you-so glance, as if it was her fault they were here and not at school. The principal raised a finger in the air.

"Yes?" Landers said.

"Shouldn't you have scheduled separate meeting times for us? I have a ton of work to do."

Freeman's rebuke didn't appear to ruffle Landers.

"I recognize the value of your time, Ms. Freeman. While I'm interviewing one of you, my paralegal will be speaking with the other person. And vice versa. I'll be focusing on your personal knowledge of the allegations, while my paralegal will be inquiring about specific documents that might be helpful to us in defending your case."

Your case. Zola didn't like his choice of words. This wasn't *her* case. She wanted nothing to do with it.

The principal would not be appeased. "I'd like to know why the superintendent isn't here. He's named in the lawsuit too."

Landers flashed that smile again. It must work wonders on juries.

"In lawsuits like this, superintendents are routinely named as defendants but rarely have any direct knowledge. I spoke to him yesterday and he confirmed that. Are you telling me that's not the case?"

Freeman responded with a huff. "I guess that's correct."

"I promise to make this process as quick and painless as possible," Landers continued. "I've handled more than three dozen bullycide cases."

Zola cringed. She'd first heard the term bullycide at a continuing education workshop right after getting hired at Parker. She'd hated it then and she hated it even more now that Bailey's death made it so real for her.

"At the moment, I have two other bullycide cases," Ethan continued, oblivious to Zola's growing distress. "One in Riverside and the other in Oakland. But don't worry, you'll have my full attention. I expect the Riverside case to settle soon."

Zola didn't know what to think. Were there that many kids killing themselves because of bullying?

Darcella reached for a bottle of water from the center of the table and screwed off the cap. "I don't understand how a parent can sue the school when a child took her own life."

"We live in a very litigious world," Landers said. "People sue even when they don't have a valid claim. But there's a very high bar the plaintiff will have to jump."

"So what does Bailey's mother have to prove?" Freeman asked.

"First, she has to show that you had notice of actual or threatened harm to her daughter. Second, she has to prove that you were deliberately indifferent to that harm. And finally, she has to produce evidence of bullying that was so severe it deprived her child of access to educational benefits."

"Well, this should be an easy win for us," Freeman proclaimed. "Because we had no knowledge of *any* bullying."

"In my experience—and mind you I've never lost a bullycide case at trial—even if bullying did occur, parents have a hard time showing that a principal or teacher was *deliberately* indifferent to it. That's a tough standard to meet."

Actually, that's precisely the case here, Zola thought.

"You mentioned that you're about to settle a case," Zola said. "Is that because you think you'll lose at trial?"

"No. The parents have been trying their case in the media, which has divided the small community. One side supports the school. The other is rallying behind the parents. The district just wants it over with."

"Well, I doubt there'll be any media attention in this case," Freeman said. "A friend of mine who goes to the mother's church told me they're trying to keep everything hush-hush. They don't want people to know that the child killed herself."

"Let's hope so. Media attention can make these cases significantly more difficult to defend."

CHAPTER

45

"YOU READY?" ANGELA asked.

Erika nodded, squaring her shoulders. Dressed in a snazzy burgundy suit, she appeared well-equipped for battle. At least on the outside. Her melancholy eyes, however, told a different, sadder story.

They were standing on the sidewalk in front of the L.A. Community School District's main office, about to commence a press conference. A few feet away, Jenny handed out copies of their complaint to reporters.

"Leave everything to us," Angela told Erika. "Other than your short statement at the end, you won't have to do any talking."

"I just hope I can get through it without bursting into tears."

Angela couldn't say it, but tears would be fine. Grieving mothers made wonderfully emotional images on TV news broadcasts.

Jenny finished talking to a reporter and returned to confer with them. She squeezed Erika's hand. "This will be over in a flash."

"I think we're ready to start," Angela announced as she stepped up to the microphones.

The motley gaggle of reporters and camera people formed a semi-circle around them.

"We're here today to announce the filing of a lawsuit against Parker Elementary School. The negligence and failure to supervise exhibited by the school and its employees was the direct and proximate cause of the death of nine-year-old Bailey Lewis." She held up a picture of Bailey, moving it from left to right before placing it back on an easel.

"This beautiful, bright, bubbly fourth grader hanged herself two weeks ago after she was viciously bullied at Parker Elementary School. Her mother's lawsuit is aimed at ensuring that no other student loses his life due to bullying and that no other parent has to suffer the pain that—"

"If you claim bullying caused the child to commit suicide," a reporter called out, "why aren't you suing the bullies and their parents?"

Angela had anticipated this question and didn't miss a beat. "Students who bully are often very troubled kids. So they're victims too. They often have emotional problems that go undetected, which manifest in cruelty to others. We're not here to compound this tragedy. We're here because the school failed to protect my client's daughter."

"So how much money are you seeking?" another reporter asked.

"Five million dollars," Angela said, standing even taller.

They'd debated that amount, with Angela insisting that a larger number would gain more media attention.

"We're seeking a significant damage award to send a message not just to Parker Elementary, but to schools all across the country. They have to start effectively combatting the growing problem of bullying. This is an epidemic schools can no longer ignore."

Angela paused to take a breath as another reporter lobbed a question at her. "How can you expect the school to know a child is going to kill herself when her own family obviously didn't know she was that troubled?"

Before Angela could respond, Erika leaned into the microphone.

"It's true that I didn't know my child was in such pain." Her voice was strong, her stance bold. "But Parker Elementary knew she was being bullied and they did nothing to stop it. If they had,

Bailey would still be here. The school's employees failed to protect my daughter from mean-spirited children who tormented her on Instagram, repeatedly telling her to go kill herself."

Erika paused as parallel tracks of tears began a trail down her cheeks. "When you go home to your own children tonight, ask them if they've witnessed bullying at their schools. I suspect they'll say yes. And I bet some of them will tell you that there were adults who witnessed it and did nothing about it. This has to stop."

Angela caught Jenny's eye. What had just poured out from Erika's heart was far better than what they had scripted for her. Erika's soundbite would be playing on every local channel tonight and might even get picked up by the national news.

Erika backed away from the microphone as Jenny placed a tissue in her hand. As she dabbed at her eyes, a couple of photographers moved in for a closeup. That shot would look great on the front page of the *L.A. Times*.

Angela fought back a smile. "Anyone else have a question?"

CHAPTER

46

IT CONCERNED ZOLA that Landers chose to speak with her first. Had Darcella already fingered her as the weak link in this disgusting chain of deceit?

She followed him from the conference room to a corner office three times the size of her living room. The photographs on the wall behind his desk displayed his many celebrity connections—everyone from Obama to Lady Gaga to Steph Curry.

"Would you like some water or coffee?" he asked. "We have tea and soda as well."

Zola shook her head as she sat down in front of a glass desk almost as wide as the room.

"So tell me what happened."

Zola blinked. His question wasn't even a question. His statement—because that's what it was—was so open-ended, she didn't know where to begin. Maybe this was the first trap he'd set for her.

"What do you mean by *what happened*?"

Landers smiled. "Well, to start, do you believe Bailey Lewis killed herself because she was bullied?"

Shifting in the huge chair, her right index finger encircled one of the bumpy gold studs that ran along the length of its arm.

Zola expected Landers to pelt her with fact-based questions. *Did Bailey Lewis complain to you that kids were bullying her?*

Did you ever see anyone bully Bailey Lewis?

Did any other student ever tell you Bailey Lewis was being bullied?

Zola wanted to provide facts. Not her opinion.

Landers waited, his eyes boring into hers. She averted her eyes and focused on his ego wall. Brock would kill to meet Steph Curry.

"That shouldn't be a hard question to answer, Mrs. Phillips." His tone was gently chiding.

Zola met Landers's gaze full-on. Barely a minute in and she already felt like a criminal cornered in a cramped interrogation room.

"I don't know why Bailey killed herself."

That wasn't a lie. Not technically. No one except Bailey could know for sure what she was thinking at that precise moment. Of course, Zola did have her assumptions.

"That's a very good answer," Landers said, nodding. "I had a hunch that you were going to be a good witness."

She did not like this man. It was almost as if he was signaling her. A *good witness* provided answers that helped their case. Weren't lawyers supposed to start by instructing their clients to tell the whole truth and nothing but?

"Did you ever witness Bailey being bullied?"

Zola hesitated. She thought about Freeman's warnings, as well as her husband's concerns about the financial implications this case could have for them.

"If we lose," Zola said, ignoring his question, "and the jury issues a verdict in favor of Bailey's mother, would I be responsible for paying part of it?"

"That's unlikely. Unless it's determined that your behavior was outside the course and scope of your employment."

"What does that phrase mean?"

"Teaching is in the course and scope of your employment. Slugging a student is not. Does that help?"

"A little."

"Now back to my question. Did you ever witness Bailey being bullied?"

Angst danced in Zola's stomach. "No."

"Did Bailey ever tell you she was bullied?"

Zola swallowed the truth deeper down her throat. "No."

"Do you have any reason whatsoever to believe Bailey was the victim of bullying?"

"No."

Zola braced herself for the seasoned attorney to call her out on her lie. To ask her the same question three different ways to trip her up.

Landers scribbled something on his legal pad. "Let's move on to your background. How long have you been teaching?"

"What?"

Zola almost wanted to blurt out, *Don't you want the truth?*

"How long have you been teaching?" he repeated.

"Um, this is only my second year."

"Okay. So Parker Elementary is your first school?"

For the next thirty minutes, Zola listened in shock as Landers asked her a bunch of questions that had nothing to do with bullying.

This man wasn't stupid and neither was Zola. Ethan Landers knew she was lying to his face and he didn't care.

CHAPTER

47

FOLLOWING THE PRESS conference, Angela and Jenny treated Erika to lunch, then spent the afternoon fine-tuning their discovery requests.

Angela arrived home around six. Stepping inside, she heard laughter. Male and female laughter. Her head went into a mini-tailspin when she spotted Hannah and Dre in the den watching TV.

"Hey, babe," Dre said, waving her over. "I recorded your press conference on KCAL and called Hannah over so she could see it. Y'all knocked it outta the park."

"Yeah, you were great." Hannah stood.

"Thanks." It thrilled her to see Dre in such a good mood. If Hannah was responsible for that, hats off to her.

"You don't have to leave," Angela said, kicking off her heels.

"I came over to drop off a few slices of the pound cake I made." She grinned down at Dre. "I'm sorry you won't get a chance to taste any."

His hands shot up in mock surrender. "I tried to save you a piece, but it didn't work out. Hannah threw down harder than my grandmama."

Their new neighbor laughed. "Don't worry. I'll make another one this weekend. And next time, I'll bring it directly to you."

Dre grunted. "That still won't stop me from eating all of it."

This was the happiest Angela had seen her man since Bailey's death. She almost wanted to ask the woman what she'd put in that cake.

"I've been talking to Hannah about Erika's case," Dre said with the eagerness of a student anxious to share some newfound knowledge. "She knows a lot about bullycide cases."

"My son also died by suicide," Hannah volunteered.

"Oh my goodness." Angela pressed her palm to her chest. "I'm so sorry to hear that."

"A big part of my healing process was helping other parents who'd lost their children to suicide. Jonathan and I decided not to sue, but some of the parents in our support group did."

Dre's face shined with excitement. "Hannah says you should file a—"

He paused. "What's that thing you told me about where the attorneys get to search the school?"

"A request for inspection of premises," Hannah said. "I know a couple who uncovered a boatload of evidence in their son's case."

"Really?" Angela said. She and Jenny hadn't discussed serving an inspection request. "Like what?"

"When the lawyer visited the classroom, he found graffiti on a desk that said awful things about the child. The teacher didn't even know it was there. But the treasure trove was in the boy's restroom. The stalls were scrawled with vicious comments aimed at him."

Angela had served inspection requests many times, most often in employment cases. Yet it had never occurred to her to do so in this case. The gentle pang of insecurity about handling a case outside her area of expertise returned. Was this the first misstep of many?

"Please excuse me." Angela took her phone from her purse and dashed down the hallway.

"What are you doing?" Dre called after her.

"Calling Jenny. We're definitely going to do this."

CHAPTER

48

"So HOW DID the meeting with your attorney go?" Brock stood in the entryway of their bedroom, leaning against the doorframe.

"Fine."

Zola lay in their king-size bed, her body splayed like a four-armed starfish. The blinds were drawn and she hadn't bothered to undress.

Since their tiff the day she'd first told him about the case, Zola had nothing but one-word responses to almost any question Brock posed. The lawsuit was doing more than tearing her apart. It was also pulling at the loose threads of their tightly woven marriage.

"We need to talk, Zola."

"Yeah, okay."

Zola often bragged to friends that her husband—unlike most—was an enthusiastic proponent of open communication. Brock could talk a subject to death. She was the one who retreated into shutdown mode when their conversation veered into uncomfortable territory.

He sat down on the edge of the bed. "I know this is tough for you."

"Yep. Sure is." Zola rolled over on her side, turning her back to him.

"I wasn't telling you to lie."

She peered at him over her shoulder, then sat up, resting her back against the headboard. "Sure sounded like that to me."

"Ultimately, it's your decision to do what you think is best."

"There you go again. If my testifying truthfully couldn't impact us financially, you wouldn't be telling me to do *what I think is best*. You'd be urging me to tell the truth."

Brock tucked his bottom lip between his teeth. "Yeah, you're probably right."

"*Probably?*"

"Okay, you're right. When I realized we could be on the hook for damages, it made me crazy. But I talked to a guy in our legal department. He said even if the other side won, it's unlikely that you'd have to pay a dime. The school would cover it."

"Oh. So now you're fine with me telling the truth? Too late. When that attorney interviewed me this morning, I looked him dead in the eye and I lied."

Brock blinked. "You did?"

"Yep. And you know what? He knew I was lying and he didn't care."

"How do you know that?"

"Because I could see it in his eyes. He's the kind of man who'll do anything to win."

Brock chuckled. "That's certainly the kind of lawyer I want in my corner."

"Well, not me," Zola snapped.

He reached for her hand, but she jerked it away.

"I'm sorry. I didn't mean to put you in this position."

"It's no big deal." A smile doused with scorn undercut the flippancy of her words. "My principal's happy because the school won't get hit with a big verdict. I'll get to keep my job and you'll get the home of your dreams."

CHAPTER

49

FOR NOW, ANGELA'S office would serve as command central for Erika's case. Once the trial got underway, they planned to transition to Jenny's office in Echo Park, which was much closer to the superior courthouse in downtown Los Angeles.

Jenny and Angela sat next to each other in the small conference room down the hall from the office suite Angela shared with two other solo practitioners.

"I'm getting excited about this case," Angela said. "I think we can pull this off."

"Hold on to that optimism," Jenny said with a grimace. "You'll need it after Ethan Landers pulls his first stunt."

"Can you please check that Debbie Downer attitude at the door? We need to wear our game faces twenty-four-seven."

"I know that man. I'm just bracing for what's to come."

Angela's assistant knocked on the door, then entered. "Sorry to interrupt, but I thought you might want to see this. It's from Ethan Landers."

She placed a large white envelope on the table. Before Angela could reach for it, Jenny grabbed it.

"It's the defendants' answers to the complaint," Jenny said, rifling through the pages. "Nothing earth-shattering. They're denying everything."

"As expected," Angela said.

"Whoa." Jenny focused her wide-eyed gaze in Angela's direction. "What?"

"They also sent a deposition notice."

"So when do they want to depose Erika?"

"It's not for Erika."

"Okay," Angela said, stretching out the word. Sometimes Jenny could be so dramatic. "Who do they want to depose?"

Jenny smiled. "Your boyfriend."

"Are you serious? Why would Dre be the first person Landers wants to depose?" Angela perused the document. "That doesn't make sense."

"Like I told you, the man doesn't play by the rules. He likes to do things for shock value. Dre needs to be triple prepared for every possible question Landers throws at him."

"What could he ask Dre about other than what Bailey might've told him?"

"I bet he's going to grill him about approaching Bailey's teacher. I wouldn't put it past Landers to accuse Dre of witness intimidation."

"Dre was such a knucklehead for doing that," Angela grumbled. "And when he starts going off about having to be deposed, I'm going to remind him that his own behavior put him in this predicament."

When Angela got home later that evening, she was surprised to find Dre across the street, chatting with Hannah as she planted flowers in her front yard. He waved and returned home a few minutes later.

"It's nice to see you being so buddy-buddy with our new neighbor," Angela teased as she pulled a bag of corn chips from the kitchen cabinet.

"I hate to admit it, but I kinda like her."

"Don't let Chester find out you're cavorting with the enemy."

"Too late for that. I tried to apologize about snapping at him the other day, but he's not hearing it. He glares at me every time he sees me talking to Hannah. How's the case going?"

"It's still early. Jenny and I are just gearing up for battle."

Dre puffed out his chest. "Well, let me know if you need some extra armor."

"Funny you should say that."

"Why? What's up?"

"Guess who the school district's attorney wants to depose first."

"Who? Erika?"

"Nope. You."

Dre didn't speak for a good five seconds. "Me? Why me?"

"We don't know. Maybe to find out if Bailey talked to you about being bullied."

Angela didn't have the heart to tell him that his stupid decision to approach Bailey's teacher was more than likely the reason he'd been subpoenaed.

"Cool. I have a mouthful to tell him."

"It's not going to be that easy. He'll be looking for information to help *his* case, not ours."

"Well, I can't help him there."

"I hope so."

"What do you mean, you hope so. I got this."

"You aren't nervous about having your deposition taken?"

"Nope. I've got truth on my side."

"Oh, my dear, dear, naïve, young man. Litigation often has very little to do with the truth. More often than not, it's about who has the best attorney and who's better at spinning the facts."

"Then we're still good. You and Jenny are gonna give that dude a run for his money."

"We'll see."

"What's up with you? Seems like you're already intimidated by the guy and you haven't even met him yet. That's not like you."

Dre was right. This kind of insecurity wasn't in Angela's DNA. She was a former federal prosecutor and had a stellar record of success in private practice. Maybe it was the way Meltzer had crapped on their case, coupled with Jenny's warnings about Landers and his unethical behavior that was causing uncertainty to seep in. For Erika's sake, she had to shake it off.

"I don't want to spend months dragging Erika through litigation only to lose."

"We ain't losing." Dre dug his hand into the bag of chips she was holding. "So chill."

CHAPTER

50

DARCELLA FREEMAN WATCHED the KCAL noon broadcast on the small TV in the corner of her office. If she could've been any madder, her head would've exploded.

The press conference with Erika Lewis and her attorneys was yesterday's news. So why were they airing it again today?

Darcella winced as the anchor feigned a grim expression more appropriate for mass murder.

> *Parker Elementary School in Los Angeles has been hit with a tragic bullycide lawsuit. The mother of nine-year-old Bailey Lewis claims that bullying at Parker Elementary drove her daughter to suicide. We have KCAL's Sandra Foley live at the scene.*

Live at the scene? Darcella thought. *Give me a break.*

Why was the brainless reporter standing in front of *her* school? This wasn't some shooting or robbery. Bailey Lewis didn't even die here.

The reporter went on to repeat all the lies laid out in the lawsuit, simply sticking the word *alleged* in front of them. Darcella shook her head. No one could have foreseen this tragedy. The girl's own mother didn't even know she was suicidal. Yet, there she was sniveling on TV.

Too bad that reporter hadn't interviewed her. Darcella would've told her how the tearful mother was too busy with her career to bring her own child to school.

Darcella picked up the remote and switched off the TV. When the story first ran yesterday, calls from parents poured into her office. Parents who'd never bothered to show up at parent-teacher meetings were yelling at her, demanding guarantees that their kids were safe. Now, her phone would start ringing off the hook all over again and she could do nothing but take it. Lord, she couldn't wait for Landers to put an end to this fiasco.

The extra demands placed on her because of the lawsuit already had her at her wit's end. The superintendent called her almost daily and ordered her to prepare weekly status reports for the school board. He professed to be concerned about negative publicity for the school. But all he cared about was how the case might impact his job.

Darcella got up to brew a cup of coffee in the small kitchen attached to her office. As she waited for it to finish, she closed her eyes and took a deep, calming breath. She would have to stay focused to get through this madness.

Coffee in hand, Darcella returned to her desk. She was riffling through her locked file drawer when a folder labeled *Bailey Lewis* caught her attention. What was a student file doing in her personal drawer?

Darcella read a Post-It Note in Blanca's neat print dated a month ago.

THIS FILE CAME FROM WEATHERTON ELEMENTARY.

She opened the folder and started reading. It was a file from Bailey's previous elementary school. Darcella began to get excited as she flipped through the pages. Had Bailey had any issues there? Maybe she'd find some evidence to help their case. But the file only contained the child's grades, vaccination record, and a few attendance reports.

Darcella didn't expect to find any information about Bailey being bullied. No administrator in her right mind would put that in a child's file if she could avoid it. The principal at Weatherton wasn't about to make herself a bulls-eye for a case like the one Darcella was now embroiled in.

She was about to close the folder when a page near the back caught her eye. She paused to read it, then turned to her computer and typed into the Google search bar.

As her search results popped up, her pulse surged with every beautiful word on the screen. She glanced at the time in the upper righthand corner, wondering if it was too late to call Landers. She snatched her phone and scrolled through her contacts, searching for Landers's number. This news was too good to wait.

Landers was going to love her. Darcella had just discovered a smoking gun that would torpedo Erika Lewis's lawsuit before it even got started.

51

ON THE MORNING of his deposition, all Dre's swagger about testifying pulled a disappearing act.

"I still don't understand why I have to be the first person to testify."

Dre was sitting at a conference table in Landers's office, tugging at his tie every few seconds. Angela flanked him on one side, Jenny on the other. The videographer and court reporter had set up their equipment and stepped out of the room.

"We've been over this," Angela said, her patience strained. "We don't get to choose the order of his depositions."

Angela was relieved that Landers hadn't subpoenaed Erika first. She wasn't emotionally ready for a deposition. They'd invited Erika to attend Dre's deposition—which was her right since she was the plaintiff—but she declined.

The court reporter and videographer returned to the conference room followed by Landers and Darcella Freeman.

"What's she doing here?" Dre muttered.

Angela covered the microphone clipped to his shirt with her hand and whispered to him. "First, lower your voice. Second, she's a defendant. She has a right to be here."

Still standing, Landers leaned across the table and extended his hand. "I'm Ethan Landers, counsel for the defendants."

Jenny and Angela stood and clasped Landers's hand. Dre remained seated, glaring up at him.

Landers extended his hand to Dre. A beat passed before he grudgingly shook it.

"Nice to see you again, counselor," Landers said to Jenny.

Jenny nodded, her smile as phony as their opponent's greeting. They'd agreed that she would defend the deposition, so Angela could focus on keeping Dre's emotions in check.

Once they were on the record, Landers quickly ran through the preliminaries, instructing Dre to answer all questions audibly and to ask for a break if he needed one.

Landers spoke in a friendly tone, more like he was interviewing Dre for a job rather than about to walk him off a litigation cliff.

He flipped through a few pages on the notepad in front of him. "What is your relationship to the deceased?"

Dre's nose twitched. Angela knew that was a reaction to Landers's reference to Bailey as *the deceased.*

"I'm her godfather."

Angela found it telling that Dre used the present tense. He still hadn't accepted her death.

"And please don't call her *the deceased,*" Dre said, chastising the lawyer. "Her name is Bailey. Bailey Lewis."

This wasn't good. Dre seemed to be itching for a confrontation. But in this arena, Landers came armed with a sub-machine gun, while Dre packed a butter knife.

"I'm sorry. I'll be sure to do that going forward."

Landers knew Bailey's name. He was just trying to get a rise out of Dre. If he went off, Landers would surely find a reason to play the video of Dre's outburst for the jury.

Angela caught Jenny's eyes and instantly read her non-verbal message. *We need to get Dre under control.*

Landers flipped through his notes again. The longer he took, the more Dre squirmed in his seat.

"Mr. Thomas," Landers said, looking him directly in the eyes. "Did you molest Bailey Lewis?"

"What? Hell no!" His face twisted with rage, Dre leaned in over the table as if he wanted to challenge Landers to a fight. "Why would you ask me some shit like that?"

"Objection!" Jenny said, almost as unnerved as Dre. "Irrelevant, outside the scope, badgering the witness."

Landers's lips angled into a smile. "My question is indeed relevant. I have to follow the evidence wherever it leads me."

"There ain't no evidence," Dre sneered.

Jenny had warned them that Landers was unscrupulous. But even Angela hadn't anticipated anything like this. Freeman was actually smiling.

"And counsel, you may want to remind your client to watch his language. Outbursts like that won't look too good when I play this video for the jury."

"Man, screw you. I should jump across this table and kick your—"

Angela and Jenny both grabbed one of Dre's forearms.

"We need to take a break," Jenny said. "My client's been under a lot of stress since his goddaughter's death."

"Sure," Landers said. "Take as much time as you need. Feel free to use the conference room across the hall."

Angela and Dre headed in that direction, but Jenny pointed down the hall. "Let's go downstairs to the courtyard."

"Why? You think this place is bugged?" Dre asked, still fuming.

"No," Jenny replied. "I don't want anyone to overhear what I have to say to you. I'm not sure I'll be able to keep my voice down."

The three of them stepped into an elevator car.

Once they were inside, Dre started up again. "Why would he ask me some shit like—"

Jenny positioned her hands in a time-out signal. "Not another word until we're outside."

"I just wanna know why—"

"Not here, Dre!" Angela shouted. "You don't know who's listening."

"But there's nobody else in here."

"That's a speaker right there," Angela said.

Dre huffed. "Oh, so the maintenance man might be listening. Yeah, okay."

They exited the elevator and made their way to a courtyard in front of Landers's office building. They found a secluded area near a large fountain.

"Sit down," Angela said to Dre.

"I don't need to—"

"Please sit down," Jenny said sternly.

Taking in the grim expressions on both of their faces, Dre reluctantly did as he was told. Jenny and Angela remained standing, gazing down at him.

Jenny put her hands on her hips. "What I need you to do right now is to shut the hell up and listen to me."

Dre blinked. He was not accustomed to anybody talking to him like that.

"We spent a total of ten hours prepping you for this deposition. And the first thing we told you was that Landers likes to unnerve his witnesses. He's messing with your head and you're letting him. When we go back in there, you need to be smarter and calmer than he is. If you let him get you riled up, he wins and we lose."

Dre massaged the back of his neck. "But he said he had evidence that—"

"Did you molest Bailey?"

"Hell naw."

"Okay, then. There's nobody alive who believes you did. Not even Landers. Can you imagine if you'd exploded like that in front of a jury? Some of them would think you got so upset because you *did* molest Bailey. We need you to play Landers's game better than he can play it himself."

Dre brushed his right palm down his face. "You don't know how bad I wanted to lean across that table and bust that punk in his mouth."

Angela grimaced. "If you want to blow this case for Erika, then have at it. And when the cops give you your one phone call, don't call me."

"Let's go back in there and fight this fight for Bailey," Jenny said. "Okay?"

"Yeah, okay." Dre sprang to his feet. "I understand what's up. I got this."

CHAPTER

52

ETHAN LANDERS AND Darcella Freeman retreated to his office during the break in the deposition.

"You're quite an attorney," Freeman gushed, her voice dripping with admiration. "I don't ever want to be on the opposite side of you."

"You're something else yourself," Landers said. "That was quite the offensive play on your part."

"What're you talking about?"

"Your call reporting Mr. Thomas to DCFS."

Darcella smiled, feigning innocence. "I did that out of concern for one of my students."

"If you say so." He eyed her suspiciously. "How's Zola doing?"

"Fine, I guess. Why do you ask?"

"She was a ball of nerves during our interview."

"Anybody would be. Litigation's no fun. I remember my first time."

"No, her nervousness goes far beyond that."

Darcella's expression turned serious. "Are you concerned about her testimony?"

"Not at this point. She ultimately echoed everything you told me."

"As I told you she would."

Landers smiled sheepishly.

"What's that look all about?" Freeman asked coyly.

"You're a lot like me," he said. "You're smart. You're ambitious and you like to win by any means necessary."

Freeman nodded. "I would have to say your assessment of me is right on the nose."

Landers's administrative assistant tapped on the door, then stuck her head inside. "They're back from the break."

Landers stood up. "Now the real fun's about to start."

CHAPTER

53

"Is THE WITNESS ready to proceed?" Landers asked in a voice so pleasant it practically chirped.

"Yes," Jenny said, eying Dre as if to confirm her response. "He's ready."

"Okay, Mr. Thomas, you indicated before the break that you did not molest Bailey Lewis. Is that correct?"

"Yeah, that's correct."

Dre was already disregarding their advice. They'd told him repeatedly to say *yes* and *no*, not *yeah* and *naw*. He gritted his teeth as his left knee bounced up and down underneath the table.

"Is that still your answer now that you've had an opportunity to consult with your attorneys?"

"Yeah. And I didn't need to *consult with my attorneys* about that." Dre spit out the words like a bad taste. "I would never molest any child. I'm not a pervert."

"Were you aware that someone made a report to the Department of Children and Family Services about your interactions with Bailey?"

Dre paused, seemingly at war with himself over his need to stay calm. "No."

Landers opened the folder in front of him and pulled out a sheet of paper.

"I'll mark this as defendants' exhibit one." He handed the document to Dre and gave a copy to Jenny and the court reporter. "Please take a minute to review it."

Angela scanned Dre's copy, her own rage settling in when she spotted Darcella Freeman's name listed as the complainant. She glanced at Jenny, who fired back a look confirming they were on the same page.

"What is this?" Dre asked.

"That's not how this works, Mr. Thomas. I'm the one who gets to ask the questions. But since you asked, it's a transcript of a report made to the Department of Children and Family Services raising concerns that you may have molested Bailey."

Angela reached under the table and placed a hand on Dre's upper thigh, hoping to calm him.

"Do you have any idea why someone would've filed such a report?"

"No." His eyes fell back to the document. "Excuse me. I mean, yes. It says here that Darcella Freeman made this complaint."

Dre's gaze shot across the table to the principal.

"She obviously did it to try to point a finger at me instead of herself. But it don't matter because it ain't true. I guess that's why DCFS never contacted me or Bailey's mom about it."

Good, Angela thought. Dre wasn't taking his bait.

"DCFS received the report the day before the deceased—excuse me—Bailey died. I suspect that's the reason no one ever contacted you."

"How about a question instead of a comment," Jenny said.

Landers continued, not missing a beat. "Did you take Bailey to school on the morning of March seventh?"

Dre hesitated. "I may have. I'd need to see a calendar to know for sure."

"March seventh was the same day Bailey threatened another student in the school cafeteria. Does that refresh your memory?"

"Bailey didn't threaten another student. She simply reacted when that girl who'd been bullying her, Kiya Jackson, squirted ketchup on her sweater. But yeah, I took her to school that day."

Angela held her breath. Dre was doing a good job of not letting Landers put words in his mouth, but she didn't have any confidence that he wouldn't eventually explode again.

"Do you recall stopping Bailey on the steps of the school and trying to talk to her?"

Dre thought for a moment. "Yes, because she—"

"That's fine, Mr. Thomas. That was a yes or no question."

"Objection," Jenny said. "You need to let the witness finish his answer. Were you finished, Dre?"

"No, I wasn't." Dre paused, then scratched his forehead. "I'm sorry, now I forgot the question."

Landers turned to the court reporter. "Could you please read back the last question?"

After the court reporter did so, Dre continued. "I was trying to talk to Bailey because she didn't want to go to school."

"Objection," Landers said. "Move to strike the witness's last sentence as speculative.

Dre looked at Jenny, then Angela, as if expecting one of them to counter Landers's objection.

Angela began to get nervous. Dre hadn't told them about this encounter. Whatever had happened, Landers was trying to make it out to be something that it wasn't.

"A witness reported that Bailey was crying and that she jerked away from you and ran into the school. Is that correct?"

"Yes, that's correct. She was crying because she was scared to go to school."

Dre was getting into a rhythm, one Angela didn't like. They'd coached him to respond with a *yes* or *no* whenever he could. If there was a need for explanation, Jenny would jump in or have him clarify when it was her turn to question him.

"And why was Bailey scared to go to school?"

"Because she was being viciously bullied. She begged me to convince her mother to homeschool her. She was so afraid I practically had to drag her from the car. I stopped her on the steps to tell her not to be afraid, that everything was going to be okay. She started crying, so I squatted down and put my hands on her shoulders. That's when she pulled away from me and ran inside."

"If you thought she was being bullied so badly, why did you allow her to go the school?"

A pained look crossed Dre's face. He'd been asking himself that question for days now.

"I didn't know kids were telling Bailey to go kill herself. If I had known it was so bad that she wanted to die," his voice cracked with emotion, "I never would've let her go in there."

Landers apparently didn't want an emotional witness on camera, so he switched topics, catching them all off guard.

"Who discovered Bailey's body?"

Dre took a second to gather himself. "My girlfriend, Angela."

"Would that be Angela Evans, one of your defense counsel, who's sitting to your left?"

"Yes."

"Where was the deceased's body discovered?"

"*Bailey* was discovered in our office and workout room."

"Our?"

"Yes. Angela and I live together in Leimert Park."

"Do you rent or own?"

"Objection, relevancy. The witness is instructed not to answer."

"Really, counselor?" Landers said with a smug look. "You're instructing him not to answer on relevancy grounds?"

"Okay, then," Jenny said, "objection, harassment, invasion of privacy. Next question."

Landers sighed. "Never mind. Walk us through the day the deceased hanged herself."

"Objection, confusing, calls for a narrative," Jenny said. "Please rephrase. And for the last time, could you please show us the courtesy of using Bailey's name?"

"Oh, yes. Forgive me for that. Please tell me how you discovered that Bailey had hanged herself."

Angela was beginning to wonder if Landers wanted Dre to relive that day solely to stoke his grief. Dre responded in a calm, monotone voice. His voice cracked at times, but he completed his response without losing his composure.

Next, Landers took Dre through a series of questions seeking to tie him down on everything Bailey had told him about being bullied.

"Did you share the conversations between you and Bailey with Ms. Evans?"

Dre was about to answer when Jenny interjected. "Objection, attorney-client privilege."

"I doubt that an attorney-client relationship existed at that time. And anyway, I'm not inquiring about the nature of the conversations, just whether he passed that information on to Ms. Evans."

Dre waited for Jenny's instruction.

"Go ahead," she said.

"What was the question again?"

"Did you tell Ms. Evans what Bailey told you about allegedly being bullied?"

"Of course."

Landers checked his legal pad. "Okay. I think I'm finished."

Angela and Jenny traded glances. The deposition had barely lasted two hours. Landers had fired his first arrow at Dre as a stunt, the molestation allegation being the kickoff play.

Jenny asked a few questions to clarify things that Dre hadn't been quite clear on, then Landers ended the deposition.

Dre and Angela rose from their seats as Jenny reached into her satchel and pulled out a document. "This is a request for inspection of premises," she said, handing it to Landers. "We'd like to inspect the school."

Darcella Freeman recoiled. *"Inspect the school?* For what? Is that allowed?"

Landers gave the principal a hard look that instantly shut her down. "I'll take a look at the document and get my response to you."

He waited until they reached the door before calling out. "Wait. I almost forgot I have something for you too." He walked over and handed Jenny a large, sealed envelope.

She stuffed it into her bag and continued out of the room.

"I'm dying to know what's in that envelope," Angela said as they waited for an elevator. "I bet it's a deposition notice for Erika."

"Nope," Jenny said. "It's some of kind of motion meant to screw with our heads."

"What makes you think that?" Dre asked.

"Because that's what Landers does. I wasn't going to give him the pleasure of opening it in front of him and letting him see the anger on my face. He totally gets off on that."

No one spoke again until they'd reached their cars, which were parked side-by-side in the underground parking structure.

"Okay, now can we take a peek?" Angela asked.

Jenny pulled the envelope from her bag and handed it to her. "Have at it."

Angela ripped it open and took her time reading it. Deep lines creased her forehead as she flipped from page to page.

Jenny leaned against her car, arms folded, a knowing look on her face.

"So, what is it?" Dre asked, peering over her shoulder.

Angela finally looked up. "I guess I should've expected this. It's a motion to disqualify counsel."

"What?" Jenny stepped over to see the document for herself.

"Yep," Angela said. "That asshole is trying to get me kicked off this case."

CHAPTER

54

ZOLA WOKE UP Saturday morning in much better spirits. She decided to hibernate in the peacefulness of her classroom, grading papers, and revising her lesson plans.

The minute she flicked on the light switch inside her classroom, the bright colors and soothing warmth embraced her. This was exactly what she needed to help pull her out of the doldrums. It wasn't right to let her other students suffer because she was in the middle of this mess.

Zola also needed some time away from Brock. They were barely speaking. She partly blamed him for her predicament. If he had stood by her and urged her to tell the truth no matter what the consequences, she wouldn't have lied to their attorney. Deep down, Zola knew that wasn't fair. She was a grown woman. Grown enough to stand up for herself. To stand up for Bailey.

After three productive hours, Zola was locking the door of her classroom, when the strong scent of paint wafting from the girl's restroom assaulted her nostrils. The custodians always reserved painting for the summertime. Both students and staff had allergies and sensitivities that made it wise to do so.

Zola hoisted her purse higher on her shoulder and was about to head out, but changed her mind. Something pushed her to investigate why they'd be painting inside the building this time of the school year.

She found Damien on his knees, roller in hand, painting the wall above the sinks.

"Hey, Damien, I never thanked you for coming to my aid the other day, when that guy approached me in the parking lot."

"No, prob, Miss Zola," he said, smiling up at her over his shoulder.

Zola thought it was cute that he always called her Miss Zola. He was younger than she was. Damien was raised in Jackson, Mississippi. She wished more young guys had his manners.

"What are you doing here on a weekend?" Damien asked her.

"Playing catch-up. Isn't it unusual for you to be painting during the school year?"

"Not really."

"Does the principal know you're painting today?"

"I doubt it. The schedule got messed up. No one painted the girl's restrooms this summer."

"Are you painting the restrooms in the other buildings too?"

"Nope. Just this one. It was the only one they missed."

"Will the walls be dry in time for the girls to use it on Monday?"

"Should be. I'll check it out before school starts. If the smell hasn't cleared out, I'll rope it off and they can use the one down the hall."

As Damien continued working, Zola stepped into the hallway but didn't leave. She just stood there, baffled. Something had drawn her there and wouldn't let her leave. After a few minutes, she peered inside again. Damien was in the stall farthest away from her.

Tiptoeing so he wouldn't hear her, Zola examined every inch of the open space, not sure what she was looking for. Teachers had their own restrooms and rarely came inside the students' facilities.

Zola noticed writing on the walls by the sinks where Damien hadn't painted yet. Nothing offensive, just a name here and there, a heart and some indecipherable doodles.

Damien stuck his head out of the stall.

"Did you need something, Miss Zola?"

"No, I was just leaving." She smiled awkwardly. "Don't work too late."

CHAPTER

55

IN THE FEW days since his deposition, Dre had stopped peppering Angela about the status of the case. Instead, he sulked around the house in a constant state of agitation.

As they sat in the den watching TV, Angela glanced over at him. Dre could tell she was about to say something. All he wanted right now was silence.

"You did a great job at your deposition. I know you wanted to go off on Landers. I'm glad you didn't let him rattle you."

That had to be the third time she'd told him that. Dre felt like a five-year-old getting a pat on the head for eating his brussels sprouts.

Why had he pushed Erika to sue the school? If his deposition was any indication, they were going to drag Erika through the mud too. Then the case would probably get dismissed on a technicality.

He was still pissed off that Landers had filed that motion to disqualify Angela.

"Do you think the judge is going to kick you off the case?" he asked, anxious to talk about something besides his deposition performance.

Angela shrugged. "We don't think so, but we're meeting with Jenny's mentor for advice."

"The dude wouldn't have filed it if he didn't think he could win it, right?"

"No, that's not right. Landers likes playing games. You saw that firsthand at your deposition. Once he realized he couldn't get you riled up again, he ended it."

"It don't seem right that he can get away with stuff like that."

"Well, he can."

"Can't you report him to the judge?"

"It wouldn't do any good. We'd look like whiny children."

"Well, I hope he loses that motion."

"Me too."

Dre picked up the remote and started channel surfing. "Why do we pay damn near two hundred dollars a month for cable TV when there's nothing to watch?"

"Are you feeling okay?"

"I'm fine. Please stop asking me that."

Angela held up both hands. "Okay, fine. You hungry?"

"Nope."

"You should eat something. You—"

Dre got up and headed out of the room.

Angela followed close behind. "Where're you going?"

"For a walk." He pulled his jacket from the front closet.

There was a look of terror in Angela's eyes. "It's almost eleven o'clock, Dre."

"I know what time it is."

He zipped up his jacket and pulled the hood over his bald head.

"C'mon, Dre. You can't be serious. You can't go out like that."

"Like what?"

"If you insist on taking a walk, fine. But please don't leave here in a hoodie."

"Why not?"

"You know why not."

"So you saying I can't take a walk in my own damn neighborhood?"

"Not wearing a hoodie at close to midnight. That's asking for trouble."

"I'm not restricting my movements because white people who don't even belong here might be scared of me."

"The black people in this neighborhood would be scared of you too. They'll be the first ones calling the police."

Dre refused to acknowledge the truth of her words. "I don't care. I need to get some air." He opened the door and stepped outside.

A soft breeze tickled his face. He moved at a slow pace, trying to quiet his mind. As he passed a house near the end of the block, he noticed someone peeking out from the curtains. As he turned to face the house, the curtains abruptly closed. On the opposite side of the street, he saw a repeat performance. He wondered if somebody was already dialing 911.

This was his reality and he hated it. Farther down the block, he spotted a white couple walking toward him.

They could take a stroll day or night and nobody would call the cops on *them*. Dre resented them for being able to move into *his* neighborhood—his *black* neighborhood—and have the freedom to do things he couldn't.

As they got closer, he was itching to ask them a question.

"Can I ask you something?" Dre said when they were within a few feet of crossing paths. "How come you're not afraid to walk down the street this time of night in a black neighborhood?"

The woman clutched the man's arm. The guy, however, showed no sign of distress at being approached by a tall, black man in a hoodie. Maybe he was packin'.

"I'm not trying to cause you any trouble." Dre removed his hood, hoping to put them at ease. "I live right up the street. I just wanna know what makes you so fearless."

The guy shrugged. "Why should we be afraid? This is our neighborhood too. We pay taxes just like everybody else."

Dre turned around and started walking alongside them, continuing the conversation. He learned that Ken and Kiley moved to Leimert Park over a year ago from the Bay Area. They had enjoyed

taking late-night strolls in their old neighborhood and saw no reason not to do the same here.

"We don't focus on the negative," Ken said good-naturedly.
"When you expect bad things to happen, they do. When you don't
allow negative energy into your lives, it doesn't come."

Huh? So that's how it works?

The next time the cops jammed him up, all he had to do was send
positive energy their way and they would back off? Dre would've
been pissed off if he hadn't been so stunned by the man's simple
explanation.

Minutes later, Dre found himself back in front of his house. He
said goodbye to the couple, trudged up the walkway, and sat down
on the porch, his mind still reeling.

After thinking about it, he decided that Ken's optimistic mantra
was total bullshit. It was his white skin, not his positive outlook, that
protected him. White privilege at its finest. Ken had a born-and-
bred sense of entitlement that Dre would never experience. The man
didn't view life through the same lens as Dre because they inhabited
distinctly different planets. A cop—black or white—would never
point a gun at Ken's head just for having the nerve to walk down
the street.

Dre should've felt as fearless as Ken, especially in his own community. And a nine-year-old child should've been able to go to school
without being so badly bullied that she didn't want to live anymore.

*Bailey, I'm so sorry you had to go through all that. Why didn't you
come to me? I would've fixed it.*

For the first time since his eruption at the repast, an overpow-
ering combination of anger and grief bubbled up from the deepest
corner of his soul. He wrapped his arms around his upper body and
rocked back and forth.

For what seemed like hours, but was probably only minutes, Dre
sat in the darkness and wept until his eyes had no more tears left to
cry.

CHAPTER

56

"THIS WON'T FLY." Sidney Meltzer tossed the motion to disqualify onto his desk. "Landers is a first-class prick. He does stuff like this just to yank your chain."

"Well, consider my chain appropriately yanked," Angela said with a mock smile.

Sidney's office was becoming a familiar place for them. She and Jenny had spent the last half-hour updating him on the latest developments in the case.

"Isn't he afraid of pissing off the judge?" Jenny asked.

"Apparently not. Landers never does anything super outrageous. He walks just close enough to the fire to feel the heat but not so close that he'll get burned."

Angela wasn't sure she trusted Sidney's assessment that Landers wouldn't prevail on his motion. Not only had she discovered Bailey's body, her testimony could be relevant as to Bailey's state of mind since they were together hours before her suicide.

"Although the case law seems to be on our side," Angela said, "it's not a slam dunk."

"Nothing about the law ever is. But my money is with you guys. What else is going on? Was your investigator able to dig up any helpful evidence or witnesses?"

Jenny shook her head. "Not yet. But he's still working on it."

"Okay," Sidney said. "What's the theme of your case?"

Angela fired back a blank look while Jenny fidgeted with her hands.

"C'mon, Jen. I taught you that from day one. You need a theme. And you don't come up with it a month before trial when you're ready to write your opening argument."

Angela never developed a case theme this early.

"We've been so busy with discovery and strategy," Jenny said, "we haven't had time to think about that."

"'That's not an excuse," Meltzer said, not letting up. "Every time you walk into that courtroom, you're playing to the judge. People like to think judges sit there giving both sides an equal shot. That's bull. You need to get him on your side early on. Every motion you file, every oral argument you make should be reinforcing your theme to the point that the judge can recite it himself by the time the trial starts."

"Okay," Jenny said. "We'll spend some time working on it this week."

"Let's see if I can help. Based on the facts you know now, let me hear your closing argument. That'll help us zero in on a theme."

Jenny screwed up her face. "Closing argument? We haven't even taken our first deposition yet."

"I know that. But if you had to argue the case tomorrow, what would you say? C'mon, you guys are bright." He turned to Angela. "You were a federal prosecutor for Christ's sake. Show me what you've got."

Angela smiled. "Okay. I'll give it a try." She stood up and moved behind her chair. "I'm winging it, so don't expect a star performance."

Sidney nodded.

"Ladies and gentlemen of the jury," Angela began, holding up an imaginary frame. "I want you to take a good look at this little girl. Bailey Lewis was only nine years old. As you've heard from the testimony in this case, vicious, unrelenting bullying at Parker

Elementary School forced her to do something unimaginable. This beautiful little girl took her own life because—"

Sidney's hands waved back and forth like a pair of malfunctioning windshield wipers. "No, no, no, no, no. That's way too bland. I need you to be more creative."

He turned to Jenny. "What about you? What've you got?"

"Frankly, I thought what Angela said was a pretty good start. Introducing them to Bailey right off the bat seems like a good thing."

"That's a closing argument an average attorney would make. You're not average attorneys. You need to make the jury *feel* your case."

Angela flopped back into her chair. "And exactly how do we do that?"

"I'll show you." He stood and walked around his desk. "Turn your chairs toward me and pretend you're sitting in the jury box."

Angela rolled her eyes. The man had a whopper-size ego.

"C'mon, I'm serious."

"If you insist," Angela said.

"I do."

Sidney paced in front of them for a good ten seconds, gathering his thoughts.

"Good afternoon, ladies and gentlemen," he began, "I'd like you to pretend with me for a minute. Pretend that you started a new job three weeks ago. You love the pay, the work, and your spacious new cubicle."

Angela shot Jenny a confused look. *Where was he going with this?*

"For the first two weeks," Sidney continued, "everything is great. You practically skip in to work every morning. Then one day you see your co-worker Dana approaching you in the hallway. You smile at her, but Dana doesn't smile back. As she passes you, she bumps into you, slamming your shoulder against the wall. Hard." Sidney grabbed his shoulder and pretended to stumble. "You're stunned.

The hallway is at least ten feet wide. What Dana just did was no accident. And you have no idea why she did it."

Angela began to understand where Sidney was headed and was fascinated by his approach.

"You ask around and find out that Dana had applied for the job you got. She's upset because you took her position. Now you understand why she bumped into you in that hallway. Do you report Dana to HR? You're new at the company. You don't want to make waves. You decide to ignore what happened and stay clear of her. But a few days later, you're in the break room about to pour yourself a cup of coffee. Dana walks up behind you and whispers into your ear. *You stupid bitch. You don't deserve to work here. You should go kill yourself.*

Sidney stopped talking, giving his words time to register.

"Okay, now, you're *really* scared because you're sure Dana is a nut job. A week later Dana sits down across from you in the cafeteria. As she opens a ketchup packet she accidentally"—Sidney stopped to mime air quotes with his fingers—"sprays ketchup all over your white silk blouse.

"The next morning, another co-worker tells you that Dana posted a picture of you on Instagram and used a filter that makes you look like a monkey. Her posts says, *Just kill yourself.*

Sidney dramatically flung both hands in the air.

"Now, you've had it. Something needs to be done about Dana. First, you go to your boss and tell her the whole story. Within hours, Dana is suspended pending an investigation. Two weeks later, HR's investigation determines that Dana has engaged in workplace harassment and she's fired."

Sidney paused and stepped closer, taking his time to make eye contact with both of them.

"And that's precisely what should've happened." He lowered his voice, but not his intensity. "Something similar happened to Bailey, my client's beautiful nine-year-old daughter."

He held up an imaginary picture of Bailey and plodded from one end of the non-existent jury box to the other.

"As you've heard from the witnesses in this case, a classmate of Bailey's slammed into her in a school hallway, injuring her shoulder. That same girl also intentionally tripped her, causing her to skin her knees. The girl posted a picture on Instagram that made Bailey look like a monkey. She constantly taunted Bailey on social media, repeatedly urging her to kill herself. The girl also sprayed ketchup on Bailey's favorite sweater—a sweater she cherished because it was a gift from her father. Her father who'd recently died of bone cancer.

"Both Bailey's teacher and her principal knew about the bullying. What did they do about it? Absolutely nothing. Why? Because she's a child. When a kid is harassed—and let's call it what it is, harassment, not bullying—sometimes schools simply look the other way. The teachers and administrators at Parker Elementary School didn't investigate Bailey's complaints. They didn't expel the bully. You know what they did? Nothing. Absolutely nothing. Bailey was so distraught by the harassment, she hanged herself.

Sidney paused for so long, it made Angela uncomfortable.

"She hanged herself," he said again, dropping his voice to just a whisper. "She was only nine years old.

"The school district's counsel is going to stand up here in a few minutes and tell you that Bailey took her own life because she was depressed over her father's death. I won't lie to you. Bailey missed her father with all her heart. But the bullying she endured—not her father's death—is what pushed her over the edge.

"Bailey shouldn't have been forced to tolerate such brutal harassment simply because she was a child and not an adult. You need to send a message to the three people sitting over there"—Sidney looked over his shoulder and scowled at the imaginary defendants—"the superintendent, the principal, and Bailey's teacher. They shouldn't have allowed Bailey to endure the kind of harassment she was subjected to. Punish these defendants for their failure to protect her."

Anguish washed over the room as Sidney returned to his chair. It was easy to see why he was so effective at trial.

"Wow," Angela said. "That was amazing."

"Thank you," Sidney said, beaming. "And by the time I'm done with the two of you, you're going to have an opening *and* closing argument that's twice as good."

57

CHALLENGING A MOTION to disqualify counsel is akin to begging an employer not to fire you. Except here, it's not your employer pulling the plug, but a nasty opposing counsel who wants to send you packing.

Angela and Jenny were seated in the gallery of Department 6 in Los Angeles Superior Court, waiting for Judge Eduardo Quintana to begin the day's calendar.

"I know you're a little upset about this motion," Jenny said to Angela. "Please let me handle the oral argument without jumping in, okay?"

"If you say that one more time, I'm going to pull out my hair from the roots. Don't worry. I'm not going to turn into Dre and cuss in the courtroom."

Jenny grinned. "Promise?"

Landers walked in and handed his business card to the judge's clerk.

"Good morning, counselors," Landers said before taking a seat in front of them.

"Morning," Jenny said, refusing to smile.

Angela remained mute until Jenny nudged her. She'd forgotten Jenny's admonition that Landers reveled in getting under his opponent's skin. They were supposed to act like the motion was no big deal. Just another routine day in court.

Angela smiled big. "Good morning."

Another fifteen minutes passed before Judge Quintana took the bench. He had a solid reputation with diehard fans on both the plaintiff and defense bar, a feat few judges could claim. After rushing through three discovery motions, the clerk called out their case.

As they strolled into the well of the courtroom, the judge chuckled. "I don't think I've ever had one of these motions before. Mr. Landers, I've read your moving papers. And Ms. Ungerman, I've read the papers you've filed in response. Is it really a good idea for Ms. Evans to be litigating this case? Am I correct that she was the one who discovered the child's body?"

"Yes, that's correct," Jenny said. "Ms. Evans gave serious thought before making the decision to co-counsel with me on this matter. Contrary to defense counsel's contention, the advocate-witness rule doesn't apply to the facts of this case."

"I respectfully, disagree, Your Honor," Landers piped in. "The rule makes it clear that a lawyer who will also be a witness in the case cannot also act as an advocate."

"Your Honor, Mr. Landers isn't quoting the rule in its entirety. It only applies if the lawyer is likely to be a witness on a *significant issue before the court*. Ms. Evans has no such knowledge. So it's highly unlikely she would be called to testify."

Landers inhaled. "We do intend to call her as a witness. Ms. Evans spent the evening with the child and was the person who discovered her body. Hence, she has knowledge of young Bailey's state of mind just hours before her death."

Angela grunted quietly. In front of the judge, she was *young Bailey,* but at the deposition, she was *the deceased.*

"The cause of death is not at issue here," Jenny fired back, "so the fact that Ms. Evans discovered her is not *a significant issue.* This is not a murder case or anything having to do with *how* Bailey died.

The issue here is *why* she died. The primary issues are whether Bailey was bullied and whether the school failed to protect her after being put on notice of the bullying. As to those key issues, my co-counsel would not be needed to testify because she doesn't possess any relevant evidence."

Landers refused to give in. "Ms. Evans's live-in boyfriend admitted under oath that he shared with her the conversations he had with Bailey. Those conversations pertain to the reasons the plaintiff alleges that Bailey took her own life."

Jenny tried to keep a straight face. "I'm sure that an attorney with Mr. Landers's experience recognizes that the testimony he just described constitutes inadmissible hearsay."

The judge tapped his pen on the desk. "What about that, Mr. Landers?"

"There are some exceptions to the hearsay rule that would allow those discussions into evidence. Also, it's not clear at this early stage, that the cause of death is undisputed." Landers glanced down at his legal pad. "Furthermore, when an attorney assumes the role of both advocate and witness, the line between argument and evidence becomes blurred, confusing the jury. That has the potential to harm the integrity of the judicial system."

Give me a break, Angela thought. The word integrity should be permanently banned from his vocabulary.

Angela did exactly what she promised Jenny she wouldn't.

"Your Honor, if I may speak." She could almost feel Jenny's hot glare graze her cheek. "If I'm barred from this case, the school district would effectively be dictating who could represent my client. We also believe that the defense is using this motion as a tactical device. Therefore, the motion should be subject to strict scrutiny because of the likelihood for abuse."

The judge allowed a little more back and forth, then announced his decision.

"I agree with Ms. Evans. It would be unfair to allow a party to disqualify their opponent simply by claiming they *intend* to call him or her as a witness."

Angela exhaled with relief. She was happy enough to float out of the courtroom.

"On the other hand, Ms. Evans did discover the body of the child. To the extent there's disagreement regarding the nature of her death or her state of mind that evening, it could be necessary for her to testify."

Angela was about to experience a crash landing. *Is he really going to kick me off the case?*

"But the bottom line is that defendants have not offered any credible evidence that Ms. Evans has relevant information regarding a *significant* matter in this case. Hence, at this stage of the litigation, disqualification would be premature. Defendants' motion is denied."

"You win some, you lose some," Landers said when they stepped into the hallway.

"Sure do," Angela gloated.

Before she could turn away, Landers shoved an envelope into her hand.

"I'd like to depose Erika Lewis. Email me some dates that work for you and your client."

CHAPTER

58

ANGELA AND JENNY spent two full days prepping Erika for her deposition. Their practice sessions went well, but there was no way to prepare Erika for the mud Ethan Landers might lob at her from left field.

As they sat in Landers's conference room waiting for the deposition to start, Erika's fidgeting was beginning to worry Angela. She would rest her hands in her lap, then massage her temples. Seconds later, she would start drumming her fingers on the table, then repeat the whole routine.

"Remember to take a breath before responding," Angela said. "And take your time. If you need to pause to think about a question, that's fine."

Erika nodded. Weariness clouded her eyes. She'd told Dre she was thinking about giving up her new manager position and going back to a less-demanding staff job.

Landers and Freeman entered the room.

"We're so sorry for your loss," Landers began, extending his hand to Erika. "I'll try to make this is as painless as possible."

That was certainly a lie, Angela thought.

They went on the record and Landers rushed through the preliminaries, then immediately moved in for the sucker punch.

"Have you ever worked as a stripper?"

Erika gasped so loud, the court reporter flinched.

Oh, come on, Angela wanted to shout. But she wasn't about to give Landers any inkling that he was getting under her skin.

Luckily, they'd prepped Erika for the question, figuring that he would try to make her out to be a bad mother. During their prep session, Erika had seemed shocked that Landers would be allowed to probe her past. The distress marring her face conveyed that she was even more shocked now that he was actually doing it.

"Objection," Angela said, her tone neutral. "Badgering the witness, argumentative, irrelevant. The witness is instructed not to answer."

Landers folded his arms. "You can't instruct her not to answer on those grounds."

Actually, Landers was right. While he might not be able to get such evidence in at trial, lawyers were given a lot of leeway in depositions. Angela made the strategic decision to call his bluff.

"I'm not going to let you harass this grieving mother. If you want her to answer that question, you'll have to file a motion compelling her to respond. So let's move on."

Landers hesitated as he locked eyes with her.

If he did file a motion, he would probably prevail. But hitting Erika with that question out of the box was nothing more than a stunt, which would make Landers look like the bad guy in the judge's eyes. So there was a good chance, he wouldn't risk taking the issue to the judge.

"Fine. I guess we'll have to file a motion to compel her answer."

Sure you will.

Landers looked down at his legal pad. "Okay then, tell me about Bailey's problems with hyperactivity."

Hyperactivity? Where was he going now?

"Objection to the form of the question, overly broad, vague, and ambiguous, calls for a narrative."

Landers smiled. "I'll rephrase. Ms. Lewis, Did Bailey suffer from hyperactivity?"

"It's Mrs. Lewis. And the answer is no."

"Forgive me for that. Was your daughter ever treated for attention deficit disorder?"

"What?" Erika paused. "No, not really.

"That's two very different responses, Mrs. Lewis. Is it *no* or is it *not really?*"

"It's no," Erika said, her tone snippy.

"If she didn't suffer from hyperactivity or attention deficit disorder, why was she taking the drug Concerta?"

"What? Bailey wasn't taking any medication."

Landers opened a folder and pulled out a piece of paper. "I'd like to mark this is as defendant's exhibit one. Please take a moment to review it."

Angela scanned the document. It appeared to be a note made by the school nurse at Weatherton, Bailey's prior school. Jenny had subpoenaed copies of Bailey's file from both schools and this document wasn't in it.

"Why wasn't this document produced in discovery?" Angela asked.

"I just recently received it."

Angela glared across the table. "Are there any other documents you *just recently received?*"

"Not that I can think of." He turned back to Erika. "Does that document state that Bailey was taking the drug Concerta?"

Erika hesitated. "Yes."

"So, are you saying you weren't aware that your daughter was taking the drug?"

"No, well...I remember now. The pediatrician was concerned about her mood after her father's death. He suggested that she start taking it to help her with her grief. But I took her off of it after a couple of weeks because it made her sluggish."

As always, expect the unexpected from Landers. They'd asked Erika if Bailey was taking any medication and she said she wasn't. Why was Landers making such a big deal about it?

"Did the doctor discuss the side effects of the drug with you?"

"Side effects?" Erika paused. "I don't know. I don't think so."

"So is it your testimony that you weren't aware of Concerta's side effects?"

"Yes. I mean no. I was not aware."

Angela opened her iPad and did a quick Google search for *Concerta side effects*. When the implications of what she read registered in her brain, she could barely speak.

Calmly raising her left palm, she cut Landers off before he could pose his next question.

"We'd like to take a short break."

CHAPTER

59

"I DON'T THINK I'VE ever attended a deposition where the plaintiff needs to take as many breaks as these people do," Freeman said with a sinister grin.

She sat on one end the couch in Landers's office, while the handsome attorney sat on the other. Bailey's mother and her attorneys were in a conference room across the hall. No doubt discussing the bombshell Landers had just dropped on them.

Landers stretched his arm along the back of the couch. "A lot of attorneys refuse to let the other side take a break at crucial times during the questioning. It interrupts the flow of things. But I don't mind at all."

"But they could be feeding that woman all kind of stuff to say."

"I hope that's exactly what they're doing."

"Really?"

"Absolutely. When a witness isn't speaking from a place of truth, it's easy to trip them up."

"As soon as you asked her about that drug, her attorney started typing on her iPad," Freeman said. "I could tell the precise moment she figured out where you were going because she looked like she wanted to barf, though she tried to play it off. I loved every second of it."

Landers's lips angled into a lopsided grin. "Litigation is a bit of a blood sport for me. I see you like it too."

"I just like being on the winning side. I'm so glad the district hired you."

"I enjoy going to bat for people who never should've been sued in the first place. The defendants I've represented in bullycide cases are good people who have the best interests of their students at heart. Their reputations shouldn't be marred by these frivolous cases."

"Well, I'm certainly glad you're sitting on my side of the table."

Darcella gave Ethan Landers a visual once over. He wasn't the type of guy she normally dated. There had been a few white guys in her past, but generally speaking, they were not her preference. But Landers's intellect, killer-instinct, and self-assurance was a turn-on she didn't want to turn off.

Her ex-husband was happy being a seventh-grade math teacher and nothing more. Their eighteen-month union had been a complete waste of her time. Darcella had picked a mate with her heart instead of her head. She wouldn't make that mistake again. A man like Barack Obama would have been the perfect match for her. Too bad Michelle got to him first.

"I have to say," Landers continued, "it was pretty sharp of you to key in on that drug when you were looking through Bailey's file. I'm familiar with Concerta from handing a ton of bullycide cases. But I was surprised you knew about it."

"I'm a member of the National Association of Elementary School Principals. A couple of months ago, they ran an article about the drug in their newsletter. So the name jumped out at me."

"You've been quite a help in this case. I'll probably be able to get rid of it by motion, thanks in large part to you."

Landers gave her a look that held more than professional admiration.

"I've enjoyed partnering with you." Darcella crossed her legs. As Landers gave them a once over, she pretended not to notice the brazen lust in his eyes. "I don't think I've ever been involved with an attorney who's as good as you are."

"Can't say many attorneys as good as I am even exist."

"Get a little confidence, will you?" Darcella joked.

"That's always been my strong suit."

Darcella daintily cocked her head. "When the case is over, you'll have to let me treat you to dinner."

"Why do we have to wait? And I'd prefer to take *you* out." Landers flashed a sexy smile. "How about tonight?"

CHAPTER

60

"I DON'T UNDERSTAND," ERIKA said, once they were alone in the conference room. "Why is he asking me about that drug? Bailey only took it for a couple of weeks. That's why I didn't remember it when you asked me if she was taking any medications."

"Have a seat," Angela said, passing her iPad to Jenny. Her friend's brown eyes expanded as she read the screen.

"I don't want to sit down. What are you looking at? Did I say something wrong?"

"No." Angela paused. "One of the side effects of taking Concerta is suicidal thoughts."

It took a moment for the meaning of Angela's words to sink in. And when they did, Erika's eyes swelled with tears.

"Are you trying to tell me I let my baby take a drug that made her kill herself?"

Jenny swallowed. "That's what Landers is trying to claim."

"Let me see that."

Jenny pulled the iPad out of her reach. "No, we can't let you—"

"Please, Jenny. I'll be fine. I need to see what it says."

"We can't let you read that," Angela said. "The first thing Landers is going to do when you go back in there is ask you if we showed you any documents."

"But I thought anything we discuss is protected by the attorney-client privilege."

"It is," Jenny said. "But if we show you that article, the fact that we did isn't protected since it's not a discussion. Once you tell him you read it, he's going to ask you a million questions about it."

"Have a seat," Angela said, pulling out a chair for Erika. "Jenny will read it to you."

As Jenny read aloud, Angela watched Erika's lips go from tightly clamped to quivering in anguish.

Doctors have commonly prescribed Concerta to children who exhibit signs of inattention, hyperactivity, impulsiveness, and/or inability to focus on tasks such as schoolwork or homework. The Concerta lawsuits claim the manufacturer of the drug failed to warn patients and physicians of the increased risks of extreme suicidal thoughts caused when younger people take the medication.

It was a long time before Erika spoke. "This is like a nightmare that won't end."

Angela and Jenny both hugged her.

"So he's trying to say Bailey took her own life because I let her take this drug and not because of the bullying?"

"It looks as if that's where Landers is going," Angela said. "But I have my doubts that it's a winning argument."

Erika pressed her palm to her forehead. "How could it not be?"

Jenny squeezed Erika's shoulder. "You said Bailey only took it for a couple of weeks. We haven't had time to research any of this yet, but I can't imagine that would be long enough for any side effects to manifest."

"And Bailey took it months before she died," Angela added.

Their words did nothing to alleviate Erika's concerns. "The minute he mentions that drug, the jury will let the school off the hook."

"We can file a motion in limine to prevent Landers from mentioning it to the jury. There's a good chance it'll be granted."

"As dirty as this man plays," Erika said, looking up at them, "we're going to need a lot more than a good chance."

CHAPTER

61

"OKAY, LET'S HEAR IT. What kind of bull did that asshole pull on Erika?" Dre opened the front door before Angela could reach for her key.

She looked at him with such despair Dre could feel it.

"Let's talk later. I need to take a long, hot bath and clear my head."

"Was it that bad?"

"Worse. I swear Landers must stay up late at night praying to the devil for ways to screw people."

Dre pulled her into his arms. "When you didn't respond to my texts, I figured it didn't go well."

Angela freed herself from his embrace and started down the hallway.

Dre wanted a rundown on Erika's deposition now, not later. But pushing Angela would be a mistake. "I'll finish whipping up dinner."

It was close to an hour before Angela emerged in a tank top and sweat pants, her hair gathered in a curly puff on top of her head. Dre found himself most attracted to her minus all the fluff: the suit, the eyelashes, the lipstick. She seemed more authentic now.

She glanced around the kitchen, finding no pots on the stove or plates on the counter.

"I thought you were making dinner?"

"I decided we should do something a little special tonight."

Angela's shoulders slumped. "No way, Dre. I don't have the energy to go out to dinner. I just want to cut off my brain and not think about this case for the rest of the day."

"Calm down, girl. I got you."

He linked his arm through hers and led her outside to the patio. "Right this way, madam."

When they stepped outside, Angela spotted the wrought iron table draped with a white tablecloth. Dre had set up dinner on the patio complete with cloth napkins, a vase with tulips, and two lavender candles.

"Oh, my goodness. You weren't playing."

Dre smiled big. "A brother's got skills. You should know that by now."

She turned around and kissed him. "Yes, you do."

He escorted her to the table and pulled out her chair. When she lifted the foil that covered her plate, she found a juicy, rib-eye steak and baked potato. A large salad bowl sat in the middle of the table.

"This looks yummy."

Dre took a seat across from her, anxious for details about the deposition but knowing it was best to let her proceed at her own pace.

"And we've got vanilla bean ice cream and Hannah's pound cake for dessert."

"Hold up. She brought you some *more* pound cake?"

Dre smiled. "She felt bad because you didn't get a chance to taste it, so she made us a whole one this time."

"I'm not sure I like the idea of you being all chummy with that woman."

"Why? You scared the white girl might take your man?"

Angela grinned. "Nope. Her ass is flat enough to iron on. She doesn't have a chance."

Dre nodded and smiled. "That would be very true."

For the next several minutes, they enjoyed their dinner, neither of them speaking.

"That was a perfect meal," Angela said, as Dre set a bowl of cake and ice cream in front of her. "I really appreciate you."

He winked. "Ditto."

"I know you're dying to find out what happened today," Angela said, exhaling a long breath. "Brace yourself."

When she told him the first question Landers asked was whether Erika had ever worked as a stripper, Dre exploded.

"What? How can he get away with—"

Angela cut him off. "He didn't get away with it. I instructed Erika not to answer and he moved on."

Next, she walked him through Landers's questions about Bailey suffering from hyperactivity and taking the drug Concerta.

"Bailey was on medication?"

"It appears so."

"Okay. So what?"

"There are a ton of lawsuits claiming Concerta causes kids to have suicidal thoughts."

Dre put down his spoon. "So he's claiming Bailey's dead because that drug made her do it?"

"Yep."

"Is that true?"

"I doubt it. She only took it for a couple of weeks. We won't know how it impacts the case until we do some research."

"That punk is a piece of work. First, he comes at me with that pervert madness, then he tries to get you kicked off the case. And now this? How can he look himself in the mirror?"

"I suspect with all the money he makes defending bullycide cases, he's quite proud of what he sees in the mirror."

"You need to hurry up and depose Bailey's teacher," Dre said. "I'm telling you, that woman knows something. Otherwise, she would've told me that Bailey had never complained to her."

"Even if Bailey did complain, it's in Zola Phillips's best interest to lie."

"I have a good feeling about her," Dre insisted. "I don't think she's going to do that. She cared about Bailey. I saw it in her eyes."

Angela stuck a spoonful of ice cream into her mouth. "We'll see."

CHAPTER

62

Darcella rolled over in the luxurious bed, loving the comfort and contrast of the silky, white sheets against her naked, copper-brown skin.

"I was wondering when you were going to wake up," Landers said, snuggling closer to her. "I enjoyed watching you sleep. You're beautiful."

He leaned over and kissed her, the stubble from his five-clock shadow lightly scratching her face. "Beautiful *and* soft," he murmured, his fingers grazing her flat stomach.

Darcella smiled. It had been quite a while since a man had made her feel so desired.

Following Erika Lewis's deposition, they left Landers's office for dinner at Culina, a celebrity hotspot at the Four Seasons Hotel in Beverly Hills. After brazenly flirting, they openly acknowledged a mutually intense sexual attraction. They'd agreed, however, to postpone acting upon it until after the case had been resolved.

But the longer they sat across from each other, the stronger the fervor grew. Halfway through a meal of Scottish salmon, fingerling potatoes, and the most deliciously expensive red wine Darcella had ever tasted, Landers put his cards on the table.

"I have to be honest," he said, his eyes thirsting with lust. "I don't think I can wait until the case ends to be with you."

Darcella wasn't sure she could hold out either. It had been almost a year since she'd shared an intimate evening with a man. "I think we're on the same page," she replied coyly.

Never taking his eyes off her, Landers pulled out his cell phone and reserved a room. An attendant delivered a key card to their table fifteen minutes later.

Loosened up by far too much wine, they skipped dessert and made their way to the elevators, clawing and kissing like horny teenagers.

When Landers threw open the door to the presidential suite, Darcella stood in the doorway with her mouth agape. She'd never seen a larger, more elegant hotel room. The muted colors, fine fabrics, and stylish furniture, were right out of some TV show for the rich and famous.

He took Darcella's hand. "I didn't come up here to admire the room."

Leading her to the bedroom, they feverishly undressed each other and fell into bed.

Landers was a slow, passionate lover. In his arms, Darcella felt like a priceless work of art. He often paused to marvel at her body, fawning over its color, texture and firmness. She loved the way he took his time, kissing and sucking and licking her with his long, warm tongue. By the time he entered her, she was gasping and clawing his back. He wasn't the best lover she'd ever experienced, but he was damn close to the top of the list.

Once they were sexually sated, they talked late into the night, sipping champagne and munching on chocolate-covered strawberries. It was an evening straight out of a romance novel.

He nudged her back to the present with a soft kiss on the lips. "Are you usually this quiet in the morning?"

"Not really. Are you usually this passionate?"

Landers smiled. "It's part of who I am. Passionate in the courtroom, even more so in the bedroom."

Darcella snuggled up against him. "You surprised me."

A self-assured smile curled the corners of his thin lips. "How so?"

The man loved having his ego stroked and she had no problem complying.

"You're such a dragon slayer professionally, I was worried you might be a fumbling caveman in bed. But you're an incredible lover."

"Thank you." Landers kissed her again. "I pride myself on excelling at everything I do."

Darcella giggled, then grew quiet. "Are you sure we're not crossing any ethical lines by not waiting until the case is resolved?"

Rolling onto his side, he propped up his elbow and rested his head in his hand. "We're on the same side, remember? But we'll make this our little secret. So relax, pretty lady."

Relaxing was not something Darcella found easy to do. Even now, on a Saturday morning, she was thinking about all of the unfinished tasks on her plate. The sooner Erika Lewis's case got dismissed, the better. She couldn't wait to walk into the next Delta or Links function with the rich, gorgeous Ethan Landers on her arm. Every last one of those bitches would die.

"I hate that we'll have to sneak around," Darcella said with a pout.

"It won't be for long. Now I have even more incentive to dispose of this case." He leaned forward and nuzzled her neck. "And until then, I plan to make every clandestine minute we spend together more than worth your time."

CHAPTER

63

WHEN ANGELA, JENNY and their paralegal showed up for their inspection of Parker Elementary School, an attendant escorted them to the principal's office. Darcella Freeman sat behind her desk, while Ethan Landers stood leaning against the wall.

"Good evening, counselors." Landers greeted them with the kind of warmth reserved for close friends.

"This is our paralegal, Diego," Jenny said, introducing a paunchy, thirty-something guy wearing a flannel shirt.

"Pictures?" Darcella said with a frown, turning to Landers. "They get to take pictures?"

"Yes," Angela responded. "We do."

Diego would be the one taking the witness stand at trial to lay the foundation for the photographs.

"Why don't you have a seat?" Landers said.

"I don't think we have time to sit and chat," Angela said. "I'd like to complete the inspection before it gets dark."

Landers rubbed his palms together. "Let's get to it."

Freeman led them out of the office. "I still don't understand the need for this," she grumbled.

"We'd like to see Zola Phillips's classroom first," Jenny said, as they walked down a wide hallway. "As stated in our inspection request, we'd also like a general tour of the school, including the cafeteria, the playground, and each of the boy's and girl's restrooms."

"Whatever," Freeman mumbled.

It was close to five o'clock, so the place was all but empty. Angela was struck by the number of anti-bullying posters along the hallway.

"Diego, let's get some shots of this hallway."

He took individual still shots of each anti-bullying poster, then walked in a slow, horseshoe shape shooting video of both walls.

"Okay, we can continue." Angela took off ahead of them as if she knew where she was going.

The principal retook the lead, stopping at the far end of the hall. "This is Zola Phillips's classroom."

When they stepped inside, the room engulfed Angela in sadness. She could imagine little Bailey sitting at one of the tiny desks. She briefly closed her eyes, struggling to fight off the return of grief.

While Diego took several wide shots of the room, followed by closeup pictures of the four walls, Angela and Jenny roamed up and down the aisles.

Freeman and Landers stood near the front of the classroom, watching them as if they were there to steal. As Angela strolled the aisles, she spotted something that made her blood rush. Not wanting to draw attention to what she had discovered, she pretended to study something on the wall.

Walking over to Diego, she whispered, "I want you to snap a picture of the back of the third chair in the second row from the window. I'm going to distract them so they don't see you do it."

Angela walked over to a bulletin board near the door. "Can I ask what this is?"

Both Landers and Freeman rushed over as Diego snapped a picture of the chair.

"I see Bailey had the highest score on this list," Jenny said.

"It's a spelling contest," the principal said. "But I'm surprised Mrs. Phillips didn't take that down. We wouldn't want to trigger another student."

"I'm glad she didn't." Landers pulled out his phone and took a picture. "The alleged bullying obviously didn't affect the girl's academic performance. This is quite helpful for our side."

Angela called Diego over to take a picture as well.

Angela started walking toward the door. "I think we have everything we need in here. I'd like to see the cafeteria next."

"We should visit the restrooms while we're here," Freeman said. "It's right across the hall."

"I'd prefer to see those last," Angela insisted.

The principal frowned as she locked the door and walked them back down the hallway. The cafeteria was about six times the size of the classroom, with dull yellow walls. Chairs and benches were lined up along the north wall, which made the room appear larger than it really was.

"Where was Bailey sitting when Kiya squirted her with ketchup?" Jenny asked.

Freeman pursed her lips. "I have no idea."

"Could you find out for us?" Angela asked, as Diego snapped pictures of the room. "I'd hate to have to depose the teacher on lunch duty just to ask one little question. I'd also like to know where she was standing."

Freeman put a hand on her hip. "Is this really necessary?"

Both Angela and Jenny ignored the question. "I think we're ready to take a look at the girl's restroom now," Angela said.

They walked back across campus and the instant they stepped inside Angela gasped. "This restroom looks and smells like it was recently painted." Her words were full of accusation. "When did that happen?"

The principal shrugged. "I'm not sure. I'd have to check with custodial staff."

Jenny ran a finger along the wall and held up a faint white smudge for them to see. "The paint is barely dry. I'd say it happened in the last couple of days."

Angela stepped in and out of the four stalls, closely examining each space.

"I've never been in a school restroom without a lick of writing on the walls," Jenny said, turning to Freeman. "This place had to be painted after we served our inspection request."

Landers and Freeman exchanged glances. "Like I said, I'd need to check," the principal said.

"You do that," Angela said, growing angry. "And if it was, that means you destroyed evidence."

"C'mon counselor." Landers folded his arms across his broad chest. "Let's not start throwing around baseless allegations."

"We'll find out soon enough if they're baseless or not," Angela continued, "because we're filing a spoliation of evidence motion."

Landers winced. "You gotta be kidding me. You don't even—"

Angela didn't let him finish. "And when we do, we're requesting sanctions against you"—she turned to point a stiff finger at Freeman—"*and* your client."

CHAPTER

64

ZOLA'S STOMACH CHURNED with trepidation. She was about to spend the next six hours with Ethan Landers, prepping for her deposition. She'd been so frazzled that morning, Brock didn't want her behind the wheel. He'd dropped her off and headed to a Starbucks across the street to get some work done.

As she waited alone in the conference room, she walked over to the window, peering down at the tiny figures twenty stories below. Some people jumped to their deaths from buildings like this. Zola had never faced a problem so severe she'd wanted to end her life. Poor Bailey.

All night long, she pondered what telling Ethan Landers the truth would mean for her teaching career. Zola couldn't remember not wanting to be a teacher. After her first day of kindergarten, she'd come home and lined up her dolls to simulate a classroom, sharing everything she'd learned that day with her imaginary students. Teaching wasn't just a job. It was her life's mission.

The door opened and Zola spun around.

"I'm sorry," Landers said, as startled by her jumpiness as she'd been by his entering the room. "I didn't mean to frighten you. Quite a view, isn't it?"

She half-smiled and made her way back over to the table. Landers sat down across from her.

"Well, you know why you're here," he began. "I'd like to go over the facts with you again and take you through some of the questions I think they're going to ask you. We'll do this again the day before your deposition. Is that okay?"

Zola nodded. *Do I have a choice?*

"First, no nodding during the deposition. The court reporter can only take down what she hears. You'll need to speak in a loud, clear voice."

She nodded again, then caught herself. "Okay."

"One of the reasons the other side wants your testimony is to find out if you have any evidence to support their allegation that Bailey was bullied. But, as you told me during our initial interview, you don't."

Zola pressed two fingers to her right temple. "Well...I...it's possible I may have something."

Landers set his clasped hands on the table and leaned forward. The shifting of his body felt like a subtle signal that her response was unsatisfactory.

"Mrs. Phillips, if you're changing your testimony on this key issue, that's something I need to know."

"Uh, no. I'm not."

"You seem pretty uncomfortable right now. Is there something going on?"

"No, I'm fine."

"If there is, I'd like to know now. Not in the middle of the deposition."

"I'm fine," Zola repeated.

"Okay then. If I think you're getting off track during the depo, I'll ask if you'd like to take a break. The answer is *always* yes. Even if you don't need one."

Zola nodded.

"No nodding. Remember?"

She smiled weakly. "Sorry."

"Let's try it again. Pretend I'm the opposing counsel. Did Bailey ever report to you that she was bullied?"

Zola waited a beat too long. "No."

Landers scratched his jaw in obvious frustration. "The attorneys on the other side are pretty sharp. They're not just going to be listening to what you say. They're going to be watching how you say it as well as observing your body language. Do you understand?"

Zola started to nod but caught herself. "Yes."

"And if I were watching you testify right now, I'd wonder if you had something to hide. So you need to be mindful of your spoken responses as well as the unspoken ones. How about sitting up a little straighter in your chair? That might help."

No, it won't. But telling me you want to hear the truth would.

Zola sat more erect, folded her hands, and set them on the table in front of her, mirroring Landers's position.

"Much better," he said encouragingly.

For the next three-and-a-half hours, Landers took her through the questions she would likely be asked during her deposition. By the fourth round, Zola felt like a well-oiled robot, responding without a hint of her earlier hesitation.

"Did you ever witness anyone bullying Bailey Lewis?"

"No."

"Do you have any knowledge whatsoever, direct or indirect, that would support the plaintiff's claims that Bailey Lewis was bullied?"

"No."

Ethan smiled and nodded. "As long as you respond the same way at your deposition, everything will be fine."

CHAPTER

65

JENNY AND ANGELA stood outside Judge Quintana's courtroom, discussing their impending oral argument. There was no way to recover the evidence they were convinced that the school had covered up. But winning this spoliation motion and getting Landers and Freeman sanctioned would be a much-needed psychological boost for their side.

Just as Angela was about to tick through the most important points they needed to hammer home, Dre rushed up to them. Angela wasn't pleased that he was there. When she realized she couldn't talk him out of coming, she gave him a stern warning that any theatrics before the judge would land him in jail for contempt of court. He promised to be a model citizen.

Still shaken by her deposition experience, Erika had decided not to come.

"You'll never believe what I just saw. I was—"

Angela held up her hand. "Not now, Dre. I'm trying to focus."

Despite all her years of practice, there were still times when Angela experienced a fit of anxiety before arguing an important motion. Fortunately, once she opened her mouth to speak, the jitters miraculously disappeared.

"But you need to know that—"

"Unless you have something to say that will help us win this motion," Jenny barked at him, "it'll have to wait until we're done."

Dre's head reared back. "Why don't I just go take a seat?"

"Great idea," Angela said, her eyes never leaving her notes.

The two attorneys collaborated a few more minutes, then stepped inside the courtroom. Freeman and Landers were already seated. Her opponent looked as confident as ever.

Angela spotted a thirty-something Asian guy sitting on the second row. Their eyes met and she gave him a slight nod, which he returned with a smile.

The court clerk called their case number and the three attorneys stepped into the well. Judge Quintana was not in a good mood.

"Counselors, please tell me this isn't going to be one of those cases where I get to see you every few days to preside over some juvenile discovery dispute you should've been able to resolve on your own? Because if that's the case, I promise you, I'm not going to be a happy camper. As you can imagine, I have far more important things to do."

"Your Honor," Angela began, "we gave serious thought before filing this motion. We're here because we believe the abuse in this case was so outrageous it warrants action from the court to discourage similar behavior from defendants in the future."

The judge huffed. "Go on, counselor."

"When we showed up at Parker Elementary School to inspect the girl's restroom—the same girl's restroom our client's daughter used every day—we were shocked to learn it had been painted. We believe that this was done to cover up relevant evidence."

Landers barely let Angela finish her last sentence. "Your Honor, this was all a big mistake that the defendants sincerely regret. No one was covering up anything. As stated in the principal's sworn declaration, she had no idea the custodians would be painting the restrooms when they did. Nor does Ms. Evans have any evidence that anything was covered up on those restroom walls."

"There's no way to know that now," Angela said, glaring over at Landers. "Because any evidence has been destroyed."

"This is nothing but harassment and intimidation on the part of the plaintiff's counsel," Landers fired back. "I also submitted a declaration from Damien Miller, the custodian who did the painting. He confirmed that he was the one who initiated it. He received no direction from the principal and knew nothing about the inspection demand."

The judge's gaze bounced back to the plaintiff's table. "Your opponent has a point. I agree that the timing *looks* pretty fishy, but I can't issue sanctions based on your gut feeling."

"And may I add," Landers said, before Angela could respond, "the custodian's declaration states that he didn't notice anything on the walls."

Angela sucked in a breath. "The point here is—"

"Ms. Evans," the judge said, not allowing her to finish, "even if I did find that the school had intentionally painted the restroom to conceal evidence, I'd have a hard time calculating the harm."

"Exactly, Your Honor," Landers interrupted again. "Their request for ten thousand dollars in sanctions against me and my client is outrageous. The law requires that sanctions have a clear relationship to the harm caused by the allegedly improper behavior. I'm not sure the plaintiff can claim *any* harm. Even if there had been graffiti aimed at young Bailey in that restroom, the defendants had no knowledge of it. So it wouldn't advance the plaintiff's case."

Angela felt like a rock climber trying to scale a mountain but unable to get a foothold.

"Sometimes, we have to look at things with a common-sense approach," she said.

"Such evidence would've been indicative of the environment at Parker Elementary."

The judge gave Angela a forlorn look. "I'm sorry counselor. Your speculation about what *might have been* on those walls isn't enough.

Without any proof of a deliberate cover-up—excuse the pun—I can't find that any misconduct occurred. Motion denied."

Landers and Freeman practically skipped out of the courtroom. Jenny and Dre trudged out behind them. Angela stayed behind to speak to the court reporter.

"I just ordered an expedited transcript," Angela said when she met them in the hallway. "It's time to play hardball."

Jenny grimaced. "Trying to reverse the judge's decision isn't worth the fight. That'll just piss him off."

"That's not why I asked for it. I'll explain when we get back to the office."

"I think you *should* fight it," Dre grumbled. "I can't believe they got away with that bull."

"Well, believe it," Angela said. "In this case, justice is indeed blind. Blind as a bat. Let's get out of here."

As they headed toward the elevators, Angela spotted Landers and the principal at the end of the hallway.

She grabbed Dre by the forearm and pulled him off to the side. "I don't want to be trapped in an elevator with them. Let's wait a couple of minutes and give them a chance to get out of the building."

He snorted. "Works for me."

As they waited, Jenny turned to Dre. "What were you so anxious to tell us before we walked into the courtroom?"

"I was trying to drop some knowledge on you." He jutted his chin toward Landers and Freeman. "About those two."

"What about them?" Angela asked as the pair disappeared inside an elevator car.

"They're screwing around."

Angela blinked. "Screwing around with what?"

"With each other."

"Dre, please," Angela said. "And how would you know that?"

"I spotted them getting into an elevator on the first floor. I saw Landers squeeze the principal's ass. And all she did about it was giggle like a teenager with a crush."

Both women guffawed in unison.

"Are you sure?" Jenny prodded.

"Absolutely."

"How close were you?" Angela challenged.

"Close enough to know what I saw."

They refused to buy it.

"Doubt me if you want to," Dre insisted. "But that white boy is definitely hittin' that."

CHAPTER

66

"Okay, everyone, let's quiet down." Zola couldn't believe she was actually smiling and feeling like a teacher again.

She'd made a vow not to think about the lawsuit during school hours. That simple mindset change was like clearing cobwebs from her head and replacing them with smiley faces.

As she looked out at her students, she saw another sign that today would be a good day. Kiya Jackson was absent.

"Who can give me the meaning of the words *greater than?*"

Treyana, a girl on the first row, shot her hand in the air. "I know, I know."

Zola pointed her finger, giving her permission to respond.

"It means you have more than something else. Like five is greater than four."

"Very good, Treyana! Now who can tell me what *less than* mean?"

Treyana's hand shot up again.

Zola smiled at the girl. "Let's give somebody else a chance to answer."

She called on a bright little boy who always second-guessed himself. "How about you, Michael?"

"Like three is less than ten?" he said, his response more of a question.

"Excellent."

The boy beamed.

"I'm going to write the symbols for *greater than* and *less than* on the board."

The door opened and the principal stepped inside. Zola froze.

"Don't mind me," Freeman said, moving to the back of the room. "I'm just here to observe."

Administrators occasionally visited Zola's classroom to monitor her teaching skills, but Freeman had never taken the time to do so. Her presence wrecked Zola's rhythm and she wasn't sure where she'd left off.

She stared at the lesson plan sitting on her desk.

"This is the less-than symbol and this is the greater-than symbol," she finally continued, writing on the board. "And I have a great way for you to remember them. The less-than symbol looks like an alligator's head trying to eat the smaller number. And the greater-than sign looks like the alligator's head trying to eat the bigger number."

A few of the students giggled. Freeman stood along the back wall, her arms folded, her expression blank.

"I have a stack of cards with three-digit numbers on them. Everybody's going to get ten cards. I want you to put the correct alligator's head between them. I'm going to walk around to make sure you've got it right."

Zola did her best to stay focused on the lesson, but the principal's presence jarred her. Somehow, she managed to keep it together.

As the students trickled out, Freeman made her way to the front. "I understand you met with Ethan yesterday."

Ethan? So you two are on a first-name basis now?

"How did it go?"

"Fine." Zola hoped Landers hadn't called the principal to complain about her.

"I hope so. This case can't be resolved unless we're all on the same page."

You've told me that a thousand times.

"Now, a few pointers about your teaching. You failed to have the students state their daily learning outcomes."

No, she hadn't done that. But how could Freeman know that since she hadn't been there at the start of her class?

"It's important that your students have learning targets. You've been teaching long enough to know that."

"I'll be sure to do that."

"And I'd like to see you do more small-group work so all students are actively engaged."

"We do a lot of group work," Zola said in her defense. "You just happened to walk in on a day when we weren't."

"And the pacing of the lesson should've been slower. You rushed through those examples on the board. I would've given four or five students a chance to answer before moving on. And make sure you give all of your students equal attention. When you were walking around, checking their work, you ignored the children on the back row. "

That's because I didn't want to get anywhere near the back of the classroom since you were standing there.

"Okay."

"I guess that's it." Freeman looked around the room as if searching for something else to criticize. "Oh, I need to assign you to morning bus duty."

"I did a month of bus duty earlier this year." Zola relished her morning time and didn't want to spend it herding kids off of buses. "Isn't it somebody else's turn?"

"Yes, but Mrs. Towers is taking on another project for me. So I'll need you to fill in for her."

Zola practically sneered at her boss.

"Good luck on Monday," she said. "They took my deposition a few days ago. It was no big deal. Ethan said I did an amazing job. I never once let them trip me up. I'm sure you'll do just fine."

Freeman turned and walked out of the door.

She fell into the chair behind her desk, fuming. Giving her bus duty was just a sample of what would follow if she told the truth at her deposition.

Zola could only take so much. And if Darcella Freeman kept messing with her, she might just break rank.

CHAPTER

67

ANGELA DECIDED TO work from home for a change of pace. She was eating lunch in the backyard when Dre and his son appeared on the patio.

Little Dre ran over to give her a hug. "Hey, Miss Angela."

"Look at you," she said, hugging him back. "I can't believe you're only ten years old. Pretty soon you're going to be taller than your dad."

"I know, huh?" he said, grinning. "I can't wait for that to happen."

"Ain't gonna change nothing," Dre said, playfully punching him in the arm. "I'm still gonna dunk on you every day of the week."

Angela was stretched out in a deck chair. Dre sat down next to her.

"We might have some evidence that can help you with Bailey's case." He turned to his son. "Tell Angela what you told me."

Little Dre scratched the top of his head. "I forgot."

"Sometimes I wonder about you, boy. When I asked you if kids bully other kids at your school, what did you tell me?"

"Oh, yeah." His face lit up. "That stuff happens all the time. And the teachers know about it too."

Angela sat up in her chair. "How do you know that?"

"Because they'll be standing right there. They would have to be blind not to see it."

"Do you ever get bullied?"

"Hell—I mean, no."

"You better watch your mouth, boy. You spend too much time with your mama's people. I told you about that."

"Sorry, Dad."

His son was the product of a short-lived liaison that was never meant to be. Dre had never had a relationship with his son's mother but always played an active role in his life.

"Why don't bullies mess with you?" Angela asked.

"Because my dad made me stand up for myself."

"I told him he could either fight the bully or get his behind whupped by me."

"That's not the way to deal with this, Dre."

When they got married and had kids, that approach would definitely be a problem.

He threw an arm around Little Dre's shoulders. "Works for us."

"My dad said bullies are punks and he's right. If you fight back, they get scared. But they ain't about nothin'."

"Don't say ain't," Dre scolded him.

Angela smiled. Dre apparently didn't realize he'd just said *ain't* a few seconds ago. "Let's get back to your teachers. I can't believe a teacher would see a student being bullied and not do anything to stop it."

"Maybe not all of them," Little Dre said, scratching his head again. "But one time, when my friend Troy was being bullied, the teacher said she didn't feel like filling out a bunch of paperwork, so they better start getting along. But the bully still messes with him. He just does it when no adults are paying attention."

"This is the kind of evidence you need in Bailey's case," Dre said. "You should interview her classmates."

If this was evidence, Dre was smoking something.

"Can I play Minecraft on the TV in the office?" Little Dre asked, apparently bored with the conversation.

Dre nodded. "Make sure you leave the door open."

Since Bailey's death, Dre exhibited more than a few nervous habits regarding his son. Whenever Little Dre spent the weekend, Dre would get up three or four times in the middle of the night to check on him. He refused to allow him to sleep in the office and rarely let him out of his sight for more than thirty minutes at a time. And he constantly asked his son if he was happy.

Dre still had more to say. "If they clamped down hard on bullies and kicked 'em out of school, there wouldn't be this problem. Those teachers don't care about those kids."

"Whoa. Let's not take it that far. I had some incredible teachers, and I'm sure you did too. We can't disparage the entire profession."

"Yeah, whatever. Once you win Erika's case, that'll send a message to every teacher at that school."

Angela appreciated his confidence in her, but it only made the pressure worse. "How's Erika doing?"

"Not good. A co-worker found her in her office in tears a couple days ago. They sent her home."

They were both quiet for a moment.

"Is her mom still here?"

"Yep. She wants Erika to go back to Oakland with her, but she won't."

Angela could only imagine Erika's pain. "I hope this lawsuit doesn't make things harder for her."

"I think it'll have the opposite effect. There's nothing she wants more than making that principal pay for allowing Bailey to be bullied so badly she..."

Dre looked away. He still loathed saying the word suicide.

The judge's denial of their spoliation motion was already one major blow. For both Erika and Dre's sake, Angela prayed there wasn't another one.

68

THE KEY TO winning or losing a case often rests in the hands of the expert witnesses. A savvy expert who gains the jury's trust can fill in evidentiary holes, slanting the scales of justice to one side or the other.

Angela and Jenny were meeting with Dr. Nadia Croton to find out if she would agree to serve as their consulting expert. As a consultant, the psychologist would help them build their case. Because their conversations with her were not privileged, a different expert would be hired to testify at trial.

They sat next to each other on a posh leather couch in the lobby of the child psychologist's Pasadena office.

"I was lying in bed last night thinking about what it's going to do to Erika if the case gets dismissed. I should've fought harder when Dre started pressuring her to sue."

Jenny shook her head in disagreement. "Erika wanted to wage this battle for Bailey. She'll be okay no matter how it turns out."

Angela wondered if she would have the emotional stamina to fight back like Erika was doing after losing both a husband *and* a child. She was almost certain she would not.

Jenny glanced at her watch. Their meeting should have started fifteen minutes ago. "I hope this isn't a sign."

Another twenty minutes later, a receptionist showed them into Dr. Croton's warm, spacious office. A sense of safety eased through Angela's body as her feet sank into the plush carpet. The wall to the left was painted sunshine yellow, with crazy, colorful swirls interspersed with multi-colored, smiley faces. Tiny chairs, building blocks, and an array of toys took up one corner of the room.

"Let's sit over here," the doctor said, pointing to a small area with a couch, coffee table, and two cushy sofa chairs.

Dr. Croton was a soft-spoken, fiftyish brunette. Her dress was colorful and free-flowing.

"First, let me apologize for the long wait," she began. "One of the schools I support had an emergency situation. And it just happened to involve bullying."

"Are you able to share any details?" Jenny asked.

"No, I can't. But generally speaking, I'm called in when a student is in crisis. That can mean anything from the discovery that a child is cutting herself or has told a classmate she's contemplating suicide."

"Have you seen an increase in those kinds of calls?" Angela asked.

"Yes. But I attribute some of it to increased awareness. Just as the #MeToo movement has shined a big spotlight on sexual harassment, media attention has heightened the focus on bullying and child suicide. Take a look at this."

Dr. Croton handed Angela a news article. She read the headline, then passed it on to Jenny.

"Since your client is African-American, I'm sure you're aware of the increase in the suicide rate among African-American children under twelve."

Angela and Jenny nodded.

"And, unfortunately, they're less likely to receive treatment for depression, suicidal ideation, and other mental health problems. There also aren't nearly enough African-American mental health professionals. These children need to see therapists who look like them and can relate to their life experiences."

"I'm just baffled about the way kids today treat each other," Angela said. "Like telling another child to kill herself. How did they learn to act like that?"

The doctor answered with one word. "Technology. More specifically, the growth of smartphones, social media, gaming, and texting. Several studies have found a direct link between heavy social media use and poor mental health."

"The suicide component is so shocking," Jenny said. "I still remember the name of the bully at my middle school. But I don't recall any kids committing suicide."

"It's better to say *died by suicide* not *committed suicide*," Dr. Croton said gently. "Using the word *committed* implies the person broke the law or a moral code. Like saying someone committed murder. That's not comforting to the family."

Jenny's cheeks flushed. "Oh, I'm sorry."

"No need to be sorry. Suicide is an unusually complex issue. While I don't like the idea of litigation, particularly after a child has died—which means we were too late to help—I do see it as a focal point for change. After a teacher or principal spends a few years embroiled in litigation, they tend to take combatting bullying more seriously."

"Some people believe litigation might cause a school to go overboard," Jenny pointed out. "Any little thing a kid does might get them sent home."

"I'll take overkill over neglect anytime."

Angela was anxious to find out if she was willing to join their case as a consultant. "Have you had a chance to look at the documents we sent you?"

The doctor nodded. "I think I can definitely help you shape your case but not in the way you may have anticipated. I did a little research of my own. Parker Elementary doesn't have an adequate anti-bullying protocol."

Angela's brows furrowed. "They have a bullying policy. We sent you a copy."

"It's not enough to just have a policy. What's important is how it's implemented."

"Okay," Jenny said. "What didn't they do?"

"For one, they don't use Educare."

"What's that?" Jenny asked.

"It's a computer program for behavioral intervention. While the school district has the program, it hasn't been diligent about ensuring their employees use it."

Angela scribbled *Educare* on her legal pad. "How does it work?"

"Teachers and administrators are required to input disciplinary issues, infractions, or any other troubling conduct by a student into the system. When an issue arises, you can open up Educare and see that child's complete behavioral history. It tracks behavior the same way schools track academic performance. It's effectively an early warning system."

"Why isn't Parker Elementary using it?"

"I don't know, but some administrators don't like it because it means more work for them. It can also highlight the things they're failing to do. As you probably know, it's rare for a school to lose a bullycide case." She paused and grimaced. "And for the record, I hate that term because it sensationalizes an extremely serious topic. In the cases I've been involved in where the schools lost, either they didn't have a behavioral tracking system or they had one and ignored all the red flags the system waved in their faces."

Both Jenny and Angela nodded.

"When a jury hears everything Educare can do and then learns the school didn't use it, they latch onto that," the doctor continued. "I've seen some brilliant lawyers make that the linchpin of their cases. You should request the records of the girl who bullied Bailey going back to kindergarten. I'd bet good money that she had some behavioral issues that were ignored."

"Frankly," Angela said, "I'm a little concerned that a system like that could be used to stigmatize kids. I would bet that black children, especially black boys, are more likely to be flagged as problem kids and pushed out of schools. That's just fueling the school-to-prison pipeline."

The doctor nodded. "You're absolutely right. That has been one criticism of the system. It's important to conduct annual audits to make sure there's no disparate impact based on race."

"From an expert's vantage point," Jenny said, "what's the weakest part of our case?"

Dr. Croton smiled. "Thanks for asking. That tells me a lot about your skill as an attorney."

Angela held her breath as she waited for the doctor's response.

"You're going to have a hard time showing a direct link between the bullying Bailey experienced and her suicide because she suffered a major trauma—the death of a parent. And she never received counseling. It's very likely Bailey suffered from depression and her father's death was the onset. The other side's going to hammer that home and the jury's going to buy it."

"Every kid who's depressed doesn't take their own life," Angela said. "We're arguing that even if she was depressed about losing her dad, the bullying is what pushed her over the edge."

"And you're probably right. If the school had had appropriate bullying protocols in place, it's possible they could've reached her in time. That's the argument you want to make."

Both Jenny and Angela furiously scribbled down what the doctor had just said.

Angela expelled a sigh of relief. "Thanks for taking our case."

"Don't thank me yet," Dr. Croton said with a stern smile. "I'm not a lawyer, but having been involved in several cases like yours, you have a tough, uphill climb."

CHAPTER

69

ALL CHATTER CAME to an abrupt stop when Zola entered the teacher's lounge. Lately, her colleagues had started treating her like a feather that might fly away if they even breathed her way.

They might not be able to see it, but Zola *was* getting better. It had been days since she'd run off to the ladies' room for a long cry. That was progress.

She poured herself a cup of coffee. Five other teachers were sitting around the long conference table.

"How're you doing?" Tara asked.

"I'm fine," Zola said, taking a seat.

But she was not fine. Brock was constantly bugging her about the status of the case. Their apartment, once a place of refuge, was now plagued with tension.

"Don't take this the wrong way, but you don't look fine."

Zola tried to muster up a smile. "Thanks a lot, Tara."

"I'm sorry. I didn't' mean it like that."

"Don't worry about it. I know I'm a mess."

"I would be a basket case if I'd lost one of my students too," Malcolm chimed in. "My heart goes out to that girl's mother. But to sue the school? I can't understand that. How could anybody here know that child was suicidal?"

The teachers then started a back-and-forth discussion on the pros and cons of suing schools for bullying. She instantly zoned out.

"Zola?"

Tara touched her on the shoulder. "So what do you think?"

"About what?"

"That lawsuit filed by Bailey Lewis's mother."

Zola shrugged. "It's her right. She thinks the school failed her child."

"But do *you* think the school failed her?" Malcolm asked.

Alarm bells clanged in Zola's head. The principal's prized pet was only asking the question so he could run back and report what she said. Freeman had probably instructed him to grill her.

Zola needed to be careful. "If the child was bullied, then yes, we failed her."

"But do you think she was bullied?" Malcolm pressed.

"I never saw any bullying take place." She sounded like one of those politicians on cable news who strayed into partisan spin to avoid answering a question.

"As that lawsuit proceeds, all of the defendants need to be on the same page."

Had Freeman fed him that line?

"That's so true," Zola replied, playing her role. "I was devastated to learn they'd named me as a defendant. Lord knows I don't want a verdict against me."

"Yeah, that's gotta be tough." He grabbed his third donut from the center of the table and stood up. "See you all later. Education awaits."

"He's such a prick," Tara said once Malcolm was gone. "Like we don't know he's Sami's spy. I bet he's on his way to kiss her ass right now."

Zola chuckled derisively. Better him than me.

CHAPTER

70

BLANCA CHARGED INTO Darcella's office. "Turn on Channel 9. You need to see this."

Freeman often kept her small TV tuned to CNN with the sound muted. She picked up the remote, fumbling to find the correct button.

An impatient Blanca grabbed it from her, changing the channel just as the camera zoomed in on a KCAL news anchor sitting on set.

Large red letters filled the right side of the screen: *The Bullying Epidemic in America.*

"Where's the darn volume button?" Blanca muttered.

A second later, the anchor's strong voice flooded the room.

Pre-adolescent suicide rates are skyrocketing and many experts are tying these deaths to bullying. Bullying is nothing new, but today's parents are no longer taking it sitting down. They're fighting back in the courtroom through bullycide lawsuits. We recently told you about the suicide of beautiful nine-year-old Bailey Lewis.

A smiling picture of Bailey took up the entire screen.

The mother of this young fourth-grader at Parker Elementary School alleges that she was relentlessly bullied. It got so bad, in fact, that Bailey hanged herself. Can you imagine? Only nine years old. What a world we live in.

The anchor paused as he dramatically swung his head from side to side.

Today our guest is Marcus Yang, an investigative reporter for the Ladera Press-Telegram who's been following the bullycide lawsuit filed by Bailey's mother against Parker Elementary School. This is quite a piece. I can tell a lot of hard work went into your story.

As she watched and listened, Darcella's face burned with disgust as the young reporter spoke.

I've taken a keen interest in this case, and I have to tell you, what I witnessed in court a few days ago was stunning.

Yang told the audience that the attorneys for Bailey's mother had filed a motion against the school alleging an attempt to cover up evidence. Yang went on to explain how the girl's restroom was painted just days before the attorneys were scheduled to inspect it.

That sounds awfully suspicious, the anchor said.

Exactly. And the judge at one point said as much. But he still denied the motion.

The anchor turned away from the reporter and faced the camera.

We tried to get a representative of Parker Elementary to appear on set, but the school district declined, opting instead to provide the following statement:

Our hearts go out to the family of Bailey Lewis. We conducted a thorough investigation into the allegations of bullying. The school's records show no official reports of bullying made by the student or her family.

"No *official* reports?" Freeman shrieked. "That implies there were *unofficial* ones. What idiot wrote that statement? This is defamation!"

"Just calm down," Blanca said, muting the TV. "At least they didn't mention your name."

"They mentioned my name the minute they said Parker Elementary," Darcella seethed. "That reporter just called me a liar."

All four lines on Freeman's desk phone lit up.

Blanca reached over and answered the first one. She put the call on hold and handed the receiver to Freeman.

"It's the superintendent. He saw the story too. He's even more pissed off than you are."

CHAPTER

71

D RE WOULD BE the first to admit that he'd messed up big time when he tried to talk to Zola Phillips. This time, though, things would be different. He'd be smarter about his plan. Not that he actually had one.

For at least half an hour, he'd been parked across the street from Kiya Jackson's apartment building just off Slauson and Crenshaw. He'd followed her home from school two days earlier, his rage simmering as he watched her. The little girl was no bigger than Bailey, yet she had completely terrorized her. The nasty stuff she'd posted on Instagram still enraged him.

Dre didn't understand why Angela and Jenny weren't going after Kiya's parents. They should've at least talked to the child's mother about her behavior. Looking at the rundown building, Dre doubted there was a father in the picture. What man would let his child live in a dump like the one he was staring at?

The only thing keeping him from hopping out of his Jeep and marching right up to their apartment door was the knowledge that Angela would kill him. So why was he even there?

Before he could answer that question, the door to apartment 12B opened and a boney woman stepped onto the second-floor walkway. Dre figured she had to be Kiya's mother. Dressed in shredded skinny jeans and a tank top, the woman shared the girl's dark, chocolate skin. They both wore cornrows braided in the same intricate pattern.

Dre rolled down the window to get a better look.

"Hurry up, fool!" the woman yelled, sticking her head back inside the apartment. "I don't have all day."

Just as Kiya appeared in the doorway, the woman snatched her by the collar, dragging her across the threshold. "And don't forget to lock the damn door."

"Okay, Mama. Okay."

After shutting the door, Kiya trailed her mother down the stairs toward a beat-up Kia sedan parked on the street. The woman slid behind the wheel while the little girl climbed into the back seat.

As they pulled away from the curb, Dre made a U-turn. He had no business following them, but he couldn't stop himself.

The Kia headed east on Slauson, eventually making a sharp right turn into a swap meet parking lot. Dre did the same, parking his Jeep one row behind them. He turned off the engine and hopped out.

"When we get in here, don't ask me for a damn thing," the woman spat at her daughter as they exited the car. "I ain't playing either."

Dre pretended to walk in the direction of the swap meet's entrance but kept his eyes glued on the pair.

Kiya's head dipped until her chin almost grazed her chest. "But you said I could get a new backpack," she whined.

"No, I didn't. I told you about lying!"

The woman reared back and slapped the girl hard across the face. Dre was so shocked he nearly stumbled over his own feet.

Kiya cupped her cheek and whimpered.

"I ain't tryin' to hear all that!" The woman spat as she dug around in her purse. "Shut up with all that crying or you can get your ass right back in the car and stay there until I'm done shopping."

All the animosity Dre had felt toward the little girl zapped right out of him. No wonder she bullied other kids. She lived with the perfect role model.

"Are you alright?" Dre called out. He was still a few feet away but could already see a red welt rising on her face.

"Mind your own damn business!" the mother shouted, before looking up to see who she was talking to. But once her eyes met Dre's, her rigid body became as soft as a cotton ball.

"We're fine," she said, her voice high and flirty as she boldly looked him up and down. The sugary smile on her face made it more than apparent that she liked what she saw.

"She's just acting up for no reason. I'm Marquita. What's your name, handsome?"

The woman disgusted him. "You shouldn't hit your kid," Dre snarled at her. "Somebody might call Child Protective Services on your ass."

"I don't know who in the hell you think you are?" the woman fired back, her left hand gripping a non-existent hip. "You need to stay outta other people's business. C'mon, Kiya."

She snatched her daughter by the wrist and started dragging her away. "See what you don' caused. You got strangers talkin' mess to me. Shut up and stop cryin'."

Dre stood there until they disappeared inside the building. He walked back to his car, his emotions a mass of anger and confusion. Kiya might've been a bully, but she was a victim too. Her life had to be hard living with a mother like that. Maybe he really would report her.

This was all so messed up. Five minutes ago, he'd wanted nothing short of revenge. Now all he felt was fear.

Fear that Kiya Jackson could very well be the next child who tried to end her own life.

CHAPTER

72

DARCELLA RESTED HER head on Ethan Landers's chest. Their bi-weekly trysts at the Four Seasons Hotel were fun, but truthfully, she was getting a little stir crazy. She hated the sneaking around and wanted to hit the town with the smart, rich Ethan Landers on her arm.

"I hope Zola does okay tomorrow," Ethan said.

"Are you worried about her testimony?"

"A little." He scratched his chin. "If she says that child complained about bullying and the two of you did nothing about it, that will definitely change the complexion of our case."

"But that's not what happened."

"Well, Zola's body language tells a different story. When I prepped her, she looked scared and indecisive. If she acts that way tomorrow, those attorneys are going to assume she's hiding something."

Darcella was quiet for a long moment. "If she says Bailey did complain to her, how bad would it hurt us?"

Ethan sat up on his elbows and looked Darcella in the eyes. "Are you telling me that happened?"

"Of course not."

Who is this man kidding? Darcella thought. *He knows the real deal.* He was just as unethical as she was, which was the sole reason they were such a good fit.

"Okay," Ethan said, lying back down.

"I hope you can get rid of this case before there're any more news stories. When do you think it might be over?"

Darcella could still hear the superintendent yelling at her.

Ethan wiggled his thick eyebrows. "Very soon." He ran his finger up her smooth thigh. "I'm about to hit them with something they won't see coming."

"Like what?"

"You'll have to wait like everybody else."

"I love the way you operate. Once the case is over, I want you to whisk me off to some exotic island."

Ethan tried to kiss her, but Darcella turned her face way. She was no longer in a kissing mood.

"Well?" she prodded.

He nuzzled her neck with wet kisses. "Well, what?"

"What about us taking a vacation together?"

"Sure."

Darcella knew when she was getting played. She was tired of driving all the way to Beverly Hills for sex and room service meals. If Landers really cared about her, he would've bought her some expensive gift by now.

"Never mind." She rolled onto her side, turning her back to him.

"What? I said okay."

"Say it like you mean it."

He sidled up closer, kissing her on the back of the neck, spooning his body against hers.

"Does this tell you how much I mean it?"

He pressed his hard length against her ass.

"No, it doesn't," Darcella said, trying to scoot away.

Ethan gently took her by the shoulder and laid her flat on her back so she was looking up at him. "I'd be crazy if I didn't want to be on an exotic island with you. Have you ever been to Seven Mile Beach?"

Darcella held onto her frown. "No. Where's that?"

"The Cayman Islands. It's heavenly. A friend of mine has a house there on a private beach. I can go there anytime I want."

Darcella's frown magically disappeared. "Really?"

"Yes, really. And I'm going to make love to you on the sand underneath the stars."

"Uh, well, I don't know about that. Sand and my hair don't get along too well."

He laughed. "We have one last leg to go before the case is dismissed."

"How long will that take?"

"A month at the most."

"I've never had a case get dismissed. Either the district settles or it goes to trial."

"That's because you haven't been working with an attorney as brilliant as I am."

"You're certainly sure about yourself."

"When you're talented at everything you do, it's hard not to be." He leaned down and took her right breast into his mouth, while guiding her hand between his legs.

"I'm going to win this case the same way I win ninety-nine percent of my cases," Ethan mumbled, moving to her other breast. "By hitting them before they ever see the blow coming."

73

"This is it," Angela said as they waited in her office for Zola Phillips's deposition to begin. They had a lot riding on what the young teacher had to say.

"I've been praying she does the right thing and tells the truth," Erika said.

Jenny nodded. "Me too. And I never pray."

They all laughed.

Angela's assistant stuck her head into the room. "Your nemesis has arrived."

When they entered the conference room, Angela took the seat across from Zola. Landers was seated to her left, with the principal next to him. The teacher looked like a scared rabbit, her hands clasped and resting on the table, her twitching eyes unable to make eye contact with anyone or anything for more than a second or two.

Landers smiled at Angela. "That KCAL story you guys obviously arranged was quite the low blow."

"Excuse me?" Angela said.

"Since you couldn't convince the judge that my client engaged in misconduct, you used the media to malign her."

Freeman sat with her arms folded and her lips locked in an indignant pout.

Angela spread her hands, palms up. "I didn't put any words into that reporter's mouth. He simply reported the facts."

It gave Angela a boost to know that the story got under their skin. "Anyway, let's get started."

After covering the basic instructions, Angela got straight to the point.

"Did you know in advance that the girl's restroom outside your classroom was going to be painted?"

As Angela had hoped, Landers hadn't prepared his witness for that question.

Zola's eyes darted to the left. Landers, however, was occupied by the principal, who was whispering into his ear.

Was she seeing things or was Freeman leaning unusually close to him?

Landers had not yet objected to her question. Nor had Zola answered it.

"I'm sorry, Mrs. Phillips, but did you understand my question?"

"Oh, um, could you repeat it?"

"Did you know in advance that the girl's restroom right across from your classroom was going to be painted?"

The principal seemed to tense up as she waited for Zola to respond.

"No, I didn't."

"Was that something you would normally be aware of?"

"Not really. The buildings aren't usually painted during the school year. It's typically done during the summer months."

Landers placed a folder over the microphone clipped to Zola's lapel and whispered in her ear.

Lines creased Zola's forehead as she repositioned herself in the chair. Whatever Landers had just said rattled her.

"Have you ever seen the custodians painting *any* building on campus during the school year?"

"No. I don't think so."

"She hasn't worked there long enough to even know when they paint," Freeman said under her breath.

"Counsel, please remind Ms. Freeman that she's not in the witness chair anymore. She should keep her comments to herself."

Freeman fired daggers across the table at Angela, who hurled them right back. "Were you surprised to see them painting the restroom?"

Zola hesitated. "Yes."

"Why?"

"Because I didn't think the paint would be dry by Monday. I asked Damien about it and he said—"

"Objection, uh...calls for speculation," Landers stumbled. "This line of questioning is irrelevant. The court has already resolved this issue."

Angela ignored him. "You were about to tell me about a conversation you had with Damien Miller, a custodian and Parker Elementary."

"Objection. Calls for a narrative," Landers yelled. "That's not a question."

"Counselor," Angela said with a smile, "no need to shout."

Landers was acting awfully touchy about this topic. That only made her want to dig in more.

"Let's slow down and see if I can get Mrs. Phillips to clarify her response. Did you ask Damien why he was painting the girl's restroom during the school year?"

"Yes."

"And what did he tell you?"

"He said he was just doing his job."

"To your knowledge, was there a schedule requiring the restrooms to be painted at that time?"

"Objection, outside the witness's knowledge. Calls for speculation."

"You can answer," Angela said, not missing a beat.

"I don't know anything about the schedule. Just that Damien—"

"We need to take a break." Landers jumped to his feet.

"Sure, but not while she's in the middle of answering my question. Mrs. Phillips, you were about to say something else about Damien Miller. What was it?"

Zola paused, confused by the back and forth between the attorneys. "I'm sorry, I forgot what I was going to say."

"Let's go ahead and take that break." Landers was already on his feet and moving toward the door.

Once everyone was out of the room, Angela turned to face a smiling Jenny.

"It's nice to give Landers a taste of his own medicine," Jenny said. "His client is ignoring his advice about not volunteering information and it's driving him crazy."

"I hope she keeps it up," Erika said.

Twenty-two minutes later, Zola, Landers, and Freeman returned to the conference room. The teacher looked more petrified than she had at the start of the deposition. Angela switched to a different subject. She'd return to the painting schedule later, after Zola had time to forget what Landers had just told her to say.

Angela handed Zola and Landers copies of a photograph Diego had taken. "Do you recognize this?"

Zola clutched her stomach. "No."

"This photograph was taken in your classroom. Are you saying you weren't aware of the graffiti on the back of that chair?"

"Absolutely not." The woman looked as if she might cry. "I would never allow something like this in my classroom."

The chair had the words *Just kill yourself Bailey* etched on the back. Angela didn't expect to gain much ground with the picture. She simply wanted to unnerve her witness.

"This is a wide shot of your classroom," Angela continued. "Can you tell me where Bailey sat?"

Zola pointed. "Right here."

"As you can see, the chair right in front of Bailey has that vile graffiti about her."

The woman gasped.

"Bailey had to look at that every day."

Landers leaned back in his chair. "Is there a question pending, counselor?"

"Did anyone ever tell you that these hateful words urging Bailey to kill herself were in *your* classroom?"

"No, I swear. I didn't know anything about this."

"No need to swear," Landers griped. "You're already under oath."

"Did you ever see Bailey being bullied?"

Zola hesitated and shifted in her seat. "No."

"Did Bailey ever tell you Kiya Jackson bullied her?"

"No."

"Did Bailey ever tell you Kiya Jackson stuck out her foot and tripped her?"

Zola's eyes shot across the table at Erika. "No. I don't think so."

"*You don't think so?* Is there anything that might help refresh your recollection?"

Confusion glazed the teacher's face. "I don't understand. Like what?"

Like looking in a freakin' mirror.

A loud screech filled the room as Freeman noisily pushed her chair back from the table.

Angela glared at her. "If Ms. Freeman continues trying to signal the witness, I'm going to ask that she be barred from the deposition."

Freeman snorted. "How dare you accuse me of—"

Landers held up his palm, cutting her off. "That accusation was way out of line, counselor."

"Just make sure it doesn't happen again." Angela glanced down at her notes, then up at Zola. "Let's try this one more time. Did Bailey ever tell you Kiya Jackson stuck out her foot and tripped her? That's a yes or no question."

"No."

"Did you ever see Kiya Jackson stick out her foot and trip Bailey?"

"No."

Liar.

"Was Bailey one of your favorite students?"

Zola smiled for the first time. "Yes, she was. She was a lovely little girl."

Then why aren't you standing up for her?

"Do you believe your principal, Darcella Freeman, takes bullying seriously?"

"Of course she does." There was conviction in her voice, but her drooping shoulders undercut the impact of her delivery.

"Do you use the Educare system?"

"Edu what? I don't know what that is."

Great answer.

"What would you expect your principal to do if a student complained of being bullied?"

Zola hesitated. "I'd expect her to evaluate the facts and conduct an investigation if necessary."

"What's involved in an investigation?"

"Objection. Outside the witness's area of expertise."

"You can answer," Angela said dryly.

"I guess an investigation would start with interviewing everyone involved."

"And then?"

Landers interrupted. "Mrs. Phillips, you sound a little sluggish. Would you like to take a break?"

"No, I'm fine," she said, waving away his concern. "I just want to get this over with."

That wasn't the response Zola was supposed to give. Either she had forgotten her attorney's instruction or she didn't care.

Judging from the twin frowns on the lips of Landers and Freeman, they were quite displeased with her answer.

74

"YO, DRE! STOP! What are you doing?"

Dre was on his knees, installing laminate wood flooring in the master bedroom of the Hawthorne duplex. His buddy Gus was standing over him, waving his hands like a crazy man.

"What's the matter?"

"Those aren't the right planks."

Dre looked down at the floor. "What are you talking about?"

"Is something wrong with your eyes? Those planks don't match. Look at the color over there." Gus pointed toward the wall. "You're using the ones for the living room."

Dre stared at the work, stunned that he hadn't noticed what was now so obvious.

"Oh." Dre got to his feet. "My bad."

"You know what? You need to take a break."

"Naw, I'm good."

Gus shook his head. "Naw, man, you're not. You haven't been good since Bailey died."

Dre said nothing.

"Let's call it a day and head over to La Louisanne's to kick it for a minute." Gus strapped on some kneepads. "But first we gotta take up what you just put down."

Forty minutes later, they took separate cars and met at the entrance of the neighborhood bar and nightspot.

"Apache's on his way over," Dre said, averting his eyes. Apache was not one of Gus's favorite people.

His friend blew out a breath. "Man, you know I don't like hanging around your lunatic cousin."

"I know, I know. He called me in the car and I let it slip that we were headed over here. I wasn't thinking."

"That's for sure."

They walked inside and took seats on the patio. Gus ordered a Cognac, Dre a Pepsi. His avoidance of alcohol was a carryover from his drug-dealing days. He had never smoked or consumed his own product or anything else that could alter his senses. He'd been a fairly savvy drug dealer. But ultimately not savvy enough to avoid getting caught.

Seconds after placing their drink orders, Apache strolled in strutting like a peacock.

"What's up, Gussy Gus?" He slapped Gus hard on the back. "Long time no see."

"Man, I told you not to call me that."

"Stop acting like a little bitch. You know you're glad to see me."

Apache turned around and waved his hand in the air, trying to flag down a waitress. When she failed to notice him, he yelled way louder than he needed to.

"Hey, sweetness. I need a whiskey over here A-SAP."

Gus swung his head from side to side, then glowered at Dre.

"What's up with the lawsuit?" Apache asked. "Y'all ready for my help yet?"

"I know you ain't relying on this clown," Gus said.

"Don't be ragging on me, bruh. I'm like the Godfather. I handle everything."

"No, I'm not relying on him," Dre said. "And since you asked, the lawsuit ain't going well at all. We were counting on Bailey's teacher to come clean. Angela called me earlier today. Her deposition was a bust."

"What's that mean for the case?" Gus asked

"It means that without a witness who can testify that an employee knew Bailey was being bullied, Erika doesn't have a case."

"I can find a witness for you," Apache offered. "What you need 'em to say?"

"Never mind," Dre and Gus said in unison.

"I'm serious. I was just telling a partner of mine about the lawsuit. His homeboy's son goes to Parker. Want me to talk to the kid? Maybe his son knew Bailey and saw something go down."

"No thanks," Dre said. "Stay out of it and let the lawyers do their thing."

"Sounds to me like the lawyers ain't doing too good."

"That's about the size of it." Dre's voice cracked. "I can't stop thinking about seeing Bailey hanging from that closet."

His eyes welled with tears and he pressed his lips together as if to keep his emotions inside. "And when I think about that teacher and principal not being held responsible, I wanna go down to that school and burn the place down with them in it."

"Hold on," Gus said. "Don't be talking like that, Dre. You gotta check your anger at the door."

"Want me to do it?" Apache asked. "'Cause you know Apache can make it happen. I know plenty of people who could get the job done."

"Man, will you shut up?" Gus yelled at Apache. "He don't want you or any of your hoodlum friends to do a damn thing. He's just blowing off some steam."

Dre rose from his chair, a bit wobbly on his feet. "I gotta go take a leak."

"You see that?" Apache glanced over his shoulder as Dre walked away. "This lawsuit's got my cuz breaking down like a little bitch. Looks like it's time for me to step in and handle things."

"Just stay out of it," Gus groaned. "Don't nobody need your help."

"Whether they know it or not," Apache bragged, "everybody needs my help."

CHAPTER

75

THE BEST THING about Zola's deposition was that it had taken place on a Friday. Now she had the entire weekend to brood over the lies she'd sworn under oath not to tell.

When Brock got home that evening, he found her in bed with the covers pulled up to her neck. It wasn't even six o'clock. Zola had closed the blinds, giving their usually bright bedroom a dark, cave-like feeling.

"Hey," he said, sitting down on the edge of the bed. "How did it go?"

"I did exactly what you wanted me to do. I lied through my teeth. So I guess it went great." She rolled onto her side, facing the wall, instead of her husband.

Brock clicked on the lamp on the nightstand.

"Look, Zola, I never said you should lie. You were under oath. If you lied, you could end up facing perjury charges."

Zola peered over her shoulder at him. "Too late."

"What did you lie about?"

"Everything."

The hardest part of the whole day was having to sit across from Bailey's mother. Zola had tried to avoid her gaze, but the woman's pitiful eyes drew her in like a car wreck on the side of the road.

Zola began to weep. "What kind of teacher am I? I didn't stand up for that beautiful little girl. I hate myself. I don't deserve to be anybody's teacher!"

Brock cradled her as he would a wounded bird. "You're a great teacher. If you weren't, you wouldn't be in this much pain." "No, I'm not! I'd want someone to stand up for my child, but I was too weak to do that for Bailey."

Brock rocked her for a long time.

"There's something I never told you," Zola said, pulling away to look him in the eye. "I have some evidence."

Brock frowned. "Evidence of what?"

"Evidence that my principal knew Bailey was being bullied and wasn't willing to do anything about it."

"What kind of evidence?"

"I recorded her."

At first, Brock didn't say anything. "Does anybody know you did that?"

"Of course not."

"When did you record her?"

"When we met in her office after Bailey had that outburst in the cafeteria. I pretended to be looking for some tissue in my purse, but I was really turning on my phone."

Zola untangled herself from Brock's embrace and grabbed her cell phone from the nightstand. She tapped the screen several times, then looked up at him. "Listen to this."

I want to make sure we're both on the same page. When you came to me this morning, you told me Bailey never said she was being bullied, correct?

Yes, but I did see Kiya Jackson trip her.

As I said before, that was most likely an accident. So are we on the same page?

Um, sure, I guess. But we spoke on at least two other occasions about my fear that Bailey was being bullied.

That's not what I recall. You simply expressed concern about Bailey being a loner and not having any friends. If you want to continue teaching here or anyplace else, your recollection had better start lining up with mine.

Brock stopped the recording. "She straight up threatened you! I'm so glad you have her on tape."

"Recordings aren't the only thing I have."

Zola tapped the screen of her phone again.

"When I saw Damien painting the girl's restroom, I had a feeling something was up. I waited nearby, hoping he would take a break. A couple of minutes later, he did. That's when I slipped into the restroom and examined all the stalls. This is what I found in one of them."

Brock took the phone from her and started swiping through the pictures. "What the hell?" he exclaimed, staring at the screen.

Bailey Lewis is a bitch.

Bailey = monkey girl.

Everybody hates Bailey. Just kill yourself.

Bailey needs to die.

"Elementary school kids wrote this stuff? I wouldn't expect to see this kind of craziness in a high school boy's restroom. They're only nine and ten years old for Christ's sake."

Zola fell back against the headboard and covered her mouth with both hands. "I don't know what to do."

"And I don't know either. Withholding this kind of evidence might even be criminal. If you hand it over now, you'll nail your poor excuse for a principal, but since you lied under oath, you're going to be at the center of a cover-up right along with her."

Brock squeezed Zola's hand as tears trickled down her cheeks. "And I won't let that happen."

CHAPTER

76

APACHE HATED SEEING his cousin's head all messed up over that little girl's death. He could no longer sit on the sidelines. Dre needed evidence and Apache was going to find it for him.

In Apache's world, filing a lawsuit wasn't the preferred way to resolve a dispute. But since Dre was on the up and up now, Apache decided not to resort to the more coercive tactics he typically employed to gather information. At least for now.

The instant he entered Cut It Up Barbershop on Crenshaw Boulevard, it was like someone pressed the pause button on a video and everybody froze in place. All conversation ended. All eyes looked away. A few guys probably stopped breathing.

"Hey, fellas," Apache called out from just inside the doorway. "What's up?"

Cut It Up was a small, oblong storefront with four barber chairs that T-boned into a waiting area near the door. Eight folding chairs framed a huge window that faced the street.

Regular trips to the barbershop were not part of Apache's routine. Thanks to his Indian heritage, his hair didn't require that kind of maintenance.

"I'm Apache," he said, for the benefit of those who didn't recognize him. Though based on their stunned expressions, no introduction was needed.

Apache had a rep for being a hothead who would shoot first and asked questions later. His appearance in the barbershop foreshadowed that trouble—most likely violent trouble—was imminent.

"I'm looking for a dude named Rosco Davis," he called out to no one in particular. "I heard he gets his hair cut here."

No one said a word.

"Relax," Apache said, smiling. He could smell the fear in the room, a fragrance sweeter than a rose. "Ain't nothing about to go down. I just wanna talk to him."

Still no takers.

"Okay, then, who's his barber?"

No heads moved, but a bunch of eyes darted toward the last barber's chair. After a long pause, a barrel-shaped guy half-raised his hand.

"What's your name?" Apache asked, taking a slow stroll to the back.

"Cliff."

"You know when Roscoe's coming in?"

"Naw, man. I don't know."

"Really, Cliff? I heard Rosco and his son come in here damn near every week right about this time. Somebody must've lied to me. Or maybe you're the one lying?"

The clippers in the big man's hands began to wobble a bit. "Uh, he might be comin' through later on. I...I don't know for sure."

"Okay." Apache headed back to the front and lowered himself into one of the metal chairs. He folded his arms across his chest and extended his legs, crossing them at the ankle. "I think I'll wait."

He wore a big smile that was more of a warning than a welcome.

The guy who was next in line suddenly had someplace else to be and hurried out of the shop. Another man walked in, made eye contact with Apache, and backed out of the door. Apache laughed to himself. Since the Nipsey Hussle shooting, which happened right up the street, dudes in the neighborhood were more paranoid than ever.

After about twenty minutes, Apache started to get antsy. For all he knew, the barber could've texted Rosco and told him to stay away. Apache had no idea what Rosco even looked like. Maybe he'd already come through and someone had slipped him a signal.

When a man entered with a boy at his side, Apache sat up. The kid looked to be around Bailey's age. Before he could ask the man his name, he received confirmation in another form. Damn near everybody in the shop seemed to be searching for a place to hide.

Rosco raised his hand in greeting. "Hey, Cliff, how long's the wait?"

Cliff acted like he was about to swallow his tongue.

"Hey, Rosco," Apache said, getting to his feet. "Let me holla at you outside."

Rosco gave him an I-don't-know-you look. "About what? And who the hell are you?"

Apache was a little perturbed that the man didn't recognize him. How many Hollywood-handsome, Indian-looking black dudes in L.A. could there be?

"They call me Apache."

To Apache's delight, the trepidation in the man's eyes told him that his reputation had indeed preceded him. Rosco reflexively put his hand around his son's shoulders, pulling him close. "What you want with me?"

"I just wanna holla at you a minute. Your kid too. Let's step outside."

The man stayed put. He looked around the shop in a wordless appeal for help from his barbershop buddies. Every pair of eyes in the place focused on anything except Rosco.

Apache had his piece in his waistband. He didn't like flashing his weapon if he could help it. Ultimately, the menace in his eyes did the job.

Rosco and his son followed him outside the barbershop. Apache led them a few yards away.

"Have a seat," he said, pointing to a small, wrought iron table in front of a soul food restaurant.

Apache remained standing as father and son complied.

"What do you want with me?" Rosco asked, the pitch of his voice several octaves higher than it had been seconds ago.

Apache felt kind of bad the little boy had to witness his father punking out like a little sissy.

"I wanna talk to your son," Apache began.

"My son? Why do you need to—"

Apache held up his right index finger, accompanying it with a scowl that mandated silence. Rosco's mouth instantly clamped shut.

"What's your name?" Apache said to the boy.

"Rosco Junior." He fidgeted with his hands, no doubt feeding off of his father's distress.

"You go to Parker Elementary?"

He nodded. "Yeah."

"You know Bailey Lewis?"

Little Rosco's eyes swelled into eight balls. "Yeah! She was in my class. She killed herself."

"Well, Bailey was a family friend of mine and I'm trying to find out whether anybody at your school bullied her."

"I didn't do nothing to Bailey!" Rosco Junior looked over at his father. "I swear I didn't."

"Okay, okay, calm down. I ain't trying to pin nothing on you. Did you ever see anybody bully her?"

"Yeah."

"Who?"

The boy looked over at his father again. "Will I get in trouble for telling?"

"No," Apache said. "But you'll definitely get in trouble for *not* telling. Who bullied Bailey?"

Little Rosco was still reluctant to speak.

"Just tell the man!" Rosco shouted.

"She was bullied real bad," he said. "By this girl in my class named Kiya Jackson. One time she even spit in her face."

Apache smiled at big Rosco, who seemed relieved that Apache didn't have any business with him.

"I'ma need a favor. I want your kid to speak to a couple of lawyers for me."

CHAPTER

77

THREE DAYS AFTER Zola Phillip's deposition, Angela and Jenny were chatting over turkey sandwiches and Diet Cokes, when they received an unexpected delivery.

"More news from the war zone," Gina joked. "And this news isn't good."

Angela put down her sandwich. "If that asshole has filed another baseless motion, I'm driving to his office and keying his car."

Gina laughed as she placed a thick set of documents on the desk. Jenny took a sip of Diet Coke. "What is it?"

"I don't believe this guy."

"What?"

"He's serving us with a summary judgment motion."

Jenny set down her Diet Coke. "Discovery hasn't closed yet. He can't file an SJ now."

"Let me be more precise. It's a *proposed* summary judgment motion. His cover letter says that as a courtesy, he wanted to give us an advance look at his motion because he thinks it will convince us to drop our lawsuit."

"Damn, he's got balls," Jenny said. "Have you ever had anybody send you a proposed motion before?"

"Never. Most attorneys would be too afraid of showing their hand. I guess he thinks his case is so rock solid that's not an issue."

"Landers is such an arrogant asshole. Let me see it."

"Hold on," Angela said, still perusing the documents. "He's claiming the death of Bailey's father and the drug she was taking are responsible for her suicide. Not the bullying."

Angela started reading the motion aloud:

First, the undisputed facts show that the plaintiff cannot demonstrate that the defendants had actual notice of an alleged threat of harm to the child. Second, the plaintiff has no evidence that the defendants were deliberately indifferent to any alleged threats of harm. Finally, the plaintiff cannot demonstrate that the alleged harassment was so severe and pervasive that it deprived the child of access to educational benefits.

Angela paused again. "He's also included a 998 offer." She tossed the papers onto her desk. Jenny snatched them up.

Jenny flipped through the document. "How much is the offer?"

"Fifteen grand."

Jenny practically spit up her Diet Coke. "That's a joke."

"What's a 998 offer?" Gina asked. Angela hadn't noticed that she'd been standing in the doorway the whole time.

"A way to paint us into a corner," Jenny mumbled.

"It's basically a tactic to encourage a party with a weak case to settle," Angela explained.

"If we reject the offer and our case is dismissed or we get a jury award that's lower than the offer, we'll have to pay any costs they incurred after making it. Like deposition costs and experts' fees."

"Wow," Gina said. "So you have to be really sure you're going to win."

Angela nodded. "Exactly. And I'm sure Landers has given his experts free reign to run up the bill."

"This doesn't scare me," Jenny said. "A 998 offer has to be reasonable and fifteen grand isn't reasonable."

"That summary judgement motion is pretty solid," Angela said glumly. "I hate to say it, but it may be time to throw in the towel."

CHAPTER

78

Brock was growing increasingly concerned about Zola's mental state.

She moped around the house the entire weekend, seesawing between fits of anger at Darcella Freeman and spurts of weepy rants about her own behavior. She'd even called in sick on Monday morning, something Zola had never done before. The guilt of not standing up for Bailey was eating away at her spirit.

When Brock arrived home from work the night before, Zola was in better spirits and talked excitedly about returning to her students. So he was surprised when he stepped out of the shower and found her still in bed.

"Hey, there, sleepyhead," Brock called out. "Time to get up."

Zola moaned, then rolled over onto her side.

"I'm going to put some coffee on. I'll bring you a cup."

Brock feared his wife was seeping into a state of depression. Nothing he did seemed to boost her spirits. Being back in her classroom was the best medicine for her.

After the coffee finished brewing, Brock headed for their bedroom, carrying the cup he bought her the same day she got the job at Parker Elementary. World's Greatest Teacher was stenciled on the side in bright yellow letters.

"Hey, wake up. Your coffee's going to get cold." He set the cup on the nightstand.

"I can't go in today," Zola mumbled into her pillow. "I need one more day."

And tomorrow you'll need another day. "You need to get back to work, Zola. Your students miss you."

"I don't know why they would. If they ever needed me, I wouldn't have the courage to stand up for them." She let out a sharp gasp, which Brock recognized as a windup to another crying spell. "Bailey would be alive if I'd stood up to Freeman."

When Zola started to sob, Brock stroked her hair. Zola needed to see a therapist, but if she did that, she might come clean about the source of her distress. They couldn't risk that.

"Okay," he said. "One more day. But tomorrow, you have to get back on your horse."

Maybe they'd take a drive down to San Diego next weekend. Zola loved the Loews Coronado Bay Resort, where they'd celebrated their first wedding anniversary. It wasn't in the budget, but if it helped Zola, he'd make it happen.

Returning to the bathroom to shave, Brock heard Zola's cell phone ring. A call this early in the morning could only be the school. He rushed to reach the phone, but it stopped ringing.

He checked the screen and saw that the missed call was indeed from Parker Elementary. He was about to return it when the house phone rang.

Brock dashed into the kitchen and grabbed the receiver. Again, the call-back number was Parker Elementary.

"Good morning, may I speak to Zola Phillips?"

"Zola's still not feeling well," Brock said. "I'm afraid she's going to need another day off."

"What's wrong with her?"

"Who am I speaking to?" Brock asked, not happy with the woman's nasty tone.

"This is Darcella Freeman, the principal of Parker Elementary. And who am *I* speaking to?"

He could almost sense her evil through the phone.

"This is Zola's husband, Brock. She's a little stressed out from the litigation as well as Bailey Lewis's death. She needs a little time to get back to her old self. I'm sure she'll be back at school soon."

"How long is soon?"

The woman was worse than Zola had described.

"Soon is however long it takes," Brock said, his chest tightening.

"May I speak to her?"

Why? So you can harass her some more?

"She's still asleep and I don't want to wake her. I'll have her give you a call when she gets up."

The principal wasn't going to intimidate him like she did Zola. He understood why the teachers called her Satan's mistress behind her back.

"Well, please have her call me when she finally does get out of bed."

"I'll do that. But if you don't hear from her later today, you can call me." Brock rattled off his cell phone number.

"That won't do. I can't discuss personnel matters with you."

"Is there some problem?"

"As I just said, I can't discuss that with you."

"Well, like *I* just said, if Zola doesn't get back to you today, feel free to call me for an update."

Silence.

"Let Zola know I hope she feels better."

"I'll be sure to do that."

Brock wished he could've told Freeman every awful thing he knew about her. The woman didn't deserve to be principal. But that wasn't how life worked. Zola was the one whose contract likely wouldn't get picked up, while the principal went on to a bigger and better position.

As Brock finished shaving, a devious thought came to him, prompting a slow smile to snake across his face. Maybe it was too risky to tell anyone about those recordings, but what if the media got a hold of the pictures from the girl's restroom? There was no way they could be linked back to Zola.

If Darcella Freeman's cover-up was exposed, her career wouldn't be toast, it would be a crispy burnt toast. So what if Zola got fired too? She was smart. Another school would snatch her up in no time.

Who was he kidding? Brock wasn't any braver than Zola. He would've folded under the pressure just like Zola had.

79

"WHEN WE GET in there," Dre said, "let me do the talking. Angela's going to go ape shit when she finds out we talked to that kid."

Apache nodded. "Okay, cuz. This is your show."

He followed Dre into Angela's office suite. The receptionist wasn't at her desk, so they proceeded to Angela's office, which was empty. They found Angela and Jenny in the conference room, sitting around a table scattered with papers.

Dre saw the surprise on Angela's face when she noticed them standing in the doorway.

"What are you guys doing here? Is something wrong?"

"No, nothing's wrong." Dre stepped farther into the office.

"Hey, almost-cousin," Apache said to Angela, then turned to Jenny. "Hey, white lightning. You miss me?"

Jenny grinned. "Hey, Apache."

"We found somebody you need to talk to." Dre hesitated. "About Erika's case."

Angela pounced to her feet. "What did you guys do?"

"*We* didn't do nothing," Apache interrupted. "*I* was the one who went out and got you some evidence for your case."

Dre glanced over his shoulder. He could've strangled his cousin. "Like I was telling you before," Dre continued. "Apache knows a guy whose son goes to Parker."

"I don't actually know the dude," Apache interrupted. "But I—"

"Can you let me finish?" Dre said, eyeing his cousin. "The kid's willing to testify that he saw Bailey being bullied."

Angela's hands flew to her hips. "Didn't I ask you guys to stay out of this case?"

"We're not *in* the case. I just think you should talk to the kid. Pretty please?"

Apache whistled. "Damn, cuz, what's up with that? I ain't never seen you grovel to no babe. You wearing panties now?"

Angela scowled at him. "Apache, I don't have time for your craziness today."

"If the kid has some evidence, I'd like to hear it," Jenny said. "When can we talk to him?"

"Now," Dre replied. "He's outside in the hallway with his father."

Dre and Apache ushered Rosco Davis and his son into the conference room and introduced them. Apache pulled out a chair to sit down as Dre was about to do the same.

"Excuse me?" Angela said. "You two can't be here."

Dre huffed and stood up. "C'mon, man. Let's go."

"Bruh," Apache mumbled, getting to his feet, "we need to go buy you a new sack of nuts because the ones you got ain't working too good."

"Shut up, fool," Dre barked.

They waited in Angela's office for forty minutes before Angela and Jenny returned.

"Apology accepted," Dre said, greeting Angela with a smug smile. "That kid gave you some good evidence, right?"

"It helps," Angela said, not nearly as excited as Dre had hoped she'd be after getting firsthand information about what Bailey had suffered.

"*Helps?*" Dre said. "Is that all you've got to say."

"The boy can't say for sure whether any teacher, administrator, or staff member saw any bullying take place," Angela explained. "And that's where our case is lacking."

Apache raised his hand. "Hey, just tell me what you need the kid to say and Apache will make it happen."

At that, Angela plopped into one of the chairs in front of her desk. "Jesus, help me."

"That's not how it works," Jenny said to Apache. "We appreciate you guys trying to help. But unless we prove that the school—meaning an employee—had knowledge of the bullying and did nothing about it, we're not going to win."

CHAPTER

80

DELIVERING BAD NEWS to a client isn't a task any lawyer relishes. But having to tell someone you care about that they weren't going to get the justice they had anticipated, made the job much harder.

"I guess we can't put this off any longer," Angela said, staring across her desk at Jenny.

She had a solemn look on her face and nodded.

Erika and Dre were next door in Angela's conference's room. They would have preferred to meet with Erika alone, but she had insisted on Dre's presence.

He was so bent on revenge against the principal and Bailey's teacher that he wasn't rational. Having him there would make what they had to do twice as hard.

Dre had pestered Angela all night about what they were going to discuss today. She'd made up some lame excuse, then left for the office earlier than usual to avoid any more questions.

Angela grabbed a folder from her desk as they both got to their feet. "Can you take the lead?" she said to Jenny.

"Why? You scared your man's not going to take this well?"

"Yep. I'll need to be focused on calming him down."

Jenny smirked. "Good luck with that."

When they stepped into the conference room, Erika and Dre were seated on the far side of the table. Angela and Jenny took seats facing them.

"What's up with all this formality?" Dre asked. "We could've done this at the house."

"We wanted to have a frank talk about the status of the case," Jenny began. "There've been some developments."

"This doesn't sound good," Erika said.

She was dressed casually in jeans and a light blue sweater. That ever-present weariness still darkened her eyes.

"Landers served us with a motion seeking to dismiss the case," Jenny continued.

"Dismiss it?" Dre interrupted. "How can he do that? Don't we get to go to trial?"

"There's a process called summary judgment," Jenny explained. "If one side can convince the judge that the other side doesn't have enough evidence to meet their legal burden, the judge can dismiss the case. And that's what they're trying to do."

"This is crazy." Dre slumped back against his chair.

"Without proof that the school knew about the bullying, we can't defeat the motion. They've made a settlement offer. If we—"

Erika cut her off. "How much?"

Jenny swallowed. "Fifteen thousand dollars."

Dre gripped the edge of the table. "Oh, hell naw!"

Unlike Dre, Erika maintained her composure. "So that's how much they think my daughter's life is worth?"

"The settlement isn't a measure of her worth," Angela replied. "They're offering what attorneys call nuisance value. Even though they think they'll win at trial, they're willing to pay something to resolve the case early."

Silence sucked all sound from the room.

"I don't care if they think we'll lose," Erika said. "I want to keep fighting. I've been praying hard about this."

Angela had prayed about some difficult cases too. God always answered her prayers, but sometimes not in the way she'd wanted or expected Him to.

"You also need to know that they've made what's called a 998 offer," Jenny said. "If we turn down the fifteen grand and your case is dismissed or we lose at trial, you could be responsible for paying the defendants' costs. Experts' fees can get pretty outrageous. I've seen some approach six figures."

Dre leaned in over the table again. "This is why the justice system is so messed up. That doesn't make a bit of sense."

Angela kept her focus on Erika. "We wanted to have this meeting to make sure you were aware of the risks of turning down the offer."

"Are you suggesting I take the offer?" Erika asked, surprised.

Angela's eyes met Dre's before returning to Erika. "In my legal judgment, with the evidence we have now, there's a strong possibility the judge will dismiss the case."

"You've told me more than once about cases you thought you were going to lose but ended up winning," Dre said, challenging her. "Maybe this is one of them. Even if it's a long shot, I don't think we should settle."

"This isn't a game," Jenny said, jumping to Angela's defense. "The evidence is what drives this case. And so far, we don't have enough. It doesn't make sense for Erika to continue spending money on depositions and legal fees if we're not likely to get a verdict in her favor."

"What about Bailey's classmate?" Dre asked. "He told you he saw the bullying. He can testify."

"We need evidence that a teacher or administrator knew Bailey was being bullied."

"Then depose a bunch of 'em. Somebody'll eventually break and tell the truth."

"It doesn't work like that," Angela snapped.

Dre wouldn't let up. "I don't understand why you can't just—"

"That's enough!" Erika pressed her palms to her cheeks. She turned to Angela, then to Jenny. "I appreciate you giving it to me straight. But I don't care about the money. Earl had a large life insurance policy as well as mortgage insurance on our old place, which is how I was able to buy the house in Baldwin Hills. I want to keep fighting. If we can make it past that motion and get to a jury, I think we can win."

Angela groaned inwardly. "If that's really what you want to do."

"It is." Erika sat up a little taller in her chair as a flash of enthusiasm ignited her sad eyes. "Even if we lose, taking the school through this lawsuit will make them think twice about letting another child be bullied. For me, that makes the fight worth it."

CHAPTER

81

"WAKE UP! ANGELA, wake up!"

Dre stood over the bed, shaking her by the shoulder.

Angela shot up, her head still hazy with sleep. "What's the matter? Is everything okay?"

"Erika's here. She has something you have to see! Get up!"

Angela had turned in early, a little down about their meeting earlier today. The clock on the nightstand flashed 11:45 p.m. What was it that couldn't wait until morning?

"Grab your robe. Hurry up."

Still woozy, Angela slipped into her house shoes and grabbed her robe from a chaise in the corner of their bedroom. She walked down the hallway, rubbing her eyes with the heels of her hand.

Erika was sitting on a stool at the kitchen island. Dre stood next to her, his face ready to burst with excitement. There were papers spread out in front of them.

"Look at this madness." Dre was practically jumping up and down. "You can't tell me we don't have a case now."

When Angela got closer, she could tell that the papers were actually photographs. She picked up one of them, still baffled as to how this would help their case. The picture seemed to show graffiti scratched onto a wall. Then her eyes focused on six words that chilled her.

Everybody hates Bailey. Just kill yourself.

Angela looked from Dre to Erika. "Where did you get these?"

"They came in the mail," Erika said. "No return address."

Angela took her time examining each picture. There were two wide shots of the entire wall and individual pictures of four slurs targeted at Bailey. The remaining three were as nasty as the first one.

Bailey Lewis is a bitch.

Bailey = monkey girl.

Bailey needs to die.

"This is the stuff they covered up in that restroom!" Dre said. "This proves that witch of a principal knew what was up."

Angela's head shot up. "Was there a note with the pictures?"

"Oh, sorry. Yes." Erika pulled another piece of paper from the envelope with the following typewritten words in the middle of the page.

DARCELLA FREEMAN LIED WHEN SHE CLAIMED THE GIRL'S RESTROOM WAS SCHEDULED TO BE PAINTED. THIS WAS WHAT SHE WAS TRYING TO COVER UP.

SIGNED, ANONYMOUS

"They blatantly lied to the court," Angela said, growing excited herself.

Dre's lips dripped with satisfaction. "And I bet I know who sent them."

"Who?" Angela asked.

"Bailey's teacher. Zola Phillips."

"What makes you think that?"

"My gut."

Angela rolled her eyes. *Yeah, I'm pretty sure I can sell that to the jury.*

"I'm serious. I looked into that woman's eyes when I talked to her in the school parking lot," Dre said. "She knows what went down."

If Phillips did send them, she was putting her career on the line. So from that perspective, Dre's hunch didn't make sense.

Erika was smiling. "I've been praying about this case day and night. This is a sign. And I think it's the first of many."

A beat of hope and fear took hold of Angela at the same time. Yes, this was important evidence, but she couldn't run into court with these photographs without someone to verify where they came from. There was no way these pictures would ever be admitted into evidence without that.

Angela looked up at Dre and Erika. There was so much excitement spilling from their eyes she didn't have the heart to dash it.

Even if the pictures were somehow admitted, their existence alone didn't prove that the school had notice of the bullying.

"Say something," Dre said. "This changes everything, right?"

"Yeah," Angela lied. "This helps our case a lot."

CHAPTER

82

FOR MORE THAN twenty uninterrupted minutes, Sidney Meltzer sat with his elbows planted on his desk, his fingers steepled, as Angela and Jenny recounted the recent developments in their bullycide case.

"I know you told us from the start that it was a tough case to win," Jenny said, "but we think this additional evidence could lead to further evidence. We wanted your advice about what steps we should take next."

Instead of speaking, Sidney swiveled his chair around and gazed out of the window. "Give me a minute."

As they stared at the back of his chair, Jenny leaned in and whispered, "He's weird like that."

It was another couple of minutes before Sidney turned back around to face them.

"On the pro side, those pictures are pretty convincing evidence that they painted that restroom to cover up that graffiti about Bailey. And as we all know, the cover-up is always worse than the crime. There are a lot of wimps on the L.A. Superior Court bench, but Judge Quintana isn't one of them. I've seen him sanction a defense counsel ten grand for hiding evidence."

Both women nodded, their faces strained with anxiety as they waited for the con.

"But these photographs still don't get you over the hump. Adults didn't use the girl's restroom. How do you prove a teacher even saw this stuff? And unless the person who sent them to you comes forward, you'll never get them into evidence."

Angela closed her eyes.

"And that summary judgment motion is solid," Sidney continued. "You still can't prove the school had knowledge that Bailey was being bullied."

Jenny blew out a long, slow breath. Silence descended over the room like a heavy tarp, depriving them of sunlight.

"Thanks for your input," Jenny finally said. "We already know everything you just stated. We were hoping that maybe you could pull some rabbit out of your hat."

"I've been known to do that from time to time," Sidney said with a laugh. "Stop looking so defeated. It's not time to wave the white flag yet. Before I tell you what I think your next step should be, why don't *you* tell *me*?"

Angela quietly inhaled. Sometimes Sidney treated them like first-year law students.

"Our first step is to reopen Darcella Freeman's deposition and confront her with these pictures," Angela said. "And depending on what we find out, we then depose Zola Phillips."

Jenny turned to face Angela. "Why not depose Phillips first? She's the weakest link and is more likely to fold."

Angela mulled that over. "Because she didn't order that restroom to be painted."

Sidney nodded. "I agree. Depose the principal first. Next, you need to find out who sent Erika those pictures."

"I'm thinking it was Phillips," Jenny said, echoing Dre's guess.

"Maybe not." Sidney leaned back in his chair. "If she knew about that graffiti, that means she lied during her deposition."

"What if the principal denies knowing about it and we can't figure out who sent the pictures?" Jenny asked.

"Then we're screwed," Angela said.

"Not necessarily," Sidney said. "One thing I've learned over the years is that when one domino falls in a case, others are poised to hit the deck. So get rid of those sad faces. You still have options."

"Name one," Angela said sarcastically.

"You could always go nuclear."

Angela huffed. "And what does that mean?"

He grinned. "I'll explain later. Depose that principal and hammer her as hard as you can. Then give me a call."

CHAPTER

83

"GOOD AFTERNOON, LADIES," Ethan Landers crooned into the phone. "I know why you're calling."

No, asshole, Angela thought, *you don't.*

After their discussion with Sidney, the two attorneys agreed that using their newfound evidence tactically was the best course of action.

"So, shall I assume you're ready to accept my clients' generous settlement offer?"

"I wouldn't call fifteen thousand dollars generous," Jenny sniped.

"In light of the facts of this case," Landers chuckled. "I would have to disagree. As you know, I've tried a ton of these cases."

"So you've told us," Jenny said. "Repeatedly."

Landers ignored the slight. "You've produced absolutely no evidence that shows you can meet your burden of proof. My clients wanted to offer Bailey's mother enough to reimburse her for the funeral expenses. They're heartbroken about her death."

Sure they are, Angela wanted to say.

"Normally, with such a solid case, I would've urged them to move forward with the motion. I did you a favor by giving you a sneak peek. Most attorneys don't do that. But I believe in full disclosure. I plan to file it the day after discovery closes in two weeks."

Angela couldn't wait to drop their bomb in Landers's lap.

"We've reviewed your motion," she said. "Of course, we disagree that it's the slam dunk you think it is."

"I never said it was a slam dunk. Just that it's a winner."

"Whatever," Jenny muttered under her breath.

"So I guess this means you're not going to accept my settlement offer?"

"No," Angela said. "We're not. Our client deserves far more than fifteen thousand dollars."

"Then what's the purpose of this call?"

"We wanted to give you a heads-up that we'll be sending you a deposition notice later today," Angela explained.

"Really?"

"We're reopening the deposition of Darcella Freeman."

"That deposition is closed."

"We didn't use the full seven hours we're allotted." Angela fumbled for her notepad. "To be precise, we only used four hours and thirty-three minutes."

"And why is it necessary to recall her?"

"We've discovered some new evidence."

"What evidence?" For the first time, the arrogance left his voice.

"Nothing we care to share right now. So can you make your client available on Monday at ten o'clock? If you decline, we're prepared to go in *ex parte* tomorrow to ask the judge to compel her testimony."

"No need to be so heavy-handed. I'll check my client's schedule and get back to you later today."

Angela didn't put anything past Landers. He was the kind of scumbag who would avoid them until discovery closed. Then try to block them from reopening Freeman's deposition.

When they hung up, Jenny smiled hopefully.

"I've already started working on a brief asking the judge to reconsider our spoliation motion." She turned her laptop around so

Angela could see the screen. "Read this and let me know what you think."

"Aren't you the hopeful one," Angela said, as she perused it.

Like their original motion, it requested sanctions of ten thousand dollars against Landers and the principal, as well as an instruction to the jury that the defense had deliberately hidden evidence.

Angela backed away from the computer screen. "This is probably our final play. Let's pray Darcella Freeman tells the truth."

CHAPTER

84

DARCELLA CHECKED INTO the presidential suite at the Four Seasons Hotel and slipped into a frilly pink teddy. She smiled as she admired her tight body in the full-length mirror. The case would soon be over and she and Ethan would be lounging on a private beach in the Cayman Islands.

After pouring herself a glass of Riesling, she stretched out in the middle of the bed. This was how she wanted Ethan to find her. Striking a seductive pose straight out of *Playboy*.

She glanced at the clock on the nightstand. Ethan was late. That wasn't like him. Perhaps something had come up. Darcella wasn't the type of woman who didn't know how to entertain herself. In fact, she loved having the suite all to herself. She could get used to living like this on the regular.

Ethan had never discussed the future of their relationship. For now, that was fine. Darcella wasn't certain he was the kind of man she could marry, but she definitely wanted to keep him around for all the extravagant perks. After a few weeks, most men bored her. Her confidence, beauty, and brains threatened them. It was nice to have a guy secure enough to want a woman who was his equal.

Darcella heard the main door open. She set her wineglass on the nightstand and resumed her pose, legs crossed at the ankle, her teddy hiked up to show just enough thigh. She propped herself up between two pillows and daintily cocked her head to the side.

Ethan charged into the room, his face flaming red.

"Is there anything you need to tell me?" he demanded.

Darcella sat up. "What? Calm down. Tell you about what?"

"About the lawsuit. They want to depose you again. Any idea why?"

She pressed both palms to her cheeks. "What? Can they do that?"

"Yes, they most certainly can."

"But why?"

"I was hoping *you* could tell *me*. They claim they have some new evidence. If there's anything you've done that you haven't told me about, I need to know about it. Now."

"I swear I have no idea what they're up to."

He pointed a long finger down at her. "You better be damn sure. Because if you're holding something back, I'm going to be the one who looks like an unethical scumbag before the judge."

"Stop shouting at me!"

"I'm your attorney first and your lover second," he said, his voice still way too loud. "I don't like surprises."

"And I told you, there won't be any." Darcella hopped off the bed, her hands on her hips. "If you're going to continue talking to me this way, I'm leaving. You owe me an apology."

Ethan tugged his tie loose, tossed it onto the dresser, and slumped into a club chair in the corner of the room.

She watched as his chest heaved up and down. His angry eyes burrowed into hers as if they were searching for the truth.

"Fine," he grumbled. "I'm sorry. Their call threw me for a loop. I don't know what they're up to and that concerns me. I'm usually the one pulling the surprise punches. I don't like being in this position."

"I promise you they have nothing. They're just scrambling because they know the case is going to be dismissed."

Darcella picked up her wineglass and took a sip, trying to figure out what evidence they might have. And then it hit her. Had Zola finally cracked? Gone to the other side in tears and spilled everything? Darcella knew she should mention this possibility to Ethan. But then again, she didn't know for sure.

She walked over and sat in his lap. "Let's forget about that stupid lawsuit for awhile."

Taking his hand, she placed it underneath the soft fabric of her teddy.

"You're something else," Ethan said, massaging her thigh. "You know that?"

"Indeed, I do."

"Nice," he muttered, licking her neck and easing his hand farther up her leg. "I love it when you don't wear panties."

She moaned as his fingers grazed her center.

"See?" Darcella purred. "Isn't this a whole lot more fun than arguing about that stupid case?"

CHAPTER

85

ANGELA HAD TROUBLE sleeping the night before Darcella Freeman's deposition. If she could get the principal to break, this would turn the tide of the case back in their favor.

To heighten her stress, Dre was barely speaking to her. He wanted to attend the deposition, which Angela firmly vetoed.

"I can be there as support for Erika," Dre had pleaded.

"Erika's got a support system. Me and Jenny. Landers will balk if you're there and I don't feel like a fight."

In truth, they probably could have allowed him to come, but she didn't trust Dre to behave.

"I promise I won't fly off the handle like I did before. I swear. The second part of my deposition went fine, didn't it?"

"You're not coming anywhere near today's deposition. So please stop asking me."

"Fine. Never mind." He marched out of their bedroom and started puttering around in the kitchen. He typically gave her a peck on the lips before she departed each morning. Not today.

Erika and Jenny were already seated in her office when Angela arrived.

"This is going to be a turning point in the case," Erika said with a hopeful smile. "I can feel it."

"They're here," Gina said, sticking her head in the door. "The videographer and court reporter are also set up."

Jenny stood up. "Let's get to it."

As Jenny and Erika headed out of the office, Angela hung back. She needed a few minutes to psych herself up. She took a series of long, deep breaths. *You're going to crush Darcella Freeman.*

When she finally entered the conference room, Angela took the empty chair between Jenny and Erika. Freeman sat directly across from her, Landers to her left.

In that moment, she remembered Dre's comment about the two of them screwing around. They were the perfect couple. Landers was probably in on Freeman's restroom cover-up.

After terse greetings, Angela turned to the court reporter and videographer. "Let's go on the record. You can swear in the witness."

Darcella Freeman folded her hands and set them on the table. She looked way too smug. Angela couldn't wait to slap the self-righteousness off her face.

"Ms. Freeman, I'm here today to ask you a few follow-up questions. First, is it still your testimony that you had nothing to do with ordering the painting of the girl's restroom outside Zola Phillips's classroom?"

Darcella smiled sweetly. "Well, yes. As I testified before, that restroom had been missed during the summer."

"And the work order your attorney previously produced to us, pre-dated our request to inspect the restroom. Is that correct?"

"Yes. That order was already in the system. Unfortunately, I wasn't aware of it, or I would have halted the painting as soon as I learned about your request."

The woman's demeanor showed not a shred of nervousness.

"How many times have you visited that restroom?"

"Never. I have no reason to go in there. I have a private restroom connected to my office. I've never been in any of the student restrooms."

"Were you aware that there was graffiti on the walls and the stall doors of the restroom?"

"No."

Landers's brows fused into one as he struggled to figure out the direction of Angela's line of questioning.

"Did anyone ever report to you that there was graffiti on the door of one of the restroom stalls?"

"No."

For the most part, Freeman was a well-trained witness. She didn't volunteer information and answered with yes or no responses whenever she could, expanding only when it helped her case.

"I'd like to mark this next document as exhibit twenty-one, continuing the numbering from Ms. Freeman's first deposition."

Angela turned to the court reporter and handed her an 8 x10 photograph. It depicted a wide shot of the four slurs on the door of the restroom stall. She slid two more copies across the desk for Landers and Freeman.

"Please take a few minutes to review the document and let me know when you're done."

Freeman barely glanced at it before splaying her manicured fingers against her chest and exclaiming, "Oh, my goodness."

"Do you know where this photograph was taken?"

"No, I don't."

"Have you ever seen this image before?"

"No, I have not."

"Do you know who wrote those words captured in the photograph?"

"No, I do not."

"How about this picture, which I'll mark as exhibit twenty-two?" Angela handed two copies across the table.

"I've never seen this either."

Angela walked through all six pictures and with each *no* response from the principal, a little of Angela's resolve dissipated. Still, she trudged on.

"Did you instruct someone to paint the girl's restroom to cover up these vicious attacks on Bailey Lewis?"

"Absolutely not. I had no idea this stuff existed."

Freeman began drumming her fingers on the table. Was that a tell that she was lying?

Just as Angela was about to ask another question, the principal placed her hand over the microphone clipped to her lapel and whispered into Landers's ear.

"Are you aware that lying during a deposition constitutes perjury?" Angela asked.

"Objection!" Landers said, waving his right hand like he was backhanding a fly. "Badgering the witness. Don't threaten my client simply because you aren't getting the answers you want."

"I'm not threatening her. I just want to make sure she understands the significance of her testimony."

"I'm her lawyer. Trust me. She understands."

Angela looked down at her notes. She had wanted these questions to unnerve Freeman. To capture her stuttering on camera. Either Freeman was telling the truth or she was the best liar Angela had ever deposed.

"And what would you say if I told you we had testimony from someone who claims they saw you go into that restroom?"

Jenny fidgeted in her chair, no doubt wondering where Angela was headed. They had no such evidence.

For the first time Freeman visibly flinched. "If someone told you that, they would be lying because I've never gone in there."

"If you'd been aware of that graffiti on school property urging Bailey Lewis to kill herself, what would you have done about it?"

"Objection, calls for speculation," Landers said.

Angela didn't take her eyes off the woman. "You can answer."

"I would have immediately commenced an investigation to try to find out who had written it."

Freeman's emphasis on the word *immediately*, almost made Angela laugh.

"But first, I would've made sure those offensive words were painted over that very same day," she continued. "And I would've notified Bailey's mother as well as the school psychologist to make sure Bailey was okay. This is awful. But I had no idea about it. And I'm sure none of my teaching staff did either."

"Did a student ever report to you or one of your staff that these comments were on the door of the restroom stall?'

"No." This time Darcella smiled.

Angela was coming up empty at every turn and the principal was loving it.

"What about your custodians? Since they cleaned the restrooms, they must've seen it. Did one of them ever report it to you?"

"No. Most of them are contractors. When those guys are cleaning up in the evenings, they're moving so fast, I doubt they have the time to read what's on the walls."

Angela's questions continued along this line for another twenty minutes.

"Let's take a short break," Angela said.

Erika and Jenny followed her back to Angela's office.

"Well, it was worth a try," Jenny said.

"So what happens now?" Erika asked. "Can we still go to the judge with the pictures and ask him to reconsider the motion?"

Angela rubbed the back of her neck. "I'm not sure."

Erika seemed flabbergasted. "Why not?"

"Because we don't have anyone to verify them. We need someone who can sign a declaration stating that the pictures were taken in that restroom stall."

"What about deposing Bailey's teacher again?" Erika suggested.

"Discovery closes in another week. Zola Phillips already lied about Bailey complaining to her. She'll probably lie about this too."

Erika's voice shook. "So it's over?"

Before Angela could answer, Jenny cut her off. "Nope. We have a few more options."

Angela glared at her friend. *Why are you getting Erika's hopes up?*

When Erika left to go to the ladies' room, Angela couldn't hold her tongue.

"Why did you tell her that? You're just prolonging the inevitable. The judge is going to grant Landers's motion and dismiss the case. Erika needs to be prepared for that."

"Are you forgetting what Sidney told us?"

Dipping her head in frustration, Angela let out a long huff.

"He told us to come back to him after the depo," Jenny reminded her. "That it would be time to go nuclear."

"Do you even know what that means?"

"Nope. But I trust Sidney. Whatever the nuclear option is, I'm more than ready to push the red button."

CHAPTER

86

LANDERS WAITED UNTIL he and Darcella were confined in the privacy of his Maserati before erupting.

"What kind of game are you playing?" he yelled, his voice so loud the windows vibrated.

"Calm down. Why are you so upset? Everything went fine in there."

"They're going to ask the judge to reconsider their spoliation motion. And when he sees those pictures, he's not going to buy your little story!"

"Okay. And?"

"Look at those pictures!" He hurled them into her lap. "Are you seriously telling me you had no idea this stuff was on that door and it was just a coincidence that it was painted over a few days after they served us with an inspection demand?"

"That's exactly what I'm telling you."

"I don't believe you! Did you falsify that work order?"

"What? No. Of course not."

Landers's lips straightened into a thin line. "I need to know the truth, Darcella! This isn't just about you lying at your deposition and signing a false declaration under penalty of perjury. I'm on the line here too. If the judge thinks you're lying, he'll assume I knew and report me to the bar."

He unloosened his tie and pounded the steering wheel with his fist.

"I will not continue to talk to you until you calm down."

Landers's head fell back against the headrest. "I'm going to ask you this one...more...time. Did you know about that graffiti before the restroom was painted?"

Darcella hesitated. "Okay. Yes, but—"

"Yes, but nothing! You've made an easy case exponentially more difficult. You shouldn't have done that. And you should've told me you did!"

"I guess I panicked. The day after they gave us that inspection notice, I went to check all the classrooms and the restrooms and that's when I saw it."

"Jesus Christ! You just testified that you never went in there. Did anyone see you?"

"No. I waited until school was out. There was no one else around. I checked the parking lot first and all of the teachers' cars were gone. It was almost eight o'clock."

"Well, they obviously have a witness who saw you go in there."

"No, they don't. Angela Evans was bluffing."

"What about the custodian who did the painting? Was he in on it?"

"Do you think I'm stupid? Of course not. I didn't tell him a thing."

"Then how did he know to paint?"

"I went into the computer and changed the schedule."

Landers pounded the steering wheel with his fist. "So now there's an electronic footprint showing that you changed the work order. Now *that* was bright. How do you know he didn't see that stuff on the wall when he was painting?"

"Damien's not the brightest bulb in the pack. I'm sure he went in there and slapped that paint on the walls so he could hurry up and go home. If he'd seen it, he would've mentioned it to me."

Landers brushed his palm down his face.

"And so what if we painted over it?" Darcella said. "They still can't prove Bailey complained of bullying."

"That's not the point! Now my credibility with the judge will be damaged. Judges don't like to be lied to."

"Who says anybody lied? They won't be able to prove I changed those records. I covered my tracks."

"Sure you did. That's why they have those pictures."

Darcella closed her eyes. She knew exactly who was responsible for that.

"I have something to tell you, but promise you won't yell at me again."

Landers looked at her with pure venom in his eyes. "What now?"

"The only person I can think of who would've sent them those pictures would be Zola Phillips. That restroom is right outside her classroom. She's the only one who would care."

"It would be crazy for her to do that. She's personally liable in this case."

"She's young and idealistic," Darcella said. "And stupid too. So what do we do now?"

"There is no *we* here. I didn't knowingly misrepresent myself to the court."

"Oh, please. Don't sit there an act like you're the epitome of ethical behavior. We both wanted to win. You've been playing hardball from day one."

"But I'm smart about what I do and I never lie to judges."

"You're overreacting."

"No, I am not. We're just going to have to play this by ear. If you're right and Zola gave them the pictures, she probably did it anonymously. If they don't ask the judge to reconsider their motion in the next few days, it means they don't have anyone who can verify them."

"Don't worry about it." Darcella placed her hand on Landers's upper thigh, giving it a sexy squeeze. "Everything's going to work out just fine."

Landers took Darcella's hand and dropped it back into her lap. "You better hope so."

CHAPTER

87

ONCE THE PRINCIPAL'S deposition ended, Jenny and Angela headed to Sidney Meltzer's office.

As was his style, he listened quietly as they recounted the details of their failed effort.

"Too bad." He shook his head grimly. "I was hoping you'd get a confession out of her. You don't have enough to get the judge to reverse his ruling on your spoliation motion."

"We know that," Angela said, dejectedly. "So, I guess we're done."

"Hold on there, counselor. The courtroom isn't the only place to try your case. You guys have been getting some nice local press. When KCAL interviewed that young reporter, I'm sure that produced a lot of pressure. Schools are notoriously skittish about bad press."

"Are you saying we should take the pictures to the media?" Jenny asked.

"That's precisely what I'm saying. That might smoke out the person who sent them to you. You don't even have to call it a cover-up. Just recount the facts. Anybody watching will reach their own conclusion. And they'll assume the school did something wrong."

"Marcus Yang will be glad to run with this," Angela said.

"No, no, no, no," Sidney said. "You ladies are thinking too small. As I said before, you need to go nuclear."

"And how do we go nuclear?" Angela asked, exasperated.

"That's where I come in." Sidney turned to his computer and started tapping keys. "You're taking this story to CNN."

"CNN?" Angela and Jenny said in unison. "You think they'd be interested?"

"Hell, yes. It's exactly the kind of sensational story they like to air. You can bet other TV stations and newspapers across the country will be picking it up after they cover it."

"And how do we get it on CNN?" Jenny asked.

Sidney tore a sheet of paper from a notepad and copied something from his computer screen.

He handed the paper to Jenny. "Here's the email address and telephone number of a college classmate of mine. Tell her I sent you."

"She's with CNN?" Angela asked.

"She's not just with CNN, she's Don Lemon's producer. I know her quite well. Almost married her. This story has all the elements she loves: a hot topic—bullying—a sympathetic victim, and a nasty school cover-up complete with pictures. Lemon will blow up this story to smithereens."

"Even if we publicize these pictures," Angela pointed out, "that's not going to help us defeat Landers's motion to dismiss the case."

"True," Sidney said with a knowing smile. "But after the rainstorm of negative national attention, I suspect the district might be willing to offer your client a whole lot more than fifteen grand to make the case disappear."

CHAPTER

88

Taking their story to CNN turned out to be excellent advice.

From the start, Don Lemon's producer was excited about the story. She had actually been researching a piece about the link between bullying and the growing number of child suicides, so their timing was perfect.

Before committing, the producer requested all of the documents filed in the case, the deposition transcripts, and the restroom pictures. It took a week for everything to come together. Erika and her attorneys would be interviewed by Don Lemon live via satellite.

A camera crew set up in Angela's conference room with Erika in the middle, the attorneys flanking her, and a green screen behind them.

Lemon stared straight into the camera.

I have three very important guests tonight. As you saw in the piece we just aired, there's a growing increase in young children taking their own lives. I'm talking about children nine and ten years old. Sometimes even younger. And in all of these cases, the parents of the children allege that they were the victims of relentless bullying at school.

He paused to shake his head.

Tonight, my guests are two Los Angeles attorneys and their client, the mother of one such bullying victim. Take a look at this beautiful child, nine-year-old Bailey Lewis.

The screen switched from Lemon to a smiling picture of Bailey, then to a split screen of Lemon and his three guests.

Mrs. Lewis, can you share your story with my audience?

Erika began by telling them what a wonderful child Bailey was and then talked about the bullying she endured at Parker Elementary.

I didn't know it was so bad that Bailey was contemplating suicide, I had no idea what was going on at that school.

Her voice disintegrated into a whimper. Lemon pursed his lips and nodded.

This is so tragic. Here are some pictures of what other students at her school allegedly posted on Instagram about Bailey. And these next pictures show a restroom stall that Bailey used every day. It's hard to believe these vicious comments allegedly came from elementary school children. We also have with us, attorneys Angela Evans and Jenny Ungerman. Ms. Evans, how did you get these pictures?

They were sent to us anonymously. When we visited the restroom, the graffiti had been mysteriously covered up with a fresh coat of paint—just four days after we notified them that we wanted to inspect the school.

Wow. Sounds mighty suspicious to me.

That's our feeling as well.

Let me ask you this. Because I also need to be fair. In their court filings, the school claims Bailey was distraught over the death of her father, not the alleged bullying.

Jenny was about to answer when Erika jumped in.

My husband died nine months before Bailey's suicide. Was she sad? Yes. Did she miss her father? Absolutely. But in the absence of the bullying, I have no doubt that my child would still be here today. It was the way she was treated at school that was the last straw, making her give up on life. She was only nine years old.

Erika broke down into a quiet sob.
Lemon turned back to the camera.

This is such a tragedy. But one that is being repeated all over the country. Take a look at these kids, all of them under the age of twelve.

More than two dozen pictures filled the screen.

Each one of these children took their own lives just this year. They were all alleged victims of bullying. This is a crisis situation, people. It's time to do something about it. If your child is a victim of bullying, here's an excellent resource for you— StompOutBullying.org. And if you or someone you know is in crisis or having suicidal thoughts, please reach out to the National Suicide Prevention Lifeline at 1-800-273-8255. You'll find free and confidential emotional support and the line is staffed 24 hours a day.

Lemon thanked them for sharing their story and the camera faded to black.

"I'm so glad we got Bailey's story out there," Erika said, dabbing her eyes with a tissue. "Millions of people saw that piece."

Jenny stared down at her phone. "I can't believe this! I have emails from six TV stations and three newspapers wanting to interview us."

Erika turned to Angela. "Why do you look so sad? I thought it went really well."

"There's only one person I wanted to see the story."

"And who's that?"

"Judge Eduardo Quintana."

CHAPTER

89

DARCELLA WATCHED THE CNN story from a small TV on her kitchen counter, her blood pressure spiking to stroke level. This was unadulterated defamation. She dialed Ethan even before the interview had ended.

"Are you watching this craziness?" she screamed into the phone.

"Sure am," Ethan said calmly.

"I'm suing them. This is defamation!"

"No, actually, it isn't. Don Lemon was very careful to repeatedly say *alleged* and the attorneys never said you or anyone else engaged in misconduct. Only that the graffiti was mysteriously covered up."

"Well, they damn well implied I did it!"

Darcella was near tears. This was her reputation on the line. "Why aren't you upset about this? What are you going to do about this?"

"Nothing."

"Nothing? Are you nuts? We can't let that interview stand unchallenged."

"Please calm down. As long as the person who sent those pictures doesn't come forward to verify them, this case is about to be history."

"We don't know that they won't."

"True. But after thinking about it, I agree that Zola's likely behind this. And you better hope that she was."

"Why should I hope that?"

"Because she can't come out of the shadows without implicating herself. And that's an excellent reason for her to keep her trap shut."

"Don't worry. I'll make sure she does."

"Oh, no, you won't," Ethan yelled. "Don't you say one word to her. You haven't spoken to her, have you?"

"No, but—"

"But nothing. If she's the one who sent them, then she probably knows a lot more than you think she does. Confronting her might push her over the edge. If she decides to go to the media, we're screwed because it'll be an insider spilling the beans, not a grieving mother."

Darcella had just hung up with Ethan, her body still raging with anger, when her cell phone rang.

"Dammit," she said after reading the caller ID. There was only one reason the superintendent was calling.

"I thought you told me the case was under control and there wouldn't be any more media attention!" he bellowed. "Do you know how this makes the district look? Were you involved in a cover-up?"

"Of course not. Those are baseless allegations. Our attorney assures me the lawsuit will be dismissed very soon."

"It better be."

"I'm fairly confident that—"

"Just get it done!"

The phone went dead.

Darcella squeezed the phone so tight her hand ached. She couldn't believe the superintendent had hung up in her face.

This was all Zola Phillips's fault. There was no way Darcella was going to sit by and let that woman ruin everything she'd worked for.

Someone needed to deliver a strong message to Zola. And despite the warning from Landers, Darcella was going to be the one to do it.

CHAPTER

90

TWO TEACHERS RUSHED up to Zola the instant she stepped into the school hallway.

"Did you see that CNN interview with Bailey's mother and her attorneys?"

She shook her head. Lately, Zola refused to watch local or cable news. It was too depressing. She just wanted to get to her classroom so she could cloak herself in the comfort of her students.

"Girl, I hear Sami is beside herself. She's the one who's going to take the fall for this."

Instead of stopping at the teacher's lounge for coffee, Zola walked right past it.

"Hey, Zola," one of the teachers called out to her. "You're not coming to the lounge this morning?"

"No," she said, not bothering to look back.

It wasn't until she reached her classroom that she realized she'd been holding her breath. She let out a long sigh and slumped into the chair behind her desk. Zola had wanted to stay home, but Brock convinced her that hiding out wasn't going to solve anything. She had to return to school and hold her head high.

There was a knock on the door. She walked over to open it, poised to tell her busybody colleagues to leave her alone. Blanca, the principal's administrative assistant, stood on the other side of the door.

"The principal wants to see you in her office."

Zola glanced up at the clock on the wall.

"Don't worry. You'll be back before class starts."

What now? Zola thought.

Strangely, rage, not fear, bubbled inside her. She was tired of being bullied.

As she marched down the hallway, Zola kept her eyes straight ahead, hoping she didn't run into any more gossiping teachers. When she entered the administrative offices, it was as if someone had pushed a mute button. All conversations ended.

Zola stood in the principal's open doorway. "You wanted to see me?"

"Thanks for coming down. Close the door and have a seat." Freeman waited for Zola to sit down. "I'm assuming you saw that trash on CNN disparaging our school last night."

"Nope. I don't watch much TV anymore."

"Well, they had pictures of graffiti about Bailey, which they claim were taken in the girl's restroom outside your classroom. Did you send her mother those pictures?"

"What?" Zola couldn't keep the shock off her face. *Had Brock...?* No. He wouldn't have done that without telling her. *Would he?*

"I don't know what you're talking about. I didn't send anybody anything." Though she wished she had.

"Well, I don't believe you."

"So be it."

Freeman blinked, obviously surprised that Zola wasn't acting like a cowering little girl anymore.

"The case will probably be dismissed in a few days," the principal sniffed. "You need to keep your mouth shut. At least you had the good sense to send those pictures anonymously."

Zola closed her eyes. *Brock, what did you do?*

"As I said, I didn't do that. And if you did nothing wrong, exactly what am I keeping my mouth shut about?"

"Don't try to bait me. You know what I'm talking about."

"Oh," Zola said, "you mean my reporting that child's bullying complaints to you and your choosing not to do anything about it?"

"You know that and I know that, but as long as nobody else knows it, everything's going to turn out fine."

"Maybe I don't care about that anymore."

"So you *do* admit sending those pictures?"

"I don't admit any such thing."

"Well, don't forget that perjury could mean jail time."

"You, of all people, should know."

"I don't like your attitude, Mrs. Phillips."

Zola glanced at her watch and stood up. "School's about to start. Is that it?"

CHAPTER

91

"I HAVE A GOOD feeling about this," Jenny said, a look of hopefulness on her face.

Once again, they were standing outside Judge Quintana's courtroom, this time to argue Landers's motion for summary judgment.

Angela started to respond to her friend, but thought better of it. Who was she to dash Jenny's unrealistic expectations?

No witness had materialized to verify the restroom pictures, so they could not use them as evidence. Although Erika, Angela, and Jenny had been flooded with media requests following their KCAL appearance, the continuing publicity had not prompted the school district to increase their settlement offer.

Angela glanced down the long courthouse hallway. Erika and Dre hadn't arrived yet. She prayed they were hemmed up in a massive traffic jam. It would be better if they weren't on hand to witness their imminent defeat.

"Well?" Jenny said, giving Angela's elbow a nudge. "Say something,"

"What's there to say? You know as well as I do how this is going to go."

"I think we have a shot," Jenny persisted. "Hopefully the judge saw that CNN piece."

Technically, judges weren't allowed to consider evidence that wasn't properly presented to the court. But underneath their black robes, judges were ordinary people, subject to being influenced by things they were supposed to disregard.

Angela arched a brow. "Quintana doesn't seem like the kind of guy who stays glued to CNN. He's known as a real intellectual. I bet he considers TV beneath him."

"Even if that's the case, he has a court clerk, two law clerks, and a court reporter. Courtroom staff tend to be pretty close-knit. One of them had to see it and tell him about it."

"We'll find out soon enough."

Angela spotted Darcella Freeman and Ethan Landers approaching from the far end of the hallway. She turned her back to them. As soon as the clerk opened the courtroom doors, Landers and Freeman walked in ahead of them without acknowledging their presence.

"You think that principal feels bad about her role in this?" Jenny asked, once they were seated in the gallery.

"Nope. I don't think she even believes Bailey was bullied."

Just then, Erika and Dre entered the courtroom and took seats directly behind them.

Dre leaned forward to whisper into Angela's ear. "I have a good feeling about today. I know you guys are about to represent big time."

He sounded like a football coach trying to pump up a consistently lousy team. Angela responded with a weak smile.

They watched three motions being argued before the clerk called out, *"Lewis versus Parker Elementary School."*

Judge Quintana began talking before they barely settled in. "I've read the moving papers as well as the opposition and reply briefs. This case seems pretty straight forward on the law."

In an instant, Angela lost all hope. The judge was getting straight to the point.

"Despite the allegations in the plaintiff's complaint, I don't see any evidence that raises a disputed issue of fact." He gazed over at Angela and Jenny. "What evidence do you have that the school had notice of the alleged bullying?"

Angela shifted her weight from one foot to the other. It was time to play politician. Ignore the question asked and instead, respond to one of your own.

"Your Honor, we supported our opposition brief with copies of multiple, vicious online threats made against Bailey by students at Parker Elementary, a declaration from Bailey's mother about her daughter's emotional state, a declaration from a classmate of Bailey's who witnessed the bullying and a photograph of a chair in Bailey's classroom that had offensive graffiti about her on it. We believe all of these things considered together put the school on notice."

Angela wished she could've added the restroom graffiti, but without someone to verify it, they could not get it into evidence.

"Counselor," Judge Quintana said sternly, "the school can't control what students do after hours on social media. And do you have any evidence that a teacher or administrator knew about the posts?"

"No, Your Honor."

"And what about that graffiti on the back of the chair? Did the teacher know it was there?"

Angela could feel her body shrinking like a punctured tire. "No."

"Your Honor," Landers interrupted unnecessarily. "This isn't a complex motion. Not a single school district employee was aware of the alleged bullying. There's no case here."

The judge turned back toward the plaintiff's table. "Your response, counselors?"

Jenny stepped in to respond. "Your Honor, there was an incident the day before Bailey's death where another student intentionally squirted her with ketchup."

Judge Quintana flicked his hand in the air, figuratively swatting that argument away. "C'mon, Ms. Ungerman. Even if the court accepted your version of what happened in that cafeteria, it doesn't prove the school had notice of any bullying and was indifferent to it. Nor does that single incident amount to severe and pervasive conduct."

Landers jumped in again, with a bunch of legal mumbo jumbo that hammered the coffin closed.

"Anything else, counselors?" the judge asked.

Angela shook her head and braced herself. "No, Your Honor."

Quintana peered down at the court reporter sitting beneath the bench. "Let's go off the record."

The court reporter placed her hands in her lap.

He turned to Landers. "A few weeks ago, I denied the plaintiff's spoliation motion because your client submitted a declaration stating that painting that girl's restroom was done based on a schedule and was not an attempt to cover up any evidence."

Jenny touched Angela's hand, momentarily excited about where the judge might be headed.

"I understand that a local TV station recently aired pictures of vicious taunts against the plaintiff's daughter allegedly written in a restroom stall. I'm assuming the plaintiff's counsel didn't bring this issue before the court because they were unable to verify the photographs. I'm not saying that graffiti would be enough to put the school on notice of the bullying, but I do want to communicate that I'm quite concerned that fraudulent declarations may have been submitted to this court. And if that's indeed the case, I would not be happy about it."

Oh, my God. Angela was afraid to breathe. Was Quintana going to deny the motion?

"Your Honor, well...I...my client," Landers flubbed. "I can assure you that neither my clients nor I had any knowledge of that graffiti."

"For your sake, I hope that's the truth. Let's go back on the record."

The judge waited until the court reporter's hands were hovering over her machine again.

"I've decided to take defendants' motion under submission for ten days. In the interim, I'd *strongly* suggest that the parties retain a mediator and attempt to settle this case."

"There is a God," Jenny whispered.

"Your Honor!" Landers bounced up and down on his tip-toes. "We've already made a settlement offer which—"

"That's it," the judge said, banging his gavel. "Next case."

By the time they gathered in a corner down the hall, Erika and Dre were so excited they could've floated back to their cars.

"That judge knows the real deal," Dre said, nodding. "He's on our side. We're going to win this!"

"I know, I know," Erika said smiling. "I prayed so hard about this last night. God answered my prayers."

Angela took in the elation on their faces, unwilling to dash their naive excitement over how the law worked.

When Angela turned to Jenny, her friend's eyes conveyed exactly what Angela was thinking. Judge Quintana wasn't going to dismiss Landers's motion. The law and facts were decidedly in favor of the defendants. While the judge suspected that the school was involved in a cover-up, there wasn't a thing he could do about it without some admissible evidence to back up that suspicion. Judge Quintana was simply applying a little judicial pressure to help Erika get a decent settlement.

And Angela had no confidence whatsoever that the school district would give her one.

CHAPTER

92

THE PARTIES HASTILY arranged a mediation, something neither side seemed optimistic about.

Jenny, Angela, Erika, and Dre were assembled around a circular marble table in a small conference room in Landers's Century City office.

Dre got up to take in the view from the twentieth-floor window. "So this is how you can afford to live when your job is screwing over people, huh?"

Angela softly exhaled. She hadn't wanted Dre here. His resentment would hurt more than help. But Erika had insisted.

"So how does this work again?" Erika asked softly.

"Right now, the mediator's in a separate room with Landers, the principal, and Bailey's teacher. Basically, she's going to find out how much they're willing to offer to settle this case. Then she'll ask us what we want. If the numbers don't match, it's her job to move both sides to middle ground."

"What about the truth?" Dre asked. "Isn't she going to try to find out what really happened?"

"No. Her primary job is to get us to a mutually agreeable number. Other than using the facts to point out the weaknesses in each side's case, the truth is almost irrelevant to this process."

"Then this is a big waste of time." Dre snatched a chair from the table and fell into it. "Offering Erika fifteen thousand dollars was an insult. They're probably going to come in here with another low-ball number."

"Whatever happens, everybody needs to keep their cool," Jenny warned.

Twenty minutes later Ophelia Conroy, a retired superior court judge, stepped into the room. She was a tiny woman, with an imposing presence. Rounding the table, she gave everyone a firm handshake.

"I'm assuming your attorneys have explained how this works," she said, directing her attention to Erika. "This case is quite a tragedy and I'm so sorry about the loss of your daughter. But I want everyone to understand that I'm not here to cast blame or to prove right or wrong. My goal today is to help you get a settlement you're happy with."

"So how much did they offer?" Dre demanded.

"Whoa, we're not quite there yet," Conroy said with a tight smile. "I understand the judge is going to issue his ruling on the summary judgment motion in a few days. And based on my reading of it, I suspect he's going to grant it."

Angela had been through the mediation process dozens of times. Conroy would spend the next several minutes pointing out all the weaknesses in their case, just as she had likely done with Landers and his clients. In theory, that would make both sides more amenable to settling the case.

"Is the district willing to put up at least seven figures?" Jenny asked.

The mediator pursed her lips. "That's unlikely. They're confident that they're going to prevail on their motion. So they aren't even in the six-figure range."

She began running through the cons of Erika's case when Angela interrupted her.

"We understand we have an uphill battle on the law. What's their opening number?"

Conroy looked irritated. "Fifty thousand."

"That's more than I thought they would offer," Dre said. "But it still ain't nearly enough."

"Do you think they're willing to go much higher than that?" Angela asked.

"Perhaps," she said, "but not anywhere near seven figures."

"Give us a few minutes to speak with our client," Angela said.

The mediator had barely shut the door before Erika spoke up. "I'm not taking fifty grand. My baby's life is worth more than that."

"The judge is going to dismiss the case," Angela explained. "So it's either fifty grand or nothing."

"I disagree," Erika said. "At the hearing, he was on our side. He was upset about those pictures."

Dre quickly backed her up. "I say let's roll the dice."

"I know he seemed to be on our side," Jenny tried to explain. "But judges have to follow the law. Judge Quintana was doing us a favor by delaying his decision on the motion to pressure the district to settle."

Erika and Dre, however, weren't budging. Angela asked the mediator to return and delivered Erika's decision. She wanted to end the mediation and take her chances with the judge.

Conroy expressed disappointment and tried to convince them to continue the mediation, but Erika wasn't interested.

They all trudged down the hallway, no one speaking. In the lobby of the building, Erika stepped inside a convenience store to buy some gum. As they waited for her, Zola Phillips walked toward them. At first, Zola didn't notice them. When she finally did, the teacher froze mid-stride.

"We know you sent us those photographs," Dre said, his tone non-threatening. "And we also know there's a lot more evidence that's being covered up."

Zola's eyes widened, but she didn't speak.

"Dre!" Angela said. "You can't—"

"It's not too late for you to do the right thing," he continued. "Bailey doesn't deserve this."

Zola took a single step back. Before Dre could say another word, she spun around and charged off in the opposite direction.

"That woman knows something," Dre insisted, staring after her. "And you'll never be able to convince me otherwise."

CHAPTER

93

FOR THE NEXT week, Angela and Jenny checked the court docket several times a day to see if Judge Quintana had posted his decision. On the morning of the tenth day, the decision still had not appeared.

"Maybe this is good news," Jenny said. "Maybe he's trying to find a way to help us win."

"Yeah, right," Angela muttered. "Whatever you're smoking, stop it."

Jenny laughed and Angela found herself joining in.

If Judge Quintana granted the motion, they could always appeal, but that would be nothing more than an intellectual exercise. They didn't have a valid basis for an appeal.

"Let's get something to eat," Jenny suggested. "I have a taste for barbecue."

Angela stood up to stretch. "Sounds good."

She bent down to retrieve her purse when her desk phone rang. Her face paled when she read the caller ID.

"Who is it?" Jenny asked.

"Landers."

Angela didn't make a move to answer the call.

"You're not going to pick up?"

"I don't want to speak to him. Let him leave a message."

"He could be calling to congratulate us on blocking his summary motion."

"No way. He'd be more likely to call if he won."

The phone rang four more times before going to voicemail.

"You're not going to listen to his voicemail either?"

Angela stared at the blinking red light on her phone. "Nope. Let's go eat first."

"Stop acting like a scaredy-cat. At least check the court docket again. Maybe the decision is in."

Angela reluctantly sat back down and pecked a few keys on her desktop computer. "Yep. The decision is posted." She slumped back in her leather chair.

"So open it."

Angela attempted to swallow, but her throat was too dry. As she clicked on the document, Jenny leaned over her shoulder, both of them peering at the screen.

In the matter of Erika Lewis v. Parker Elementary School, et al., Defendants' Motion for Summary Judgment is granted.

Neither woman made a sound. Angela hit a button on her desk phone and played Landers's voicemail message.

Hello, counselor! Don't know if you've got word yet, but our motion was granted. Just wanted you to know the school district has decided not to go after your client for costs. I guess that's it.

"Asshole," Angela muttered. "He could've sent an email."

Jenny sat back down. "I was really hoping against hope."

A sly smile appeared on Angela's face. "I have an offer for you. I'll deliver the news to Erika if you tell Dre."

"I don't think so," Jenny said laughing. "And I'm vetoing barbecue. We need to go someplace with alcohol. How about Mexican food? I could use a giant-size margarita."

"Sounds like a plan."

As they stood to leave, once again, the phone rang. Angela was about to let it go to voicemail, but something made her pick up.

"Hello?"

"I have some evidence in the Bailey Lewis case," said a male voice.

Angela sat back down and put the call on speakerphone.

"Who is this?"

"I don't want to say just yet."

Angela looked at Jenny.

"What kind of evidence do you have?"

"Evidence that the school—mainly the principal—lied to the court."

"Okay. Can you send us this evidence?"

"I'd like to meet with you. In person."

"That's fine," Angela said. "When are you available?"

"I can be at your office by five."

CHAPTER

94

DARCELLA WAS REVIEWING the school's latest state test scores when Ethan Landers called.

"It's a done deal," he said, unable to contain his excitement.

Darcella snatched off her glasses. "Are you telling me what I think you're telling me?"

"I sure am. Case dismissed."'

Darcella shook her fist in the air. "Hallelujah. This nightmare is over!"

"Yes, it is. Can you get away to celebrate with me?" Ethan said in a seductively husky voice. "I need a fix of the sexiest woman on the planet."

Darcella giggled like a teenager as she glanced at her calendar. "I can make it to our spot by seven."

"No. I need to see you now. Right now."

She giggled again. "It's the middle of the day, Ethan. I can't just leave."

"Sure you can. You're the head honcho. You can do whatever you want."

"I have a four o'clock meeting that I can't miss. And there's no way I can make it all the way down to the Four Seasons and back by then."

"Then meet me at the Airport Hilton. That's only fifteen minutes from the school. I'll have lunch waiting."

Ethan's pleading made her tingle all over. The idea of a lunchtime tryst sounded so exciting. They'd never done that before.

"Pretty please. I'll bring some pictures of my friend's place in the Cayman Islands."

"You're not playing fair," Darcella teased.

"How can I when I'm dying to hold you in my arms again? If you come, I promise to make you come."

Darcella giggled. "Okay, okay."

An hour later, they were relaxing on lawn chairs on the balcony of the Airport Hilton's penthouse suite, having satisfied their sexual hunger as well as their appetites.

"I'm so glad that case is over and done with," Freeman said. "And I owe it all to you.

"Yes, you do."

"Is there any chance of them filing an appeal?"

"They're free to do that, but they don't have any valid grounds. Put the case out of your pretty little head. The only thing I want you to think about right now is me."

Freeman stepped up to the edge of the balcony and stared down at the city below. Ethan walked up behind her and kissed her slender neck. "You're so beautiful."

"I don't think I'll ever get tired of hearing you say that."

He lifted her sheer teddy and pressed himself against her bare ass.

"I could make love to you nonstop for the rest of the day."

"I bet you could. But I have a four o'clock meeting, remember?"

He nuzzled her earlobe. "Cancel your meeting. Let's make it an all-nighter."

"Ethan, you're going to cost me my job."

"So what? If they fire you, I'll represent you for free and get you millions."

"I'm going to hold you to that. But I really have to go."

"No, you don't." He snaked his left arm around her waist and used his right hand to massage her stomach. As his fingers crawled lower and lower, she gasped with pleasure.

"C'mon," he whispered into her ear. "You know you want more of this. I certainly do."

CHAPTER

95

FOR NEARLY TWO hours, the male caller sat in Angela's office sharing his shocking story.

By the time the talking stopped, Angela's mind was whirling like an out of control ceiling fan.

The new facts were more than enough to get the spoliation motion reversed and the dismissal of their case set aside. Darcella Freeman could also be facing perjury charges. Too bad the man didn't have any concrete evidence linking Landers to the principal's shenanigans.

Angela and Jenny stepped out of the conference room and headed back to Angela's office to speak privately.

"I can't believe it," Jenny said.

"I can. Darcella Freeman is pure evil. She cared more about her career than making sure Bailey was protected. I think we should go straight to the media with this."

"Agreed," Jenny replied, "but not CNN."

"Why not?"

"We don't have a week for the producer to do her fact-checking and squeeze us in between the political news. Let's call Yang. I bet he can help us get this story on KCAL tonight. We can promise him an exclusive for his newspaper."

"You're right," Angela said. "Even if KCAL runs it first, CNN may still pick it up later."

"Not just CNN. This story will go viral. Should we call Erika?"

Angela shook her head. "Not yet. Let's make some calls to be sure KCAL's on board before the man has a change of heart."

Two hours later, Angela and Jenny drove the man to KCAL studios, where they were scheduled to be guests on the ten o'clock broadcast. They were sitting in the green room, when a young producer walked in.

"We'll have all three of you on set," she said, looking down at an iPad. "I'll run through the questions with you in just a second. I'll be right back."

"How are you doing?" Angela asked, after the producer left. "Are you okay?" She couldn't shake the fear that any minute he might bolt from the room.

"I'm fine. This is the right thing to do."

After reviewing the questions with them, the producer escorted them into the studio and positioned them in tall chairs around the anchor desk.

"Just relax." The news anchor flashed a comforting smile. "Keep your focus on me and forget about all these lights and cameras."

They nodded.

"Okay," the floor director called out, raising his hand in the air. "We're on in five...four...three..."

The anchor's smile disappeared, replaced by a solemn stare.

Good evening. For several weeks now, we've been following a lawsuit filed against Parker Elementary School by a mother who alleged that bullying pushed her nine-year-old daughter to take her own life.

And now, in this exclusive report, a whistleblower has come forward with shocking allegations that the school's principal engaged in a blatant cover-up.

CHAPTER

96

DARCELLA AND ETHAN lay sprawled on opposite sides of the bed, exhausted from hours of blissful lovemaking. Not only did Darcella skip her four o'clock meeting, Ethan begged her to stay overnight. When she protested that she didn't have a change of clothes, he'd treated her to a shopping spree on Rodeo Drive.

Around ten that night, Darcella's phone dinged with a text message. She ignored it. Then it dinged again. And again and again. The succession of text messages came in so fast they sounded like a musical selection.

"What the hell?" Darcella grabbed the phone from the nightstand.

"Oh, my God!" she gasped as she read the growing string of texts. It was as if everyone she knew was texting her at the same time. "Oh, my God!"

Ethan groggily propped himself up on his elbows. "What's going on? Did something happen at school?"

"Where's the remote?" Darcella scampered naked around the room.

"What's going on?" Ethan asked again.

"KCAL is running another story on that stupid case. Don't they know it's been dismissed?"

"Calm down." He spotted the remote and handed it to her.

Darcella flicked on the TV.

My name is Malcolm Lawson. I've been a fifth-grade teacher at Parker Elementary for over nine years.

Tell us why you're here today.

I've been following the lawsuit filed by the mother of Bailey Lewis. It's a shame what happened to her. My wife was the one who convinced me that I had to come forward. So I'm here to tell you everything I know about the cover-up by the school's principal, Darcella Freeman. And it's pretty ugly."

"You fuckin traitor!" Darcella yelled at the screen. "I trusted you!" Ethan was fully awake now, sitting on the edge of the bed.

One of my students complained to me that she was getting a headache from smelling the paint in the girl's restroom. I was surprised that the restroom had been painted. They never paint during the school year because so many kids have allergies and sensitivities. And I knew for a fact that they'd painted that restroom a month before school started. So I spoke to Damien Miller. He's the custodian who did the painting. After a little cajoling, he told me that our principal ordered him to paint it. He said she did it to cover up graffiti about Bailey Lewis. He showed me some pictures he took before he started painting.

The screen switched to a wide shot of the inside door of the restroom stall, then zoomed in for a closeup of the words, *Everybody hates Bailey. Just kill yourself.*

So you're alleging the principal knew those vicious threats were in that restroom stall and forced the custodian to participate in a cover-up?

Yep. She also made Damien sign a false declaration claiming the bathroom was already scheduled to be painted. He was the one who sent the pictures to Bailey Lewis's mother. Damien also saw that little girl being bullied multiple times and reported it to the principal. Freeman told him that if he didn't keep his mouth shut, she would claim she'd seen him put his hand underneath a student's dress. He was scared to death of being framed for child molestation. I was so disgusted about the principal's behavior, I had to come forward.

As Darcella stared at the TV, she wasn't sure she would ever be able to breathe again. The idiot hadn't just ruined her career. He'd destroyed her life.

"Is any of that stuff true?" Ethan asked, furious. "Did you really do that?"

"Oh, shut up," she snapped. "I was doing what I had to do."

"I don't believe this!" He hopped off the bed and snatched his boxers from a nearby chair. "I can't believe you forced that custodian to sign a fraudulent declaration. Judge Quintana will think I was in on this. What you did could get me disbarred."

"This is not about you, okay?"

"Like hell it isn't! And when the time comes, you better make it damn clear that I played no part in any of this."

"Don't you dare stand there acting like you didn't know what was really going on."

"What?" Ethan almost lost his balance as he struggled to step into his slacks. "Are you crazy?"

"You may not have known the specifics, but you knew you weren't getting the full story from me. You would have to be stupid not to know. That's the reason you never asked me any probing questions. You were too busy trying to get into my panties. Can you also get disbarred for screwing your client? Maybe I'll report *that* to the state bar."

"You're nuts!" Ethan zipped up his pants and threw on his shirt. "You're going to have to find yourself another attorney. And it's going to be on your dime because I doubt the school district will pay for it. Threatening an employee and covering up evidence are definitely outside the course and scope of your employment."

Panic spread across Darcella's face. "I don't want another attorney. I want you. You can get me out of this."

"Lady, there's not an attorney alive who could save you."

Darcella grabbed his forearm. "Ethan, wait. I need you to—"

He shoved her away as if repulsed by her touch. Snatching his wallet from the nightstand, he stuffed it into his back pocket and stomped out of the bedroom.

"C'mon, Ethan, you have to hear me out," she begged, trailing after him. "Please, Ethan. Just hold on a minute. Let me explain."

Darcella's tearful pleas went unanswered as Landers opened the door of the hotel suite and slammed it in her face.

CHAPTER

97

ZOLA AND BROCK sat on their couch dazed and motionless, seemingly hypnotized by the television screen. The revelations coming from the mouth of Malcolm Lawson were better than a plot twist in a big-budget movie.

The day Darcella accused Zola of sending the restroom pictures to Bailey's mother, she'd immediately called Brock, who swore he hadn't sent them to her. Zola suspected that maybe Damien had, but she didn't know for sure. As she watched the newscast, Zola was stunned to learn that Damien had also witnessed Bailey being bullied and had reported it to the principal.

After Malcolm finished telling his story, the anchor turned to Angela Evans.

What's the current status of the case?

Unfortunately, it was dismissed earlier today. Of course, we had no idea about this evidence. We plan to file a motion asking the judge to set aside the dismissal based upon this new evidence.

What are your chances of prevailing?

Because we now have proof of the principal's blatant cover-up of crucial evidence, we're very hopeful that the case will eventually proceed to trial and Bailey's mother will receive justice.

The interview ended and the anchor tossed to a commercial break.

Brock reached for the remote and muted the TV. "Well, you have to feel better now, right?" he said to Zola.

"Better?" Zola's voice trembled. "Why in the world would I feel better?"

"Because your principal's going to get what she deserves. And you won't be implicated."

"That doesn't make me feel good! If anything, I feel worse. I'm embarrassed that Malcolm, of all people, had the courage to do what I couldn't."

Brock took her hand. "You shouldn't look at it like that. You heard that attorney. The bottom line is Bailey's mother is finally going to get justice."

"And I could've made sure that happened weeks ago," she said, tears flowing. "I made her loss a whole lot worse than it had to be."

Zola pressed her head against Brock's chest and wept.

"The case is going to trial. You'll get your chance to help her then."

"Everybody's going to attack me for being as much of a liar as the principal. If she gets charged with perjury, I will too!"

"Everything's going to work out."

Zola pulled away from him. "No, it's not. You don't know that woman. She'll lie on me. If she goes down, she's going to make sure I go down with her."

98

"I'M GOING TO say this one more time. I strongly recommend that you don't do this."

Darcella leered at the attorney standing in her kitchen, talking to her like she was an errant child.

"You've said that more than once," Darcella bristled. "This is still what I want to do. It's my reputation on the line. Not yours."

Everything about Monty Clark irked her. His small stature, his cheap suit, his beady, roving eyes. He was nothing like Ethan Landers.

Because of Malcolm and Damien's stupidity, Darcella had been placed on administrative leave and forced to retain her own counsel. Clark was the best her money could buy.

"But this is not going to help you," he insisted. "You're better off fighting the case in court. Not this way."

"Malcolm's interview is all over the internet. People are making me out to be a villain. I have to fight back."

As they stubbornly squared off, a KCAL cameraman was busy setting up his equipment in Darcella's living room.

Erika Lewis's bullycide lawsuit was now a national headline and Darcella Freeman was at the center of it. There were even trending hashtags targeted at her: #PrincipalNoMore, #PrincipalFromHell, and the one she hated most, #PrincipalWithNoPrinciple.

The cameraman stepped into the kitchen and asked Darcella to have a seat on the couch so he could frame his shot.

"When is the reporter getting here?" Darcella asked as she sat down.

"I just got a text. She's five minutes away."

"I still don't understand why I couldn't be live on the set."

"That wasn't my call."

Minutes later, a young reporter floated through the front door. "Let's get started with some cutaways."

Darcella frowned. "Some what?"

"My photographer's going to shoot some pictures of me from that direction." She pointed to the side of the room where Darcella was sitting. "That way, if we need to edit the interview we can insert a few seconds of my face."

"I don't want to be edited," Darcella said, smacking her lips. "That's why I wanted to do this live."

When the cameraman finished the cutaways, he positioned himself behind the reporter, his camera aimed at Darcella. Her attorney stood leaning against the wall, shaking his head.

"Ms. Freeman, you have the notoriety of being the most hated principal in America on social media right now. How did this all come to pass?"

What?

If the camera wasn't rolling Darcella would have slapped the woman. Where was her objectivity?

She took a calming breath and smiled. "This all came to pass because an employee at my school took it upon himself to go to the media with blatant lies. He—"

"I assume you're referring to Malcolm Lawson, a teacher at Parker Elementary. He alleges that you concealed evidence that Bailey Lewis was bullied and forced another employee to sign a fraudulent declaration. Why would he make that up?"

"You'll have to ask him about his motivation for lying. I'm just telling you nothing he said was true. At no time did Damien Miller tell me about that graffiti or notify me that Bailey Lewis was being bullied. If someone had, I would've put an immediate stop to it. Parker Elementary is a California Distinguished School, which means—"

"So you're saying you weren't aware of the graffiti in the girl's restroom?"

"That's correct."

"And you didn't force the custodian to sign that declaration."

Darcella sat up even straighter. "No, I did not. And you won't find any evidence to the contrary—other than Damien's blatant lies—because none exists."

"Is it true that the school district has placed you on administrative leave?"

"Only temporarily. Once the district completes its investigation vindicating me, I'll be filing a lawsuit against both Malcolm Lawson and Damien Miller for defamation of character."

The reporter asked three more questions, then ended the interview.

"Wait a minute," Darcella protested. "I still have a few more things to say."

"I'm so sorry. I have another story to cover. We have to run."

Within minutes, the reporter and cameraman were all packed up.

"Your producer told me the story will air on tonight's five o'clock broadcast," Darcella said, following them to the door.

"I doubt it'll run tonight. There's another crazy car chase going on right now," the reporter said. "When that happens, the whole show is scrapped. Just pray there isn't another one tomorrow."

Once they were gone, Darcella relaxed on a lounge chair on her patio, sipping a glass of red wine. It didn't taste nearly as smooth as the expensive wines she'd grown accustomed to during her trysts with Ethan.

What had she been thinking to involve an imbecile like Damien in her plan? She should've grabbed a can of paint herself and tossed it around the restroom and claimed the place had been vandalized. That would've been a much better plan to hide that graffiti. Without Malcolm's prodding, Damien probably never would've told anybody about reporting to her that Bailey had been bullied. Never in a million years would she have expected Malcolm to be the lead backstabber. She would never trust *any* man again.

As her perfectly crafted world threatened to crumble, Darcella was determined to maintain a positive attitude. She was a survivor. She would surely overcome this madness just as she had surmounted every other struggle in her life. No one could dispute that she was a talented administrator, as evidenced by the success of Parker Elementary under her leadership. Even if the school district fired her, she'd find another job in education, even if she had to leave California to do it. Hell, she might start her own charter school.

Everything would be fine.

As long as Zola Phillips continued to keep her damn mouth shut.

CHAPTER

99

THE DAY AFTER their appearance on KCAL, Angela and Jenny got to work drafting their brief to set aside the dismissal of Erika's case.

Damien Miller provided them with a new declaration recanting the one Ethan Landers had submitted to the court. They'd also helped the custodian retain an attorney who agreed to represent him *pro bono,* in the event he faced perjury charges. If the school district was dumb enough to fire him, he'd have a great retaliation case.

To their delight, Damien also gave them the names of three teachers who also reported instances of bullying of other children to the principal. Each one claimed Darcella Freeman downplayed their concerns for fear of jeopardizing the school's status as a California Distinguished School. Once the case was revived, they planned to subpoena the teachers for depositions.

"This is pretty good," Angela said, reading the section of the brief Jenny had drafted.

"Thank you very much, counselor." Jenny tapped the document she was holding. "Your arguments are pretty darn amazing too."

In the past few days, they'd been swamped with media inquiries. A dozen invitations for speaking engagements came in and twice that many calls from parents from all over the country who wanted to sue their child's school. They were getting so many calls that they had to team up with Sidney Meltzer to handle the volume. Angela didn't want to make bullycide cases her specialty. She preferred to represent bullied kids *before* they acted out of desperation.

Angela's assistant stepped into the office and shut the door behind her.

"You two must be the luckiest attorneys alive."

Jenny glanced up at her. "What's that big grin on your face all about? You look like you're about to burst."

"I am," Gina said, her smile so wide it threatened to stretch off her face. "Someone has some additional evidence for Erika's case."

"Who?" Angela and Jenny said in unison.

"Bailey's teacher, Zola Phillips."

Jenny stood up. "Are you kidding? Is she on the phone? Put the call through."

"She's not on the phone." Gina pointed a thumb over her shoulder. "She's right out there in the lobby. So is her husband."

Angela's brain struggled to process what Gina was telling them. "Are you serious?"

"As five heart attacks."

Jenny darted for the door, ready to head out to the lobby to greet them.

"Hold on," Angela said, stopping her. "We can't talk to her. She's a defendant in this case and she's represented by counsel."

"After all the stunts Landers pulled on us, now is not the time for us to start acting like saints."

Angela got to her feet. "C'mon, Jenny. It's best to play this by the book."

"It's not like *we* approached *her*," Jenny insisted. "She came to us."

Angela hesitated, then turned to Gina. "Tell them to give us a minute."

"What are you doing?" Jenny asked, as Angela started tapping keys on her computer.

"I need to research this to make sure it won't come back to haunt us. I don't want Judge Quintana to have any reason to be pissed off at us when we walk back into his courtroom."

Jenny fell into her chair and stewed. "I don't believe this."

Five minutes later, Angela glanced across her desk at her friend. "According to the ABA rules, we can't talk to Zola. At least not without Landers's consent."

"Have you lost your mind?" Jenny yelled. "Are you telling me we're not going to hear what she has to say? Show me the rule. I want to read it for myself."

Angela turned the computer screen around until it faced Jenny.

ABA Rule 4.2 Communication with Person Represented by Counsel

In representing a client, a lawyer shall not communicate about the subject of the representation with a person the lawyer knows to be represented by another lawyer in the matter, unless the lawyer has the consent of the other lawyer or is authorized to do so by law or a court order.

"Crap." Jenny still wasn't ready to give up. "I don't think that applies if we didn't initiate the contact. Zola came to us."

Angela turned the monitor back around, patiently scrolled down the screen, and highlighted a single paragraph.

"Read this." She turned the screen back toward Jenny.

The rule applies even though the represented person initiates or consents to the communication.

"It's not worth it to push the envelope on this," Angela insisted.

"Okay, fine. We can't talk to Zola, but there's nothing preventing us from talking to her husband. I bet he knows everything."

Angela thought for a moment, then browsed the screen again. "Nope. The husband would be considered Zola's agent. Talking to him about what Zola knows would be prohibited as well."

"Give me a freakin' break!"

"Hold on," Angela said. "I have an idea."

She picked up the phone and buzzed Gina. "Bring in Mr. Phillips. Tell him we want to talk to him. Alone."

Seconds later, Gina escorted Brock Phillips into the office. He took a seat in front Angela's desk, adjacent to the sulking Jenny. Zola's husband appeared to be as young as she was. The uncertainty in his eyes undercut the confidence of his dark gray suit and military-rigid posture.

"I understand from my assistant that your wife has some evidence she wants to share with us," Angela began. "Unfortunately, there's a rule that prevents us from talking to her because she's represented by counsel."

Brock's face twisted up as if he was in pain. "Are you serious? Zola saw Damien's interview on Channel 9. She's ready to come clean about everything. There's still a lot you don't know."

"I'm sorry," Angela said. "It wouldn't be appropriate. Whatever evidence Zola has, she should give it to Ethan Landers."

Brock threw up his hands. "This is nuts! Zola wants to talk to the two of you. Not him. He's nothing but a whore for the school district. Zola has recordings. Recordings of Darcella Freeman. He'll probably destroy them."

Recordings?

Angela swallowed and tried to ignore Jenny's pleading eyes. She wouldn't put it past Ethan to do exactly that. Regardless, she refused to stoop to his level.

"I don't believe this," Brock said, rubbing his forehead. "Zola finally gathered the courage to come here, and now you're telling me you don't want to hear what she has to say?"

"For the record, I don't agree with her," Jenny said in a salty voice. "I think—"

Angela raised both palms in the air as if she were trying to tamp down the tension in the room. "Hold on. There is another option. That rule only applies to lawyers, not to their clients."

A mischievous smile danced across Angela's lips. "So there's nothing preventing Zola from telling Bailey's mother everything she knows."

CHAPTER

100

ANGELA AND JENNY barricaded themselves in Angela's office, waiting for Erika's call. They'd ordered Cobb salads for lunch, but the food sat untouched as they watched the phone as if it were a priceless jewel under threat of theft.

"Maybe they changed their minds," Jenny said, fidgeting.

"I doubt it. Zola's husband was dying to get everything off his chest. I'm sure she was too."

Angela had given the couple the address to Erika's home in Baldwin Hills. Erika promised to call as soon as their meeting ended.

Three hours and fifteen minutes later, Erika's name flashed on the screen of Angela's cell phone. She answered before the second ring.

"Tell us everything," Angela said, placing the call on speakerphone.

"You won't believe this," Erika said, breathless. "It's far worse than we ever imagined."

As Erika began to recap her conversation with Zola and her husband, both attorneys grabbed a legal pad and started jotting down notes.

"Did they play the recordings for you?" Angela asked.

"They didn't just play them for me. They gave me a flash drive with a copy of everything. Listen to this."

As they listened, Angela and Jenny went from shaking their heads to cupping their mouths in astonishment.

"You couldn't make this stuff up," Angela said.

Jenny nodded. "I wouldn't want to be in Ethan Landers's shoes when we go back to court. Judge Quintana is going to be extremely pissed."

For several minutes after ending the call, the two women sat facing each other, stunned into stillness.

Jenny was the first to break the silence. "I guess Dre's going to be one happy camper tonight."

"That would be true." Angela started straightening up her desk. "I'm almost afraid to leave the office. What if another witness walks in ready to tell all?"

Jenny laughed. "That might give me a heart attack." She eyed Angela with a cagey smirk. "There's somebody else we need to talk to."

"Who?"

"Ethan Landers."

Angela smiled. "For what? To throw sand in his face?"

"Yep."

Angela handed Jenny the receiver and dialed. "Go for it, counselor."

When Landers answered, Jenny took great pleasure in advising him that they planned to file a motion to set aside the dismissal based on concealment of evidence.

"That custodian is lying," Landers said, his bravado still on full throttle. "It's his word against the principal's and she has far more credibility than he does. And if the judge does set aside the dismissal, I'm more than prepared to try the case."

Liar, liar pants on fire, Angela thought.

"I doubt you'll want to go to trial when you see the additional evidence we have," Jenny taunted him. "Or should I say, *hear* the evidence?"

"Is that right?"

"Yes, that's right. We now have irrefutable proof that Darcella Freeman submitted a false declaration to the court. Proof in the form of her voice on tape. As a courtesy, we'll be sending over a copy for your listening pleasure."

Landers audibly gulped.

"And after you take a listen, I'm sure you'll be talking to your clients about settling the case. And your opening offer should be at least seven figures."

Landers chuckled. "This must be some awfully good evidence."

"Trust me, it is. Your client is definitely going down for perjury. And if you were part of her little cover-up, you'll be going down right along with her."

"I've been completely ethical in my handling of this case. I knew absolutely nothing about the principal's conduct."

"Hmmm," Jenny continued, having way too much fun. Angela could tell from the gleam in her eyes exactly what she was going to say next. "Forgive me if I'm a little skeptical about that since you've been sleeping with her."

Landers sputtered like a car on empty. "I...I...when will I see this so-called evidence?"

Jenny flashed Angela a knowing look. He didn't even try to deny his affair with the principal. So Dre was right.

"You'll see it soon enough," Jenny said. "If you don't want to wait for us to send it, talk to your client Zola Phillips. I understand she's preparing a little evidentiary gift bag for you as we speak."

"If you've been talking to my client without my permission, I'll report you to the bar! I need to know what evidence you have," Landers demanded. "Right now."

"I'm sorry, but you're not calling the shots anymore."

She slammed down the phone and gave Angela a high-five.

"That felt soooo good," Jenny gushed. "I think I deserve a margarita."

101

DARCELLA WAS MORE than psyched. It had been two days since the reporter taped her interview, leaving her to wonder if they ever planned to run the story. But all afternoon, KCAL had been teasing it.

Principal in bullycide lawsuit
goes on the offensive. Story at six.

The shot of Darcella sitting on her living room couch looked pretty amazing if she said so herself. She was glad she'd chosen her fuchsia Carolina Herrera blazer, setting it off with pearls and a light pink, matte lipstick.

Finally, the public was going to hear her side of this awful story.

Earlier that morning, Blanca had called to check on her. "How are you doing?"

"I'm great. Thanks for asking. I'm enjoying the time off. I'm sure I'll be back at work in no time. How's Ms. Anderson doing?"

A vice principal from another elementary school in the district had taken over as interim principal.

Blanca snorted. "She's running around here like a chicken with her head cut off."

Good, Darcella thought. *Let them miss me.*

As Darcella had expected, Blanca confirmed that the rumor mill was running rampant. She was just grateful that Zola Phillips was still playing along.

At ten minutes to six, Darcella grabbed a glass of red wine and a bowl of popcorn and positioned herself in front of the big screen TV in the den. Her story was the lead.

After the anchor read a short intro, the shot widened to include the reporter who'd interviewed her, standing to the right of the anchor desk.

Our investigative reporter, Jana Villanova is joining me live on set with an update. Jana, what's the latest?

The reporter looked much prettier than she had the other day. The wonders of a good makeup job. The camera moved in for a closeup.

As we've been reporting, the increase in child suicides linked to bullying is on the rise nationwide. In a bullycide lawsuit filed against Parker Elementary School, there have been shocking allegations of a cover-up by the principal of that school, Darcella Freeman. I sat down with Ms. Freeman to discuss the case. Tonight, she seeks to set the record straight.

Darcella took a sip of wine. "I love it!"

The piece included several soundbites from Freeman, including her vehement denial of the allegations. By the time it ended, Darcella was almost cheering. The reporter closed her story with a strong soundbite from Darcella.

The education of children has been my life's work. I love what I do and once these fraudulent allegations have been investigated and I've been vindicated, I look forward to returning to Parker Elementary to resume my spotless career.

Darcella raised her wineglass in the air. "Now *that's* what I'm talking about." She grabbed a handful of popcorn and tossed a few kernels into her mouth.

But seconds into her celebration, Darcella saw something on the screen so shocking that her hands began to tremble. Her wineglass slipped from her grasp, crashing against the shiny maple floor.

Zola Phillips was live on set, sitting inches away from the news anchor.

You're a teacher at Parker Elementary School and you're also a defendant in this lawsuit. Is that correct?

Yes. And what you just aired in that piece isn't the truth. Our principal was not a champion of children. I made repeated reports to her about Bailey Lewis being bullied. And she ignored me every time, simply because she feared an investigation might mar the school's reputation.

You're making some pretty serious allegations here.

They're not allegations, they're fact. I have recordings of the principal that back up everything I'm saying.

"You stupid bitch!" Darcella hurled the bowl of popcorn across the room.

A recording began to play as the screen filled with a transcript of their words.

Darcella Freeman: This case will probably be dismissed in a few days. You need to keep your mouth shut. At least you had the good sense to send those pictures anonymously.

Zola Phillips: As I said, I didn't do that. And if you did nothing wrong, exactly what am I keeping my mouth shut about?

Darcella Freeman: Don't try to bait me. You know what I'm talking about.

Zola Phillips: Oh, you mean my reporting that child's bullying complaints to you and your choosing not to do anything about it?

Darcella Freeman: You know that and I know that, but as long as nobody else knows it, everything's going to turn out fine.

The camera returned to Zola and the anchor on set.

That was pretty shocking.

That's only a tidbit of the evidence I have.

Have you turned this evidence over to the school district?

No, not yet. I gave it to Bailey's mother first. I'm here tonight because I'm also to blame. I was too weak to stand up to the principal and get Bailey the help she needed.

The camera zoomed in as Zola began to weep.

Darcella pressed both hands to her mouth. How could Zola do this to her? She was a superior educator who cared about her students. This was so unfair!

Now it wasn't just her word against Damien's. There was no way she could refute those recordings. Her reputation was destroyed. Her career in education was over. She might even be charged with perjury.

Darcella wasn't sure how long she had sat there shaking. At some point, she rose from the couch and marched into the kitchen. She needed a drink far stronger than wine. Tequila bottle in hand, she walked back to the couch and took one sloppy swig after another.

Thirty minutes later, fueled by the alcohol, Darcella picked up her phone from the coffee table and dialed.

"If you think I'm going down by myself, you're wrong," she seethed into the phone.

"Somehow that's exactly what I expected you to say," Zola said calmly. "But you don't scare me anymore."

"You stupid little girl, why couldn't you just keep your trap shut?"

"Because it wasn't the right thing to do."

"Whatever comes down on me, is going to hit you ten times as hard. I'll make sure of that."

"But I didn't do anything wrong besides letting you intimidate me into not protecting Bailey."

"No one will believe that once I'm done telling my story. If I have to lie to make sure you go down for perjury too, I will."

"That's fine. I'll deal with it."

"Is that all you have to say?" It irked Darcella that Zola was being so matter of fact about her threats. "I'm serious. I'm coming after you."

"I know," Zola said, "that's why I'm talking to you on speakerphone. My husband is recording this call on his phone. You're a complete disgrace to the teaching profession and you deserve every bad thing that's about to happen to you."

Darcella gasped, slapped the screen of her phone ending the call, and hurled it onto the couch. She cried and shrieked in anger, yelling and pounding her fists on the couch. This was not, could not be happening to her.

She had to speak to Ethan. No one else could save her. Darcella dried her tears and picked up her phone, praying that this time, he would answer. For the past several days, all of her calls had gone straight to voicemail.

"Hello."

Darcella silently yelped with joy.

"How are you, Ethan?" She tried to muster up a sultry voice that would remind him of the incredible intimacy they'd shared.

"What do you need?"

The aloofness in his voice chilled her.

"So it's like that?"

"Yes, it's like that. What do you want?"

"I was hoping we could talk. I miss you. Maybe we could meet at the Four Seasons. I promise to make it worth your while."

When Ethan didn't respond right away, Darcella interpreted his silence as a positive. She closed her eyes and held her breath.

"C'mon, Ethan," she cooed. "You know you want some more of this. Just admit it."

"I'll pass," he said finally. "What you did was stupid. I'm not putting my career on the line for you. And by the way, I'm married. So don't call me again."

The phone went dead.

Married?

The indignation Ethan invoked in her at that moment was more intense than the animosity she felt toward her backstabbing subordinates. Ethan Landers had used her. And now he was tossing her aside like a dirty washcloth.

Darcella took in a long, deep breath, determined not to let this break her. She was strong. She was smart. She was beautiful. She was going to come out on top.

Not Ethan Landers, not the lawsuit, not even the school district would bring her down.

And as soon as this mess was over and done with, Darcella planned to look up Ethan's wife and have a nice, long chat.

EPILOGUE

In the days following Zola's appearance on KCAL, a flood of additional evidence came to light about the principal's attempts to cover up multiple instances of bullying at Parker Elementary.

Two school district psychologists and three teachers reported that the principal had pressured them to downplay clear incidents of bullying. Dr. Andrews also disclosed a disturbing call she'd had with the principal after the filing of Erika's lawsuit. According to the psychologist's handwritten notes, Freeman had ordered her to deny that she'd ever proposed convening the threat assessment team or drafting a bullying-prevention action plan for Bailey

A week after a front-page, investigative piece by Marcus Yang detailed Freeman's long history of intimidating, harassing, and retaliating against teachers and staff, her leave of absence was converted to a termination. She was charged with perjury and pleaded no contest, receiving six months' probation. As part of her plea deal, she was prohibited from ever holding a position in education.

While Malcolm walked around enjoying his hero status, Damien and Zola avoided perjury charges by providing evidence against Freeman. Damien managed to keep his job after threatening a retaliation lawsuit. Zola quietly resigned. With the help of her pastor, she landed a job teaching first-graders at a local Christian school.

During a disciplinary hearing before the state bar, Freeman testified against Landers, accusing him of pressuring her into a sexual relationship. Thankfully for him, her credibility was shot. Landers was able to prove that he had no knowledge of his clients' misconduct and received a three-month suspension for violating California

State Bar Rule 1.8.10, *Sexual Relations with Current Client.* That rule bars an attorney from having sex with a client unless the intimate relationship preceded the representation.

Angela and Jenny never got the chance to file their motion to set aside the dismissal. The story of the cover-up at Parker Elementary School went viral, airing nationally, as well as on newscasts in England, Australia, and Japan. The school district fired Landers and their new attorney offered Erika $2.5 million dollars to settle the case. She accepted. Erika used part of the settlement to create a foundation—Bailey's Gift—to educate kids and parents of color about childhood depression, bullying and suicide. She quit her job and began speaking about bullying and child suicide at schools, churches and community meetings all over the country.

Once the case was wrapped up, Dre and Angela took a short vacation. During their drive to Palm Springs, Dre said something that took Angela by surprise.

"I think I need to talk to somebody."

Angela wasn't sure she'd heard him correctly. She took her time responding. "You mean somebody like a therapist?"

"Yep."

"I think that's a great idea. "

"Erika's been bugging me about going to her grief class, but I ain't down with the group thing."

"What made you change your mind about seeing someone?"

Dre half shrugged. "I was listening to talk radio and—"

"Hold up. Since when do *you* listen to talk radio?"

He smiled. "Since never. That's why I know it had to be some kind of divine intervention. This therapist chick said something that clicked for me. She explained that the saying *Time heals all wounds* is a bunch of crap. She said an emotional trauma is like having a flat tire and not worrying about it because over time air will somehow get back into it and everything will be okay."

Angela could see that the analogy had truly resonated with Dre.

"That's crazy, of course," he continued. "And it's just as crazy to ignore grief and pretend you're not hurting, like I was doing. She said emotional healing takes work. That made a lot of sense to me."

Angela nodded. "Me too."

"I've tried, but I can't stop blaming myself for not knowing how unhappy Bailey was. I feel like I should have been able to keep her from"—he paused, still having a hard time with the word *suicide*—"from doing what she did. I didn't just fail Bailey and Erika. I also failed Earl. Big time."

"No, you didn't. It's not your fault."

"I know that in my head." His voice quivered with emotion. "But in my heart, I feel like I should've been able to save her."

Angela didn't try to offer any words of comfort. She reached over and entwined her fingers with his. Dre's willingness to talk to a therapist was huge. He was going to be okay.

They drove for several miles without speaking.

"I have something else to tell you," Dre said.

"Okay."

"Promise you won't get upset."

Angela eased her hand away from his. "What did you do, Dre?"

"Dang girl, give a brother a break. I don't know why I'm even telling you this. But I guess I just want to get it off my chest."

"Okay, I'm listening."

"A few weeks ago..." His voice trailed off.

Angela waited.

"I went to Kiya Jackson's apartment."

Angela flinched. "You what? Why would you do that?"

"Calm down. I didn't go to the door or anything. What I saw changed my whole perspective about that little girl."

Dre described the callous way Kiya's mother talked to her and how she had slapped the girl across the face.

"I felt sorry for her," he said. "She's a victim herself."

Angela nodded. "That's one of the reasons we didn't pull her into the case."

"I did something else too," Dre said, grinning.

Angela eyed him warily. "What?"

"I called Child Protective Services on her ass."

They both burst out laughing.

"I ain't mad at you for that. But promise me you won't interfere with one of my cases ever again in life."

"You got it," Dre said with a devious grin. "Now, it's your turn. You owe me an apology too."

"For what?"

"When I told you that lawyer and the principal were smashin', you didn't believe me."

"Okay," Angela said, more than contrite. "Please accept my apology." She clasped her hands in a prayer pose, then leaned over and planted a kiss on his cheek.

"Next time, you better recognize. I'm so glad they fired that principal. I only wish you could've gotten that asshole attorney disbarred. I still get pissed when I think about the questions he asked me."

"Just forget about it, Dre."

He glanced over at her again, his grin now twice as wide. "If I go down to his office and punch him in the face, will you defend me?"

"Boy, stop talking crazy."

"Never mind." He picked up his cell phone from the center console. "You ain't the only attorney I know."

"Who are you calling?"

Dre ignored her question.

"Hey, Jenny," he said, putting the call on speakerphone. "I was thinking about going over to Ethan Landers' office to kick his ass. If I catch a case, will you defend me?"

Jenny's girlish laughter filled every crevice of the car. "Absolutely. I might even go down there with you and get in a punch or two for myself. But I just have one request."

"What's that?"

"Please leave your cousin Apache at home."

AUTHOR'S NOTE

It's rare for me to remember when or how a story idea comes to me. With this book, however, I will never forget the precise moment that the plot began to percolate in my brain.

A dear friend and elementary school teacher, Pamela Goree Dancy of Marion, Alabama, told me about the tragic deaths of two beautiful, nine-year-old girls—Madison Whitsett of Birmingham, Alabama, and McKenzie Adams of Linden, Alabama. It was Christmas Day and the girls' deaths had been weighing on my friend's mind as they would soon weigh on mine.

When I read the news stories about their suicides, I was stunned. The very idea that children that young could take their own lives was incomprehensible. I couldn't stop thinking about Madison and McKenzie, and cried myself to sleep that night. The next morning, I was determined to write a novel dealing with this heartbreaking topic as a way of educating myself and my readers.

I spent the next few weeks researching bullying, childhood depression, and suicide. I read books, online materials, and talked to educators and mental health professionals. I learned that suicide among children is far more common than I realized. The Congressional Black Caucus, in fact, has identified suicide among African-American children as a national emergency and created a task force to address this health crisis.

If you think bullying is no big deal, you're wrong. If you think childhood depression is not real, you're wrong. If you think suicide can't happen to someone you love, you're wrong.

It's my hope that *Failure to Protect* moves you to action. Saving our children will require the collective efforts of each of us. Do your own research and share what you learn with family, friends and co-workers. Talk frankly to the kids in your life. Partner with schools. Volunteer with an organization.

For more information on bullying, suicide and childhood depression, I've included a few helpful resources. You can find many, many more on the internet.

RESOURCES

If you or someone you know is in distress or having suicidal thoughts, call the **National Suicide Prevention Lifeline at 1-800-273-TALK (8255)**. Callers are routed to their nearest crisis center to receive immediate counseling and local mental health referrals. The Lifeline, which is staffed 24 hours a day, is free and confidential and supports people who call for themselves or someone they care about.

Organizations

Bystander Revolution
Bystanderrevolution.org

Child Mind Institute
childmind.org

The Jed Foundation
thejedfoundation.org

Kind Campaign
kindcampaign.com

Stomp Out Bullying
stompoutbullying.org

Stop Bullying.gov
topbullying.gov

Black Mental Health Alliance
blackmentalhealth.com

National Alliance on Mental Illness
nami.org

Centers for Disease Control and Prevention
cdc.gov

National Organization for People of Color against Suicide
Nopcas.org

Books

Why People Die by Suicide
By Thomas Joiner

The Truth About Suicide
By Donna Holland Barnes

Dear Bully: Seventy Authors Tell Their Stories
Edited by Megan Kelley Hall and Carrie Jones

Bullycide in America: Moms Speak Out about the Bullying/ Suicide Connection
Compiled by Brenda High

Silent Souls Weeping: Depression-Sharing Stories, Finding Hope
By Jane Clayson Johnson

Documentaries

Bully (YouTube, Amazon, iTunes)

Audrie & Daisy (Netflix)

Boy Interrupted (Amazon, YouTube)

The Bully Effect (YouTube, Cartoon Network)

Not Alone (Netflix)

If You Only Knew: The Journey Through Teen Depression and Suicide (Amazon)

READING GROUP QUESTIONS
FOR *FAILURE TO PROTECT*

1. What meaningful steps can teachers and principals take to prevent bullying in schools?

2. Were you ever bullied in school or has a child in your life been bullied? If so, how did you handle it?

3. Is bullying a bigger problem now than it was years ago? Or is it just that we pay more attention to it today?

4. Do you believe teachers and school administrators should be held legally responsible for failing to protect children from bullying?

5. Do you believe social media is partly to blame for the increase in bullying and child suicides?

6. Do you agree or disagree with Dre's view that today's children are shielded from the realities of life to their detriment?

7. Is the threat of a lawsuit an effective tool for making teachers and principals more accountable for preventing bullying?

8. What can be done to make people more aware of childhood depression?

9. What can be done to encourage people to pay as much attention to their mental health as their physical health?

10. Does the fact that some religions view suicide as a sin hamper us from dealing with suicide in a more open and honest manner?

11. Should Kiya Jackson and her mother have been included as defendants in the lawsuit despite their lack of financial resources?

12. How do you feel about the gentrification of many African-American neighborhoods across the country? Are you pro, con or neutral?

13. Would you be comfortable with your mate having a close female friend like Erika?

14. Have you ever felt pressured by a superior to refrain from reporting something that violated the law or your company's policies? How would you have handled Zola's situation with the principal?

15. What did you like most/least about *Failure to Protect?*

If you enjoyed *Failure to Protect,* be sure to check out Pamela's other novels, which are available in print, e-book, and audio book formats everywhere books are sold. Here's an excerpt of one of her popular legal thrillers.

IN FIRM PURSUIT

PROLOGUE

KAREN CARRUTHERS HAD never thought much of women who filed sexual harassment claims. A woman who couldn't hold her own with a man—any man—simply didn't have balls. But now, Karen was one of them.

Gripping the gearshift of her convertible Mustang Cobra, Karen pressed down hard on the gas and didn't let up until the speedometer hovered near eighty-five. At this time of the day—only minutes before sunrise—L.A.'s 405 Freeway resembled the flatlands of some Midwestern highway. The road was all hers, so she took it.

Whenever trouble loomed, Karen did the one thing that soothed her. She drove. For the past few weeks, anxiety had crept into her every thought and buried itself there. But during her freedom drives, as she liked to call them, she felt fearless. Invigorated. Fulfilled. All those *empowering* words her therapist insisted that she *embrace*.

As the Mustang glided past ninety, the crisp air fanned Karen's face and she inhaled a healthy gulp that a New Yorker would have considered warm for a February. Despite the cool temperature, she felt a hot exhilarating rush. Not all that different from what she experienced during sex. Really great sex.

Zooming past the Santa Monica exchange in a nearly drunken state of euphoria now, Karen almost missed the Mulholland exit. Imitating a stunt she'd seen in a Bruce Willis movie, she laterally zipped across three lanes, just in time to make it to the off ramp. As Karen ascended the short incline to the traffic light ahead, she combed her fingers through her thick mass of strawberry blond hair, then rubbed her emerald green eyes.

When Karen first reported her allegations of sexual harassment against Henry Randle, she had expected that the man would be fired. But she had not anticipated that Randle would turn around and sue Micronics Corporation. Now, Karen was her company's star witness in his wrongful termination case. A case she wanted nothing to do with.

Leaning forward, Karen pressed the CD button and began singing along with Faith Hill. Not until she had made a left onto Skirball Center Drive and a right onto Mulholland, did she notice the black sedan a couple of car lengths behind. A longer glimpse in her rearview mirror told her that the car was a BMW with a lone occupant inside. Karen punched off Faith mid-chorus and picked up speed. Her pulse did the same. She passed the University of Judaism at close to seventy. The sedan sped up as well.

And then it hit her. *The documents!* Karen snatched her purse from the passenger's seat, fished out an envelope, and stuffed it down her sweater and into her bra. She had known all along that they would eventually come looking for the documents. Feeling them against her skin sent an icy chill through her body.

Karen inhaled and tried to think clearly as trepidation gradually sucked the air from her lungs. The two-mile stretch of Mulholland that lay ahead was interspersed on both sides with outrageously expensive homes and cliffs with made-for-Hollywood views. A sharp turn down one of the long driveways would leave her trapped, making her an easy target for her pursuer. A wrong turn in the opposite direction could send her into a nosedive off one of the cliffs, finishing the job for them.

Though fear now coursed through every vein in Karen's body, an odd smile graced her lips. There was no way the BMW would be able to keep up. Her breathing slowed ever so slightly after another glance in the mirror confirmed that her pursuer was losing ground. Karen had cruised Mulholland so many times she could almost drive it blindfolded. She only had to make it down the hill to Beverly

Glen. Somebody was bound to be walking a dog or taking an early morning jog. *They* would not want witnesses.

Karen patted her breast, confirming that the envelope was still there. Still safe. Just then, another car shot out of a driveway several hundred yards ahead and Karen's heart slammed against her chest. Instinct told her the BMW to her rear was not working alone. She anxiously felt for the envelope again and concentrated on her next move.

She took another quick glance in the rearview mirror. *The BMW wasn't there.* When she looked to her left, her eyes bore across the empty passenger seat of the BMW and directly into the barrel of a gun.

Time froze for a second, then a piercing scream left Karen's lips, reverberating into the early morning air. Karen stomped on the brakes and the BMW, unprepared for her sudden stop, darted ahead, just as she had anticipated.

What happened next, however, had not been part of Karen's plan.

She jerked the steering wheel sharply to the left and hit the gas. But instead of making a full U-turn, the Mustang headed off the road, straight toward a thin patch of bushes where a guardrail should have been.

Karen's hands flew to her face, barely muffling her futile screams.

For what seemed like minutes rather than seconds, the Mustang floated across the reddish-orange sky like a wonderfully woven magic carpet. After a moment of calm, Karen felt the sharp pull of gravity, then braced herself for a landing that turned daybreak into darkness.

CHAPTER 1

"THIS CASE SHOULD be settled," barked the Honorable Frederick H. Sloan. The judge's demanding baritone required a response even though no question had been posed.

I looked over at Reggie Jenkins, my spineless opposing counsel, seated to my left in the judge's private chambers. The petrified expression on his face told me I would have to speak for the both of us.

"Your Honor," I began, knowing how much judges loved to hear that salutation, "we're just too far apart. My client is ready and willing to try this case."

Judge Sloan rolled up the sleeves of his crisp, white shirt, revealing more of his flawless tan. Most of the federal judges who sat on the bench in California's Central District did not fit the typical stereotype of a jurist. Sloan was both tall and handsome and had probably hit the gym during the lunch hour. If it weren't for his lush grey hair, it would have been hard to tell that he had bypassed sixty a few years back.

"How about you, counselor?" The judge swiveled his chair away from me and zeroed in on my opponent. "Are you prepared to try this case, too?"

Jenkins inhaled and scratched the back of his neck. A chubby, middle-aged black man, he had chronically chapped lips and wore a short Afro that always looked uncombed. His beige linen suit needed a good pressing and his tie was as crooked as he was.

"Oh, no, Your Honor." Jenkins cracked the knuckles of his right hand against the palm of his left. "I don't like wasting the taxpayers' time and money."

I wanted to bop Reggie on the head with my purse. He settled all of his cases because he was too incompetent to go to trial.

Judge Sloan swung back to me and smiled heartily. "I've seen very few cases that were slam dunks. You sure you want to try this case, little lady?"

Little lady? I hated it when judges talked to me like I was some bimbo. After only eight years of practice, I had some pretty impressive stats on my Bar card. I was a senior associate at O'Reilly & Finney, one of the most respected trial firms in L.A. I had also won a five-million dollar verdict in a race discrimination case and defended a high-profile murder case. But taking crap from judges was par for the course.

Before I could respond, the judge returned his focus to my rival. "Mr. Jenkins, what's your client looking for?"

"Your Honor," I interrupted, "my client really wants to try this —"

Sloan held up a hand the size of a dinner plate, but did not look my way. "I'm talking to Mr. Jenkins right now." He grabbed a handful of roasted almonds from a crystal dish on the corner of his desk and tossed a couple into his mouth.

"Well, Your Honor," Jenkins stuttered, "my client, Henry Randle, was fired based on trumped up charges of sexual harassment. He was really terminated because he's a black man and because he refused to turn a blind eye to the company's fraudulent billing practices. He —"

I couldn't contain myself. "That's not true. Your client was fired for grabbing Karen Carruthers in an elevator and trying to kiss her. And there's absolutely no evidence that —"

This time the judge cut me off with a raised hand *and* a stone-hard glare. "Ms. . . . uh . . ."

"Henderson," I said, annoyed that he couldn't even remember my name. "Vernetta Henderson."

"Ms. Henderson, you will speak only when I ask you to."

I locked my arms across my chest and slumped a little in my chair. When a federal judge called for order, he usually got it.

"Mr. Jenkins," the judge continued brusquely, "I know the facts. Let's cut to the chase. Make Ms. Henderson an offer."

Jenkins looked timidly in my direction and took a long moment before speaking. "I believe I could get my client to accept five hundred thousand," he nearly squeaked.

"Out of the question," I said, ignoring the judge's gag order.

Judge Sloan leaned forward and stroked his chin. "I'm afraid I would have to agree. Give us a more realistic number, Mr. Jenkins. What's your bottom line?"

Reggie looked down at his hands. "I . . . uh . . . I guess if my client received something in the neighborhood of thirty thousand, he might accept it."

Thirty thousand! I mindlessly doodled on the legal pad on my lap. That was a good offer. My client, Micronics Corporation, would easily spend ten times that in attorneys' fees by the time the trial was over. But Micronics' litigation philosophy mandated trying winnable cases, even when they could be settled for nuisance value. They firmly believed that if a plaintiff's attorney litigated a case for months or years and netted nothing for his efforts, he would think twice before suing the company a second time, knowing the battle that awaited him.

Truth be told, I was psyched about trying the case for reasons of my own. If everything remained on schedule, my anticipated victory in the Randle case would come about a week before my law firm's partnership vote. Having another big win under my belt days before the vote would cinch things for me. I would soon become O'Reilly & Finney's first African-American partner. I was not about to let Judge Sloan steal my thunder.

"Your Honor," I said, looking him fearlessly in the eyes, "Micronics Corporation isn't interested in settlement."

Sloan propped an elbow on the desk and pointed at me with a finger the size of a wiener. "You *and* your client are making a big mistake," he said with a controlled fury.

I swallowed hard and said nothing. Pissing off a judge, particularly a federal judge, would mean hell for me the next time I appeared in Sloan's courtroom. He could be as retaliatory as he wanted with no fear of repercussions. One of the many perks of having a job for life.

Sloan snatched a legal pad from his desk and started writing. "You want to try this case?" he said with a cruel smile, "then you've got it. I'm expediting the filing of the pretrial documents. I want the trial brief, the jury instructions and all motions filed by Monday morning. And I'd like to see you two back here Tuesday afternoon for another status report."

"Your Honor!" Jenkins whined, cracking the knuckles of both hands this time. "I'm a solo practitioner. There's no way I can get all those documents drafted in four days." He took a ChapStick from his jacket pocket and nervously dotted his lips.

"That's not my problem, Mr. Jenkins. Perhaps you'll be able to talk some sense into Ms. Henderson before Monday morning." The judge grabbed another handful of almonds. "You can leave now."

As I followed Jenkins down a long hallway that led back to the main courtroom, a flutter of apprehension hit me. *What if I didn't win?*

Luckily, the flash of self-doubt did not linger. Reggie was a lousy attorney. Going up against him would be like trying a case against a first-year law student.

The Randle case was going to trial and I was going to win it.

CHAPTER 2

REGGIE JENKINS MADE it back to his office on the low-rent end of Wilshire Boulevard in less than thirty minutes. Instead of getting to work drafting the pre-trial documents for the Randle case, he gazed out of a window clouded with years of grime and sulked.

He could not understand why Vernetta Henderson was so adamant about trying the case. Especially after he had made a perfectly reasonable settlement offer. Women attorneys, particularly the black ones, always made everything so personal. The girl acted like she wanted to punish him for even filing the case.

The view of the alley two floors below did nothing to lighten Reggie's sour mood. To the right, three bums nodded near a metal trash bin overflowing with debris. The stench managed to seep into Reggie's office even though his windows had been glued shut for years.

Reggie regularly fantasized about having an office with a real view, in a swanky downtown high-rise with marble floors, round-the-clock security guards and windows so clean you could see yourself. His name would appear on the door in fancy gold letters: *Reggie Jenkins, Attorney-at-Law*. Or better yet, *Jenkins, Somebody and Somebody*.

His secretary, paralegal and sometime girlfriend, barged into his office without knocking. "I just wanna make sure you gonna have my money on Friday," Cheryl demanded. Her fists were pinned to a pair of curvy hips.

Reggie's teeth instinctively clamped down on the toothpick dangling from his thick lips. "I told you I would, didn't I?"

"You said the same thing last month, then you didn't show up at the office for three straight days."

Reggie snatched his checkbook from his briefcase and scribbled across one of the checks. "Here," he said, thrusting it at her. "Just don't cash it until tomorrow."

As Cheryl sauntered out, Reggie shook his head and frowned. One day, he was going to have enough cash to hire a real secretary.

He stared down at his cluttered desk, realizing that he was about to lose another one and there wasn't anything he could do about it. Although he had promised Henry Randle his day in court, Reggie had never actually intended to make good on that vow. It was much easier to settle cases — the winners as well as the losers. He'd only had six trials during his thirteen years of practice and had lost every single one of them. He thought about calling Randle to update him on today's court session, but what would he say? *You'll get to tell your story to a jury, but you're going to lose.*

Reggie had checked around and learned that Vernetta was an excellent trial attorney. *He* clearly was not. Juries unnerved him. Whenever those twelve pairs of eyes focused on him and him alone, something inexplicable happened and he turned into a bumbling idiot. If a witness responded with an answer he had not expected, it startled him and he froze up. When an opposing counsel yelled *Objection – hearsay* in the middle of his question, it wrecked his rhythm, causing him to stumble like an old drunk taking a step off of a curb he didn't know was there. By the time the judge had ruled on the objection, Reggie did not know what to say next because he could not even remember what question he had asked.

He rummaged through the unruly stack of papers in front of him and pulled out the *Randle vs. Micronics* complaint. The day Henry Randle had walked into his office and told his story, Reggie felt like someone had handed him a blank check. He had never had a case with allegations of race discrimination *and* whistle blowing. Randle swore that he had never even laid eyes on Karen Carruthers before running into her in that elevator, and he certainly had not grabbed the woman or tried to kiss her. And Reggie fully believed his new client's claim that Micronics trumped up the whole thing to silence his complaints about the company's fraudulent billing on some multi-million-dollar contract with the Air Force.

But as the litigation progressed, Reggie's enthusiasm for the case waned. Just as it always did. Now, he simply wanted his thirty-three percent of whatever settlement he could get so he could move onto the next one.

He turned on his ancient computer and prepared to get to work on the pre-trial documents. Before he could open a blank screen, an idea came to him and his dour mood immediately brightened. After mulling it over for a few minutes, Reggie grabbed his car keys, checked his breast pocket for his cell phone, and rushed out of the door.

If his brilliant little plan actually panned out, he was about to turn the tables on Ms. Vernetta Henderson *and* her scheming client.

CHAPTER 3

AFTER BEING RELEASED from detention in Judge Sloan's chambers, I headed back to my office where I checked my voicemail messages and quickly browsed through twenty-three new emails. Finding nothing that couldn't wait, I made my way to Haley Prescott's office on the other side of the twelfth floor.

Haley was a second-year associate assigned to assist me with the Randle case. She had only been with the firm for six months, having clerked for a federal judge in D.C. after graduating from Yale Law School.

The sweet smell of lavender prickled my nose the minute I stepped inside Haley's office. The place smelled like a florist's shop. The oversized bouquet sitting on the corner of her desk looked like it had just been picked from somebody's garden. Haley's fingers were gliding across her computer keyboard, her eyes glued to the monitor in front of her.

"Hey," she said flatly, not bothering to look my way. Haley saved her more enthusiastic greetings for male attorneys. The partners in particular.

"I just got back from court," I said, as I walked up to her desk. "I hate to deliver bad news, but Judge Sloan wants all the pre-trial documents in the Randle case filed by Monday."

Haley's fingers stopped in place. "That's not possible. I'm spending the weekend at my condo in Mammoth."

As hard as I tried to like the girl, she never failed to get on my last nerve. What bothered me most was her air of superiority, something that was no doubt bolstered by having a mother on the Ninth Circuit

Court of Appeal, a politically connected father, and the looks of a runway model. Almost every attorney in the firm – partners and associates alike – treated her like she was rainmaking royalty. Considering the potential clients she would likely attract to the firm because of her parents' connections, she probably was.

But ruined travel plans came with the territory. So I ignored her grousing. "Which documents have you drafted so far?" I asked.

Haley rudely went back to typing. "None of them."

"I thought you told me you had already started drafting the trial brief and jury instructions."

She paused to tuck one of her curly, blond locks behind her left ear. The girl had long, feathery, Pamela Anderson hair. And from what I could tell, it was the real thing, not that dull, pasty shade that came from a peroxide bottle or years of overexposure to the sun. It was no doubt the only genuine thing about her.

"This isn't the only case I have," Haley snapped. Her voice took on a Bostonian pitch that hadn't been there a second ago.

"I don't know what other cases you have," I snapped back, "but I'm sure they aren't going to trial in a matter of weeks."

All I could do was stare at the girl. It was times like this that I really missed my friend, Neddy McClain. She'd been the only other African-American attorney at O'Reilly & Finney besides me. Neddy and I had started out on rocky ground, but ended up getting pretty tight after defending a big murder case together. She had recently moved to Atlanta, where her new fiancée, a former police detective, had opened his own private investigations firm. I would've loved to see Haley give Neddy the kind of attitude she was throwing my way. Neddy would've had Haley running from her own office in tears.

Haley's lips remained pursed into a tight pout. "Like I said, I really can't work this weekend."

My right hand unconsciously went to my hip. "And, like *I* said, the documents have to be filed by Monday."

As far as I was concerned, the fact that Haley's mama was one step below a Supreme Court Justice, did not mean she didn't have to work just as hard as everybody else. I was actually glad to be throwing a wrench in her plans.

Haley allowed several beats to pass, then fixed me with an infuriated look that didn't need translation. "Fine," she said tightly.

I turned to leave, but Haley stopped me. "I forgot to give you this." She shoved a document at me. "One of the secretaries from Micronics' HR Department faxed it over this morning."

I quickly scanned the four-page fax and felt a heavy pall come over me. It was a memo to file written by Bill Stevens, Micronics' former in-house attorney. When Stevens left the company, the Randle case was transferred to O'Reilly & Finney. The memo briefly summarized allegations of sexual harassment made against six Micronics employees, not including Henry Randle, during the past five years. Most of them had been accused of misconduct far more egregious than what Henry Randle was accused of doing. One of the men allegedly grabbed a woman's breast. All six were white. To my dismay, even though an HR investigation confirmed the charges against each of them, none had been fired.

I looked at the date in the upper left-hand corner of the page and thought I was seeing things. "This document was written months ago," I said, more to myself than to Haley.

"The secretary said the memo was misfiled with another case," Haley explained, her full attention still on her computer screen.

"Why didn't you call me the minute you got this?" I paused and tried to collect myself, not wanting Haley to pick up on my rising stress level. "You knew I had a court appearance in the Randle case today."

Haley huffed out a breath of air. "Actually, I tried," she said. "But you apparently didn't have your cell phone on. I didn't leave a message because I figured you were already in court."

I felt a light pounding in my chest. I walked over to close the door, then turned around to face my subordinate. "I just passed up a chance to settle this case," I said. "Something I probably wouldn't have done if I'd known about this fax."

Haley shrugged. "I was out when it came in and I didn't think you'd be discussing settlement at a pre-trial conference. It wasn't scheduled until two o'clock. If you'd come into the office this morning, you would've known about that fax."

"I had a dental appointment," I said testily. *Why was I explaining myself to this child?* It took most junior associates until their third or fourth year before they stopped being intimidated by the partners and senior associates. But my senior status apparently meant nothing to Haley.

She tucked another loose curl behind her ear. "How much did Jenkins want?"

I exhaled. "Thirty thousand. And I should have taken it."

"I thought you were so eager to try the case."

"I *was*." I waved the fax in the air. "But this changes everything. This memo basically proves Randle's discrimination case. Every one of these guys – who all just happen to be white – got off with a mere slap on the wrist. We can't take a chance of going to trial with these facts."

"Well, I can tell you one thing, Porter's not going to be happy when he finds out you passed up that settlement offer."

Tell me something I don't know.

Porter was the partner in charge of the Randle lawsuit. He'd been riding me ever since we got the case, something he seemed to enjoy doing to most associates.

"Well, look at the bright side," Haley said. "That document is attorney-client privileged so we don't have to produce it. And the odds are pretty good that Jenkins won't find out about those cases on his own. He didn't even ask for information about prior sexual harassment claims during discovery. The man is totally incompetent."

I suddenly felt protective of my fellow black brother. *I* could call him incompetent, but I didn't like hearing him criticized by this pompous little sorority girl.

I reread the fax and my rage slowly shifted from Haley to Micronics. *Why hadn't somebody at Micronics told me about these other cases?* I was certain that I had asked HR about prior sexual harassment claims. *Hadn't I?*

"If you ever get another fax or letter or telephone call or anything else with important information about a case I'm working on," I said, "I want to know about it. Right away."

"No problem." Haley gave me a *Cover Girl* smile.

I headed for the door and did not bother to look back. "I'll expect to see a draft of the trial brief and jury instructions by noon on Saturday."

CHAPTER 4

THE CEO OF Micronics Corporation strolled down the spacious hallway of the Cypress Club with a decided, purpose-filled gait. His eyes bore straight ahead, ignoring his elegant surroundings. The rich wood paneling, the expensive Oriental rugs, the Picassos and Monets that lined the walls. Any other time, J. William Walters would have taken notice of the Pavarotti aria wafting from the expensive Bose speakers. Not today.

A casual observer might have assumed that Walters' brain cells were consumed with annual reports, stock prices or one of his company's newest inventions. But in reality, unshakable images of newspaper headlines and prison cells had been his primary focus for several weeks now. At night, it was becoming increasingly impossible to shake the visions—he refused to call them nightmares—of SEC agents raiding his posh office, slapping handcuffs across his meaty wrists and taking him on a preplanned perp walk as cameras from all the major networks shined blinding lights into his eyes.

Making a sharp left, Walters headed for the Ronald Reagan room, one of a dozen or so private meeting places reserved for the Cypress Club's most exclusive members. Exclusive in Walters' world meaning not just rich, but rich and powerful. When he reached his destination, he did not bother to knock before thrusting the door open and stepping inside.

It took a second for Walters' eyes to adjust to the near darkness. The ominous room seemed more suitable for a late night poker game than clandestine corporate decision-making. He nodded in the direction of the room's sole occupant, sitting in a red velvet club chair. Rich Ferris, Micronics' Vice President of Human Resources, was a fair-skinned black man who was as buttoned up as a born-again preacher. Ferris nodded, but did not otherwise greet his boss of the last seven years. Instead, he quietly took a sip from his second vodka of the evening.

The CEO was a long time member of the Cypress Club. Thanks to Walters' connections, Ferris had recently been extended an invitation to join the elite society. Unlike some of his colleagues, Walters had not raised a fuss when the club finally gave in to outside pressures and began actively complying with its non-discrimination provision. No matter how many blacks or Jews walked through the door, it would have no tangible impact on his life. Certain people were impervious to change. At least, that was how it had been.

"Well, let's get to it," Walters said, wishing he had a drink, too. He eyed the fully stocked bar in the far corner of the room. The thought of getting up to fix one for himself had not occurred to him. An attendant would arrive shortly. He would wait.

"How're we going to fix this?" Walters' harsh eyes rested pointedly on his subordinate.

Ferris did not rush to respond to the question. In his own right, he was a well-educated, impressive businessman whose innovative workforce strategies had earned him profiles in publications like *Forbes, Black Enterprise,* and the *Wall Street Journal.* At the instant, though, he looked like a scared little boy.

The CEO let the silence linger to the point of punishment. "You don't have any ideas?" The sarcasm in Walter's voice failed to mask his anger. "Let's not forget that we're in this together. If the feds come calling for me, they're eventually coming after you, too. So, I'll ask the question one more time. How do we fix this?"

Ferris sat forward and cleared his throat. "I've taken care of it," he said. He raised his glass to his lips, but did not take a sip. "In fact, everything is well underway."

"Go on," Walters said.

"I don't think I should say anymore than that. The less you know the better."

The CEO grimaced. He wanted to hear the specifics, but Ferris was right. If somebody sat him down in front of a polygraph machine, he liked the idea of being able to honestly plead ignorance. Too bad he had not taken that approach months ago.

"When will we know for sure that everything's been resolved?" Walters asked.

"A month at the most, maybe less."

"What about the media?" Walters absently rubbed his jaw. "Are you certain there's nothing out there that some over-ambitious reporter won't uncover?"

"There's no paper trail to speak of," Ferris said. "We've covered our tracks."

Walters wanted to explode. Ferris had just lied to him. Intentionally, no doubt. There was indeed a paper trail. A very troublesome one. But Walters had already put his own clandestine clean-up plan into motion, knowing he could not leave something this serious up to his circle of incompetents. If and when real trouble surfaced, the minions he had carefully positioned on the front lines would be there to take the fall.

The CEO had personally picked each of his nine direct reports as much for their shrewd business acumen as their unique personal frailties. They were all yes men. Brilliant yes men, but clearly followers, not leaders. Intellect without strength. At the time, Walters had not wanted an equal among his inner circle. Now, he could have used one in the room.

"What about the Randle case?" he asked.

"That's being taken care of as well." Ferris spoke with genuine confidence for the first time.

Walters nodded again. "Who's handling it?"

"O'Reilly & Finney has the case now. If something goes wrong, it'll look better if an outside law firm has a hand in it."

"Good," Walters said, nodding.

"I had them assign the case to Vernetta Henderson. She handled that wage-and-hour lawsuit at our Long Beach facility last year," Ferris said proudly. "She also defended a big murder case a few months ago." He paused. "And she's African-American." Ferris actually preferred *black* over *African-American*, but was trying to sound politically correct.

Walters had made it known that he liked having African-American attorneys heading up Micronics' defense team when black plaintiffs sued the company. In the CEO's mind, having a black mouthpiece diffused the issue of race for the jury. Ferris wholeheartedly agreed.

"Good," Walters said again. He glanced at the door. He could not wait much longer for his drink.

"The trial's just a few weeks away," Ferris continued. "According to Ms. Henderson, a defense verdict is all but a certainty."

A stunned look glazed Walters' face. It took a moment before he could speak. "Are you out of your mind? That case can't go to trial."

Ferris clenched his left fist, then set his empty glass on the table to his right. "We already gave Ms. Henderson the go ahead to try it." His voice came out in a near whimper. "It's going to look pretty strange to suddenly ask that it be settled."

"Not half as strange as you and me sharing a prison cell!" Walters yelled. "If this thing gets out they'll hang us all out to dry!"

Ferris pinched the bridge of his nose. "Ms. Henderson's a real go-getter. She's going to ask a lot of questions."

"I don't care about her questions," Walters said through clinched teeth. "Just get the damn case settled. Now!"

Books by Pamela Samuels Young

Vernetta Henderson Series
Every Reasonable Doubt (1st in series)
In Firm Pursuit (2nd in series)
Murder on the Down Low (3rd in series)
Attorney-Client Privilege (4th in series)
Lawful Deception (5th in series)

Dre Thomas and Angela Evans Series
Buying Time (1st in series)
Anybody's Daughter (2nd in series)
Abuse of Discretion (3rd in series)
Failure to Protect (4th in Series)

Young Adult Adaptations
#Anybody's Daughter (1st in series)
#Abuse of Discretion (2nd in series)

Lawyers in Lust Series
Dangerously Sexy Romantic Suspense
by Sassy Sinclair
Unlawful Desires: An Erotic Suspense Novella
Unlawful Seduction: An Erotic Suspense Novella

Short Stories
The Setup
Easy Money
Unlawful Greed

Non-Fiction
Kinky Coily: A Natural Hair Resource Guide

ACKNOWLEDGEMENTS

Each book I write is truly a labor of love. Like my thriller about child sex trafficking, *Anybody's Daughter,* my goal in writing *Failure to Protect* was to open eyes, change perspectives and, hopefully, save lives. I had a lot of help in trying to achieve that goal.

I'd like to begin by thanking the educators and mental health professionals who took time out of their busy schedules to answer my questions, provide me with resources and, in some cases, critique an early draft of this book: Monique Fordham-Jackson, Assistant Principal, Los Angeles Unified School District; Dr. Marcia Smiley, Perry County (Alabama) Board of Education; Dr. Donna Holland Barnes, Associate Professor of Psychiatry, Howard University and Co-founder of the National Organization for People of Color against Suicide; Victor Schwartz, M.D., Clinical Associate Professor of Psychiatry, New York University School of Medicine and Chief Medical Officer of the Jed Foundation; Faye Mandell, Licensed Clinical Social Worker/Psychotherapist; Richard Lieberman, MA, NCSP, School Psychologist/Consultant, Loyola Marymount University; and Dr. Marleen Wong, Senior Vice Dean and Clinical Professor, University of Southern California. Thanks to all of you for sharing your expertise and for the work you do on behalf of children.

A big thanks to two book clubs for their no-holds-barred critiques: Joy Book Club of Jackson, Mississippi (Keneasha Clark, Kimberly Harris, Cnevovia Burnes, Shontia Morris, Leona Bishop, Kim Mathews, Nikeya Brown and Avril White) and Victorious Ladies Reading Book Club of Durham, North Carolina (Shavonna Furtrell, Michelle

Chavis, Venita Alderman Brandon, Asha Jones-Wade, Sharea Myers, Nichole Page and Carla Lipscomb). I pray you will all be fans for life!

Finally, I want to thank those friends and family members who gave me their honest assessment of the various drafts of this book: Cheri Reid (your candidness, empathy and insight helped me produce a much better book), Tyrone Devezin (thanks for your encouragement and mind-boggling attention to detail), Cheryl Mason (I owe you big time for saving me on multiple fronts), Olivia Smith (always on hand when I need a fast read), Jennifer Stone and Willette Hill of Go On Girl Book Club (y'all really rolled out the red carpet for me in Ft. Lauderdale!), Molly Byock (the coolest white chick I know), Dawn Clark (one of the fastest readers I know), Donny Wilson (thanks for the male perspective), Darlene Hayes (thanks for suggesting that I add Apache), Julie Ungerman (the real "Jenny"), Jerome Norris (who always gives it to me straight even when I don't want to hear it), Donna Lowry (thanks for the last-minute test-read), Pamela Goree Dancy, Arlene L. Walker, Cynthia Hebron, Janet Swerdlow, and Linette Carey. As always, your feedback—both pro and con—was much appreciated.

Last but not least, thanks to Lynel Washington, my virtual assistant; Ella Curry of Crown Holders, my long-time social media publicist and unofficial developmental editor; and the newest members of my team, editor Kiera Northington and publicist Pamela Broussard of BNM Publicity Group. Thanks for helping me get the job done.

ABOUT THE AUTHOR

Pamela Samuels Young is an attorney and award-winning author of multiple legal thrillers. A passionate advocate for children, Pamela speaks frequently on the topics of child sex trafficking, bullying, sexting, online safety, fiction writing and pursing your passion. Pamela is also a natural hair enthusiast and the author of *Kinky Coily: A Natural Hair Resource Guide*. The former journalist and Compton native is a graduate of USC, Northwestern University and UC Berkeley's School of Law. She is single and resides in the Los Angeles area.

To schedule Pamela for a speaking engagement or book club meeting via speakerphone, Skype, FaceTime, Zoom or in person, visit her website at www.pamelasamuelsyoung.com.

Pamela loves to hear from readers! There are a multitude of ways to connect with her.

Email: authorpamelasamuelsyoung@gmail.com
Website: www.pamelasamuelsyoung.com
Twitter: www.twitter.com/authorpsy
Instagram: https://www.instagram.com/authorpsy/
Facebook: www.facebook.com/pamelasamuelsyoung and
www.facebook.com/kinkycoilypamela
LinkedIn: https://www.linkedin.com/in/authorpamelasamuelsyoung/
YouTube: www.youtube.com/kinkycoilypamela